THE GOLDEN THREADS TRILOGY BOOK ONE

THREAD
∙
SLIVERS

#29 of 50 First Run

Leeland Artra

LEELAND ARTRA

DEDICATION

This book is dedicated to my children Lewin & Sapphira: may you both always stay sharp; and to my beautiful wife Evelina for putting up with my late nights dreaming at the keyboard.

NORTHERN ICE FIELDS

Skogen Hoit Forest

DUIANNA

Gredria

NAE-RAE   RHONIA

YALTHUM

OCCIDUUS OCEAN

LAEUSIA

OSLAD

NASUB

Ulno

AELARGO

Circumveni Desert

KARAKIA

DABIAN OCEAN

Ustra

DULGRIUM

Niga-Yur: Duianna Continent

0   1000

SOUTHERN ICE FIELDS

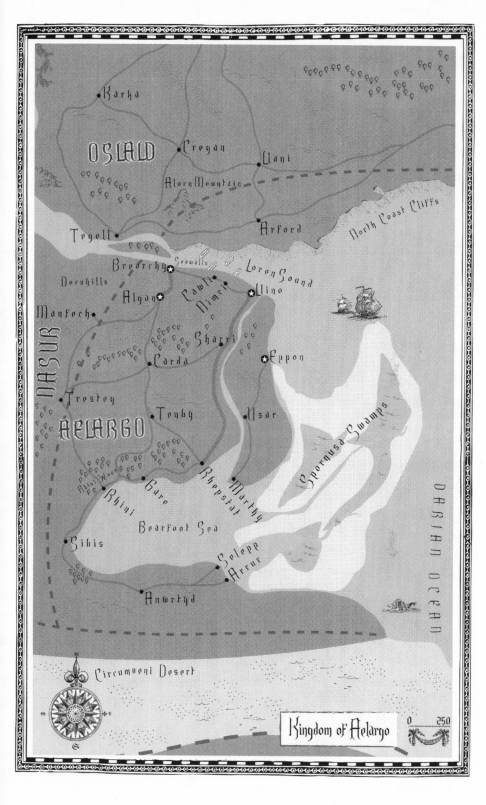

Kingdom of Aelargo

Ticca the Hunter

CHAPTER 1

BOOTS ON THE GROUND

TICCA MOVED SLOWLY AND CAUTIOUSLY over the roof, making sure she stayed in the chimney's long shadow as she inched towards it. She kept a watchful eye on the traffic in the street below. *I can't be spotted, or someone will try to kill me; and worse, I'll miss Sula's target.* Her cloak had a little magic that helped her blend into the shadows, but she knew it didn't make her invisible. It was a dangerous task to spy on these powerful people. But, she wanted to earn some respect as a Dagger, and Sula was her first big client. Ticca had managed to earn a solid reputation in a dozen or so small jobs before Sula, who had been using more senior Daggers, unexpectedly sat at her table. This was her fifth assignment for Sula, and she was earning a lot of respect and coin for her successes.

Her timing was perfect. She was in position, in the darkest crook of the chimney, as the sun started to touch the western horizon. Nervously, she scanned for any signs she had been spotted, moving into her vantage point. Everything was normal; it was business as usual for the merchants here in the Day Market. From underneath her cloak, she pulled the solid cylinder out and held it firmly in her left hand. *Hopefully, that courier will be back.*

As the darkness deepened, Ticca became the hunter; waiting, watching the traffic moving through the only known entrance to the market square. The majority of the more upstanding merchants had already locked up their wooden stalls and carted off as much as they could in their push carts, past the beautiful entry statue. Hands on their sword hilts, in their banded leather armor, the last three remaining city guards left for more respectable parts of the city. A few late shoppers moved about the remaining merchants, who were trying to evacuate the square before the sun finished setting. The Day Market was closed; this was about to become the Night Market.

A stout, confident man walked into the market wearing a dark, charcoal grey cloak. Ticca's heart rate picked up with excitement as she recognized him as the hired assassin—or Knife, as they were called—that Sula had had her identify a few days earlier. *What are you doing here personally? What have you been up to the last few days?* She held her breath as the Knife scanned the market for someone, and then looked up at the roofs, his gaze passing over her. Not finding who he was looking for, he moved into a dark shadow by the wall and pulled his hood up over his head, blending very well into the shadow.

Ticca stared intently, trying to find his outline. *Damn it, don't lose him now. If he is here, then the courier isn't coming.* She considered leaving, but her instincts were telling her to stay. *This might be important to Sula. Maybe worth a bonus.*

She couldn't make out if he was still where she last saw him. She had to decide if she should move to a new position to try and locate him. *From where he was, he can see the entrance and me, if I'm not careful. I know he won't take kindly to seeing someone on this roof. He probably won't move far. He wants to meet someone.* She started taking careful tally of the rest of the square's occupants in her mind, thankful she'd picked a location to both remain unseen, and yet, be able to view the majority of the square. The courier she was expecting still had not arrived, and she kept her attention primarily focused on watching for the Knife to move. In her peripheral vision, she saw the odd twilight shift of the statue, signaling that the Night Market was in business.

When Sula's first mission for Ticca had brought her here to the Night Market, that statue had seemed so out of place, it shocked her. During the day, it was an amazingly good portrayal of a young elven lass, shopping basket hung loosely on her left arm, her right arm lifting ever-so-slightly in friendly greeting, and a warm, expressive smile, welcoming market visitors.

It was the kind of statue only the wealthiest could dream of commissioning for their estates. Yet here, it sat in the middle of the only entrance to a medium-sized, dead-end square, just inside the lower area of town, which had been a market for as long as anyone could remember.

The night patrons began to arrive slowly, and the evening's dealers materialized from the darkened alleys, moving past the statue to enter the square quickly. People in long, expensive rain capes mixed easily with dock workers in their dingy clothes and thick coats. Everyone pulled coats, capes, and collars tight; more to avoid too much exposure to each other, than to keep the rain out.

Watching the deals for the past few nights had given Ticca a good idea of the basic rules of engagement here. Once the sun had set, the market was too dangerous for honest city guards. This was the legendary Night Market, which she had heard tales of long before she came to the city. She'd thought its reputation for having drug dealers, pawn brokers, and facilitators of any act, was exaggerated. But the merchants, or 'Hands,' as they like to be called, really lived up to that reputation. She shuddered as she remembered some of the breath-taking and brutal things she had witnessed passing through here; the worst, being a bag of what she was sure were fresh body parts. *I would like it if this place shut down, but as my Uncle says, 'People will always be capable of evil, and some will always choose to be evil.' Maybe containment here really does keep it in check.*

A dignified Hand who dealt in secrets, and a regular visitor to the Night Market, strolled past the statue. The stone figure now held its basket tight, eyes wide with fear and warning, right hand held up, as if to warn visitors of the danger within. She still didn't understand why they bothered to put that statue there, but it did make a good signal for whether or not it was safe to enter.

The shadow she had been watching split in two, with the real shadow seeming to reluctantly release its twin. *That's a neat trick you didn't have last time.* The Knife kept the hood up and drifted gracefully to intercept the newest arrival. They met, like all the others, a safe distance from everyone else, and started negotiating. It did not take long before the Knife passed a small package to the Hand, who put it in his coat.

Even in the rain-cloaked night, she could clearly see the small package was tied with a glinting golden thread. Her heart skipped a beat as she realized the implications. *Sula mentioned there might be something tied with gold. He is the contact Sula wants identified. The Knife didn't use the courier; he brought it himself. That has to be unique.* She smiled, knowing she had succeeded again. *One week, and I have found the Hand.*

When the Hand's fingers came out of the coat, they passed over the Knife's palm, dropping a small bag that vanished instantly. *Probably going to waste that coin on something stronger than hyly at a Red-Door. No matter, I have my quarry.*

The deal done, the Knife drifted off to the left. She didn't bother to watch; her attention was fixed on her new target, the Hand. *Be sure, Ticca; be real sure you can pick him out again,* she cautioned herself.

Once she had his walk, shape, and features down, it was time for the odd part. Under her cloak, her left hand squeezed hard on the small, solid metal tube it held. Although physically impossible the solid tube became slightly smaller activating the spell. She felt the small tingle of released magic flow up her arm. It wasn't unpleasant, but she was glad she had been warned; otherwise, she might have looked down at her hands, which could have been disastrous. Trying to ignore the sensation, she kept her eyes locked on the Hand, as if her very life depended on it, which it likely did. The spell moved through her veins, and up through her neck, to her head, and she felt it rush from her eyes. *This doesn't seem to be doing anything, but Sula insisted it be done before tracking the next link in her chain.*

After the spell was released, Ticca didn't wait to see the result. She reached back, grabbed the top of the roof line, and levered herself over the top, staying low and not allowing her own cloaks to flutter. Once over and out of sight from the market, she hurried until she was a few streets away. Checking that she had not been spotted or followed, she lowered herself, unseen, into another small alley. Rapidly, she stripped off her thin, outer cloak and folded it into a tight bundle. The evening chill instantly began to bite through her normal cape, which had been hidden underneath. She carefully placed the folded cloak into her secure satchel, in the chain-lined pocket. Again, she marveled that a full cloak could become such a small package of cloth, that it easily fit inside one of her hands.

Now all I need to do is report to Sula, as instructed, that I can identify the Hand. Maybe tomorrow, I can start tracking him. Flipping her cape collar into a more respectable position, she pulled the hood out slightly over her head to keep off some of the rain, and stepped boldly out into the lamp-lit road. No longer wrapped in her hunter's mindset, she allowed herself to contemplate recent events. Turning east, she started walking towards the docks. Her destination wasn't too far; after all, Llino was built around its docks.

From listening to her uncle's Dagger stories, Ticca knew Llino was about as interesting a place as any in the world to be. The Three Princes, who jointly ruled the kingdom, kept it tightly under control, just as their massive fleet kept the sea lanes and trade routes under control. Being a pirate was very hard work, and being a shipping merchant was equally hard, especially if your ships happened to be near a Three Princes' ship without the proper tariffs paid. With hundreds of patrol ships and no other navy to contend with, the Three Princes ruled the waterways and demanded a high tax on everything flowing. Of course, the fact that your goods were well protected generally made it worthwhile. Llino, being at nearly the center of all the major empires with sea trade, was a natural stop and central trading location.

As she passed the white arches of The Wizards' Guildhouse, she unconsciously shied to the far side of the street, as nearly everyone did. It never paid to be too close to a wizard. Ticca had never met a wizard she could call 'nice,' and stories of sudden executions by offended wizards made the unspoken rule of the common folk to give all wizards a comfortable space just sound thinking. Still, the building was beautiful to look at. Somehow, it was always visible, no matter the weather or light. Yet, it didn't actually glow. If it had, she would have spotted the motion from the alley's shadow, a moment sooner.

A strong hand closed hard on her throat, choking off any chance of calling for help. The attacker's other hand didn't waste time either; it grabbed her arm through the cloak and threw her deep into the alley. Ticca landed face first on the dirty, uneven cobblestones. A pain shot through her left side as the air and rational thought were momentarily knocked from her. Gasping for breath, she tried to move. She realized her right arm was being held twisted behind and so far upwards, she felt like her shoulder was about to be dislocated from the strain.

Her attacker was fast. He reversed his stance, never letting go of her right arm, as he jammed it painfully higher. He dropped one knee into the center of her back, putting his full weight down and preventing her from being able to take in a much-needed breath. All she could manage was a small squeak of pain.

"Who are you working for, missy?"

Ticca marveled for a moment at the oddly beautiful sound of that soft whisper.

"You tossed a spell from your perch. What was it?"

She heard the sound of glass tinkling. Fear, adrenaline, and years of training finally took over. Somehow, Ticca knew the elixir being pulled was deadly. With fear-fueled strength, she braced her right foot for leverage, and kicked her left foot up towards the back of her head. A crunching sound ripped the air as her foot hit something that gave in slightly, before she made full contact with her attacker's body. He fell forward, letting go of her arm, as a small glass vial bounced away on the cobblestones.

I might as well make this look good, she thought. Swinging her right foot up to join the left over her head, she moved her freed arm to the ground, and completed the reverse roll by pushing with her arms, and rolling to her feet in a maneuver that would have made her trainer smile.

The attacker rolled away and started to stand. Noticing the telltale movements that he was pulling a weapon, she considered the small knives in her belt. *It's him or me. I don't think I can beat him in a knife fight with this pain in my arm. 'Action is better than reaction,'* her trainer's voice said in her memory.

Her moment of surprise was slipping away—time was essential and short. *Need to end this now. Have to use my right arm for the hook, because it's hurting too much to brace with. Damn, this is going to hurt, but at least, it'll hurt him more than me.*

Grimacing against the coming pain, she jumped over her attacker, kicking off to spin as she launched. Her combat-trained body automatically followed through with a twist in the air, to land with her right arm looped around the man's neck. She slid down his back, locking her right arm with her left. Just as she felt the pull on her arm, she twisted hard in the opposite direction with her weight leveraging against his body. As she tightened her arm ripples of sharp pain shot through her back and neck from the shoulder. Ticca clamped her mouth shut to keep from screaming out. Her momentum was arrested with a loud crack from the man's neck.

His body jerked, and she thought she heard a hiss of surprise as they fell in a pile. Her nose confirmed he was dead a moment later. Her right arm and shoulder screamed with pain, her back hurt, and she was sure she was bruised over the majority of her body. But he was dead, and she wasn't—in short, the best outcome possible.

Damn it, how did he spot me? She swallowed hard a few times to get control of her emotions and thoughts. *Lady, he was going to kill me, wasn't he?* Looking over the first person she had ever killed, her heart raced and her hands shook uncontrollably. She wiped her hands on her pants as she breathed deeply, trying to find some balance. She looked at his tanned, rough-shaven face. Except for the angle of his neck, he looked like he was sleeping. It was definitely the Knife she had just spied on. *I should get away from here fast. But first, I might need some clues as to who exactly he was, and he surely won't need his gear anymore.*

Making sure that no one was watching, she grabbed his boots and dragged him deeper into the alley. Once a reasonable distance from the street, she started checking him for valuables. The boots felt like some of the finest leather she had ever touched, so she pulled them off and tucked them under her cloak first. She noticed that one of the two pouches smelled awful and was soaked in something that fumed, with wispy smoke tails curling to the sky. She realized that it must have been holding more elixirs, and she had broken them when she kicked him. Ignoring the smoking pouch, she took the other one, and the belt it was attached to, as it also had a few knives and a short sword. He didn't have anything else on him.

Ticca inched towards the alley entrance. *I know it has only been a few minutes since he grabbed me, but it feels like it has been a whole mark, and his neck breaking was pretty loud. Why is the guard never there to help, but always to arrest?* Her thoughts raced over the events as she passed the point where they had fought. On the ground, was a small glass vial. Picking it up carefully, she turned it over, inspecting the seal. The seal was tight, and there was a semi-clear, brownish liquid inside. *This might be something interesting for later*, she thought, as she slipped it into her own belt pouch. Thankfully, the shiny wet street was still not busy; no one was close by. No longer feeling the cold, and with a quick glance to insure no one was looking her way, she stepped out and continued on her original path in a confident walk.

With the attack replaying in her head over and over, she was surprised to find herself standing in front of her destination, the Blue Dolphin Inn. Collecting her thoughts, she stepped up to the door of the massive three-story, two-block-wide tavern. Her eyes momentarily took in the large platform jutting out of—and towering four stories over—the tavern, with its massive, gleaming, six-foot-wide, metal hoop set into the stone. Legend, and the tavern owner, claimed that it was a favorite moorage port for the *Emerald Heart*, Damega's flying ship. The only thing that made her accept the story was that absolutely no one she knew questioned it, and many more had relatives or friends who claimed to have some connection to the *Emerald Heart*. Of course, Damega and his famous flying ship hadn't been seen in many generations.

The Blue Dolphin's large double doors were both closed against the evening's cold. She easily pushed the left one open and stepped into the din. The scents and sounds of the room threatened to knock her back out into the street. The smoke was filled with many odors, including a hint of some less than legal substances. Of course, the room's main smell was the sweet scent of copious amounts of hyly, being served from the large kegs behind the bars. Her nose adjusted quickly, although she still occasionally rubbed it as the smoke tickled it. The three large fires were well stoked, keeping the room warm. Two bards had taken up places at opposite ends of the large room, and were still in no danger of interfering with each other over the loud conversations.

Ticca scanned the tables, hoping to find an open one, which of course, there wasn't. A handful of the tables had rather nice-looking daggers stuck into them, standing straight up. She noted all the Daggers sitting at those tables. Not recognizing any of them as friends, she moved stiffly towards the left-hand side of the room. Finding a place at a communal table, she sat down. Within a few minutes, one of the serving girls came by with a tray of hyly mugs. Ticca helped herself to one and ordered some of the evening's meal. The girl nodded and moved off.

Sighing loudly, Ticca took a full mouthful of the sweet liquid. As she swallowed, she enjoyed the warm, burning feeling that spread rapidly through her body. Without looking around, she took a couple more deep draughts, leaving the mug almost empty. As the warmth of the room, the melodic lute music, and warm hyly seeped into her bones, the aches of the attack and the numbing cold of the night abated, while the fight continued to replay in her mind. It took a while to relax. Shoving the feeling that everyone was watching her aside, she let the music and mood of the room soothe her.

Smiling, she straightened her back and began identifying the room's occupants. A traveling merchant or six were always here, and tonight was no exception. The local merchants were feeding them and plying them with hyly, looking for the best deal on whatever stock they'd brought in. Of course, there were the dozen or so Daggers, all trying to upstage each other with drinking, wrestling, and knives. The card players' tables were all over full tonight, with dozens of spectators, signaling that some big game was playing out.

Just as she was a little relaxed, a loud *thunk* announced her food had arrived and made her nearly jump out of her seat. Under the table, her hands had already drawn her dagger and knife. Looking up, her heart racing, she saw it had been Ellar, one of the many servers, who'd brought her meal.

Relax Ticca, relax, the dead stay dead, and it's safe here. Ellar was very young, maybe twelve years of age, and had been acting increasingly shyer around her for the last few weeks. She looked directly into his eyes and smiled warmly in thanks, as she slipped her weapons back into their sheaths. He turned a bright red, gave a nod, and dashed behind another table with his large tray of plates. His reaction somehow made her feel almost human again. Her mood finally lifted as she watched Ellar retreat. She started giggling. *Yep, he has definitely taken to me.* Looking at the food, she was surprised to see it actually consisted of some very good cuts of meat, and there were two small loaves, instead of one. *I guess there are benefits to giving him a little smile.* She grabbed her knife and began eating the fine meal for which this evening's work was sure to compensate.

It was no surprise that as she was finishing the meal and a second mug, Sula appeared and sat across from her. *How does she do that? I would have sworn she wasn't even in the room a minute ago.*

"You're eating well tonight."

"With the bits you pay, I can finally afford to not starve." Looking into Sula's dark eyes, she smirked. "Course, I'm doing a lot better than your previous thugs."

Sula looked directly at her and tossed the same insult she had been using since Ticca's first rapid success. "Yes, using an inconsequential thug has worked out." A hint of humor tinged the emerald pools of Sula's eyes. "You can track the next link."

That was not a question. *She obviously can detect that bit of magic she insists I use,* Ticca thought, not for the first time. *I know she doesn't follow me. But her information is sometimes too good, especially about what to expect or look for.* Again, Ticca worried about exactly what was playing out. Sula had a lot of coin, and the senior Daggers acknowledged her as a serious client. *I hope I am working for the right side. My gut says I can trust Sula, but there is something unique about her.*

"When you're done, meet me in your room." Sula stood. Her clothes were nondescript, neither rich, nor poor. Her cream-colored blouse was loose cut, but not so loose as to hide her obviously large, well-proportioned breasts, as she leaned in closer to say softly, "You might consider a bath and change of clothes first." Her green skirt matched her eyes and swept all the way to the floor, yet it showed off both her very fine female figure as well as her graceful moves, as she glided away into the crowd around the bard.

Stunned for a moment, Ticca looked down at herself. The whole front of her shirt and pants were caked in drying scum. Her cloak's edges showed that it, too, was in need of a cleaning. *Oh my. I didn't even notice the alley sludge. I must have it all over my face and neck, too. No wonder, I haven't had to fend off any drunks yet.* Looking around, she realized that nobody cared; after all, dirt was part of life here. Still, it was a little embarrassing, especially after working for cycles to establish herself as a real Dagger.

Shrugging, she decided it was too late to do anything about it. *No rush tonight, and I earned this.* She leaned against the wooden back of the bench, which was smoothed and rounded from years of customers doing just this. Ticca slowly finished the remains of her meal and savored the last half of her mug of hyly.

Standing, she maneuvered over to the bar. Genne, the owner, came over, after a minute. He looked her over very slowly from head to foot. *Any other man, and I'd be pulling my dagger for taking that long a look. But from Genne, I know it's an assessment of performance.* "Trust d'work was good tonight. D'ya wanna bath or jus' t'bed?" She felt taller at his tone. *He thinks I did well enough tonight.*

Smiling with satisfaction, she asked, "Is the water hot?" She pulled a pence from her purse and held it where he could see it.

"Ah, d'boy c'n add more coal if'n ya want."

She handed over the coin with a smile. "I want. Let Ellar know I'll be there shortly." Genne closed and opened his hand, and the coin was gone, replaced by a silver key stamped with a pattern. Taking the key from Genne's palm, she turned and started climbing the six-foot-wide stone steps that started next to the bar, and circled all the way up to the platform four stories overhead. Where the coin had vanished to, she wasn't sure. *I know Genne was raised in this inn. His family has owned the Blue Dolphin for generations, and he is an important part of Dagger actions here. Still, he must have had an interesting past, to be able to pull little tricks like that.*

She climbed three stories to the pair of large, warehouse-style, sliding doors at the top, which had an aging sign warning people to clear the platform as fast as possible, should the Emerald Heart pull into port. She smirked at the sign. *As if that would ever happen again.* She walked down the quiet hall to her room. Seeing her hair check still in place in the upper corner, she unlocked the door. As she opened the door, her left hand gripped her knife hilt, and she cautiously checked for intruders before stepping in.

A little paranoid tonight, she thought as she lit the small oil lamp that served as the only light source in the room. She pulled out some cleaner clothes from her pack on the floor. Laying the newly-acquired boots, belt, and pouches on her bed, she exited again, putting the hair check in a different spot, after the door closed. Turning to the stairs, she saw a couple of people heading down the opposite hallway. She locked the door again and went back down to the baths.

She found the door with a matching symbol to the key Genne had given her. She unlocked the door and stepped in quickly so as to not let too much steam out. Ellar was there, pouring some steaming water into the tub. Finishing, he turned to go down the back stairs to the kitchens, and let out a small squeak of surprise at seeing her in the room, which made her giggle warmly.

"I...I...I... Um, I'm sorry m'lady. I... I didn't hear you come in." He obviously wanted to move, but his body was frozen in fear.

"Ellar, relax." She sighed and stepped toward him. That unfroze his body, and he practically jumped through the back door.

"I...the... I mean, the bath is full an' hot, lady. Jus' put your clothes through the panel, and I'll have them clean for you by morning." At the mention of clothes, he went an amazing shade of pink. He closed the door so quickly, it caught his foot, which he rapidly extracted.

Smiling, she stripped and put her clothes through the panel, into the waiting basket on the back wall. Then she slowly stepped into the very hot water. After a good cleaning, she examined herself. She had a large bruise that went all the way around her arm, where her attacker had grabbed her. Her right shoulder was slightly swollen, with a number of broken blood vessels causing more areas of darkened flesh. Most of her front was also a patchwork of discoloration. She was sure her neck was just as ugly, and the constant ache in her back told her there was a very large purple area on her back, where he had planted his knee.

She massaged her shoulder and back in the hot water, then relaxed and soaked in the warmth for a time. When the water became cool, she stepped out and rubbed herself down with the coarse towel. Feeling much better, she dressed and went back up to her room.

The hair check was right where she left it. Unlocking the door, she checked the room again, and her gaze fell on the small pile of stuff she had left. *Sula should be coming up in a little bit. Now is as good a time as any other. Besides, if I don't keep busy, I'll fall asleep.*

Since she had light and time, she could see right away that the equipment she had taken from her attacker was not simple fare. The belt was a very fine grade of leather, expertly stitched. The inside of the belt was a soft cloth, in which were various evenly-spaced pockets and bulges. Removing the knife sheaths and pouch from the belt, she knelt on the floor and laid the belt out the length of her bed, with the cloth side up. Feeling along the stitching, she located each item and carefully removed it, placing it on the bed above the pocket it had come out of. Once done, she looked over the assortment of tools. They were all metal with a dull, black patina. She tested each one. Some were very flexible and smooth edged, others had teeth, some were sharply pointed, and others had stiff, but thin, points or teeth of various sizes.

I've heard of thieves' picks, but these are amazing. I doubt this is a beginner set, or even a common set. She went back down the row of tools, picking each tool up and examining it carefully again before putting it back in its assigned pocket. *Not sure what I should do with these. I am pretty sure, getting caught with them would be a criminal offense.* She rolled the belt up and put it on the bottom of her pack. *I am not even sure if I can sell them for anything, or even where it would be safe to try to sell them, except at the Night Market.*

Next were the knives. There were five total: four small, identical-looking ones, and one that might be considered a sword, as it was too long to really be a dagger. It was made of an unusual metal with dark, wavy lines running irregularly down the length of the blade. It had the same black patina as the thieves' tools. *It is very light; adjusting for the length, I could use this in a knife fight as easily as a fighting dagger.* The knives were typical small knives that could be used as hand tools or thrown. These, she knew how to use. She checked the balance and edge of each knife, smiling the whole time. *Very fine knives, I can use these for sure.* She spent a little time figuring out how to best arrange the extra knives on her belt. *This might work, or I could get one of those cross-chest belts with some hold points for them.* Her eyes twinkled, imagining how she'd look with four fine throwing knives on a cross belt. *I'll definitely look a bit more experienced, or at least, more impressive, that way.*

She pulled his pouch over. It, too, was very fine quality. She admired the clasp, which was silver with a geometric pattern. It was slightly distressed with age and use, giving it an antiqued look. *This is nice; I like the pattern and the look.* Opening it, she sat and stared in disbelief. *It's empty! Where did the things I felt in it go?* Looking around her room, she couldn't help feeling a little worried. *If someone got in here and stole this, why not take everything else? Why leave the pouch?* Her mind was buzzing with a new rush of adrenaline, when a knock on the door made her jump. As she went to the door, the real worry dawned on her. *Whoever did this was able to put my hair check precisely where it should be, and at exactly the right length!*

The next knock was louder and broke her out of the stupor she was in, staring at the closed door. Shaking her head, she put her key in the door. "Yes?"

Sula's voice came through the door. "Was the bath hot?"

She opened the door, and Sula stepped inside. Closing the door again, she tried to regain her composure. "Yes, it was extremely hot, and I really needed it." She locked the door, leaving the key in the lock.

Sniffing the air, Sula nodded. "Yes, you did. So what happened to get you so filthy and not even notice it?"

Shrugging, she stepped back to the bed and plopped down on it. "I was mugged on the way back by the Knife from three days ago." Sula's eyes brightened. *Is she curious or mad?*

"You were tagged. Are you sure it was the Knife?" Her voice was as steady and calm as ever but her eyes were slightly narrowed.

"Absolutely positive; he asked who I was working for and what the spell I tossed was."

"What happened? Would you please tell me every detail?" It sounded like a question, but it was an order, like many of the other things Sula said. She always sounded so polite and never demanding, but there was never any doubt, one should do as she asked. Sula sat down in the room's only chair, by the small table. Her back was as straight as a sword, feet tucked just so, and her hands were folded perfectly in her lap.

She has to be from a very high family. That kind of relaxed perfection is trained over a lifetime. Shrugging, Ticca explained, starting at the market. She had been expecting this, and had put together the narrative while bathing. Sula listened patiently and only interrupted to ask for more details, or to double-check a fact. When she was finished, Ticca reclined leisurely on the bed, and Sula sat, thinking quietly for several minutes.

"This might not be a total disaster."

"Look, there was no way anyone could have been more careful," Ticca started, defensively.

"No, no. That isn't what I mean," Sula cut her off. "He must have been better than we estimated. He probably only picked you up because of the spell. That he sensed it, is a real surprise." She held her hand up to prevent Ticca from interrupting again.

"If the Knife sensed the spell, then the Hand might have sensed it, too." She shook her head. "I doubt he had time to tell anyone, which is the one really good luck point here." Looking at Ticca, her eyes softened for the first time in the cycles Ticca had known her. "You've never killed anyone before."

Again, it was a statement, not a question. Ticca couldn't help it. She looked down as her throat closed up, and her eyes watered at the thought. She tried hard not to let Sula see the slight tremor that occurred in her hands, as she first looked at them as the hands of a killer.

Reaching over, Sula put a hand on her knee very gently. "I am truly sorry. But you should know you did the right thing. I am sure he would have killed you without any remorse."

Sula withdrew her hand and pretended to think for a few minutes, giving Ticca time to regain control.

Ticca straightened up. "It was bound to happen sometime." Instead of the never-you-mind tone she was aiming for, it sounded more like a squeak.

Smiling, Sula pretended it had come out as Ticca had intended. "May I please have the spell vessel back?"

Ticca pulled the small, bronze-colored cylinder from her pouch by the bed. In the light, it looked like an ordinary metal tube, but when holding it, Ticca could feel where her fingers should go, and it was sized perfectly for her hand. Ticca knew that was no accident, as Sula had measured her hand the day she hired her. She handed it over, and Sula carefully accepted it without actually touching it. Instead, she took it using a shiny white cloth, which she then wrapped around it carefully and tightly, before putting the package in her belt pouch.

"May I please see this elixir the assassin was going to use on you?"

Ticca produced the glass vial and handed it over.

Sula examined it carefully and sniffed at the seals. After holding the vial upright and tapping it, she pulled the stopper off. Ticca jumped up in surprise and moved away. Sula looked at her with amusement. "If I was going to kill you, I'd do it someplace less obvious, and in a way that would give you no chance to react."

"Yes, well, that stuff is likely dangerous, and you just broke the seal."

"True, but this particular vial is designed to be opened and resealed many times." She continued to examine the liquid, very carefully smelling it from a distance before putting the seal back into place. "Vanedicha."

"Huh?" Ticca looked curiously at the resealed vial and sat back down. *Tonight has had way too many surprises.*

"Vanedicha is a poison that induces a kind of trance if a small amount is inhaled. It kills, if you actually get a large dose." Surprisingly, Sula handed the vial back. "A couple of drops on the upper lip under the nose are enough to cause one to become like an empty shell for about three marks. When you start to wake up, you are amazingly cooperative, forthcoming, and honest for about a mark. Three or four doses within a week will cause death. It is very sweet, and will mix with hyly or a sweet wine almost imperceptibly, and cause a painless, sleeping death in about three minutes."

Ticca sat there holding the vial, staring at Sula. "How...? Why would you...? Am I to use...?" was all she could manage to say.

A charming, musical laugh filled the room. "Oh my dear, no. I just don't want you misusing it or experimenting with it."

Shaking her head to clear it, she stared at the lady. "Why not take it?"

"Well, that would be impractical. It does answer some questions, though."

"What questions?"

"For one, if he had told anyone of you yet, and the answer is no. Otherwise, he wouldn't be trying to capture you." Sula's smile turned a little knowing. "If he had, they would have told him to kill you outright." Sula stood up. "I have to report in myself, and there are a number of things to be done."

Ticca stood, as well. "I'll pick up the Hand tomorrow and start tracking him."

Sula walked over to the door and held up a hand. "No, I think it best if you find something else to do for a while. We have to determine if the Hand sensed the spell." Sula considered a moment. "It will take up to a week, possibly a cycle, to determine if anything has changed unexpectedly. In the meantime, it would be best if you went about your business as usual, so as to not attract undue attention. In fact, it might be good for you to take on small tasks while we check on the results of this evening's turn of events."

Ticca felt a sharp pain of concern. "You mean I should put up my dagger?"

Sula reached into her purse and produced a fistful of something, holding it out. "Yes. However, I am in no way finished with your services. I promise I'll be a repeat client."

Ticca held out her hand, and Sula opened hers, dropping four small, gold coins into her hand. Ticca's mouth dropped open. "Four crowns! Are you serious? I was only expecting a cross."

Sula smiled. "Of course, I am serious. I want you to keep a room here at the Blue Dolphin, where I can find you when I need you. After all, only the really talented Daggers can afford to rent a permanent room at the Dolphin." Sula turned and unlocked the door. "Doing so will let me find you, and will get you some nice local jobs with silly nobles, both of which will likely help when I come looking for you again."

With that, Sula slipped out of the room, gently closing the door behind her.

Ticca locked the door. She laid out the coins on the table. Touching them in order, she counted again. *Four crowns so she can find me again! If I get a small room here, this will last almost six cycles. If I start Daggering, I can probably earn enough to stay here as long as I stay alive.* Touching the coins, she thought, *Gold crowns. Now I know she is nobility. Even high-earning merchants don't normally carry gold.*

Ticca took the coins, put them in the new pouch, and set it aside. She looked at the glass vial on her bed. *How did Sula know all that about the poison? Where could someone with such an obviously good upbringing go to learn such things?* Shaking her head, she picked up the vial and examined the stopper again. *So I can open and close this many times. With an average dose being only a couple of drops, there is enough here to last almost forever.*

She put the glass vial on the table and picked up the new boots. She loved beautiful boots, and these were unbelievable. The leather felt soft and warm. She ran her hands over every inch, examining all the beautiful handiwork. The stitching was fine and even, running together in an endless string. The interior was lined with an unusual kind of fur. She wasn't sure what it was. Being raised as a trapper and skinner made her wonder how far these boots had come. *A real shame, they were made for a man's foot. I bet they'd be comfortable and warm year round.* Looking at the boots more closely, she noted that they really weren't much bigger than her own.

Slipping her foot into one was like putting on a well-worn and loved glove. It fit perfectly. She slipped on the second. They fit like they had been made for her alone. *How can this be? It was dark, but what are the odds, a random Knife bent on capturing and killing me would have feet exactly the same size as me?* She stood up and moved around the room. They really did fit, and they felt amazing. The unique fur lining made them very comfortable, and it was on the interior bottom too, which she thought was odd, as it would wear quickly. But it didn't compress as much as she thought it would, and felt almost like walking on soft, grassy ground.

I am too tired to reason this through. Feeling warm, clean, well fed, and comfortable, she lay down on the bed and fell asleep, still wearing her new boots.

Lebuin's Trial

CHAPTER 2

CLOAKS IN THE DARK

SOMETHING PASSED CLOSE ENOUGH TO his face that it brushed his beard and momentarily blocked the spinning mass of energy from sight. Thankfully he had spent the entire day using magical sight, so the fine flows of energy he was controlling remained constant. As he tied off one of the flows so it looped around the construction and fed from the artificial artery of power he was building, he spared a bit of concentration to glance at what had touched him. One of the masters was swinging a sword, and was coming back around for another pass. *Seriously, you expect me to worry about that? Every wizard knows how to—and does—maintain a personal shield all the time.*

A split second later, another thought brought a healthy dose of real fear. *That damned sword passed within my shield, and this isn't a training exercise!* He was in serious trouble.

Holding the minute flows under control, Lebuin diverted more power to his shield and shifted his attention fully to the attacker. *Cune! When did he get back?* His mind raced for more defenses as he realized who was attacking. A smirk grew on Cune's face as he saw that Lebuin now knew this wasn't going to go well. That pass had been just a warning, so Cune could more fully gloat over Lebuin's failure. The one rule to this test was that some effort should be made to not kill the candidate. *Damn it, I thought he was out of the country. How did he get back here so fast? For that matter, how did he find out I was going to take the trial?*

Cune did not give him any further time to wonder about the situation;

he struck hard, fast, and on target. Lebuin dodged while simultaneously sending a hard blast of energy, as much as he could spare without losing the artifact he was constructing. Brushing aside the magical blast as if it were nothing more than a fly sent to pester him, Cune finished his strike. His blade sang as it passed, totally unhindered by Lebuin's strengthened shield, right through his left sleeve, cutting a deep gash in his arm as it passed. Pain exploded from the wound, and his hold on the artifact's power flow wavered, threating to ruin the entire construction and thus signal a complete failure.

Looking down, he saw that blood was already soaking into the fine goldenrod silk of his shirtsleeve and some had splattered on his doublet. *You ruined my best doublet!* He thought. *And I almost dropped the power flow. No you don't, you bastard, you're not going to take this from me!* Reaching out to the earth line, he tapped it, adding its power generously to the air and water energies he was already channeling. Spinning around to face Cune, he waited for his opponent's next move.

Cune either didn't detect the additional power he was now pooling, or more likely he didn't think Lebuin would be able to do much with it. He danced the dance of a highly-trained Blade, his weight and balance shifting smoothly, remaining well-distributed and low. Cune brought the sword around again for another attack, lunging hard and fast. Almost too late, Lebuin released all the pooled earth mana, aiming for the floor where Cune's front foot was going to land. The ground disintegrated in an explosion of dirt and rock. Cune, caught totally off-guard, dropped halfway into the hole before his forward momentum brought his gut into contact with the edge of it. He hit so hard he folded in half, causing his face to slap the stone floor with enough force to smash his nose. The sword broke free from his extended hand and skittered to the far wall.

Dirt, dust and debris parted smoothly around Lebuin as it moved to fill the room. A murmur from the observation deck could be heard as Lebuin cautiously waited for Cune's next move. As the dust started to settle, he saw Cune still lying where he hit. Expecting a surprise attack at any moment, Lebuin approached his nemesis, who lay half in the deep hole, half face-down on the stone floor, with blood pooling around his head. *Lords, have I killed him?* Bending down, he could see Cune's chest rising and falling with breath. *He knocked himself out!* A real laugh escaped his mouth. "He's knocked himself out!"

The murmur of conversation in the observation deck got slightly louder. "Laughing over a fallen enemy is not finishing the work. He might have had some hired Blades with him, or worse, Daggers," came the sobering comment, reminding Lebuin this wasn't a simple practice session.

Turning, he scanned the area for any signs of additional attackers. Seeing none, he looked back at his construction and was proud to see that some of the effects were already manifesting, as the dust hadn't touched it.

"Is he the only threat, then?"

"Life is ever shifting and the world is full of dangers." A chuckle or three floated down from the observation deck.

Meaning yes, he was it. They didn't expect him to knock himself out cold, especially after only one real strike. All that remains is completing the construction and I am a full Journeyman. Smiling to himself, Lebuin turned his attention back to completing the artifact. The energies were still holding. *Good thing Cune's strike didn't come a few seconds earlier; I might not have been able to hold it together while dealing with his attack.*

Keeping an eye on the unconscious figure on the floor for any sign of movement, he returned to the fine work of tying all the pieces together to make the incantations hold their shape. Working with air and water magics was tricky. Still, he had spent a great deal of time figuring out this particular set of incantations, and had been practicing them for almost a year now. Next he took up the carefully selected gems he'd spent two days creating as part of these trials. Each gem was carefully cut to the precise size and shape for the incantation it needed to hold or focus. He arranged the gems on a clasp of silver in the predetermined pattern. The silver clasp had been ordered to exacting detail and carefully adjusted earlier that day by Lebuin as the initial part of this final segment of the trials. Holding the physical pieces together, he moved the energy construct down and into alignment with the clasp and its gems. With an almost audible snap the incantations bound themselves to the gems, the flow of energies melding gems and silver into one; the energies that once existed only because of his will burned their patterns into the gems and silver. The individual parts of matter and energies became a single artifact.

Taking a moment to relax, Lebuin looked closer at Cune's unconscious form. He remained right where he had been, except now the blood was dried. *He'll never forgive me for this. Not that he needed much else to hate me for.* Looking down at his own dried blood on the fine goldenrod silk, he sighed. *My best doublet ruined; what am I going to wear to the ceremony? Cune owes me far more for this. It will take years and a few more humiliations to make up for it.*

He turned and saw his master, Magus Andros, approaching the doorway to the chamber now unsealed. Looking up, he saw that most of the Magi there had already left; the rest were chatting as they filed out.

Servants rushed around the master to Cune, lifted his body out of the hole and carried him out of the chamber. The master simply walked up to the silver clasp on the bench and began to examine it in detail.

"You realize Magus Cune will retaliate for this."

"He had to have volunteered to be part of the test."

"True. In fact, he practically demanded it. I believe he was planning on bleeding you nearly to death and smashing your construction."

"As I have said before, Magus Cune has purposefully set himself against me and has taken active steps to cause me … issues."

"You did notice that Magus Cune did not just spear you. You were totally unaware of his entry, approach and initial attack. He would have been allowed to stick you like a pig on the first strike."

"Yes, I realized that," Lebuin lied. *Damn it, even when I beat him he still manages to ruin my efforts. Come to think about it, how* did *he get that close to me? I should have sensed his approach.* A quick mental tour of his now practically unconsciously maintained incantations found everything as it should be. *My alarm incantations and shields are still up.*

With a start Lebuin realized that his master was still talking. "… volunteered to be tester, he lobbied hard to convince the council to choose him; understandable, considering your long standing adversarial relationship." Magus Andros looked over his shoulder to make solid eye contact. "If he was truly the evil nemesis you claim he is, would he not have simply poked you in a non-fatal but painful spot first?"

· He shook his head. *None of you understand it—he is more than evil, he is devious, intelligent, and calculating to a fault.* "You may have a point." Keeping eye contact with Magus Andros, Lebuin decided to continue planting the alternative seeds he had been working on for the last few cycles. "After this embarrassment he will not be helpful to any of my endeavors. He might even actively attempt to undermine me." Lebuin couldn't help showing small smirk, and his master didn't miss it, either.

Magus Andros smiled himself. "You really have an interesting mind." Turning back to the silver clasp, he continued his examination. "I must say, this is rather more extravagant than most candidates manage to create. I note a number of formulas which I would venture to guess are completely unique."

Lebuin puffed up in pride slightly. *Yes, it does have a number of entirely new formulas. I have been developing those for years. I think you are going to be impressed when you notice the twist. A twist that isn't exactly new, but a variation on a little-known pattern.*

Lebuin recalled the day, many years ago, when he had returned to his rooms to find three very old tomes. Attached was a note instructing him to keep them hidden, take care of them faithfully, and to pass them on in turn, with wishes from an anonymous supporter that they'd help with his "challenges". All three books were copies, and yet they were faded and crumbling with age. They were the research memoires of a Magus Seriel of Eralci, who lived so long ago that no records existed in the Guild libraries of either him or the city he had come from.

Thankfully they had been written in the Magi's language, or at least an early root of it. It took him nearly two years of intense page-by-page work to copy, cross-reference, and translate them into his own journals in the modern Magi's usage. After that he had read them again and again, each time writing hundreds of notes and ideas of research to do. Those books had provided the foundation for many of his innovations, most especially the workings of his trial artifact. Not once in his twenty years of study at the Guild had he seen another formula similar to the key of his artifact.

Lebuin again wondered who his anonymous supporters were. There had been times when he had nearly failed, or when Cune had thwarted one of his tests or projects; each time some small trinket or library book had appeared, with a note suggesting it might help with his difficulties. The notes were all in a different hand, using different grammatical patterns. Each time, he had found a way to use that aide to overcome the difficulty, or at least rebalance his course. He often suspected one or two Magi, especially when the anonymous support stopped coming after Magus Gezu died. Of course, he also hadn't had a near-total defeat or even a serious challenge since the Magus's death.

A soft grunt of surprise pulled Lebuin back to the present situation. He smiled wider, knowing that Magus Andros had found the key. "This is remarkable work, Lebuin."

Magus Andros picked up the clasp and fastened it to his tunic, which Lebuin noted was made from wool. *A perfect, if not exactly elegant, conduit. I have a beautiful light samite and ermine cloak ready for this.* Lebuin relaxed his mind and flexed his vision into magical sight. He watched the clasp begin to work, the energies subtly flowing down the tunic. The way it moved was interesting, and he concentrated on areas where the effects pooled moving in an odd path. He noted that the energies moved well through the cloth's weave, as he expected. However, there were places where it had been mended with a cotton thread, and in those places the incantation had to move around the repair, causing odd anomalies. *I've never seen it do that before. But of course I don't have any clothes with repairs. He has had that tunic a long time. I never noticed it had so many rips and repairs; I wonder that he hasn't replaced it by now. He certainly has no need to be a spendthrift.* Eventually the entire garment was evenly infused with the energies of the incantation. *Praise the Lords and Ladies; at least it eventually reaches full coverage. I need to not show surprise on the pooling effect initially around the repaired locations.* Lebuin carefully schooled his look to appear interested and slightly worried, as anyone in a testing situation would be.

Magus Andros was also watching the effects. When the energies had stabilized, he nodded. "This is very interesting, very interesting indeed. I am surprised you held the construct together as it was when Magus Cune attacked. The only poor mark from today is that you failed to notice Magus Cune until he purposefully got your attention. Still, this was an excellent test, with a remarkable defense and an extraordinary construction. I presume the council members will be as impressed as I am." Patting the clasp, he added, "I shall have to take this construct with me to show them. I'll return it to you, along with their ruling, later tonight. I don't think it is too far out of line to congratulate you now,

Lebuin. You should have your archive token with you, unless you want to use this."

Lebuin's thoughts spun fast. *He liked it! I passed! After today I can choose my own lines of work. After all this time, I am finally a Journeyman.*

Turning and walking out through the portal, Magus Andros shook his head, looking back at Lebuin. "Only you would put so much effort into creating a device to keep yourself dry, clean, and at a comfortable temperature. Most would have tried to make a protective shield with this formula, given the tasks ahead."

Lebuin's thoughts were so far distracted by the compliments and his likely achievement of Journeyman status that he didn't even register Magus Andros' parting comment. *I need to change before anyone sees this mess on my sleeve.* Checking the hall, he hurried out and moved like a ghost towards his rooms. Oddly, the corridors were very empty. *I wonder what time it is. I know construction takes time, but most of the work was already finished. I thought I'd be done before sunset. This feels more like late night.*

He reached his room without seeing anyone but servants. Stepping into the small chamber, he moved to the second of his two fine wooden armoires. Pulling a key from his pouch, he unlocked the brass-inlaid lock. The doors swung open on their well-oiled hinges without a sound. Inside were four cabinets, two large drawers on the bottom, and a full-length silver mirror attached to the inside of the left door.

Looking at himself in the mirror, he shook his head. He was marginally above average height at five feet, eleven inches. His dark green eyes looked tired, and his normally pale skin looked a little whiter than usual. Without thinking, he took the brush and worked it through his sandy brown hair, fixing it to fall mostly on the right. His hair fell to just past his shoulders. Putting the brush down, he stripped off his clothes and threw all of them in the trash basket. Looking back at himself, he sighed. *I wish I wasn't so skinny. Without clothes on, I look like a starved beggar.*

He moved over to the water bowl. He warmed the water with magic before taking a hand towel and moistening it. As he scrubbed the wound, he saw it was actually pretty shallow. It still stung. He moved back over to the open armoire, pulling out a small vial of clear fluid. He dripped some on the wound, watching it bubble a pinkish-white. Wiping the foam from his arm with the wet cloth, he then took another vial with an oily pink fluid, which he opened and drank fully, placing the empty vial and cap in a special basket on the desk for just such items. The warmth spread through his system quickly. He watched as the wound on his arm slowly closed, still bubbling slightly. After a minute he wiped it with the cloth again, removing all the foam and blood. The wound was gone, and no scar remained. He finished cleaning up.

Unlocking the other armoire revealed two cross-sections of clothes hanging on bars, with another set of four drawers on the bottom, as well as another full-length silver mirror. He examined the clothes and selected a sea-blue shirt, matching loose trousers, and a fine sleeveless doublet of grey silk, with silver cording that would show off the shirt's pleated sleeves. To this he added riding boots which had never seen a horse—or a dirty road, for that matter. Pulling down the samite and ermine cloak, he put it on and admired the results in the mirror.

A skeleton with large, tired-looking green eyes, lovely sandy brown hair neatly parted, dressed as fine as any baron, stared back at him. *Why can't I bulk out like my brother?* he wondered again. His brother was a real bull of a man, standing a full six feet tall and weighing in at two hundred pounds of pure muscle. Practically every girl in town swooned when he walked by. They barely acknowledged Lebuin's presence, which was why he had started paying attention to fashion. By dressing with clear fashion sense, he had managed to find a means to attract some attention from the ladies. Of course *now* it was more than a means to attract the ladies. He truly loved his clothes, and was immensely proud of his fashion sense. In fact he had broken up with his last girlfriend because, in spite of her amazing beauty, she refused to dress well in private, which drove Lebuin crazy. *I really wished she wouldn't just wear those frumpy old clothes at home all the time.*

He added a complementary blue ribbon to tie his hair back and nodded to himself in the mirror, satisfied. *It's silly for journeymen to gift the Guild with a token that is never used. Traditions can be so silly; it is a wonder we continue to uphold them.* Still, reaching to the top cabinet he took out the crude artifact that he had selected long ago to be his token, when he had learned that all journeymen gift a trinket of their own making to the Guild. He hadn't given it a second thought since. It was a small silver ship, fused to a piece of dark-blue geode, which reminded him of his family. He had made it as part of his training in artifact creation. It contained a simple incantation so that the crystal glowed slightly, making it very beautiful at night. Putting the glowing ship into his pouch, he closed the doors and carefully relocked them.

He walked to the library slowly and in a slight haze. He could have ordered some food and dined in his room, but he truly lived in the library. Since the age of three when he first entered the Guild, the library had been a place of comfort and enjoyment for him. He spent every spare minute there.

Finding one of his favorite nooks empty, he sat down in the large, comfortable chair. His thoughts roamed over the trials. The tests had been difficult, but now the very last test he would ever have to take was over. From now on he was a Journeyman Magus, able to choose his own work, able to set his own path, under the direction of no one except himself. He wasn't worried about passing. The construct demonstrated techniques only few Magi had ever mastered, such as the ability to bind and draw the energies necessary from anyone, so long as they were within a few feet. The other incantations were all variations of the minor comfort formulas taught to every candidate, to help them remain healthy, as well as provide safe practice for maintaining continuous incantation and energy-channeling. Of course he had added some nice twists, such as the self-adjusting temperature, which shifted back and forth between warming and cooling as needed; strengthening the dirt repellent to the point that the protected cloth would remain sterile; and causing all the effects to spread out enough that a medium-length cloak would provide the protection to the entire body.

A servant silently placed a glass of wine on the table next to him. As the man started to move away, Lebuin pulled his attention to the present and raised his hand. The servant stopped. "Do you require anything, sir?"

"Yes; bring me some fresh-cooked meat, cheeses, fresh fruit, and a full loaf of bread. Also, bring me bottle of sharre."

"Hello, mighty Master Magus Lebuin." As the servant moved away, a sandy-yellow head of hair appeared, leaning into the nook's entry, accompanied by the very sarcastic greeting.

Lebuin laughed and gestured at the adjacent chair. "Hello, Finnba. Sit down."

Finnba said mockingly, "Am I now only an apprentice to be ordered around, SIR Magus Lebuin?" He plopped down in the indicated chair, smiling.

Lebuin took in his friend's appearance, noting that he was still wearing the same leather slippers, old, soft brown pants, patched gray linen shirt, and tired, loose, sleeveless green cotton doublet he always favored. He shook his head, thinking, *The man has no sense of style. I wish I could get him to wear some of those nice outfits I gave him. I can't believe he dresses like this even when we go out in the city.*

"You'll be taking the examination yourself pretty soon. Then we'll be able to speak more like equals. But don't forget I will still have seniority over you."

"You'll have seniority over me forever. Of course, a year's difference won't mean much after ten years or so. I bet I am promoted to a higher position than you before too long."

"You can have your bureaucratic office. You always were a quill boy. Also, you might be only a year younger than me, but I entered the Guild a full five years before you did."

"Ah yes, well, we can't all come from fabulously rich merchant families with noble-house relations. Besides, you are only one year ahead of me in training. Don't forget you had to grow up a bit first."

Lebuin didn't comment on that; it was an old jibe. His family was wealthy and owned many ships, and yes, his cousin had married some remote relative to a barony. His mother had died giving birth to his sister. He was so excited to see his baby sister for the first time that lights danced around the room. Lebuin was three years old. His shocked father had called the Guild for help, unsure of how to deal with a magical son so young. The Guild had taken control of him, and he had grown up in this very Guildhouse. He visited, and was visited, by his large family but although he loved his father and siblings, he only ever felt at home here in the Guild.

He knew he was unique in his abilities and powers. In fact, he was extremely proud of how much power he had to control. Every so often someone was born with magical abilities from the very start. These people usually became great wizards. As one of these unique people, Lebuin knew that his early training had been more about controlling him than teaching him how to use his powers. His first eight years at the Guild had been spent in a private wing, being taught individually by two instructors at a time. He was never allowed to play with the other kids alone. He recalled that many of the other kids had avoided him out of jealousy, and he long ago decided he didn't need them either. So he learned to live in solitude, which became a theme for his time there. Even after he had learned enough control of his emotions and powers to be moved in amongst the normal students, he was shunned by his peers. He had mostly ignored everyone else, staying in the library reading and researching when not required to be in classes. Only Finnba had managed to get to know him and become a friend.

He had spent so much time at the Guild with Magi and Journeyman that initially the Guild had skipped his introductory training, thinking he had already gotten it. It was discovered in his third year of training that he actually had not learned some of the anchoring techniques, so he had been put with the entry-level classes just as he was starting on his fourth year. Thankfully, the teachers rotated so much that he didn't actually repeat anything specifically. In fact he was grateful for the restart, because it gave him the knowledge that there were in fact numerous points of view to magic. *I liked the repeat lessons—they were not boring because the different instructor brought an entirely different view to the lessons, giving me a better grasp of magic than others. Perhaps when I am more respected I might recommend making that repeat loop part of the normal training for most. Of course, it would add three years to the training time.*

"Is Magus Cune really so smashed up you can't recognize him?"

Finnba's question brought Lebuin back to the present. "What? No. He did smash his nose pretty badly and bled a lot from it before it stopped."

"Huh, I figured the rumors were a bit exaggerated."

"Rumors? Really, there are rumors already? We finished the exams not more than a mark ago."

"Are you daft? You know a mark is ancient history in rumor time."

"No, I just can't believe I am the subject of one."

"You mean 'again.' Well, of course you are—when someone manages to blow a full Magus totally out of their construction trial without losing the construct, people are going to talk."

Rolling his eyes, Lebuin looked closer at his friend. *He isn't exaggerating, that is really what they are saying. How could a full Magus spread such an exaggeration? Maybe it was the servants. Cune is going to be impossible to avoid after this. I'll have to find some way to distract him from seeking vengeance.* "I didn't blow him out of my test. I made a hole for him to fall into. He knocked himself out on the floor falling into it."

"Seriously? Oh, that is so much better." Finnba's eyes brightened with humor. "Tell me what happened."

A servant brought in a platter of food with two glasses and a bottle of sharre already opened. The food was set on the table between the two magicians, and the wine was poured. Lebuin barely noticed, but did start eating as he related to Finnba the events and Magus Andros's comments.

After the story, and when, unsurprisingly, the bottle of sharre was empty, Finnba stood up. "Well, I'm off to set some rumors straight. This is far more entertaining than the whole 'flamboyant Magi battle' described to me."

Lebuin pointed at his friend, laughing fully. "Don't blow it too far out of proportion. I still have to deal with Magus Cune for many, many years."

Smiling, Finnba gave him a fake shocked look. "Blow it out of proportion? Me? I only tell the precise truth, especially when it is far more entertaining than some silly yarn." With that he stepped out of the nook.

Hunger satisfied and mind clear from the talk, Lebuin considered what to do next. He stood and stretched. He needed to do something while waiting for the council's decision. He walked over to the window and looked out on the south street. Leaning comfortably against the sill, he slowly drank from his still full glass of sharre and watched the people two stories below moving back and forth on the road. It was interesting to imagine what each person was like, what they did, and what they might be up to, although it wasn't hard as most were sailors, workers or peasants.

Lebuin was just about to go to his room when he noticed a rather graceful lady walking down the street past the Guild. What really caught his eye was the smooth flow of her calf-length cloak, with its rust colored, fur-trimmed collar matched perfectly to the dusky, almost black-red cloth. The hood pulled fully over her head was of the same material, but lined with a dark grey fur which set off the entire look. It was an unexpectedly elegant but functional cloak. Safely out of her line of sight, he watched her moving past, enjoying the flow of her movements and the shifting of the cloak. She wasn't someone he had seen before, he was sure of that. That flowing movement was very unique, especially in this city of hard-walking, jostling dock workers and merchants.

Just as she was directly across the street from him, passing the narrow alley, someone hidden in the shadows grabbed her violently and threw her to the ground, out of the light. Lebuin yelped in surprise and stood up to get a better view. In the near-perfect darkness he couldn't see the assailant or the lady. He immediately, almost unconsciously, invoked another long-practiced incantation to enhance night vision. His vision instantly became far better than an owl's and sharper than a hawk's. Everything about the scene below became crisp and clear.

The lady was totally helpless, face down four feet into the alley. The man attacking her was kneeling on her back with one knee, his other leg braced to hold her in place. He had her right arm twisted cruelly up and behind, being held by both his arm and knee. The attacker pulled a glass vial from a pouch and was concentrating on opening the stopper with his thumb and forefinger. Something else bothered Lebuin; his vision slid from the man's cloak, and the cloak itself appeared to merge with the dark shadows on the pavement making it impossible to tell where the cloak stopped and the shadow began, even with his enhanced vision. This was not an ordinary mugger or rapist.

Lebuin was preparing one of the few offensive incantations he knew when the totally unexpected happened. The lady bent herself backwards, practically in half, kicking the assailant off of her back. Lebuin was so shocked all he could do was stand and stare with his mouth open like a fresh-faced school boy. Her attacker, caught off-guard, landed badly in a heap, his cloak making half of his body seem to be missing as if he was some kind of creature crawling out of the shadows themselves.

Lebuin stared dumbfounded, incantation totally forgotten, as the lady continued the back-folding motion completely over her head. She pushed off with her free hand, snapping over to end up standing in an attack posture facing the villain. Her cloak spread out behind her from the motion like some silly romantic bard's tale. The villain started to stand, the effect not unlike a demon dragging itself into reality from the shadows. The lady, unfazed, took a step towards him and then jumped sideways directly over him. As she passed over him she caught him in a neck hold, braced by her other arm, which must have been screaming in pain from the abuse it had just endured. Her weight, motion, and hold did their job efficiently, obviously breaking the man's neck.

She stood over the body for a moment and then grabbed it by the boots and dragged it further into the alley. Lebuin was still trying to come to grips with a brutal attack being turned totally on end by this amazing woman. She efficiently stripped him of a belt, a pouch, and for some reason even his boots. However, she left the cloak. She then moved back to the alley entrance and glanced nervously around. With no one really looking, she stepped back onto the main street. She pulled her hood—now soiled with alley grime—back up to cover her dirty elegant oval face and continued walking in the direction of the docks.

Lebuin watched her go and then looked back at the body in the alleyway to confirm what he'd just seen. There was a pouch still on the body and it was smoking. Within moments the body was completely consumed in a strange green fire that didn't burn *up* so much as *in*. A minute later both fire and body were gone. All that remained was the cloak and a black charred spot on the alley floor in the shape of a body. The cloak still faded into the shadows. If it wasn't for the impossible shadow it caused it would have been totally invisible.

Lebuin glanced around; he was still alone in his safe library nook. He reached up and unlatched the window. Cautiously swinging it open so as to not make noise, he cast another incantation. He watched the street, picking a moment when no one was looking, and then reached his mind out to that cloak. With a perceptible reluctance the shadows released their cousin and the cloak flew rapidly to the open window and his waiting hand. Once he had it in his hand he let it dangle loosely outside the window as he extended his incantation for dust and dirt repellence to it. Ashes, dirt, and slime fell from it to the grounds below.

Once it was clean, Lebuin pulled it inside and closed the window. In the library light it was a very fine, dark-gray silk cloak with a hood. Lebuin looked it over closely and smiled. He even liked the color. Folding the cloak into a neat packet, he started back towards his room.

I cannot believe what it must be like to live out in this city. People always out to one up you if you let them. Pick pockets, thieves, muggers, rapists, and worse prey on the innocent. Shaking his head, he replayed the memory of the lady flipping up backwards. *From helpless victim to efficient killer in less time than it took for me to decide what incantation to use to help her. I am so glad I don't have to live out there. I am too much the scholar to try to deal with those kinds of challenges.*

On his way back he met a well-dressed servant coming from the opposite direction. "Master Lebuin," the servant said softly, stopping him.

For a moment he panicked, like a child caught stealing biscuits. He clutched the cloak a little tighter. *Get a hold of yourself, you've done nothing and this is just a Guild servant.* He forced himself to relax, so his voice was only slightly more excited than normal. "Uh, yes, do you need something of me?"

"Yes, Master Lebuin, I am instructed to bring you to the council immediately."

Thoughts of the incident in the alley were pushed away suddenly as he recalled that he was waiting for news on his Journeyman trial. "Oh yes, of course, let me drop this package off in my room and I'll go to their chamber presently."

The servant nodded and fell into step with him. "I could have someone take that for you."

"We are only a moment from my door. No reason to bother anyone with this."

The servant simply followed him to his room and waited outside while he quickly put the cloak into his armoire. Then, despite the fact that he knew where to go, the servant led him through the corridors to the main stairs and down to the first floor. Instead of turning towards the council's chamber, the man indicated he should follow him towards the main audience chamber. That could only mean one thing, and Lebuin stood a little taller as he walked behind.

Lebuin smiled as they approached the great doors. Before the doors stood ten Magi in two rows, who watched as he approached. He scanned the Magi's faces, recognizing almost everyone. Oddly, Cune was not there. A gong sounded and the doors silently swung inward. The servant who had escorted him stepped forward. "I present Apprentice Lebuin of Llino." He turned and made a sweeping gesture to Lebuin.

Lebuin looked into the large hall. It could hold a full two hundred people easily, and he was shocked to see it was full of other Magi and apprentices. *I really should have attended some of the other candidate trail ceremonies.* Laughing at himself inside, he managed to maintain a straight back and only smiled wider. *You'd think in twenty years I would have had time to go to at least one. But they always sounded boring, and I always had three books waiting in the library which were far more interesting. From what Finnba said, all I have to do is follow their lead.* Looking around, unsure about what to do next, he was grateful when the servant smiled and indicated he should walk in. *I know him from somewhere.* He rarely noticed servants; they came and went like ghosts. However, this one was about his height, wearing a very well-fitting Guild uniform of traditional dark gray pants and a soft, light gray button-down shirt with purple piping. On the front left and right chest corners of the shirt was the Guild sigil: a stylized dragon with the five waves behind it, embroidered in silver thread. The servant had light brown, almost golden eyes, and was a middle-aged Karkaian. As Lebuin recalled, his name was Ditani, and he was the personal servant for Magus Gezu. *Ditani, I haven't seen him in the three years since Magus Gezu died. He cried at his funeral pyre. After that he disappeared. I wish I could talk with him, but this is not the right place or time. I'll have to find him after this is done, but right now I have more important things to pay attention to.*

Taking the cue, he walked straight down the middle of the chamber. He heard the Magi who had waited outside fall in behind him. *What are they all about?* he wondered. Ahead, at the end of the aisle, were the five seats of the council set in a semi-circle on a raised dais. The council members stood before four of the seats. The fifth seat was always mysteriously empty. It had a large Guild sigil at the center of its backrest, and was really more of a throne. *I don't think I should kneel; only foreign trade ambassadors have done that.* So he stood tall and looked at the council members.

"Apprentice Lebuin," Councilor Nillo said in his deep baritone. "We have reviewed the reports of all your trainers, your mentor, and the trial coordinators." The councilor's eyes locked onto his. "In all cases you have been deemed ready and worthy of the badge of Journeyman to the Guild. The council itself has reviewed and inspected your works through the Journeyman trials and found your craftsmanship to be of a worthy level." Breaking the eye contact, Lebuin could swear something slightly more than ritual words and a hard stare had just happened. Councilor Nillo looked around the room. "Do any Guild Magi have cause or concern with advancing Apprentice Lebuin to the rank of Journeyman?" When no one answered, Councilor Nillo gestured to his right. "Magus Cune, you were the final trial judge; do you approve the advancement of this Apprentice?"

What! The trial judge has direct approval of advancement? So that was his game. I should have guessed he wouldn't simply stand by and let me advance. A shuffling sound came from his left, and Lebuin looked over. Magus Cune stepped down from the platform where he had been standing and approached Lebuin, where he stood shoulder to shoulder with him, facing the council.

Cune smiled and gave a slight bow to the council members. He then turned and faced Lebuin directly. "Council of the Guild, I wish only to publicly acknowledge Apprentice Lebuin's achievements here, and I am pleased to report he is ready to hold the badge of Journeyman."

There go my chances for another year. Lebuin sighed in acceptance of defeat.

"Apprentice Lebuin, you are found ready, worthy, and recommended for the badge of Journeyman. You will now deposit with the Guild a token of your own creation."

Wait, what just happened? Lebuin's thoughts raced in circles. *Cune didn't veto my advancement? But that means I am going to be a Journeyman. Why wouldn't he stop it?* Looking at Cune, he saw the same evil smirk the Magus had worn during the test. This was another moment of extreme pleasure for Cune, at Lebuin's expense. But Lebuin couldn't figure out why.

Realizing the ceremony would be stopped until he produced a token, he pulled the ship out of his pocket and held it out. Two of the council members, Nillo and Crawstu, smiled at it. After a moment it floated from his hand and hovered between him and the council. Cune moved back to his position in the crowd, as all four of the council members held up their right hands and an aura of power enveloped the ship. It reached out then to all the assembled Magi. At last, it reached out for Lebuin. When it touched him he felt it lightly resting on his shields, which he dropped, then it connected with his skin at the center of his torso. The energies filled his whole being. His vision shifted involuntarily to Magi sight and his little ship was enveloped in a sphere of energies with tendrils floating out to all the Magi present, himself, and one extra, almost invisibly thin, which went straight up. Glancing up, he noted that it went up through the ceiling and beyond his ability to perceive.

Councilor Crawstu spoke first, her voice bouncing off the walls with a resonance Lebuin had not heard before. "Do you, Lebuin, voluntarily accept to abide by, support, and if necessary enforce the Laws of Magic of the Guild of Argos Magi, from this day until the end of your days?"

"Yes, I do," Lebuin said, and he felt a vibration in the magical connection through the token.

Councilor Dicha's light tenor voice also vibrated off the walls. "Do you, Lebuin, voluntarily accept the duties, badge and rank of Journeyman to the Guild of Argos Magi?"

"Yes, I do," Lebuin said, and felt another vibration.

Councilor Mica's normally silky-soft voice practically shook Lebuin to the floor. "Do you, Lebuin, voluntarily accept the rule of Lord Argos and this, the Guild of Argos Magi, in the name of Lord Argos, from this day until the end of your days?"

"Yes, I do." This time something almost tangible was pulled from Lebuin, passed through the connection to each Magi, and as it came back to him, a small fragment broke off and went up the tendril through the ceiling. The remainder returned to Lebuin. Lebuin was shocked to have a general feeling for where every Magi in the area was. It wasn't like being able to see them, but more a general feeling that someone was close and a sense of their direction.

Councilor Nillo's deep baritone voice practically shook the foundation of the building. "In so accepting the Laws of Magic, the rule of the Guild, and the duties and rank of Journeyman of the Guild of

Argos Magi, you are so made Journeyman to the Guild of Argos Magi."

The connection swelled with power and then all of the threads snapped into the small geode ship like a frog's tongue. For a moment the ship and geode glowed with a faint white radiance. Then everything returned to normal.

The Council Magi each stepped down in turn, touching their right hand to the small ship still floating in front of Lebuin. They then each touched Lebuin and offered congratulations or wise-sounding advice.

Councilor Nillo was last, and he plucked the ship from the air. "Congratulations, boy! You finally managed to get out of this place. You'd think after more than twenty years you'd be stark raving mad. I look forward to hearing what you're planning for your Journeyman quest. You can tell me in the morning. I expect you'll be leaving tomorrow or the day after at the latest." He laughed and moved on as the procession of other Magi lined up to congratulate him.

Lebuin stood there, trying to recover from the final pull of whatever that incantation had been. It wasn't until the half Magi had congratulated him that Nillo's words sank in. *I have to leave on a quest by tomorrow! What quest? What was he talking about?* Lebuin wondered if he had misheard it; then he realized many of the Magi congratulating him on the badge were also wishing him a safe journey.

Then Magus Cune was before him, with that smirk. He congratulated Lebuin quite loudly, then leaned in close and said softly, "To make things more interesting, I placed a rather large bet with a less-than-upstanding but influential friend of mine that you could complete the quest." Then he turned, laughing, and walked away.

As the rest of the Magi and apprentices congratulated him, he realized that he didn't know a single Journeyman Magi who had ever stayed at the Guildhouse before being made a Magus. As he realized he would have to go out into the world for something as yet unknown, Cune's parting words fully registered. *Lords of Light, what just happened?*

Jicca's Dagger

CHAPTER 3

FOREST FOR THE TREES

BIRDS SANG IN THE DISTANCE as Ticca moved carefully along the game trail. The traps needed to be checked every day to prevent any accidental miss causing unneeded grief. The next trap came into view; it had been tripped, yet was empty. Ticca paused, listening to the sounds of the forest for anything out of place. Her hearing identified many animals living and dying in the pattern of the woods. Sensing nothing out of place, she approached the trap cautiously.

Scrapes on the tree bark told the story. Laughing, her bell-like voice moved off through the forest. Most animals didn't even bother to pause to listen. She moved in more confidently. A bear had helped itself to the bait meant to attract the large red squirrels she needed to harvest. Examining the marks on the tree told her it was a half-grown cub. *Well now I have a saboteur. Not the first bear to learn it's a tasty treat.*

Enjoying the late afternoon warmth and filtered sun, she went about moving, fixing, and resetting the trap. From her large pouch she pulled a leaf-wrapped package containing the squirrel bait made of sweet nuts mixed with seeds and sweet resin. Putting the remaining bait away she jumped the twenty feet to the forest floor. Looking around a second time for bear's signs, she fished in her pouch for the small vial of grizzly musk. Her hand didn't find it so she was forced to pull the pouch around, holding it open with one hand while peering in and looking more vigorously. Finally she found it wedged at the bottom under her notebook. *I don't use this too often but is sure is handy to have.* Opening the vial, she carefully applied a few dabs of the musk on the base of the traps' new tree and rubbed it into the tree bark hard using the bearskin leather cloth she carried for this purpose. *That should warn off my little friend from climbing.*

Running through the trapping checklist in her head, she reassured herself she had done everything needed. *Of course I need to note where I put it; not that I have ever lost a trap.* She smiled to herself. *Well, at least none that I remember.* She sat down as she pulled out the notebook. The book was a beautiful traveling journal, bound in fine leather. It was lightly engraved with her sign on the front and back. The paper was of a strong fiber plant that made it impervious to moisture and which gave the trader's ink a perfect surface to adhere to. Both the paper and ink were made by their respective families in town. She had made the leather cover and sewn the book together herself. She lovingly caressed it, remembering how making such a book had been used as training on strong stitching and leather preparation by her mother. Now, of course, she made them much better—this was her tenth such journal and the best she had made yet.

Sitting and dreaming of the past is not going to finish the day's work. Opening the journal, she flipped through the pages, a combination of journal, accounting log, and map book. Identifying the page for this trap, she marked out the trap's prior position and recorded a fresh entry. She was surprised to note that this was the third time she had to move this particular trap. *I have a real stubborn bear cub hereabouts, or at least one with a serious taste for sweet nuts.* Reading some of her entries for the last few cycles' work, she smiled. *At least this is the only one for this season, so far.*

She went back to the original tree and climbed up to the old location. Pulling the sweet nut bait back out she left a small portion in the nook of the limb and tied a leaf over it to protect it from the rain. *There. I hope that will stop him from hunting down the new location.* With the small offering ready she said a small prayer to the Goddess Dalpha to thank her for the challenge, and ask that the bear not harm itself in the trap should it still find it. She jumped to the forest floor, jogged back to the game trail and followed it to the next location. If she moved fast enough she could complete the trap circuit today.

Her energy increased in anticipation of coming home after running the two-day trap circuit. The soft red pelts were tied into a tight bundle that bounced on her hips as she moved through the woods. The shadows were already very long as she approached the edge between the deep forest and the open lake glade near her home. Sitting by the lake in a suspiciously leisurely pose was the man her heart and soul agreed should be her life mate. She paused to observe him. Her heart was already racing, as it always did when she saw him. He was very tall, even sitting. His long, silky black hair flowed in the soft breeze. He wore the simple green leggings he preferred. He sat with his legs pulled under him so she couldn't see if he was barefoot or not, although it was likely he was in those horrible old boots he loved so much. His figure was striking in the brown tunic with long tapered cuffs she had made for him for Midwinter's Night.

He was gazing across the lake to the southeast. *Always thinking and planning, as if he can alter the future to meet his desires.* He hadn't noticed her and was sitting such that she could pass only a few dozen feet to the left and come up directly behind him. Smiling deviously, she cautiously moved to a better location for a stealthy approach. Softly setting down the satchel of squirrel carcasses and her pouch in a spot just behind a tree, she edged out of the forest. Her devious smile and her forward motion froze as she registered that he wasn't where he had been a moment before.

"My lady needs a bath after such a work-filled day. Allow me to assist."

She screamed as strong hands grasped her hips from behind. Lifting her as if she was a leaf, he crossed the thirty feet to the edge of the lake in a couple of heartbeats at a dead run. She kicked and squirmed wildly, hoping to throw his balance off. Their speed did not abate on reaching the lake; instead, holding her high, he jumped, carrying both of them far out over the water. Midflight she managed to twist around and grab hold of him with both arms and legs. They held on to each other tightly, laughing together as the cold water welcomed them into its embrace.

- - -

Sputtering for air, Ticca sat up in bed. Her heart was pounding hard. *Where am I?* Shaking her head, she looked around the dimly-lit room. Sunlight was filtering in past the cracks in the shutters over the small window. The room smelled of dust and the faint hint of a musky perfume was teasing her nose. *Sula's perfume. I am in Llino. This is my room at the Blue Dolphin. What the heck was that dream all about? I've never experienced anything in it at all; nothing even close, except maybe the hunting and tracking.*

She moved shakily, her new boots silently hitting the hard wood floor and giving her a more grounded feeling. She bent over, holding her head for a minute as the final cobwebs cleared from her mind. *That forest was so real. But I have never been in it before. Those squirrels were huge. And who was that man who carried me into the lake? In the dream I knew him. Except I don't think I have ever met anyone that looked like him before.* Standing, she stretched and twisted, feeling great. *Amazing what a good night's sleep can do.*

Then she remembered the crowns. *Maybe the whole night was a dream.* Looking quickly at the table she sighed. *Well at least some of it was real.* She reached for the new pouch, grateful it was still there and real. Opening it, she pulled out the four shiny gold coins and small glass vial. She sat back down on the bed and placed the vial on the small table, playing with the coins in the sun's rays coming through the window. *Four crowns in one night; I am going to make it here. I proved I'm a capable Dagger. Sula is no fool—that she paid me this means I proved myself to her.* Smiling to herself, she stood, putting the coins back into the pouch.

Carefully and slowly she went through her ritual morning stretches as best as she could in the small space. Her body virtually flowed through the movements without any complaints. *Wow I am feeling amazingly good considering the beating I took last night.* When she stretched her arms behind her she gritted her teeth, expecting the sharp pain her poor shoulder should have given her. Instead she was able to complete the back stretches without anything more than the normal slight pains of muscles loosing up.

Confused, she took off her shirt and examined her arm where the night before the large bruise had been. Her skin was a healthy dark olive. Stunned she looked over every place she could get to where there had been damage the night before. After careful examination she couldn't find a single blemish. All of the abuse from the night before had vanished as if it never happened. Even more interesting was that her skin was a fairer, more uniform color, as it had been when she was a few years younger before coming to the city.

I know I didn't dream the fight, and I had dozens of bruises in the bath last night. Seriously, I should have been hurting for at least a few days. Putting her shirt back on, she sat down on her bed, thinking through everything that had happened. *I have never healed this fast.* She looked down at the boots and thought about it for a minute. *Could these boots be magical? I've never heard of healing boots. Actually, healing boots would be very practical and not likely to be suspected or taken if captured.*

Taking the boots off and opening the shutters she examined them very closely once more, this time with the help of sunlight. They were still of the unusual very fine leather lined with a dense reddish brown fur with the best stitching she had ever seen. *Now I know where the red squirrels in my dream came from. Dreams are funny, oversized squirrels instead of a bunny or an ermine, this fur is like a denser rabbit fur.* Laughing at her imagination she looked closely at the stitching. *I know I have seen stitching like this before. But I can't place it.* Shrugging to herself and turning the boot over, she examined the sole's construction. It was made from semi-hard leather that had been treated with something that made it glisten in the light and felt slightly tacky like tree sap, but not so tacky as to pick up dirt or dust. *That is a neat trick.* There were no raised heels, but the heels were stiffer with some internal support under the fur. She flexed the boots and found that the front of the boots were as flexible as her toes. *I can climb with these. With the tacky sole treatment I bet I can climb even better with these on then off.*

The fact I am alive is all the magic I need for now. Magical or not, these are the finest boots I have ever seen. Putting the boots back on her feet, she stood and gathered her belongings. She slipped her belt through the solid loops on the new pouch. It took a few minutes of playing with the throwing knife sheaths' arrangement on her belt before it felt comfortable and she was satisfied with the impression it would make. Putting the belt on over her shirt, she wiggled to be sure it settled comfortably onto her hips. She slipped the knives into the sheaths, trying not to look. *This needs to be automatic and look smooth.* She took the knives back out again without looking. Practicing drawing and sheathing each knife in turn, in groups, and at random took a little while. Eventually she was sure she could make it look good when needed. *Forget the cross-belts; this is a good set-up, now it's time to see if I can make these work for me.*

She put all her weapons around the room and stood in the center. Slipping sideways, she stretched her foot out; angling her boot toe under one throwing knife edge, she kicked it into the air. She turned around, caught it with her off hand, and sheathed it in one motion. Bending backward she scooped another knife from the table and one from the chair with both hands. The knives were sheathed before she had finished turning to step over the new short sword. Sweeping down, she picked up the short sword and then used it to flip the final throwing knife in the air and towards her from the far corner of the room. She sheathed the sword as she caught the knife. Sheathing the throwing knife she spun, grabbed the dagger from where it laid on the floor and brandished it in a single motion ending in a defensive crouch with another throwing knife in her other hand. Stepping forward, she spun and sheathed the dagger and throwing knife together as she straightened. *Not bad, not bad at all.* She started smiling at what she imagined that had looked like. *With so many knives I might get mistaken for a Blade. 'Course with my cloak hiding some, this will do very nicely.*

Feeling great, she grabbed her pack and dropped it on the bed. Not much was actually left out. Still it took a minute to pack everything else efficiently into the pack. Giving the room one last check, she checked that the new belt pouch was properly latched closed, and tied her pack closed as well. She slipped her shoulder pouch over her head and let herself enjoy the anticipation. *Today is going to be so much fun. I have wanted to do this for cycles.*

With a very wide smile, Ticca locked the door, dropped the key into her new pouch, and then went down the three stories to the common room. Naturally the room was already busy. Genne was talking with two merchants, and three girls were moving around the room cleaning tables as well as serving new breakfasts with hot arit or jeel. Looking around the room, she saw that there were as yet no Daggers present. In fact there were only a handful of local workmen present; most workmen who breakfasted here had likely already been and left for the docks due to the early tide today. The few merchants present were all locals.

The tradesmen had likely already headed to set up their goods in the trade square.

Ticca turned and walked the short distance to the very specific table she'd dreamed of sitting at for cycles. The table was one of the many open tables used by known Daggers. It was also one of the eight that could be permanently designated to a Dagger or Dagger fire-team. It was not a large table, just big enough for maybe two Daggers and a client or two to share. It had the advantage of being near the bar and the stairs, yet still commanded an excellent view of the left main room. It was also close enough to hear clearly the left room's performing bard which was important to keep up on the best tales, news, gossip, and of course enjoy the entertainment. It was also far enough from the bard's platform to allow conversing with clients. Most importantly, the table backed to a shallow nook so she could sit with her back to a wall so no one could come up from behind. *It pays being an early riser. I beat Hairy and Frumpy again. But today I am going to move up a notch.* Licking her suddenly dry mouth, she took some deep breaths to try and slow her heart, which started racing as she approached the table. Glancing around out of the corner of her eyes, she boldly sat down at the small table.

Even though no one looked as she sat down, she was sure a few took note. Genne didn't even stop his conversation and she'd half-expected him to protest. *Genne hasn't kicked me away from here, so he at least is willing to let me sit here.* She let her pack fall into the shallow contour of the wall, which meant it was out of sight from the most of the room. She watched the room and shifted to get more comfortable; her shirt was sticking to her back a little. *Damn, I was more nervous than I expected,* she thought as she covertly pulled her shirt away from her back. Leaning back against the wall, she felt her smile grow now that she had successfully taken a more prominent Dagger table. *A couple of notches higher on the Dagger scale, now I need to earn it.* It only took a few seconds before one of the serving girls came over and put down her breakfast in front of her.

"Which would you like this morning, your hot arit or the milk we got in? It's real fresh."

Ticca smiled at her for the courtesy of the total lack of acknowledgement of the significance of her chosen location. "Actually this morning I'll take both." The serving girl stood for a second to see if she was going to be asked for the price of the milk. When it was obvious Ticca was not going ask she looked a little curious, but nodded and moved off towards the kitchens. *Ah that got you a little curious.* She let her smile turn to a smirk.

As Ticca was taking her third bite, the serving girl came back with her milk and hot arit. Setting down the drinks, the girl moved off to take care of other customers. The expected familiar pair of young men came in the door and headed straight for her table. But, seeing it occupied, they stopped for a second and then turned, taking a different table. Ticca watched as they said something to the serving girl that made her shrug as she gave them their breakfast. *Asking if I am an ignorant merchant's daughter or something I bet. I know who you are and I know who you tend to work for, but you haven't been paying much attention to anyone other than the big league Daggers, have you.* After the girl brought back some hot arit for the two Daggers they drank deeply and then the hairy one put a highly polished dagger into the dagger holder in the center of their table. It had a wide winged hand guard, and a simple circular pommel; its hilt was wrapped with a blacked iron cord. *Interesting, that is new. You two have only been doing simple patrol and guard stuff. Trying to move up to bigger jobs is risky. Especially since neither of you really look like the heavy fighting types.*

A soft thud announced Genne's arrival at the table. She looked at him as he leaned back in the chair. He had taken the other Dagger chair which kept most of his back to the wall with only the kitchen door a serious approach threat. *Always got your back covered, don't you.* She smiled as winningly as she could, causing him to frown and cross his arms.

His tone was a little tired, like a scolding father, "Ya knows d'rules."

Taking another bite of the breakfast, she kept smiling and chewed for a moment before answering, just to try and draw him in a little more. "Mm, been meaning to chat with you about them, I think some things need to change."

Genne's face actually scrunched to that as if the mere thought of a change to the Blue Dolphin's rules caused him physical pain. Hairy was nudging his companion and indicating her direction in anticipation of the show. Genne's voice changed to lower than normal, still calm and somehow very scary as he answered, "D'rules aint chang'n, m'lass."

Bait, loop, and trap all in one shot. Keeping her winning smile she unlocked the pouch at her belt and reached in for the crowns. Except instead of feeling the four coins she expected, there was a couple of small cloth bags and other items she couldn't identify by touch. She heard her trainer's voice in the back of her head saying, *'Never let them see you flinch.'* Looking back at Genne she saw she must have reacted somehow for him to pick up on as he began to frown even deeper. Now Hairy and Frumpy were smiling themselves, seeing Genne's obvious growing annoyance.

She tried not to sweat or look confused. One of the small bags was obviously a coin purse, and felt heavy with coins. *Oh Lady, what has happened to me? Please be enough.* She brought the coin purse out and opened it. Trying to act casually as if nothing was wrong she looked down and her heart skipped a beat or two. Shining back were more than fifty crosses, as well as some cheras, bells, pence, rings, and even three crowns. One slightly worn crown was sitting boldly on top like it was the king of the bag, which it was. *Lady, thank you.*

In the back of her head her trainer's voice continued on. *'Always go for the greatest impact.'* Reaching into the purse and grabbing a crown and twenty crosses, she continued. "I meant," with deliberate motions putting the coins on the table, crosses first, punctuating her words, "changing our arrangement and my room."

Genne's eyes took in the purse and she was sure he could somehow sense the precise value of its contents. He then leaned forward and just as deliberately took the crown. He examined it, tasting first and then checking the heft against his years of experience handling such coins. "Well, d'night was good for you." Looking down, she saw that all the coins had vanished. "Der is a few Dagg'r rooms open."

"Yes, well I want a small one, preferably not too close to the stairs or baths."

"I'v jus d'one." Patting his pouch, which his hands had not gone close to prior, "Dis will give ya three cycles if'n ya don'wan food, two if'n ya wants all meals with'n hyly, arit, an yer milk."

Doing some unexpected counting in her head she considered it. She knew it would likely be reasonable for the Dolphin because Genne never inflated or cheated. Knowing it wasn't a bad deal made her pause. *That is*

49

higher than I expected. I know the Dolphin is one of the best Inns in the city and also one of the most costly to stay at. At twelve—no, thirteen—crosses a cycle for the room and another seven for food I know I'll be eating full hot meals as I please. But if I get some good work soon I'll be able to maintain that rate. If I up my fee from a chera a day to a cross a day or six crosses for a week I would be just under the rate of some of the best in this room. I certainly have enough here to give me plenty of time to prove I can. Looking at Genne, she saw he had a slight smile in his eyes. *He's scheming and I'm obviously on course. I need to be sure the stable fees are in this too.* "Twenty-one crosses a cycle with stable, meals, hyly, arit, and milk for me and clients; but, as I don't drink much I also want baths and," sending up a small prayer to the Lady, "this table."

Genne's brows moved up and down a little as he obviously thought it through. His eyes told her he wasn't as surprised as she expected. *You've been watching me closer than I thought. You knew I was going to ask for this table.* Ticca had to remind herself to breathe as he thought it over. Genne was reputed to be one of the hardest men to cheat or negotiate with. Standing up, he held out his left arm. "Done."

It took a moment for her to recover from the shock of the quick agreement. She had expected to be bartering down to the threads of the bed cloth. Standing, she grasped his left forearm with her left hand. "Agreed." Across the room the two other Daggers had stopped mid-bite and stared.

Genne's large hand closed on her left forearm and he grabbed her left elbow with his right hand and held her there for a moment. Before he released her he whispered, "Ya done good lady. Try t'stay alive, I likes ya." Releasing her, he started to turn to go.

"Genne, one more thing." As he turned back to her she pulled another four crosses and two crowns out. "Make it four full cycles."

Smiling, he took the coins, nodded, and headed back to the bar.

Ticca knew the room was watching now for sure. Smiling, she did the maneuver she had dreamed of doing at the Blue Dolphin since she was a child listening to the stories the bards told. Years of practice had made the choreographed sequence seem gracefully nonchalant. As she turned and sat she put the coin purse back into the pouch and drew her dagger. It spun around her hand before drop silently into the table's holder where it stood boldly for all to see. It was a slightly longer than normal dagger polished to a mirrored surface, with a small brass cross guard etched with two packs of hounds running away from the blade, a fine bone hilt, and a diamond-shaped pommel. She smirked at the two shocked Daggers, who sat with their mouths hanging open, staring. She admired how nice the dagger looked standing straight up from the center of the table. *That's right boys, this girl is an experienced hunting Dagger and dangerous.* In the back of her head she heard her Uncle's voice when he was questioned about a Dagger story he was telling: *'It ain't braggng if you can do it. And let me tell you, Daggers can.'*

Trying to not to pay too much attention to the room, she finished her meal. A few merchants openly inspected her dagger from a respectable distance, making a note in a journal or notepad before they left. She acknowledged them with a nod or smile. Some veteran Daggers came into the room for morning meals. She didn't catch a single one of them inspecting her like the new arrival she was and a few even nonchalantly acknowledged her with a nod, wave, or morning greeting. Overall it was quiet and a little anticlimactic.

When she finished her meal Ellar appeared by the table as the serving girl carried off the empty platter. Placing a square paper-wrapped package and an odd-looking key close to her hand, he said, "M'lady, for you."

Looking at the key, she thought about her next actions. *I need to figure out what in the Lady's name is going on with this purse. Might as well inspect the room Genne thinks is right for me.* Standing, she reached out for her dagger and in a fluid swirl pulled it from the holder, looped it over her hand, and let it drop lightly in its sheath. Packing up her bag and slinging it over her shoulder, she grabbed the key and moved toward the stairs.

Hairy and Frumpy stood up as she moved off and grabbed their dagger. Before she realized what they intended Genne's voice rang out clear and loud in the otherwise quiet room. "Oi, ya c'n plant yer selves back down lads. Dat table is Ticca's from now on." Hairy and Frumpy almost fell over backwards complying. Thankfully no one laughed too loudly. *I didn't mean to embarrass them. Last thing I need is enemies right now.* She noticed a number of Daggers, merchants, and workman now looked her over fully and openly. *Well that should spread the word better than anything I could do. Bet I get something to do pretty soon.* Keeping her posture straight and casual she started up the stairs.

"Ta da right"

Jumping at Genne's voice so close, she turned. "Sneaking up on a Dagger isn't exactly safe."

He smiled as he gestured down the hall. "Dagg'rs pay 'tention, or dey die."

Ignoring the obvious jibe, "I thought you were dealing with customers."

"How'd ya fine yer room?"

She looked at the key; it was more complicated than she had seen before, there were two parallel rows of teeth and the tip was hollow on the end. Also it had no sign on it at all to indicate a room. She looked up at the hall of nearly identical doors that differed only in distance between them and color. The stone hall went a short distance from the stairs then did a gentle forty-five degree turn to the right, where it continued for some distance before ending. There were twelve doors in this hall, four on the left towards the rear, city-side of the tavern and eight on the right towards the front, wharf side. Each door looked completely solid, with a smooth surface, no handles, and each had an inlaid square brass plate in the center. Four parallel sliders moved horizontally, centered just above an engraving shaped like a keyhole for the key she held. The only exception was the door to her immediate left. That door didn't have a brass plate, instead the whole door was a glossy iron-colored metal with five sliders and three engraved circles around the keyhole engraving. Confused, she looked at Genne who had stood there watching her with a proud little smile.

"You have a point."

"Taint all dat hard. Yer key is fer d'purple door," he indicated the second door on the right. "D'sliders is a'secon lock. I'll hel'you t'set it. Den only you an' I will know it. I've a few keys t'each," he continued, gesturing at the row of doors. "If'n ya rent due an' ya don come ba' n'six cycles I call d'key, store everyting n' secret place. If'n ya don come ba' n'fifty years it's me family's clear. If'n ya come ba' you owe six cycles' rent plus a chera a cycle for safe store. Ya know how safe it tis here an' mos Dagg'rs pay tention for udder Dagg'rs. Still we ain't responsible if'n a thief gets inna your room." Looking her square on, he added, "An if'n ders a fight cuz o'you," he pointed a finger square at her chest, "yer ta pay fer damage. Clear?"

The price I agreed to is more than what I thought it was for a small Dagger room. We already agreed and nothing here will change it really; it is an interesting arrangement. I wonder if anyone has come back within fifty years. Looking straight back at him, she said, "Clear." Looking at the stone walls and running the new information through, she looked at the doors again. She glanced at the door on her immediate left that looked like solid metal. If it was painted it was the best job she had ever seen, but the locking mechanism wasn't a brass plate and something else was a little different. Pointing with her chin, she asked, "Whose room is that?"

Genne didn't even look. "Damega's. He's paid up clear for nodder few undred years. An glad I am, I don' wanna be d'one ta try an open it. Ta be honest I dou' we'll ever try ta claim it. See, he is d'one who designed d'locks an some of our udder features." Her eyes locked on the door, stunned as if it was a mythical monster come to life. Taking the key from her limp hand Genne stepped up to her door, moving the sliders to different spots. He waited a couple of seconds, then a soft click came from the panel and an interior cover slid out of the way, showing that the engraving was a real keyhole but with some kind of very tight-fitting internal cover. Genne stuck the key in and turned it to the right. A couple of clicks came from the door, and he pushed it open. As he removed the key another snap came from the lock as the sliders all returned to the far left and the interior cover slide back into place, turning the keyhole back into an engraving on the panel.

Stepping in, he motioned for her to look at the back of the door. Edging into a much larger room than she expected, she turned her attention to it. There was a handle in the middle of the plate which had another slider that moved vertically next to it.

"Ya c'n keep d'door open by mov'n dis up," indicating the vertical slider, which was currently all the way down. "Up an any'one c'n come in. Down an' its locked. Ya don need d'key ta get out." He paused, looking at her. She nodded that she understood the basic workings. Genne pulled a different key from another pouch, moved the sliders again to open the keyhole. This time he stuck the different key in and turned it hard to the left and held it there. "Move these how ya wan dem t'open d'key'ole."

She changed their positions and made sure to remember it. When she nodded to Genne he turned his key back and withdrew it from the door. Again the sliders all returned to the far left and the keyhole snapped closed. Closing the door, he handed over her key. "Les' see ya open it."

It took a couple of attempts to get the hang of the lock but she eventually passed some level of competence because Genne grunted. "Ya'll do." He gently put his hand on her shoulder. "Ya moved up a notch ta day, lady. Dagg'rs are m'family's tradition an'trust. I thin' yer ready. Ders an ancient Dagg'r say'n from afor dey came here," he indicated Damega's door with his head. "'Heros get remembered, legends live forever.' It's yer turn ta add ta da Dagg'r legend." He stood looking her in the eye for a minute, then nodded as if she had made the mark. "Dro' d'udder key off when yer don mov'n." He turned and went down the stairs without another word.

Well, I wanted to be a Dagger, and I am. Honor, courage and commitment will win, just like you said, Uncle. In the back of her mind she heard her Uncle's voice: *'Nobody ever drowned in sweat girl, so dig in and work hard.'* With a nervous glance at the metal door across the hall from hers, she stepped into the room and closed the door. *I just rented the room across the hall from Damega's, in the biggest trade city of the realm. Uncle, you wouldn't believe this in a million years. Lady forgive me, I don't believe it myself.*

She checked that the door was locked and stepped over to the large bed which was in a small alcove with an armoire on the right. Turning, she felt giddy looking at the magnificent room she could call her own. It was larger than she'd expected, with a dining or planning table filling the recess that jutted out to the left of the doorway. She stepped over to the street-side window and brushed her hand along the empty bookcase next to it. She plopped into one of the four overstuffed chairs in front of the bookcase and enjoyed the feeling of her own space.

There was a door behind the entry door. Curiously, Ticca stood up and opened it. She stood, shocked for a moment that she even had a private toilet with a clothes storage room big enough for dozens of outfits with room to spare. *Wow, I have running water in my room and I don't have to use the communal toilet. I'm not even going to try to explain this to Uncle. If he comes he'll be shocked silent.*

Wandering over to the window, she looked out on the street in front of the tavern. Merchants and workmen moved back and forth along the wharf road. Large carts were being pushed or pulled in every direction imaginable. She noted that the window could be opened inward and had outer shutters. The view was amazing, the glass was almost flawless. Something about it made her look closer and she found that the frame was made of metal and the glass was an unbelievable inch thick. The security of the window was made even stronger by a set of inner shutters made of iron which could be closed and bolted shut.

Turning around she took in her new room again from the window. *Now I know why the rate was higher than I expected. This is more than I ever imagined. To think this place has been here for hundreds of years. I wonder who has used this room, if I ever heard of them in a bard's tale.* Smiling widely, she laughed. *I wonder what the bards will do with a name like Ticca.*

She shook her head. *I have things to do and I need to get back down there to get work to keep this place.* She quickly found a place for most of the stuff in her pack. Then she took off her belt and pulled the mysterious pouch off of it. Laying her belt out on the bed she took the pouch over to the low table and sat down in one of the stuffed chairs. *Oh Lady, these are comfortable.* She leaned back and enjoyed the comfortable feeling. Then she noticed a low stone table, just the right height for a drink... or her feet. So she put her feet up on it, finding it solidly in place. Holding the pouch with both hands, she started looking at it again, more closely this time.

It seemed a simple, medium-sized pouch. *You know, this is just the right size for a small travel book. And the package the Knife handed over in the Night Market would have fit in this perfectly, if nothing else was in it.* Opening the pouch, she discovered that it still had the coin purse and other items, which she now pulled out. There was a flint pack, some string looped so that so it could be pulled out easily, a small red wax candle, a small high-quality mirror in a silk sleeve, three circular stones that looked like fat coins but which stuck together quite strongly, and a second purse of brown silk that held five gems. Taking the cloth coin purse, she emptied it and counted thirty-two crosses, six cheras, nine bells, sixteen pence, and five rings. *The gems have to be worth at least fifteen, maybe twenty crowns. Lady, that wasn't just any simple Knife! He had thieves' tools, was carrying as much as a noble would, and wearing a pair of magic boots.*

Looking at the now-empty pouch, she turned it over and over. It was well-made but there was nothing extravagant about it. *Where did that vial and my shiny four crowns go? This is the stuff I saw in it when I took it from him.* That thought stopped her for a moment. *This means that no one got into my room but somehow the items vanished and reappeared.* Looking at the clasp again she noticed that its inscription was circular. In fact it had an inner and outer ring that split what was already a very nice geometric pattern. Feeling the clasp she noted that it was very smooth, that the geometric pattern had five distinct outer areas, and that in each of these there was an invisible deformity in the surface. Her fingertips could feel slight indentions in each of the five areas and each section had a unique feel to it. *It must have something to do with these patterns I can feel.*

Feeling along the center section shifted it slightly under the pressure of her finger. Sitting up, she looked closer. It was almost imperceptible, but the center of the pattern could rock back and forth slightly and it locked into position, requiring specific pressure at the top or bottom to shift it into the other position. Looking into the pouch with the center section pressed on the top or bottom changed nothing. *Why cut the pattern in half with a circle?* She looked closer and realized that if she rotated the outer portion of the clasp, each of the five outer areas where the circle cut them would still interconnect, making a slightly different but complete pattern. Meaning the pattern would be complete, but slightly different, in any one of five points if the outer portion was rotated. *Maybe it is meant to rotate.* Grabbing the clasp she tried to turn it without success.

Dang, I thought I had it. She sat back, looking at it; then an idea came. *A rotating lock?* She pressed the bottom half of the center section. It rocked into place. Grabbing the outer ring she found it resisted moving slightly at first and then moved very easily. She turned it one fifth of a turn. It actually snapped into position, leaving the geometric pattern complete but slightly altered. In fact if she hadn't been studying it for these minutes it would seem unchanged. She opened the pouch and looked inside. The pouch was no longer empty; it now held five vials with liquids in a wooden holder that had three empty slots, an assortment of cloths, and a set of quills tied with string. *Lady, this is amazing!*

She tried to turn the outer ring again but it wouldn't move. Closing the pouch, she tried again and it moved as easily as the first time. Opening the pouch again revealed it was full of papers. She pulled them out and found none of them made any sense. *I know I am not great at reading, but I don't recognize anything here.* She spread the papers out on the large table. She could tell there were four separate authors by the handwriting. Beyond that there was not much else she could read. The only item she *could* read was a set of five rough maps drawn in an elegant hand. Two of the maps had reference points she recognized, one was of an area a long way west in the neighboring kingdom, and another map was of the part of the great forest to the north.

She stacked the papers and set them aside on the table, then closed and turned the latch again. It was still empty. Not sure if anything had happened, she repeated the process. This time she opened it and sighed with relief—there where her four shiny crowns, the vial of poison, and the key to the upper floor room. *This is really going to make carrying everything I need a lot easier.* Taking out the vial of poison, she scooped some of the coins back into the purse and put the purse and keys into the pouch. Turning the clasp to the next point she put everything back in except for the poison and notes. Then she turned the clasp to the next point and added the vial of poison to the other vials in one of the empty slots. Looking at the notes, she though, *No reason to leave them behind;* turning the clasp to the next position she put all the papers back inside. Finally, she turned it back to the position with the coin purse and the keys.

With a large smile she slipped the pouch back onto her belt and put the belt back on. Confirming the pouch was still holding her coins and keys she pressed the center of the clasp on the top. With it rocked into position the outer ring would not turn. *I was just rotating that outer part by accident. Lady, thanks to you for this good fortune.* She felt the indentions in the uppermost section. *These indentions are to tell which section is open without looking. I need to get three identical coin purses and maybe a pair of identical journals. I can keep different but reasonable amounts of coins in each purse but have one special one with the large value coins. With two identical journals I can have one which has very bad notes, hard to read maps of no value and pair it with one coin purse with a few rings and pence in it and leave that where the pouch is locked to normally. If I get captured or robbed they'll get what they may have seen me with but it will be worthless. I can easily shift this to the more valuable purses or journal when I need to. With this I need give nothing away even if captured.*

She thought back on the Knife. *I hope not every Knife is so well-equipped.* With that thought bouncing around in her head a shiver passed through her. *I really got lucky killing him the way I did. Now the world has one less Knife in it.* Feeling a little less remorse over her first kill, she stood and went to the door. Stepping out of her room, she made sure the door closed behind her. Glancing at the metal door opposite, she thought, *I really have bumped up to a new level. First a little shopping, then it will be time to earn some more coin and prove I really belong here.* She walked down the stairs and entered the main room. There were more Daggers present, and a few even acknowledged her directly. She returned the same courteous acknowledgements, which drew the attention of some other Daggers. Hairy and Frumpy were gone. *Hope they do well on their first fighting Dagger exercise.* She placed the upper room key on the counter near Genne, who nodded to her, took the key and continued his conversation.

"... can tell em' jus' what I said. I 'avn't seen Vestul n'two days, an' his stuff is still up der an I'm clear ta nex' cycle."

The man Genne was talking to was obviously not taking the news well; in fact he looked a little sick. "But, he missed the meeting. Are you sure he didn't come back?"

Genne's look hardened, and the slightly shorter man caved in on himself. "Right, right, I got it, he went up for the night and left in the morning, didn't return and isn't in his room." He pushed away from the bar and went out the door, mumbling, "Oh Lord he isn't going to be happy; he really isn't going to be happy."

Missing customer, that can't be too unusual. I need to find some coin purses. With that thought she stepped out onto the now-busy main road and turned left to head for the market.

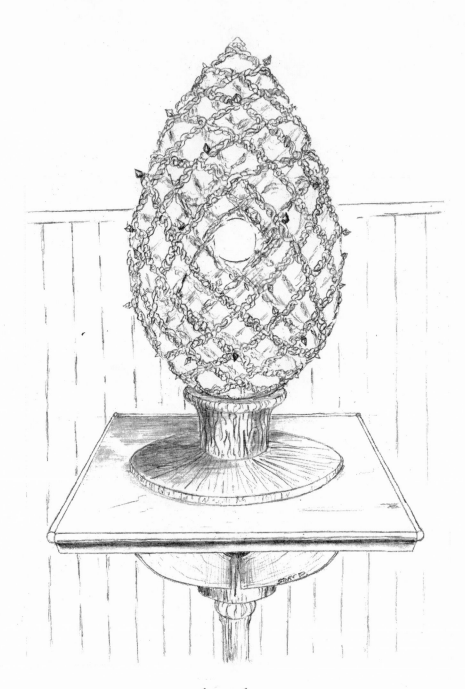

Argos Artifact

CHAPTER 4

DAGGERS ON THE TABLES

TWO KNOCKS BOUNCED AROUND THE room. Opening one eye brought sharp pain from the too-bright sun shining in the half-open shutters. Closing his eyes, Lebuin rolled over, pulling one of the soft down pillows over his head. The coolness of the cream silk cover felt good. Two knocks again. *Maybe whoever it is will give up and go away.* Waiting for the expected knocks was dragging his mind out of the unconsciousness of sleep. The previous day's events rolled around his head.

Oh Lord, what am I going to do? I have no idea what to do next. I have to leave, but, for what? Concentrating, Lebuin tried to pull back any memories of what the teachers might have said about Journeyman requirements. Nothing was coming up. The effort brought him fully awake. *Why did no one mention this? Or was this something else everyone thought I knew so no one told me?* Too many questions, not enough answers. The bed was comfortable, the silk sheets resting on his skin, and it was warm. Closing his eyes he started to drift off back to sleep.

Two knocks bounced around the room. *Dang it, I don't have classes, go away.* He waited, remembering Magus Cune's evil smirk as he walked away after the ceremony. *The ceremony, that incantation with my creation was unexpected. It linked us somehow.* Remembering the feeling as the link was established, his training took over and he broke the memory down, recalling the precise feelings of the power and its interactions with his physical and mental bodies. With the interactions recalled he examined himself mentally and found the connection. A slim thread of a channel was present where none had been before. The incantation had imprinted on him just as if he had been an artifact.

Curiously he fed a little power from his core into the channel. A new awareness was added to his list of senses. *Interesting, I can feel every Magi around.* Playing with the new sense he realized there were slight flavors or colors or scents to each feeling. *Ah; I bet I can tell who is who if I pay enough attention to this and keep it active.* Deciding to refer to the variations in the sense as 'scents', Lebuin adjusted his mental state adding this new channel to the incantations he maintained continuously. *Now I just need to pay careful attention when I meet each Magus to learn their scent.*

Two more knocks bounced around the room. Groaning, he sat up. "Who is it? I was asleep."

"Journeyman Lebuin, please, your breakfast."

Breakfast? I didn't order any food. I thought it was another Mage. Reaching out with his mind he released the inner locks on the door. An immaculately dressed servant smoothly opened the door while balancing the tray of food. *He is certainly well dressed. He looks quite respectable in the Guild uniform.* Looking a little closer, he thought, *And that is a very tidy uniform.* Closing the door behind him the servant moved to the side table and put the tray down. Handing Lebuin a cup of dark fluid he said, "Sorry it isn't hot anymore. I have been circling for a mark waiting for you to answer the door."

"I can warm it up." Looking at the cold cup of arit Lebuin used a little magic to warm it. *Circling for a mark? That doesn't make any sense. I know I am not fully awake yet.* He looked at the servant. "My Lord, Ditani, what are you doing here? I don't recall seeing you for more than a year."

Ditani smiled. "At least you remember me. Gezu wasn't sure if you'd ever remember a servant."

Lebuin's back stiffened at the snide comment, the familiar use of Magus Gezu's name, and the easy, familiar way Ditani spoke to him. "I can have you dismissed for that comment."

Chuckling nervously, which made Lebuin even more irate, Ditani made a painful-looking smirk. "Wouldn't it be most difficult to dismiss someone who doesn't work for you?"

The majority of his conscious thoughts stopped on that comment. Taking a deep drink from the hot arit to give himself time to recover, Lebuin's memory recalled Magus Cune's last statement. *'I placed a rather large bet you could complete the quest with a less-than-upstanding but influential friend of mine.'* Looking at the now-empty cup of arit, panic struck him. *Lord, did I just drink poison? Would he strike me so fast, and in the Guild itself?* Looking at Ditani closer, he saw what he had registered nearly unconsciously earlier—the uniform was immaculate. It had been carefully maintained in pristine condition. Further it fit Ditani extremely well, far better than most servants' uniforms fit. Servant uniforms being standard, the Guild simply bought them in quantity in various sizes and the servants could pick and choose the closest fit. They rarely took the time to correct the fit. Ditani's uniform had none of the normal signs of wear or stains. Obviously not new, it had been precisely tailored to Ditani's form some time ago. *Would an assassin take the time to tailor a uniform?*

Ditani simply stood watching Lebuin. *He doesn't look malevolent. In fact he looks worried.* Lebuin felt more awake as the arit flowed into his system. Ditani's eyes had deep bags as if he had not had much, if any, sleep. His complexion was also far whiter than would be normal, especially for a Karkaian. *No, he isn't an assassin; in fact he is scared and worried about something. He dresses well and takes care of his clothes. Maybe I can help.* "Well if you aren't a Guild servant, then you might as well sit down and tell me why you are here."

Ditani looked timidly around and Lebuin helped him decide by pointing at a chair which slid a few feet to Ditani. Sitting, he looked pleadingly at Lebuin; then like a cork popping from a bottle of chantrose, he burst out, "I don't know who to trust. I am not even sure if anything is wrong. He has only been missing since yesterday morning. Still he said he'd meet me and he didn't. Then he didn't make the appointment. When I checked the room he wasn't there. I had to seek help. So I came here. I don't know why, but I stopped at my cousin's place to get one of my old uniforms. When I got here everyone was talking about how you had nearly killed Magus Cune and were going to advance. I wanted to talk to Varni to get help. But she has been dead since just after I left with Gezu's last letter. Dead—first Gezu, then Varni is dead. It can't be coincidence. I found Magus Crawstu, but she was talking to Magus Cune and I heard them say that with Magus Gezu dead there was none left to shelter you, leaving you in the dark. I fled and then I didn't know who to trust. But, I remembered Gezu and Varni saying they liked you. They had to, what with the notes and all. With your new status I thought maybe you might be able to help. But then the ceremony was announced and Councilor Nillo ordered me to fetch you in the hall. Me, he just stopped me in the hall and asked. Can you believe that? He didn't even notice who I was or that I had been gone. After that I couldn't get you alone..."

"Whoa, stop. Calm down, Ditani." Looking at the tray, Lebuin selected a glass of juice and carefully floated it over to Ditani, who just looked at it apprehensively. "Here, drink this slowly and relax a little. I need to get dressed and then we'll go through all of that again, except slower, and with more detail."

Nodding, Ditani plucked the glass out of the air with a small grateful smile and a slightly shaking hand. He sipped some of the juice and sat quietly, tensely watching as Lebuin stood up and stretched. *He is spinning faster than a top.* Looking at Ditani, he smiled widely. *Just give him a few minutes to calm down. He must have been thinking he'd get murdered for sneaking in here.* Stretching again, he moved to the two armoires and opened them wide. Grabbing his brushes, he stepped to the basin and poured some water into it. He didn't bother warming it up, letting the fresh cold water help rinse the remaining cobwebs from his mind. Glancing at Ditani, he thought, *I'd better do a rush job, but not too fast; he looks like he is starting to unwind a little.* Tilting the shaving mirror, he cleaned his teeth, brushed his hair, trimmed his beard, and corrected his bangs. He examined his various outfits. *I need to look dignified, but not too formal. I have to go shopping.* His eyes selected a beautiful pair of grey trousers. Slipping into them, he pulled out a comfortable maroon silk shirt with silver embroidery, loose sleeves, and long stiff cuffs. Over that he slipped on a sleeveless doublet of brushed suede, dyed a forest green with gold and silver geometric patterns embroidered tastefully along the center line. To this he added a belt, into which he slipped his utility knife and small pouch before securing it in a looped fashion.

Selecting complementary tall riding boots, he slipped into them and arranged his trousers artfully for best effect. Finally he put everything away exactly where it belonged and took the light gray samite and ermine cloak from the hanger. Putting on the cloak and fastening it with the artifact from his trial, he watched as the incantations began their work on his clothing. He smiled as he watched small bits of dust falling to the floor in the sunlight. Turning, he admired the results in the mirror. *I still look like a well-dressed skeleton. But at least a good night sleep has removed the haunted look from my eyes.*

Feeling completely comfortable and clean, he closed the armoires, stepping over and looking at Ditani. Ditani was still tense but had shifted to a more comfortable position and had drunk most of the juice. *Good, at least he looks a little more relaxed now. But he needs some sleep. He's about to drop.* Not sure why he cared so much, he sat down on the edge of his bed. "You look a little better. Why don't you eat..." Realizing belatedly that it would make Ditani nervous to eat in front of a mage, he decided to adjust course. "I mean, please join me in finishing off these biscuits and fruit you were kind enough to bring." To emphasize the point, he flexed his always-active telekinetic incantation to bring the side table with the tray to sit between them. Reaching out, he took an apple from the top and bit into it. Ditani took another apple but instead of biting it he held it in his slightly shaking hands for a few minutes, looking a little out of place. Lebuin shifted to a more comfortable pose. "You mentioned someone was missing. Who exactly is missing?"

Ditani looked at him as if he had missed some vital clue. Then he sighed, "Magus Vestul is missing. We came here to meet with a Duke. I am not sure which one. Magus Vestul only called him 'Duke' when he talked about him or sent him messages."

Nodding to encourage Ditani to keep going, he took another bite. Ditani bit into the apple and chewed slowly. He swallowed. "Magus Vestul sent me out to get a special gift for this Duke. Apparently he has a taste for very old sharre."

Interesting and expensive. Aged sharre is difficult to find. "Did you get the sharre?" he encouraged.

Ditani nodded. "Yes, we had ordered it weeks ago, before coming here. He was supposed to meet me at the inn but he never came. I went up to our room, but without the key I can't open the door. I knocked and knocked with no answer. When the time for the meeting came I went, expecting to find Magus Vestul there." Taking another bite, Ditani chewed and swallowed. "At the Duke's residence I wasn't allowed to meet the Duke. I offered my apologies on behalf of Magus Vestul and delivered the gift. I was fed an excellent early dinner, alone. When Magus Vestul still had not come, I was escorted out and asked to help try to find him. So I went everywhere I could think of, but no one had any knowledge of where he could be. No one had seen him since the day before."

Nodding, he took a few nuts from the plate and popped them in his mouth, savoring the flavor a little. "Then you came here to see if any Magi had seen him?"

Ditani nodded. "Magus Vestul missing the meeting has me very worried for him, and a little worried that he was doing something dangerous. I felt I should try to be nondescript. So I went and got one of my old uniforms to blend in a little. When I got here I found out Varni was dead. Vestul had asked me to help Gezu and Varni for a time, but when Gezu died Varni stopped their work and sent me back to Magus Vestul with their notes. Vestul had planned on stopping to see Varni while back in Llino, so he didn't know she was dead. To discover Varni dead was too much. Then I got pulled into your ceremony."

"*Magus*," he emphasized the word, "Gezu died of a heart failure in his sleep, and *Magus* Varni died a little later, also of heart failure. There was nothing anyone could do by the time either was found. They were both very old and their deaths were not suspicious."

"I would accept that if Magus Vestul wasn't missing." Ditani straightened slightly and looked pleadingly at him.

If I help him I might be able to coax him into my service. He obviously knows how to dress well, he is experienced with mages, and I bet he knows things that will be helpful. "Well, I can do anything I want now, and Magus Vestul would certainly have some good ideas for my Journeyman quest. I need to speak with the councilor first, then I will help you look."

Ditani practically leapt over the table to clasp Lebuin's arms. Tears were showing in the corners of his eyes. "Thank you, Master Lebuin, thank you. I really need your help. I don't know what to do."

Standing up awkwardly, Lebuin grasped Ditani's arms in his hands too. Giving his best warm smile, he said, "You're welcome. I'll be back.

In the meantime you can stay here and rest." He pointed at his bed. "In fact, why don't you lie down and take a nap while I attend to my meeting. Then we'll go out and see if we can't find Magus Vestul together." *He really is scared. Is it that dangerous outside these walls?*

Locking the door behind him, Lebuin moved through the halls towards the main offices. When he arrived a secretary nodded to him from behind a neat and tidy desk. His shirt, however, was a little crumpled around the neck and the elbows were wearing thin. *You really shouldn't wear the same shirt so frequently. Heavens, you look like a poor person, and I know you get paid well.*

Indicating the open doorway beyond his desk, he said, "Journeyman Lebuin, thank you for coming. Magus Nillo asked me to send you in as soon as you came by."

Stepping around the desk, he smiled at the secretary. "Thank you."

He stopped in the doorway and peeked in. The office was lined with shelves, every one filled to brimming with folders, books, and assorted collectables. A table with three old beaten-up chairs sat by the doorway next to a chalkboard that was so clean it might never have been used. Opposite the doorway sat a rather large desk in the shape of a large 'L'. The desk was as tidy as the secretary's, with a number of stacks of papers each held down with a collectable statue or split geode.

On one corner of the desk near the tip of the 'L' there was an unusual hollow device made of gold, silver, and numerous gems. It was shaped like an oversized egg and made entirely of a loose weave of gold and silver. It had an organic feel and the gems cut as the leaves of the twisted vines. The center of it was an area in the shape of a perfect sphere. It rested on a simple wooden base. *Every time I ask about that, he avoids the question. Maybe now I can find out what it is.*

Seated in an oversized stuffed leather chair behind the desk was the bear of a man who ran the entire Guild from this office. Councilor Nillo stood at least six inches taller than anyone else Lebuin had ever seen. Although bald on top, he had nearly a lion's mane of silver hair, which he kept a medium length and which stood straight out from his head, almost giving him a halo. His beard was a dark black, in complete contrast to his hair, and he kept it in a sharp, perfect goatee. Today he was wearing a tired grey robe over a new white linen shirt. Looking up from the papers he was reading, he smiled, and his deep voice was surprisingly soft and melodic. "Ah, Journeyman Lebuin. You are up earlier than I expected." Smiling wide and showing a set of sharp, white teeth, he pointed at a chair. "Please, sit down."

Lebuin moved to the chair and sat down. At the same time, Councilor Nillo stood up and pulled something from a high shelf. Sitting back down, the councilor produced two crystal glasses. In his hand the bottle of sharre looked like a toy. He poured two half-glasses and then resealed the bottle, putting it aside on his desk. Handing a glass to Lebuin, he held his up. "To the rather impressive end of one life and the beginning of a new one. May you serve Argos well."

Lebuin smiled. "Thank you, Councilor." He took his glass up, clinked it with the Councilor's and took a mouthful. The strongest, warmest sensation he had ever experienced nearly caused him to sputter. Warmth spread through his whole body faster than he thought possible. All the minor aches from the week's trials vanished at the same time and he completely stopped caring that the highest Councilor the Guild was dressed like a sheep herder.

Shaking his head, he looked at the Councilor, who was smiling the happy smile of a trickster. "How old is this?"

Councilor Nillo examined the bottle for a time. "I recall that this particular bottle was in my predecessor's storage. I would imagine it is likely at least a hundred years old. It doesn't yet have the feel of the good two-hundred-and-fifty bottle I shared with Prince Mory."

Even with the calming effects of the sharre Lebuin gasped. "One hundred year-old sharre—that has to be worth ten crowns!"

Without flinching, he said, "More likely twelve or thirteen." His smile widened dramatically. "Per glass. Nice, isn't it?"

"Nice doesn't begin to describe it." In spite of himself he took another drink. His tired channels filled with energy, and he felt as if he had just finished a week in a health retreat eating good food, resting, bathing, and being massaged until every ache was gone and all tiredness removed. "If this is what one hundred year-old sharre is like I can see why it is so expensive and hard to find."

"It has been said that five hundred year-old sharre can restore youth." A little twinkle in his eye showed he didn't believe it himself. "Keeping it that long in the right conditions would be tricky, if not impossible."

Another mouthful of the amazing liquor brought more feelings of well-being and confidence. "Councilor, I never thought I'd have to leave this place. I knew journeymen were to do research into various magics—in fact I was looking forward to spending my time in the labs and library doing just that. Why do I have to leave?"

He leaned back in his chair, and the door behind Lebuin closed softly. "Lebuin, I know you never once came to a Journeyman ceremony. I also know you labored under the idea of staying within these walls your whole career. You had to be kept here through your youth because of what you are. However, that also cut you off from your peers, and sadly it seems most of the world. You might make an amazing scholar someday. However, Argos himself insists that all his Magi spend a significant amount of time in the field. It is important to know the world and people whom we live to protect. This is why the rank of Journeyman is required and it is not just a name," the Magus leveled a finger at him, "it is a description of the requirements of the rank which you agreed to last night. You are to be the eyes and ears of the Guild and Argos in the world."

"So I am just kicked out until I find something new?"

"Oh no, you are not kicked out, you are only required to journey most of the time. Your research must be out there," he said, waving at the window. "It takes years of work as a Journeyman to achieve enough experiences to advance to the rank of Magus. Contribution to the Guild in the form of new knowledge, be it magical or mundane, is just a side effect of your own experience." Looking sternly at Lebuin, he continued, "Lebuin, you now directly work for Lord Argos. He is not so heavy a taskmaster as some other Gods, but he does have goals for all his mages. For now your task is to go out, experience the real world, learn about the people, and find some new magic or a new way to apply magic. When you have done that you will be ready for the next task already set out for you. Do not believe you are so unique; all mages have done this, since the founding of the Guild."

Another swallow kept the warmth flowing through his veins. "What if I am killed in this work?"

"This is not the end of our adventures. Death has its own... paths.

You may come back to research what you have learned in the libraries and with the Magi present to determine if you have found something new. Once it is agreed, you may then stay here and assist in preparing a manuscript, or an update to an existing manuscript, with your new knowledge. But you cannot stay here longer than absolutely necessary to make such determinations and updates. You will know when it is time for your next task."

Thinking of Ditani, he asked, "Can I have help outside of the Guild? Assistants, other journeymen?"

"Of course; you can even spend your family's small fortune trying to speed it up if you desire. There are no limitations on how you go about your work. Just remember, you are bound by the Laws of Magic far more now then yesterday, and Lord Argos is not forgiving of violations by his mages. The Gods long ago declared that ignorance is not an acceptable defense for any violation of their laws. Many countries have adopted this into their own legal systems. So beware of local laws, as ignorance is not likely to be forgiven, especially from a Journeyman. Don't worry, we will know where you are and if you are still alive. Should the need arise we will be able to find you quickly, no matter where you may find yourself traveling."

"That was the incantation at the ceremony, wasn't it? All those channels, they are links so I can be traced. Or so I can trace others."

The Councilor sat up straighter. "You detected the threads? You recognized their purposes?"

"Of course, why shouldn't I? I have even activated the channel within me imprinted by the ceremony."

The Councilor stood up and came around the desk, placing his hands on Lebuin's head. Seeing no reason to resist he just relaxed and waited. "You have done that. But how did you know to do this?"

"It just seemed the right thing to do. I followed the feelings of the ceremony to find the channel."

"You are only the third Journeyman in the history of the Guild to do this. That channel was not meant to be shown to you until you were made a Magus. Activating it is part of the Magus ceremony."

Sitting up himself, he said, "But that is the purpose of using my artifact, isn't it? An artifact can identify its owner."

"Yes, I see no reason to hide this from you now. You'd discover it shortly anyway. Any magical artifact can be used by a Magi to trace its maker if they are still alive. Most artifacts cease to work once the maker has died, unless a trick is employed to make the artifact independent. However, even independent artifacts can still be used to trace their maker. In some cases, with certain knowledge, the artifact can also be used to breach the maker's defenses."

Lebuin thought about that. "So if another Magi got any of my existing artifacts they could find me and affect me through any defenses I might have."

Nodding, the councilor moved back to his seat. "Yes, it can be very complicated. I know you are not yet certain of what to do first. So I suggest you go out on the town, find a guide, and go explore something, anything you want. I am sure there were odd questions you had about things in your training—now is the time to go and answer those. You also have full access to the entire library now. So before you spend cycles trying to answer a question, it would be best if you asked if it has been researched yet. Good luck, Lebuin, you have given us all a lot of surprises. I suspect your results will likely be just as unique. Do you have any questions?"

"I am sure I will have more later, but since I can come back and ask I only have one. What was that one thread at the ceremony that went to the ceiling?"

The Councilor looked at him for a minute and took a swig of his own glass before answering. "You detected that one. You really are a wonder. It didn't go to the ceiling, it went *through* the ceiling. In fact I have seen it go in many directions, which makes me happy. To answer your question, that thread went to Lord Argos."

Lebuin blinked; even with the ancient sharre in his system the shock was immense. *I am truly bound to a real God, a God that can smell me out no matter where I may go. I wonder how much can be done with this connection.*

"You're white, finish your glass. It does take some time to get used to this knowledge. Now, you have earned this." He pulled a flat leather case from his desk and handed it to Lebuin.

It was an ornate folded leather case slightly smaller than his palm, inscribed with the Guild's seal. It opened easily on one side. With the front cover opened a silver and gold inlaid disk mounted to the stiff leather backing was revealed. The disk was artistically engraved with his name, the Guild seal, and the word "journeyman" in four languages around the edge.

Lebuin looked at the Councilor questioningly. "It's your Journeyman badge," he said.

Laughing, Lebuin said, "So last night when they congratulated me for earning the badge of Journeyman it was not just figurative." Standing, he nodded at the Councilor. "I will find something to do soon. In fact, I already have a small quest in mind to perhaps get some ideas on what to really do."

The Councilor didn't stand, just made a shooing motion towards the door, which now opened quietly behind Lebuin. "Yes, go, go, and find your first task. Argos will guide you."

Before I go out I need to get a few defenses ready. I can't be caught stunned like I was last night. Stopping in the library, he reviewed some defense tomes. He chose a couple rather crude but easy attack formulae from the ones taught to all mages. *Yes, these will do just fine.* Remembering the lessons, he pooled the energies needed and prepared the incantations, adding them to his memorized incantations. *Now I can at least defend myself rapidly.* Pleased with the preparations, he left the library and headed for his room.

Entering his room, he saw Ditani was napping in the chair where he had left him. As he came in Ditani snapped to standing, looking embarrassed. "Master Lebuin, my apologies. I didn't mean to fall asleep." He looked better for the food and the short nap.

"Ditani, you have nothing to be embarrassed about. I have discharged my only duty for the day. Come, let us see if we can find Magus Vestul." Holding the door open, he motioned to get Ditani moving.

Instead of heading out to the hall Ditani stood still and, quietly, so no one beyond the open door might hear, asked, "Um, if you'll forgive my forwardness, Master Lebuin. Might it not be wise to bring some money?"

Oh my, he is good. "Thank you. Yes, I should bring some money. I have some things I'll need to buy, so I might as well do some shopping while we look. Also, I assume you mean some tokens might also help restore lost memories?"

Ditani nodded agreement. *I must remember everything will cost a coin or three. I might have to stop by my father's office and withdraw some funds. I wonder how much a nice comfortable cart will cost. I need to be able to take my clothes with me.* Opening a locked drawer, he pulled out his coin purse and examined it. *Well, I assume eleven crosses and change will take care of the day.* He put the coin purse into his belt pouch.

He turned to the door. Ditani was standing there waiting, and seeing that Lebuin was now prepared he opened the door for the Journeyman. *Yes, indeed he would be a very welcome companion for the next few years. That is, of course, if I can hire him away from Magus Vestul.* As they left the Guild he strengthened his shields as much as he could while holding the other incantations at the ready.

Ditani took him first to the Blue Dolphin Inn. Lebuin had never been inside it but had walked past it dozens of times on his way to the docks and his family's offices. Ditani again held the door for him as he entered. The smoke parted around him as he entered. Even through the filtering of his shields he could smell the various scents of tobac. Smiling, he decided he should also get some of the better leaf today as he was running low. He took a minute to let his eyes adjust better to the dimmer room. It was much larger than he expected, taking up slightly more than half of the central section of the building, and stretching all the way front to back. A large bar stood across the back wall. Halls led off out of the room from the back right and left sides. There were three large fireplaces, now burning low. Next to the bar on the back wall was a wide table with a cloth covering that had the box symbols for card games. Some tables had a metal scissor-like apparatuses mounted in them which, observing a few of those tables with occupants, was for holding a dagger upright. Some of the other tables also had a dagger stuck right into the wood of the table.

Looking at the people sitting at the tables with upright daggers he found they all were looking back at him with assessing eyes. Not one of them embarrassed and most met him eye to eye. *These are Daggers for hire. I forgot the Blue Dolphin is supposed to be where the best of the Daggers hire out.* Looking at the daggers in the tables he saw that they were all functional weapons, but each was very distinctive. *I need to ask Dad what the protocol is for hiring a Dagger. I might need one, and I probably can afford one of the best.*

Ditani motioned for him to follow and led him to the bar, where a large muscled man was talking to a couple of well-dressed gentlemen. A lady dressed more like a city guard stood in the middle of the bar facing him, leaning back against the counter with a heavy mug in one hand the other resting on the hilt of a sword. The bartender was dressed well, but his clothes had dozens of stains from the food and drink he served. Trying to not look too out of place, Lebuin sat down on one of the many stools at the bar. He then looked back around the room. The Daggers had gone back to whatever they were doing when he came in. Some were writing in journals, others had an array of objects on their tables and were using them to work on one weapon or another. Still others were just talking. It was busier than he expected for midmorning. A few people, mostly reasonably well-dressed, vacated a table after looking him over. He noticed that a group of workmen who came in behind him walked past empty tables with the dagger holders and chose to sit at the communal tables. *Why not sit at the empty table? Can only Daggers sit at those tables?*

Looking at the daggers, *not exactly good behavior sticking a dagger into a table especially when there are empty tables with dagger holders for just that purpose.* There were three empty tables with holders and they were all near one wall or another. As he watched, a well-dressed man handed a couple of bells to one of the Daggers sitting at a table with a holder near the center of the room. The Dagger and his companions stood up, taking his dagger from the holder, and they left with their employer. Immediately there was a silent exchange of looks between the Daggers at tables without holders and one stood up, pulled his dagger out of the wooden table, walked over and sat down, placing his dagger into the holder. *That was interesting. There must be a ranking order. Those other empty holder tables must signify something that these others don't feel up to challenging or claiming.*

"Master." He remembered he was here for a purpose and while he had been staring at the unfamiliar room Ditani had been talking in soft tones with the bartender. "Magus Vestul has still not been seen."

"Let's go check the room."

"I don't have the key."

"Well we can still knock; won't the inn keeper open it for us?"

"No, that isn't how it works here. Blue Dolphin rooms are for key-holders only. If you don't have a room key or are a known invited guest they won't let you go upstairs."

Thinking of Magus Gezu, he asked, "What if Magus Vestul died in the room overnight of a heart problem like Magus Gezu?"

Ditani looked worried at the new thought. "I don't know. It is not very likely."

Lebuin turned around to the bar and signaled for the barkeeper to come over. After a minute he did.

"Yes, m'lord. Wha' can I getcha?"

"I'd like to speak to the innkeeper please."

The large man stood still staring at him for a minute as if he was an interesting new insect. A shiver ran down his back and he strengthened his shield a little more. The barkeeper's voice remained calm, even friendly. "M'lord, I'm da inn keeper, owner an' enforcer. How may I serve you?" The last had only a slight accent.

Oh great, I have insulted one of the most influential people in the city and I have only been a Journeyman here for a few marks. Smiling as nicely as he could, he covertly pulled a chera out and placed it on the counter near his hand—and, he hoped, out of view of most of the room's occupants. "My apologies. I am worried about a friend, Magus Vestul. He was not exactly young; is there any way to check his room to be sure he hasn't had an accident?"

The large man considered the idea for a minute. "Wait here." He then walked around the end of the bar, crossed the room, and went up a set of circular stone stairs which Lebuin had not noticed, as the entrance was hidden from the main door but visible from the bar. All of the Daggers watched the innkeeper as he left, then looked back at Lebuin. He felt like a specimen on display, so he casually as possible turned his back on the room and leaned on the bar. Ditani stood next to him, facing the room.

Smiling he reached for where his coin had been on the counter. *He didn't take the coin. I thought bribes were common.* His hand came up empty, and he looked at the bar in shock. *Wait, where is the coin?* Lebuin looked at the other people near the bar; none of them were close enough to have taken it. Thinking back, he mused, *I'd swear on a stack of crowns he didn't reach for the coin, and no one else could have either.*

He looked at Ditani, confused. Ditani stood there looking at the room. "Do you think he'll open the room?"

"Of course, but where did my chera go?" he asked softly.

Ditani glanced at him with almost the same look as the innkeeper before answering, "Genne took it, of course."

Turning slightly, he was able to watch the room. As he waited, well-dressed folks came and went pretty often. Almost every merchant or noble actually walked around the room, boldly examining the daggers in the tables and the Daggers sitting at them too. "Is that normal?"

Ditani looked at what he was watching. "Of course. Merchants need specific services, so they have to find the right Dagger for their needs. No Dagger will ever take offense at being sized up by a client."

The innkeeper returned. "M'lord, ya needn't worry, yer friend ain't dead in da room. Der ain't no-un in da room. Can I getcha any ting else?"

Well, so much for an easy solution. Now what? Disappointed at the lack of a simple solution, he shook his head no. "Thank you, no. Can you tell him Journeyman Lebuin would like to speak with him as soon as possible at the Guildhouse when he comes back?"

"O'course m'lord. Ri'after I tell im of all da udder request. Very popular, dat one. I'ave ta' charge him more nex'time."

Now that is interesting. "Uh, popular? I take it there are a lot of people asking to see him."

The innkeeper looked at him for a few moments before he realized that nothing more was going to come without some coin. Sighing, he fished out another chera. This time he left his finger on it. The innkeeper smiled a friendly smile and gave him a wink. "Ya might say dat. Been tree udders askin' after him."

Beginning to get the feel for this, he left the coin where it was but added another one. Smiling, he leaned a little closer. "Anyone I might know?"

"No m'lord, 'least, not likely. One was a friend o' Duke, a'nudder was a recent regular, Sula by name, and da last was a Knife, stake me rep on dat, I would."

I know about the Duke, and what a Knife is I don't think I want to know. Maybe I can meet this Sula and we can help each other. Nodding as he added a third coin, "Sula is a new regular? Where might I find him?"

The innkeeper's hand came down, covering his hand and all three coins. It was heavy, muscled and coarse on the back of his hand. "M'lord, be careful o'dat one. Ya can fin' 'er at da Temple o' Dalpha. Dats al'I can do for ya." He turned, lifting his hand, and moved to some customers who were trying to dress well but failing miserably. Looking down, he saw all three of the coins were gone. *Now that is an interesting trick.*

Standing up, he motioned for Ditani to follow and he walked out, trying to look confident. On the way he took note of some Daggers he might come back and talk to later, after he had a chance to get some advice on hiring them. Both of the Daggers he was most interested in nodded politely to him as Ditani opened the door for him. *Damn, how did they know I was thinking of them?*

Once outside he started walking towards the docks and the main market. "This Sula sounds like she might be able to help. We can get to the Temple of Dalpha through the market." Ditani simply nodded and followed.

The market was as busy as always, buskers screaming their wares, merchants in booths vying for the attention of anyone who even glanced at their stalls. Temple Street was on the far side of the market, so they simply began maneuvering through the stalls on a general course for the temple district. As they moved through the market he paid closer attention to the mundane things he had never considered buying, like the leather backpacks and the more sturdy boots. *I need some boots that will not wear out, but I can keep looking respectable.*

As he rounded a stall he caught sight of a serviceably but beautifully dressed woman wearing a dusky brick-red cloak with a rust-colored hood and fur-trimmed collar. The woman was just turning away from him, heading down another row. Her tanned skin and curly dark brown hear were perfectly suited to the dusky colors she wore. *My Lord, it can't be. That is the girl from the alley!* She had already stepped out of sight with a sweetmeat in one hand and a pack swung over the opposite shoulder.

"Come on, I think I know her." Stepping faster, he dodged around some other shoppers, not sure what he would do when he met her. But still, he knew he wanted to at least talk to her. He moved so fast Ditani was left behind. She was a few feet down the aisle when he rounded the corner. Smiling, he moved hurriedly to get close enough to say hello.

An explosion of light and sound hit him from behind, pushing him forward violently. His shield buckling under the force, he stumbled and tried to stay up. *What the hell was that?* Rebounding off the girl, knocking her forward as well, he managed to regain his footing. At the same time he pushed what energy he could through his channels to recover the protective shield. The sudden rush of energies was slightly more than needed, and the excess burnt as the channels allowed what they could to flow through. Turning around, he looked for the source of the force that had hit him.

Everywhere people were running and screaming, except for one man only a few paces away. The man was rough looking, wearing all black from neck to foot. He held a rod that was pointed straight at Lebuin. The man looked mad, and his eyes burned with a hatred Lebuin found hard to stand against. *Gods, an assassin!* Panic welled up inside Lebuin as lightning leaped from the rod, striking him again. His shield was not enough, and he felt like a fire had exploded inside him as the energy channel was forcibly disrupted. Worse, the energies he was trying to send through the now-destroyed channel began pooling and burning. The shield was gone, and he was burning inside from energies that no longer had a place to go, as well as from the tag end of the attack that had charred his arms and chest.

The man in black looked momentarily amazed and then moved rapidly towards Lebuin. His voice was husky but chilling. "Damn it!" was all Lebuin heard as he saw him pull a knife with the other hand and threw it into his chest.

The pain from the knife snapped something in Lebuin. Looking at the approaching assassin he released all the energies that were burning in him and connected a ley line in the air to the attack formula he had prepared before leaving the Guild, targeting the assassin. *You can join me.* As he started to collapse, golden energies leaped from his hands, arcing to the assassin. Some energy jumped to the rod in the assassin's hand; as the darkness came, Lebuin smiled that his last sight was of his killer exploding in flames. Screams echoed down into the dark as he fell. Faintly he heard Ditani screaming his name, then nothing at all.

Racing Death

CHAPTER 5

KNIVES ARE OUT

ENJOYING THE SWEET AND SALTY flavor of the sweetmeat, Ticca strolled through the marketplace. Comparing the morning's purchases against her list of needed items, she smiled. Her new pouch had two separate compartments with identical sets of items. The exception was one had practically nothing of value, while the other held the real items. She was particularly pleased with the set of journals she'd found. It would take a little work to transfer her notes but it would be worth it. The sun was warm, and all her main objectives for the day were dealt with. She considered the future. *I should go back to the Blue Dolphin and put my dagger out. But I think I can afford to take a short break. After all, I have been working for years to get here. I think I deserve a break.* Ignoring most of the barkers vying for her attention, she thought maybe she should get a few extra supplies now that she had a safe place to store them. *Always a good idea to be prepared for having to leave on short notice.*

Her eyes were slightly dazzled by a flash of bright light and her ears started ringing from a sound not unlike a near thunderclap. Something hit her hard from behind, and her skin prickled at the contact even through her leathers. *That feels like the magic Sula made me use.* She was pushed forward with considerable force and her feet automatically shuffled, keeping her balanced. Her heart started racing as the memory of the previous evening's sneak attack made a pit in her stomach. She dropped her pack as she executed an about face into a battle-ready crouch, with knives in a defensive position.

Dagger in one hand and a knife in the other, she took in what had hit her. Instead of the expected opponent she was looking at the back of skinny, medium-height man. He was himself just finishing turning around, looking away from her. His cloak was smoking slightly from whatever had happened to his back. *Must have been blown into me, but by who or what?*

Lowering herself slightly and stepping an inch to the right, remaining ready for a fight, she was able to see past the man who had run into her. Fifteen feet away and closing was a Knife, or at least someone who really wanted to make that impression. Except this Knife was using an ebony rod, which he pointed threateningly at the other man. Looking at the singed cloak in front of her again, she thought, *This guy must be a wizard, to have withstood a surprise magical attack. That feeling when he touched me must have been his shielding. My Lady! This is an assassination attempt against a wizard in the middle of the market. Who would dare try this?*

Nearby people began to react to the events, most bolting away screaming. The few remaining that were watching the events like a busker act changed their minds and ran too when lightning leaped from the rod, striking the wizard. The wizard was pushed further back and Ticca deftly stepped backwards with the motion to keep a workable distance between them. The hair on the back of her neck stood up and her heart started racing from being in the line of fire. *This is not a good place to be.* Looking around, she saw there was no cover other than tents. *Those tents aren't going to stop a missed shot. Maybe staying behind this wizard isn't such a bad spot; he's holding up to the abuse pretty well.* The Knife was also impressed, and actually looked mad. *More than you bargained for, I bet. Now for the execution everyone always says happens when wizards are crossed.*

The wizard slowly, almost arrogantly, lifted his hands. The Knife's eyes showed a touch of fear. The Knife tried to move, shouting, "Damn it!" In a last desperate effort he threw his knife at the wizard. But he wasn't fast enough. *Nice try, but I doubt anyone can move fast enough. Throwing stuff at wizards just makes them madder.*

As expected, an over-the-top reaction came, in the form of a blaze of orange and red lights from the wizard's hands. The wizard's right hand had targeted the center of the Knife's chest, and his left the rod. In an amazing burst of blue fire the rod exploded as the Knife was engulfed, screaming, in red flames. The exploding rod blew the right hand and forearm away, leaving a stump of an arm. Small bits of meat and blood rained on the stall fronts. Ticca's stomach threatened to eject the recent meal and she had to swallow hard to stifle the sick feeling the slapping meat sounds gave her. She wanted to stop watching but the scene was too amazing. She held her mouth tightly closed, resisting the gagging sensations as the Knife fell to his knees screaming before melting into a charred pile roughly resembling a man.

My Lady, I hope I never have to fight a wizard! This is unbelievable, and it happened before my very eyes. She was totally unprepared, staring at the charred pile, when the wizard fell backwards, the thrown knife protruding from his chest with blood running out of the wound over his clothing to the ground. The wizard's arms and chest were also badly blackened and smoking. *Is he dead too?*

"Lebuin! Lord, no! Lebuin!" An older man ran to the wizard, kneeling and picking up the wizard's head. Shouting, "Guards! Anyone, help! Please Lord, we cannot let him die!" the man looked around pleadingly at the empty area, his eyes falling on her. Eyes filled with tears, he looked at the dagger in her hand then at her. She hadn't moved, and was still in a fighting posture. "Dagger? Are you a Dagger?!"

Straightening up, she sheathed her knives automatically. Stepping up to the fallen wizard, she answered, "Yes."

"Are you under coin? Name your price, he can pay, please help!"

Looking around, she saw there was no one else even remotely close. People milled at the edge of the scene, many others were beginning to gather to find the source of the commotion. *Temple Street is not far.* She looked at the wizard again. *Lady, is he thin; I bet my saddle gear weighs more than him.* Looking at the older man again, she realized he was about to grab the knife sticking out of the wizards chest. Ticca snapped her hand around his wrist, pulling it away from the knife. "Don't be a fool. If you pull that now there is no chance he'll live. I accept the terms." Pointing at her pack, she added, "You bring that and don't fall too far behind."

Squatting down, she carefully lifted the wizard into her arms. She stood and measured his weight; he was almost as light as he looked. *I can do this. For his life I have to do this. Lady, lend me some strength.* She ran full speed for Temple Street, screaming oaths at anyone in her way, effectively clearing a path and giving her precious oxygen.

Exiting the market directly onto Temple Street, she continued screaming, drawing as much attention as she could. Most people turned and watched, and anyone in her way quickly stepped aside. The wizard felt like he was getting heavier. *OK, he weighs more than my gear, but not by much.* Sweat was running freely down her face and back and her breathing became harder. Her muscles complained making her very glad the Temple of Dalpha was the second temple on the street and that the hospice entrance was on the market side. Taking the wide steps two at a time she screamed for help as she barreled into the main room. Two acolytes jumped at the sound and pointed at an empty cot and rushed to meet her there.

Laying the wizard on the cot, she stepped aside and leaned against the wall, breathing hard. One of the acolytes ran out, while the other began examining the wizard, careful of the protruding knife. Ticca watched and decided it might be good to let them know what he was. Trying to keep her breath under control, she managed to get out, "He's a wizard; he was attacked, in the market."

The acolyte nodded and looked at the doorway the other acolyte had gone through. A tall man in rich robes hurriedly entered with the other acolyte. The acolyte went back to caring for others while the tall man came directly to the wizard's bed. Ticca listened as the two men spoke in the unfathomable medical jargon these types favored. *Good Lady, how many possible treatments can there be, the man is bleeding to death.* Looking at him, she noted that the blood didn't smear or soak into his clothes but instead pooled or ran off it, staining the bed. The older man who'd hired her finally came running into the room with her pack. She waved and he came over, trying to breathe himself.

After what felt like a full mark but was only a minute at most of talking and prodding, the old man shook his head sadly and looked at her. "I am sorry, lady, there is little we can do. This is too grave a wound. I doubt if he'll even wake up."

The old man next to her snapped straight. "Surely you can heal him.

This isn't a simple hospice. Please, you must save him," he pleaded.

The healer laid a hand on the old man's shoulder. "I am sorry; this wound is beyond our abilities. I will do all I can, but I doubt it will be enough."

The old man snapped. He pushed the healer's hand from his shoulder and bolted through the inner doorway, yelling, "Lady, save us! Lady, save us..."

The healer motioned for the acolyte, who was looking at him for guidance, to follow. The acolyte ran after the old man, calling out for him to stop. Turning back to Ticca, he shook his head. "Are you alright M'lady?"

She nodded, "I'm just the hired help to get him here to save him. What if he woke up? I have heard wizards can mend themselves?"

"Alas, very few can do so, and also I seriously doubt he'll ever wake again."

If he doesn't wake then I probably won't get paid. Not that it was really that big of a deal. She mulled over staying or not as the tall healer turned his attention back to the wizard.

Ticca watched curiously as he retrieved a basket filled with bandages and surgical tools. He then carefully cut open the wizards clothing around the knife before laying out a number of bottles on a small table brought by an acolyte. Taking a long, thin, hollow reed that had a bulb on one end, he squeezed the bulb, inserting the end of the reed into one of the smaller bottles. He then carefully inserted the tip into the wound next to the knife and squeezed. The wound began to bubble pink-white liquid mixed with blood. The healer then took a longer, flexible reed and pushed it carefully down the wizard's throat; quickly, the healer used another bulb to push fluid through the reed. The wizard coughed a little as the healer carefully pulled the reed back out.

Waiting for the coughing to stop, he checked the wizard and frowned deeper. The wound had stopped bubbling out the pink foam. Looking concerned, he took yet another small vial and moved to a position where he could pull the knife out and pour the contents of the vial on the wound at the same time. Just as he grabbed the knife a cry came from the doorway, "Healer Antis, STOP!"

Looking annoyed for a moment he turned, and seeing who had

addressed him, he went a little white. The healer straightened and bowed his head, "Your will, Great Lady. I am doing all I can to save this man."

Curious, Ticca leaned around him to see the newcomer better. It was a noble lady, followed by several other acolytes. She was Ticca's height, with a round, pale face and long, thick, slightly curly black hair. She was in a long, forest-green robe, decorated with flowers and fruit hanging from the borders. She also wore a dark green mantle, drawn from behind, over her shoulders and up from behind her waist knotted in an X on her chest. Her arms were bare and muscular. On her forehead was a slim silver tiara with a fine oak tree for the center piece. Balanced in her hand sat an oversized, delicate-looking egg of gold, silver and gems. The egg was not solid; in fact she could easily see through it as it was a complex of gold and silver threads. As she strode up to the bed Ticca noticed that the device was actually an intricate sculpture with small leaves and vines. What was wondrous was that the device held a glowing yellow sphere of light that felt oddly warm and comforting, like lying out in the sun on a warm day.

The healer openly stared at the device. "Great Lady, you would gift this mage with Dalpha's Light?"

The Lady smiled. "This man is a direct servant of Lord Argos." Looking back at the doorway, she added, "I was told of his need, asked to assist, and personally deem this a righteous act of charity."

Ticca glanced at the doorway and straightened up at the hint of a green skirt, cream-colored blouse and auburn hair slipping quickly back through it. *Was that Sula?*

Stepping out from behind the Great Lady, the older man who had cried for help looked worriedly at the wizard. Taking note of the gesture, the Great Lady turned her attention to the wizard as well. "Yes, well, you have done an admirable job so far. Let us finish this together; I need assistance." The five acolytes with her moved to positions around the bed. She moved to stand next to the wizard on his right, leaving the healer where he was. Everyone but the healer knelt; Ticca, deciding it was best to not look out of place, also knelt.

The older man stepped up. "May I assist?"

The Great Lady smiled. "Any servant of Lord Argos is welcome. Kneel at his head, hold it steady and offer up any prayer you may have."

The old man took his position as instructed.

Then the Lady held the glowing egg over the center of the wizard's chest and began to vocalize, a pure beautiful melody of sounds. All the acolytes present knelt and joined in. The glowing light grew brighter and brighter until Ticca had to look down. The warmth of the light was wonderful to feel, and Ticca felt uplifted and joyful at the sounds of the chant, the warmth of the light, and even the light's intensity.

When the light became too much to bear she closed her eyes and felt a presence growing closer.

- - -

The sun was full in her face, its warmth comfortably baking her. Sighing, she knew she should finish the work, but it was so nice. From a short distance away the children were playing with a fox, their laughs like delicate silver bells ringing joyfully through the glen. Sitting up, she opened her eyes. Before her, the boots had not miraculously finished themselves. The low table was organized with her leather tools and materials. *I really should finish those boots for him. Then of course I'll have to get him to wear them.* Laughing at the absurd look she knew she'd get for suggesting he discard his favorite boots, she picked up the almost completed journal.

Marks flowed by as she wove the materials together into another fine journal. She enjoyed the comfortable feeling the energies of her people and the world gave her as she worked. The energies bound the woven paper, leather and resin glues into a single whole object. She smiled as she carved the intricate looping knot patterns into the covers. Finally, she held the completed journal up and inspected it in the late afternoon sun. *A beautiful work; it will make an excellent gift for our guest.*

Taking the journal with her, she left the unfinished boots for another day and moved through the forest village to the gathering place. Laughter, music, and talk could be heard long before getting to the feast. The tables were set out in the open with large fires at each end. The smell of roasting vegetables and meats made her mouth water. Naturally the Shar family had brought significant amounts of sharre to the feast, and it was being enjoyed by all. At the high table sat most of the family elders.

She took a place at the makers' table and enjoyed the evening's entertainments. Dancers, acrobats, and bards flowed throughout the evening as easily as the sharre and platters of food. As the feast went on she kept looking for her love but she could not find him, nor was he with the servers. *He must be here someplace, how could he miss this?* Then she noticed one of the masked acrobats dressed in flowing saffron silks and her heart told her it had to be him. She clapped and yelled support as his troupe performed amazing feats with ropes, knives and balancing. At the climax she laughed as he showed off performing the difficult knife dance of the firebirds with his silk costume streaming in intricate patterns. She even gasped with everyone else when he ended it with a mighty show of knives and torches spinning so fast that the mirrored edges flashed like the stars in a wind storm of fire and silk. He ended it by throwing all six knives high in the air and letting them come down blade first around him as he bowed. The knives passed his head and arms close enough to flutter the silk sleeves and his long hair. He remained looking down until the last knife had passed, embedding itself at the end of the neat row of hilts at his feet. She blushed when he winked at her as he exited.

As the evening wore on it came time to present her gift. She stood and made her way to the high table. Giving appropriate nods to the heads of the families, she stepped up in front of the great mage. He looked to be about middle-aged, for a human, though she knew that he had been coming to their forest for more years than most humans could hope to live. He looked at her and laughed his deep, full-bodied laugh. "My word! Can this be Kliasa, who bounced on my knee and wouldn't let me stop?"

She blushed and bowed appropriately. "Great Lord Magus Vestul of Argos, you do me honor to remember me. I have made this for your honor and for my family's thanks to you for helping end the war and save our forests." Placing the journal on the table, she bowed again.

The great mage actually looked slightly embarrassed by the act and his eyes showed a hint of tears. Magus Vestul reached out and picked up the journal and inspected it as she awaited his word. He carefully inspected the binding, cover, materials and then he noted the engraving of Lord Argos's seal on the front. His hands almost lovingly traced the patterns. "This is a wondrous work! I am most pleased with this gift. In fact I declare this to be my most prized gift of the feast. I shall use this only for the most important of research and notes, and will treasure it for all my life. Thank you Kliasa, daughter of House Elaeus." He stood and put the journal in his pouch of fine leather with the silver disk clasp. "It fits perfectly." Smiling, he reached out. "May I have the honor of the Moon's Dance with you?"

Glancing right, the matriarch looked like she was so proud she would burst. The matriarch nodded affirmative and she bowed again and accepted. The Magus was amazingly graceful as he danced the Moon's Dance with her. At the end he gave her a fatherly embrace and whispered in her ear, "I think someone is awaiting the next dance." Winking, he motioned with his head to his left. Looking the way he motioned she saw her love smiling and clapping to the music but his violet eyes were following her every move.

She walked with the great Magus, who limped slightly, back to the head table. She looked at him for a moment and he waved his hand. "Don't worry, it is just that my feet are killing me! These shoes are just too tight." Kliasa smiled to herself. *I'll fix that on your next visit.* Bowing a farewell, she said, "Thank you for honoring us, Great Lord Magus Vestul of Argos." He smiled and she turned back to the dance circle, looking for her love. He was there waiting, he had changed back into simple green leggings and the horrible boots. *I really need to finish those boots for him. Maybe I can steal those ugly worn things when he is asleep. I bet his grandmother would help me.* She approached him and he bowed deeply. "You do me honor to allow me to follow our Great Lord Magus."

Smiling, she took his hand and he pulled her suddenly very close. His warm breath sent shivers down her spine as he said softly in her ear, "Your gift really was magnificent, it must be your finest work ever."

She closed her eyes and let the exhilaration of pride lift her to the heights as her heart pounded thunderously in her ears and his breath warmed her soul.

- - -

A soft musical voice came to her. "You may stand." Ticca opened her eyes, her heart still racing. She looked around, confused for a second. *This is Dalpha's Temple. Something just happened. I was dreaming again.*

A couple of acolytes were cleaning blood from the floor, two others were helping the healer who looked like he was drunk or about to pass out towards the inner door, the old man was still kneeling at the wizard's head obviously praying, and standing next to her was the Great Lady of Dalpha herself with four other acolytes in attendance. She held the golden forest egg, which still glowed with an oddly warming soft, white light.

Ticca stood up a little shakily. *What happened? Did I pass out?* Looking at the wizard she saw there was a scar in his chest where the knife and once been, and his chest was rising and falling normally. He looked like someone who was just taking an afternoon nap, if it wasn't for all the blood that surrounded him on the bed and floor. "I'm sorry Great Lady, I didn't mean to be inattentive."

Smiling, the tall woman looked her over fully, stopping for a moment at the dagger hanging on the front of her belt. "You are a Dagger. Are you employed by Journeyman Lebuin?"

"Actually by his servant I think. I am not exactly sure at the moment. Things moved a little fast."

Nodding knowingly the Great Lady placed a hand on Ticca's shoulder. "You are touched by Lady Dalpha and Lord Argos. I believe greatness awaits you...?"

"Ticca of Rhini Wood."

"I know Rhini Wood. Are you related to Faltla?"

Ticca's eyes snapped to look at the Great Lady. "Yes, he is my Uncle. You know of him?"

Smiling widely, the Great Lady nodded. "I knew I had seen your dagger before. It's his dagger, isn't it?"

Ticca nodded and touched it lovingly.

"Actually I know Faltla personally. He was a great Dagger himself until he lost his arm and toes in the war. I was a healer then and treated him and many of his companions. In fact I was the field healer that sewed him back together and brought him here when he was injured in that last battle. Did he train you?"

Ticca was in shock. "Um, yes, Great Lady. He trained me from a babe in the ways of tracking. When I was ten years old my father died, and I stopped pretending I wanted any other life than that of a Dagger.

Uncle taught me everything he could. When it was obvious I had talent and was going to do this he called on an old friend to train me as he could not."

"Who did he call on?"

Looking around Ticca noted who was listening. "I cannot say, Great Lady. I called him only Trainer."

The Great Lady looked at her thoughtfully for a second then drew a line from her left ear down to the base of her neck and said softly, "With wiry silver hair?"

Ticca tried to hide her surprise but the Great Lady nodded knowingly. "Indeed, you will do well here." Looking at the wizard she nodded again, "Yes, I believe this is right. Ticca, when you come to the end—and you will know when that is—should you still live, please come back and see me. I wish to know the results, and I do dearly wish to hear of your Uncle."

Ticca nodded agreement. *That sounds ominous. But this is already a surprising couple of days. What more can happen?*

"When Journeyman Lebuin wakes he will be weak. Also he will be unable to use magic for a time. Please tell him to not push it too fast. Mages are a stubborn lot and often injure themselves again by too soon trying to control their magics. We have done all we can. He will live, be healthy, and in time be able to do all he was able to this morning and likely more."

The Great Lady put her hand on Ticca's shoulder again. "Ticca of Rhini Wood, although you already have been touched by Lady Dalpha, I give you my own blessing. Be well and come back when you can." With that she walked away through the inner door to the Temple.

Looking at Journeyman Lebuin, she saw the old man had stopped praying and was looking at her.

"You said something about payment?"

Laughing a little, he said, "You did get him here pretty fast. Yes, but I have little of my own. You may have it all if you desire."

Shaking her head, she pointed at the sleeping mage. "He can pay when he wakes up. If he cannot use magic for a time I think he would like my services, especially if there are more Knives out to cut him up. I doubt he'll get so lucky a second time. So for now I'll assume I remain in his service through you. What is your name, by the by?"

The old man stood up and formally held out his arm. "I am Ditani of Agash, servant to Magus Vestul and currently in service to Journeyman Lebuin while we hunt for Magus Vestul."

Ticca looked at him as if he had two heads for a moment, making him look nervously back. *Magus Vestul, like the one in my dream?* Taking his arm, she said, "I am Ticca of Rhini Wood, Dagger in your service." Letting go, she squatted by him as he kneeled at Lebuin's head. "So tell me, what is going on?"

Ditani told an amazing tale. Ticca memorized the whole story and probed for more details. In the end she was still not sure if Magus Vestul was the one from her dream. She wasn't even sure if her dream was real, but it felt real. "Well, I think you have found the right Dagger for your needs. Why don't you stay here and tend to our employer and let me do what I do best, meaning track down your missing Magus Vestul."

"That sounds like a good plan to me."

"I need some coin to grease the wheels."

Looking a little nervous Ditani shook his head and pulled out a neat little coin purse. "I have not much."

Ticca eyed the pouch. *Lady, I cannot take this poor man's last coin.* Then looking at the belt pouch still on Lebuin, she smiled. "Lebuin has already dropped coin to help, yes?"

Ditani nodded. "Yes he paid Genne three chera to learn who was asking after Magus Vestul."

Trying not to laugh, Ticca looked at Ditani and then at the sleeping Lebuin. "Three chera! Are you serious! Lady help me, that is ridiculous. I'll have to have a word with Genne and get some back. That was far too much." Reaching out, she flipped Lebuin's pouch open and pulled out the coin purse.

"Ticca! You cannot do that!" Ditani protested.

"I'm not taking it all. Just ..." Looking inside she practically choked on the amount of silver it held. *Oh my, he must be really rich. I'll have to think about what to charge him.* Of the many coins she spied a number of silver crosses, "... two crosses." She plucked out the two silver coins and put the purse back in Lebuin's pouch. Ditani was practically stuttering with outrage.

"Look, you can have an accounting of it. Plus I should have an upfront fee. We'll get this all sorted out later. First I need to change these to smaller coins. Stay here. I don't want him traveling outside unprotected. When I get back we'll go to my room at the Blue Dolphin and talk the rest of this through." Standing, she moved to grab her pack.

"Wait, did you say your room at the Blue Dolphin? You live there?"

"Yes, I have a room and table. Anything more, or can I get to work?" Ditani looked thoughtful for a minute and then he smiled the first smile she had seen on him. *He actually looks a lot better with a smile. Funny how so small a thing can change a character so much.* Looking at the sleeping wizard, she thought, *Actually when he isn't burning people to char he's kinda pretty. I think I'm going to enjoy this commission.* Pointing at Lebuin, she sternly added, "I'm serious, don't let him leave here. I'll be back in a few marks." Grabbing her pack she strode out without looking back. *This should be easy. A great mage cannot just disappear.*

Looking down the street she saw a detachment of guards walking straight for the hospice. *And now I earn my coin.* Swinging her pack over her shoulder, she took up a position at the top stair, right in their path. Standing authoritatively, she rested her hand lightly on her sword hilt and put on the carefully practiced 'military commander' face she had been taught. Speaking first, as the guards climbed the steps, she took the initiative away from the captain. "Captain, glad you made it here. Have you taken care of the trouble in the market?"

The captain scowled at her commanding tone and stopped, looking her over, his eyes landing on her dagger. Looking up directly at her face from his position two steps down, his scowl remained as he took another step up, but did not step up on level. *Good boy, stay in the junior position. That will make this easier.*

"Ma'am, were you the one who took the wounded mage away?"

Nodding, she took in the other five guards. *Bringing a lot of backup with you. Must be a little worried. I would be too if I had to follow someone who made that pile of char in the market.* All of the guards looked a little stern and tense. *They are expecting a fight. A proper explanation should put us all at ease.* "Yes, I witnessed the whole thing. A Knife attempted to kill the Journeyman with a hard attack to his back. When confronted, the Knife actually stood and tried a second time. The Journeyman defended himself and was wounded badly enough to need assistance. He hired me to get him here and to deal with the situation." *A bit of a stretch, but I don't want anyone to know how bad he really is.*

The captain considered the explanation, and then looked at her dagger again. "Can I find you again?"

She gave him a long cold stare as if he were stepping over the line and really should know better. *I need the Knives to come after me first; so here is a good opportunity to let them know I'm in the way now.* "I'm Ticca. You can find me anytime you like at the Blue Dolphin, just leave a message with Genne."

He weathered her look well and wasn't fazed. "Show me your key."

Smart and brave lad this one. Need to get to know him a bit better. He'll be promoted soon. She covertly set the clasp to the right point while toying with her sword with the other hand. All of the guards were following the sword's motion. Opening her pouch, she produced the key. All of the guards' eyes went a little wider seeing the special key, including the captain. "Anything more, Captain?"

He considered it for a moment. *Now he isn't so sure which way to jump.* "May I know the Journeyman's name?"

Ticca considered the question. *A fair question, and whoever hired the Knife already knows who he is. Plus they'll know he hired me by now, there is really no need to conceal it.* "Journeyman Lebuin of the Guild of Argos. He is of this Guildhouse. As long as we are exchanging names, I didn't catch yours, Captain...?"

He smiled, "Forio. I'll report this as reasonable defense. Thank you, Ticca. Mayhap I'll see you again." The guards visibly relaxed. Forio turned and motioned for them to follow. *And that takes care of any further interruptions for the afternoon, I hope.* She watched the guards turn back towards the market and walk out of sight before she moved. Slowly, and with authoritative steps, she strode down the stair and turned toward the market. *First, need to turn this coin into something spendable. Next, I need to talk to the people this Magus Vestul went to see.*

At the edge of the market she saw it had already gotten back to full swing. Looking around she saw a well-dressed sweetmeat vendor in a clean painted cart. *Just what I needed.* Walking up to him she saw some noble ladies moving away with sweetmeats in hand. He saw her coming and had a fresh strip out on the small counter. "Sweetmeat, M'lady?"

he smiled.

Pouting slightly, she eyed the candy. "I'd love one, but I only have a cross left after all my purchases."

He smiled. "Oh, that is no problem M'lady, the price is only a pence but I have sold enough to make change."

A full pence, oh my you are used to higher-class customers, aren't you. Still, not arguing would make this faster. "Oh wonderful." She batted her eyes at him. Producing the cross for him to see, she added, "Can you give me all pence?"

His eyes looked surprised but his smile never wavered. "More shopping in order, I presume? In fact I can." He counted out the change with experienced hands, didn't cheat, handed her the sweetmeat, and gave her a cheerful farewell in the space of a few moments.

Choosing a route that would not take her past where the attack had happened, she moved through the market efficiently. A few simple inquiries provided the leads she needed and in only a couple of marks she had reconstructed the old wizard's day before he vanished. Standing where she was sure he had been, she scanned the area for what could possibly attract him next. *OK, old man, you have spent the day pulling together essentially nothing important. It is still early evening, the sun would be slipping down, putting the street in shadows. You're probably a little tired from carrying a sack over your shoulder—where do you go next? You have a room at the Dolphin. Dinner is soon and you haven't eaten since morning... and you have little to worry about, being a powerful wizard.*

Turning in the direction of the Blue Dolphin, she walked slowly, trying to imagine herself as the old wizard. In a short distance a possible stop came up. There was a corner arit and tobac shop with some tables in a little fenced off area adjacent to the street. She walked over and sat down, and a very short woman shaped like a hyly barrel came over.

"Ullo, ullo! Bid thee welcome. Arit? Tobac? Offer thee excellent cigar."

Ticca smiled warmly at the lady. "Arit and a very excellent, but smooth cigar." Showing a handful of pence, she added, "An excellent cigar."

The lady smiled deeply and rushed off. Moments later she was back with a tray on which sat three cigars, a thick walled cup that smelled wonderful, a cigar knife and a miniature brazier. Ticca picked up the cigars each in turn, examining them and smelling the fine tobac.

Selecting one with a scent that reminded her of her Uncle, she cut the tip and the lady assisted her in lighting the cigar with the brazier. The lady left the cup on the table and took care of another customer, and came around refilling and warming her cup of arit as needed. When her cigar was down to the final third, she came back and stood politely to one side, not blocking the view of the street.

"Lady, offer thee another?"

Smiling, she said, "Please wrap three of them up for me. I really like them."

The lady left and came back with a small parcel wrapped in thick paper. "Lady, three pence each, if you please."

Ticca counted out the twelve pence and then added three more. "For your fine service; this was marvelous."

The lady bowed. "Pray thee return anytime. Offer thee something else?"

"Actually, I am curious, day before last, did an older man in dark violet shirt, brown leggings, and worn shoes stop by here? He may have been wearing a straw hat and carrying a sack."

The lady smiled wide. "Indeed yes, he was such a gentle soul. Enjoyed sweet, sweet arit and like our pipe tobac much. He bought fine grey pipe and some tobac. You know him? Please bring him 'round again. He told me funny stories for almost two full marks past closing."

Got your trail, wizard. She smiled. "I am glad to have found where he got that tobac. I thought maybe so, as you have such a good reputation. Might I have some of that as well? I have a friend that would enjoy it."

She nodded and went inside for a short span, returning with another paper-wrapped package. "It is our finest. For you, I ask only another pence."

Ticca paid her and stood up, smelling the packet of tobac. *Oh, it does smell wonderful.* "Which way did he go from here? I am a little turned around."

She smiled and pointed across the street and down a bit toward an alley. "Through there. Fair night to thee, lady."

Ticca put the tobac and cigars in her pack. Swinging it over her shoulder she walked down the street and turned into the narrow alley, looking for signs. *At night this would have been totally dark. It is the fastest way back to the Dolphin, though, so he was heading that way.* Halfway between streets the alley twisted through a quick elbow bend where the buildings didn't line up straight. Just around the corner there was a slightly blackened spot on the ground next to the building. Something about it was out of place, so she bent down for a closer look.

Squatting down, she looked it over carefully. The coloration was from blackish soot mixed by the rain with the dust and dirt; it looked like a fire had been lit there some time ago. Small items poked up from under the layer of soot. Using her dagger she poked around in the ashes. The first things she found were some bits of violet cloth, badly charred. Looking around again at the patch she was squatting in, she saw it was large enough to have been a body. Remembering the Knife from earlier, she felt a little queasy. Picking up the cloth, she sniffed it and was revolted by the same stench of charred flesh she had smelled earlier in the market.

Standing, she moved out of the patch respectfully, setting down the burnt violet cloth. *Lady of Light, is this all that remains of the wizard? Everyone thinks they're so invulnerable.* Another ripple under the ashes caught her eye, and this time she remained off the patch while poking at the spot with her dagger; it was the clay bowl of a fine-looking pipe. Looking around for some explanation, she saw the faint signs, mostly washed away by the rain.

Her mind pulled all the signs together into a clear picture. Attacked from behind, he'd stumbled, bleeding, against the building. He was slashed again from behind. He tried to brace himself against the building, turning to face his attacker, and then fell forward face down. At the edge of the building just next to where Magus Vestul had braced himself, hidden slightly by some garbage, was an open brown paper packet. Picking it up, she smelled the same pipe tobac she had just bought.

Looking back at the black ashes, she thought, *This has to be the Night's Fire that assassins and spies use to eliminate bodies. I didn't believe Uncle or my trainer when they told me it would remove the body and evidence so fast it couldn't be stopped. The only reason this is still here is because it is sheltered from the wind, and it rained, cementing it here instead of washing it completely away. A couple more days and there would have been nothing to find here. Lebuin is in real danger, having been targeted. I need to be careful getting him out of there.*

Moving fast, she went to the Dolphin, dropped off her pack and purchases and changed into her night-hunter's shirt and leggings. Leaving her full cloak, she chose to wear the camouflage cloak only. In the light it looked like a simple full-length dark grey cloak with a soft knit pattern of darker threads, but if she found the right spot she could look like a rock or shadow and be practically invisible. It was also slightly magical, so it kept her dry and warm against the elements. It had been a gift from her trainer when she left for Llino. She kept the new boots on, too; they would make climbing much easier. From her pack she added a blow gun with drugged darts, which she tucked into a special pocket at her back that kept it out of sight and comfortable; unless she had to lay down flat on her back. Putting the knife-belt and the new pouch back on over the shirt, she left with a purpose for Temple Street.

It was still early evening; the sun had only just started to head down over the horizon when she came to Temple Street from the market. Instead of walking on in she milled at the edge of the market with some shoppers and critically evaluated every possible hiding spot and person present. *You are here, I know it. There was too much public activity for even a new Knife to miss.* She bought something from a vendor and then crossed to another vendor, covertly throwing the purchase between the tents. As she haggled with the other vendor over the price of some silly earrings she spotted what she was looking for. A peasant worker who had earlier left came back around carrying the same heavy bag. Except he wasn't sweating and spent a lot of time moving down an aisle that gave him full view of the temple hospice's entry stairs. When he turned off at the last aisle, obviously moving fast to circle back she spotted another. A man sat leaning against a pole and he stood up and took over the watch while the other circled. When the bag carrier came into view, the second man stretched, yawned, and sat back down, going to sleep.

She maneuvered to a position where she could see both and get a clear shot off at the sleeper. When the one with the bag turned out again the sleeper awoke, stood and leaned against the pole. She slowly drew the blowgun behind her back, under the cloak, pretending to look at some jewelry. Loading it, she waited. As the bag carrier stepped out, the sleeper laid down to doze again. She moved casually into position, brought the blow gun out, and shot the sleeper square in the back. He jumped and reached back, pulling out the needle. The bag carrier didn't see this, hidden as he was from the view by the tent flap until the end of his circuit. The sleeper, seeing what it was, groggily tried to get up, but fell flat—well and truly asleep now. Ticca smiled as she put away the blowgun and casually strolled back toward the market entrance. The moment the bag carrier turned out of sight she sprinted to the hospice. Stepping inside the hospice door she carefully looked back, remaining hidden, and made sure that the bag carrier had not come back in time to see her. Smiling as she saw him continue his observation loop, she turned to where Lebuin was sitting up, talking with Ditani.

Both men stopped talking as she walked up. Lebuin stared at her as she approached. She noticed his eyes roamed her body like greedy hands. *Well now, aren't you just the typical male. You're going to have to work real hard if you want more than a look.* Snorting at his reaction to her tight clothing, she took on a more commanding posture. *Hope this works. I need to be seen as an authority up front or else I'll be his work horse.*

Using the 'commander' tone and inflections, she informed him, "There are Knives on your tail already. Of course, that wasn't really all that hard with the commotion you made. Our next trick will be to get you out of here without them seeing it."

Ditani looked at her hopefully. "Did you find anything of Magus Vestul?"

My Lady, please, not right now. I need them both to be thinking about now, not two days ago. Keeping her voice even, she said, "We can talk about that when we are someplace safe. I took out one of the two observers. The Knife is likely waiting to ambush you on the way back to the Guild; instead I am going to take you by a longer, more circular route to the Dolphin. We can plan your next move there." Her Uncle's voice echoed in the back of her head. *'Establish the relationship and price; and then do the work.'*

Remembering his purse, she sent up a small prayer this would work. *I need to earn the wages due a Dagger table-owner.* "Journeyman Lebuin, your man authorized any price to get you here, and then to help with your search. I don't expect that offer to extend beyond this moment. I took two crosses, one for my services today, and the second to cover needed bribes. If you desire me to remain your Dagger, I expect six crosses a week, in advance. Agreed?" Lebuin inspected her dagger. She kept her eyes calm. *Please say yes, or at least don't demand something much less.* He looked her in the face and nodded. Hiding her pleasure, she thought, *Oh Lady, thank you. Now let's stay alive long enough to spend the coin.*

Looking at Lebuin's condition, she frowned. *I doubt he can move fast enough to get safely out.* "Do you think you can run right now?"

CHAPTER 6

TIME WILL TELL

THERE WAS ONLY THE VOID, but he wasn't scared anymore. There was no sensation at all other than thought. *Where am I? Is this death?* Time passed, or maybe it didn't. Lebuin considered the situation. He recalled being attacked by an assassin. The memory of it brought it clearly to his mind. He was able to examine it in detail. The girl, the energies, his responses, the details of a man burning into a pile of coal...It was all clear to him, all of it.

What was the reason for it all? More images; he recalled classes at the Guild. He remembered marks spent pouring over old tomes. He also remembered other classes where there were more than just a student and teachers. Memories he had forgotten came back clearly, as if he were reliving them. The time he was five and he started exploring the Guild. He found he could use a little magic to unlock the door the teachers used. There was a lot more to the place than the little wing where he lived. He spent weeks sneaking around exploring before he was caught. Instead of being angry, they just left the door unlocked, with the condition that he not play with the other kids unless two teachers were present. He was young and didn't listen. One of the bigger kids pushed him, as kids will do, he had gotten mad and magic flowed. Magi had come pouring out of every doorway at the sounds of kids screaming and five of them quickly blocked his view of the results. They had rushed him off, lightly chastising him for not listening, but smiling and making him feel better. He hadn't thought of that event again, but after that none of the kids would play with him and most ran away when he appeared.

Now that he could replay the memory in detail he saw that the five mages who had taken him away all had fear in their eyes. It wasn't until the Grand Magi had appeared with some candy to soothe him that they relaxed. Looking back over that memory with his more experienced and adult point of view, he knew he had released a tremendous amount of energies, more than should have been possible for such a young child. Three of the other kids had been seriously wounded by the backlash. The older boy who had pushed him looked like Magus Cune, except much younger. He had seen that boy thrown back into a wall like a doll before tears had blurred his vision. A young Magus Cune had rushed out in the yard and been screaming for help as he had picked up the limp body of the boy. *My Lord, did I kill Magus Cune's son? Is that why he hates me so much?* Going over his memories, he couldn't find any others of an older apprentice that looked like Magus Cune.

They had kept me isolated for everyone's protection. That is why there were always Magi nearby. The other apprentices must have been talking about me for years. Fear in the eyes, smiles on the faces, always soft tones, always careful handling. It wasn't until he had matured and gained control of his emotions that they slowly began to relax, to trust. Eventually they put him in the regular programs. *They needed to train me but were afraid of the results. I was so isolated; no friends, no companions, just the older mages and my family.* The thought of his family brought images of his father and surprisingly his real mother; she sang a strange lullaby in the void. If he could he would have smiled at the memory. More came—he remembered how she prepared his meals and how she always sang as she worked. She was an amazing seamstress; she wove her own cloth, singing songs to him in his cradle. He remembered her talking with his father, both of them buzzing with happiness about her pregnancy. For nine cycles he had shared his mother's joy and happy songs. But, even now, the songs were in a language he has never heard since. He wondered what language it was.

A presence joined him. He didn't know how he knew it, he just did. He wasn't alone.

"Lebuin, hold, you must hold." It wasn't a voice, but it had a sound, if sound could move in this place. It also had emotion. Lebuin could feel the anguish, worry, and sorrow that the other felt.

"Where am I?"

"Between. You must hold. You must fight back. Lebuin, hold." Anguish and a deep regret at having to make the request came as well.

"I don't understand."

"Look for the thread. Hold, you must hold."

Concentrating, he tried to see, but there was only the void. "I can't see anything. Hold to what?"

"Open yourself, you will find the thread." Like a sharing of memories and experiences, he understood then that he had to share himself with this place. Now that it had been explained he realized he was actually shielding himself unconsciously. Opening himself, the void was replaced by a mesmerizing swirl of colors, feelings, and energies. It was beautiful; he relaxed and simply enjoyed the flows.

"Hold, you must hold." Lebuin recognized love under the anguish and guilt and knew the presence was deeply concerned for him. The presence was a bright swirl of energy with four tendrils wrapped around him, as in an embrace. "Do you perceive?"

"I don't understand."

"Here. You must fight, follow this, you must hold." And with those words came understanding.

Finally, he saw the faint, silvery thread. It looked very fine, like a spider's thread. He didn't have a body here, yet the thread came out of him and it stretched off into the distance. The thread was playing out like a fishing line. He tried to grab it, but nothing really happened. *Thoughts are what rule here. This is not a physical place.* He tried again; this time he used his will, as he would to use a telekinetic formula. It worked, and immense pain flared through his mind. He screamed but no sound came. He felt the burns on his arms and chest, and worse, the knife in his chest. He let go and the pain vanished.

"Hold, you must hold."

"The pain is too much. I'm dying. It's done."

"No. We act." He understood; many entities were pushing at agents, urging haste to his aide. He understood that this was immensely dangerous to all. The presence was being careful to not share how. "Hold. You must hold."

"Why? What is going on?"

"In time..." He understood something important was coming and it needed to be in the flow of things. The entities were trying to not cause a catastrophe while trying to avoid a catastrophe. "You have it in you. Hold, you must hold."

He grabbed for the thread, the pain was almost too much. He held. "Hold. Fight. Follow it back."

He screamed, although there was no sound. He screamed and he pulled. It took every ounce of energy and concentration he had. He pulled. As long as he held the thread he could feel everything. Someone was carrying him, bouncing along, the knife in his chest moved, causing even more pain. He screamed and pulled, screamed and pulled.

"Yes. Fight. Hold." Pride and love, guilt and anguish mixed in the entity's communication.

The pride and love gave him energy and he used it to pull.

Someone was tending to him. Something moved the knife, *pain too much pain.*

I wish screaming did something, this is too much.

His mind focused on the task of pulling. Worldly things began to come to him.

Pull—*Pain* and he could smell the medicines and linen bandages.

Pull—*Pain* and he could feel the stiff cot under him.

Pull—*Pain* and he could feel that his left boot was tighter than his right.

Pull—*Pain* and his awareness of the presence faded slightly.

"Don't leave me."

"I will not, I will remain until conclusion. Hold... Fight... She comes."

Other presences. There were three new entities. Two he knew to be in both realms at once. One was female, very powerful, and yet he was comforted by her closeness. The second was male, also very powerful, and he understood they were there to help. Last there was another powerful being, she existed only in the physical realm; she also was comforting. Lebuin tried to look at them but could not see them with the senses of the physical world, only feel their presences. In trying to see he found two other entities, both female; one was in the worldly realm, the other was in this realm. Both of the women were powerful, but not at the level of the others, and they both were simply watching.

Warmth washed over his body, the pain eased, and without warning the knife was pulled out. The warmth in his chest blazed into a searing heat. He screamed and felt a disorienting lurch as he slipped out of the void and into the world he knew.

As he lost the sense of the other realm he heard the entity's parting words, "Well done," and felt a tremendous flood of pride from the entity.

He was back in the mundane world, more tired than he had ever been in his life, but he could breathe and there was no more pain. Exhausted, he simply fell asleep.

Voices floated into his dreams. The first, a melodic female voice, spoke softly. Groggy, he only caught the end. "...Unexpected."

A male voice answered, also melodic... a wonderful tenor with an odd accent. "Yes, but in this case the unexpected could be a sign we are finally on the right path."

"This was too close, and I had to ask."

"Me too... Time will tell."

"That is my worry. Shhh, he awakes." The female voice came closer, and he felt her warm breath on his ear. "Shhh, Lebuin rest now, all is well." She sang then, softly, in a language that reminded him of the songs his mother used to sing. He couldn't fight it; he fell back into sleep, feeling totally warm, safe, relaxed, and happy.

- - -

When he opened his eyes, he found himself in a large room, lying on a cot. Dust motes swirled in a light breeze as they fell through warm sunlight streaming through some high windows.

"Master Lebuin, how do you feel?"

Looking up he saw the upside down and worried face of Ditani. *That is a very good question. I should be dead. I had a knife in my chest.* He couldn't feel any magic flowing in him. "Good question, Ditani. I'm not in pain, but I cannot feel any magic. Help me up."

Ditani moved to his side, helped him sit up and turn, putting his feet on the floor. He felt slightly dizzy; an acolyte in smudged light green robes, which fit moderately well, came over with a look of concern. "Journeyman Lebuin, please don't move too fast. You need to recover. It is uncertain how much strain your body can handle. Also, I am instructed to warn you that you could become forever powerless should you try to use magic at this time."

Frowning at the news, he looked at the man, who was about the same age as he was. "How long before I can try to channel my power?"

Looking sternly at him like any good physician, he spoke in what was probably his most professional voice. "It is suggested that you do not try to channel for at least a cycle. The Great Lady also recommends that when you begin to practice, you start slowly, first with air, then water, and then earth, moving on to each when the previous ones are re-mastered with ease. Only when all three of the other elements are effortless, is it her recommendation, should you attempt fire."

He put his head in his hands and looked down. *Well, I am alive, and that was the strangest experience I have ever even heard of.* Thinking back over his memories, he wondered if it had all been real. Wiping his eyes, he saw that his wonderful doublet and shirt had been cut open down the middle of his chest. Sputtering, he managed to get out, "My clothes! What did you do to my clothes?!"

Ditani just looked at him, wide-eyed.

"Seriously, what happened to my clothes? Ruined! My two best outfits, in two days, totally gone!" Looking down again, the anger faded into nothing as his fingers came upon and traced the vertical scar on his exposed skin. Looking down at the cot, he saw where the blood had soaked through the canvas to pool on the floor; it was hastily cleaned, but the signs were still there. Sighing, Lebuin looked back at Ditani. "Sorry, I guess this really did happen," he said, his fingers resting on his first real scar. "I don't understand what is happening. Is every Journeyman's life so dangerous?" *I was dying. If not for swift action by beings who shouldn't have cared, I'd be dead now. My skills meant nothing—a single knife in my chest and it was almost over.*

"I have heard that some are, others are not." Ditani gently placed his hand on Lebuin's shoulder. "I don't understand why someone would attack you like that."

"I think it might be Magus Cune trying to exact revenge."

Ditani looked at him, shocked. "Master, that cannot be! Magus Cune has always loved and protected the Guild. He would not attack a Journeyman unless that Journeyman was a traitor."

I bet he is involved in this. "What can I do? I cannot use magic for at least four weeks, which means I might as well just walk naked through the city."

"Master, I hired a Dagger to get you here. By sheer luck, I believe she is one of the best in the city. I may have overstepped my place acting on your behalf. It was just that I didn't know what else to do to save you."

Lebuin's hopes jumped. "No, no that is perfect! You really are a Godsend, Ditani. I wanted to hire a Dagger guide to both guard and help me with my Journeyman quest."

"In that case I am pleased. Except, well…" Ditani looked a little worried and embarrassed.

"Yes?"

"Well, the Dagger took your money and left to try to find Magus Vestul. She ordered me to not let you leave here until she gets back."

Astonished, he looked at Ditani. "Did you say 'she'? This Dagger is a woman?"

Ditani nodded. "I thought you'd be upset about her helping herself to your purse."

Lebuin instinctively pulled the purse out. It didn't feel empty. "How much did she take?"

Looking at the floor, Ditani said, "two crosses."

Lebuin laughed for a moment. "That's it? Two crosses? You made it sound like she took my whole purse!"

Ditani looked up, surprised. "You're not angry? Master, two crosses is a lot of money!"

"Is it? I thought I would be spending dozens of crowns to hire a Dagger for any length of time."

"Master…" Ditani stopped and looked at the doorway. Lebuin, following his eyes, could not believe what he saw. *I must be dreaming, that is the lady from the alley and market. But Lord, look at her.* She wore boots that were a dull grey, with a hinted pattern done in forest green. Above the boots she wore leather pants which were tailored perfectly to fit her. They were not new, but the pants were well-maintained and would likely last a very long time. The leather had been treated so that it was a dusky grey, smooth but not polished. *I bet it repels water*, he thought. Over her pants she wore a thigh-length shirt, also expertly tailored. The shirt had shifting patterns of grey and was made of a tight woven cloth that absorbed the light to excellent effect. Over the shirt was a leather belt, in nearly a charcoal gray; on the belt were a short sword, four knives, and a medium-sized pouch that blended in to her clothes. The focal point of this entire outfit, he noticed, was an ornate dagger. Her grey, patterned cloak flowed behind her, like the wind itself was personally escorting her. Every inch of her outfit spoke volumes of the wearer. *How can she pull off that kind of perfection with such simple materials?*

The Dagger stopped in front of Lebuin and put both hands on her hips, her feet shoulder-width apart, back straight, and looked him full in the eye. He felt like he had just been caught doing something naughty. *I have never seen a woman with so much authority, or presence. She could probably stand toe-to-toe with anyone.* Looking down at her boots, he realized they must be the boots she took from her assailant. Now that he could see them up close he could see why she had taken them. *I would have taken them myself, even if they do look a bit small for me.*

Her voice was pleasant but every bit as authoritative as her stance. "There are Knives are on your tail already. Of course, it wasn't really all that hard with the commotion you made. Our next trick will be to get you out of here without them seeing it."

Lebuin shifted focus from her boots to the dagger that was only about a foot from his nose. It was beautiful; the hilt was diamond-shaped, with a bone hilt polished to a glossy shine. The cross guard had a hunting motif with hounds that appeared almost alive. The dogs faced in both directions and could have been running down their quarry or attacking an enemy. *It is very suggestive of a guard or hunter. But that is the point, isn't it? The dagger describes the Dagger. Impressions, first impressions are the key. The tables by the walls, means they have their backs covered and are in a stronger position, hence are more experienced or capable. It is so simple a code.*

Ditani asked, "Did you find any news of Magus Vestul?"

"We can talk about that when we are someplace safe. I took out one of the two observers. The Knife is likely waiting to ambush you on the way back to the Guild; instead I am going to take you by a longer, more circular route to the Dolphin. We can plan your next move there." She shifted stance slightly. "Journeyman Lebuin, your man authorized any price to get you here, and then to help with your search. I don't expect that offer to extend beyond this moment. I took two crosses, one for my services today and the second to cover needed bribes. If you desire me to remain your Dagger, I expect six crosses a week, in advance. Agreed?"

Lord, she took out more people already? She is killing things hunting me. Whatever payment she wants she can have; I can spare it, and it is far less than I was already planning on paying. It's a bargain either way. Looking into her eyes, he nodded agreement.

Her reaction was hard to read, but something in her eyes came alive with speculation. "Do you think you can run?"

She is actually excited by the danger. Guess that would be a reason to become a Dagger, but how could a woman get the kind of training she must have had?

"I can barely sit up, so I doubt I can move very fast."

Her eyebrows tightened with concern, but looking at something behind him, she smiled slightly. Turning, he saw a doorway, presumably to the Temple. "Get up. We'll get you a change and go that way." She reached down and grabbed his arm with a strong hand.

He stood and felt a little dizzy but managed to stay in place. "Um, what do I call you?" She started to turn away and then looked at him in surprise; something passed through her mind, and she smiled. Her smile was like lightning. *Oh Lord she is beautiful. That someone so beautiful can be so dangerous is a wonder in itself.*

Face to face she was slightly taller than he was. She held out her arm. "I'm Ticca of Rhini Wood, Dagger in your service."

Taking her arm, he locked it with his. "Journeyman Lebuin of the House Caerni; I am pleased to accept your service." Her eyes widened only a hair's width at the name of his house. *Well, she knows us. She is really good at hiding her emotions; I bet she would do well at the tables.* "Ticca, please call me Lebuin; and I assume you already know Ditani." He gestured to the other man.

Nodding, she pointed to the inner door. "Now that we are all formally introduced, can we please proceed with getting to someplace safe?"

They made their way to the Temple's inner door. Lebuin had to lean on Ditani a little to stay steady, and they were soon intercepted by an acolyte. "That way is not proper."

Ticca looked at the acolyte sternly and said nothing, and after a moment the young man, looking more than a little nervous, decided it might be best to let a higher authority take care of the matter. "Please wait a moment, I'll get a Healer." He went through the door and closed it behind him.

Looking around near the door Ticca picked an empty cot and pointed at it. "Rest there while I make some arrangements." She then boldly stepped to the door and opened it, stepping through. Lebuin sat down with Ditani's help and they waited.

"Ditani what is a Knife, in the context that Ticca was using?"

Ditani looked at him, his eyes going a little wide. *Yes, I am totally ignorant, please don't belabor the point.* Ditani seemed to read his mind. "Milord, a Knife is a professional assassin, just like a Blade is a professional soldier, and a Dagger is a warrior-specialist."

Lord, she is killing professional assassins for me?! I might pay her a bit more just to keep her happy.

Ticca was back in about a half-mark, her arms loaded with the light green robes worn by initiates in the Temple. Ticca had already gotten rid of the fine cloak she had been wearing, and was followed by an older woman wearing the dark green robes of a priestess of Dalpha. Coming over to the cot, she tossed the robes on the end. "Here, get into these."

Ditani stood and started picking through them quickly and efficiently, selecting one for him and another for his master. Lebuin looked at the robes he was handed in disdain. "You want me to wear this in public?"

Ticca stopped in the middle of stepping into a robe herself and gave him a look of disbelief. "Are you serious? Would you rather walk out on the street with that target spot already nicely laid open for the next Knife?"

Lebuin felt a little ashamed at his reaction. *What in the world am I thinking? Damn it! Something dangerous is going on and I am complaining about the clothes. I must look the total fool.* "Sorry, I am not thinking clearly; of course I'll follow your lead." He put on the new robes and found a way to fasten his pin on the inside so it didn't show. *No reason I can't at least stay clean and comfortable.*

When they were dressed the Priestess checked them over. She made some minor corrections to their belt knots and then standing back, she nodded. "This will be just fine. You must wear the hoods up at all times; and you should not look around. Keep your hands loose at your sides. Stay in formation behind me. I will take you to Gold Street, about half a mile from here, where we have a small hospice. From there it would not make sense for us to travel this way."

The priestess looked at Lebuin, concerned. "I want you to follow behind me. Should you find that you cannot continue, pull on the back of my robes. I will find an excuse to stop. Please don't try to push through, let me know as soon as you begin to feel a little tired."

Lebuin nodded. "I understand."

"Good. Now you stand here, and you two walk side by side behind him; keep two steps distance between us and try to stay in step. I will go slowly, so this will take quite some time. No one will be able to tell that you do not belong here. Some priests think deeply while traveling from place to place." The priestess opened the door. "Now, while in the Temple, it is practice. When we exit by the main door your lives will depend on looking the part."

Gravely, they put their hoods up and fell into the measured step set by the priestess. From time to time she would glance at them as they walked and corrected them on various small points. By the time they approached the main doors, Lebuin felt like they might have a good chance at surviving this. In the main hall the priestess stopped. "Lebuin, are you well? Can you do this for a full mark more?"

This is no time to be boastful; our lives depend on me not falling on my face. He looked within himself and considered what he had done since waking up in the Temple. "Yes, I can do this; I know our lives are on the line. Thank you, Lady, for your aid."

"Service in the Lady's name is my reward. The time for practice is done; Come." And turning, she led them out of the main doors.

Lebuin's heart raced as they stepped over the threshold. *No shields, only thin cloth between me and the world*, and then another thought occurred to him, *and this is how most people live every day.* He concentrated on staying in step and at the correct distance from the others. He found that while looking straight down, he could just see the front edges of Ditani's and Ticca's robes. Lebuin was surprised to see that Ticca had found time to exchange her boots for a different pair; they were made of supple leather, dyed a soft green that matched the robes very well. *That is an amazing lady. She must have spotted the boots when she found the robes. I can't believe she would just leave those other boots.* He pondered the day's events as they walked. He found that although he was tired, he could push himself further. *I have never had so much strain or trouble. This whole day makes all the troubles at the Guild silly in comparison.* For the first time he felt vulnerable and mortal. As they walked, he tried to find any time in the Guild that had threatened and frightened him so much, but no problem or slight—even by Magus Cune—compared.

After what felt like forever, they climbed the steps to another building. The smells of the herbs and incense found in a hospice were a welcome relief from the fear of attack. Lebuin was about to pull back his hood when the priestess quietly commanded, "Follow me, I must present the three of you." Her tone clearly worried about something.

They stayed in step as they moved through the hospice room; they did not get very far before the priestess cried out, "You would dare attack inside the house of Dalpha?! Lebuin, get behind me!" and spinning, she lifted her staff high. As Lebuin pulled his hood back to find the source of the priestess' alarm, the light in the room took on a greenish tint.

A simple workman dressed in smudged brown and worn clothes with a soft gray wool cloak was diving to the side as knife rebounded off a shield created by the priestess.

Ticca spun, pulling her robe open down the front. She pulled her dagger and another knife as she jumped between Lebuin and the man before his knife had a chance to hit the floor. "Lebuin, run! Follow the priestess!"

The man rolled to his feet, facing Ticca, and smiled. "You think you can best me, girl?"

The priestess repeated Ticca's command. "Lebuin, come, now." She grabbed Lebuin's collar and tugged him away from the fight. *I can't help, I'm powerless! Lord, help her!* Turning, Lebuin grabbed Ditani's robe and pulled him along too. The priestess kept the shield up and backed them towards a doorway.

Ticca and the man approached each other cautiously at first. They said something to each other in low tones, which he couldn't make out.

Lebuin didn't see who moved first but their knives flew, filling the room with the ringing sounds of metal hitting metal. As he went through the doorway he saw the man entangle Ticca's robe with one hand and yank her off balance. He heard Ticca yelp in pain before the priestess slammed the door closed. Turning, she pointed down a hall. "This way." And she ran faster than Lebuin thought was possible in all those robes.

Although tired, he had no problem finding the energy to run after her. Ditani remained right behind them. At the far end of the hallway the priestess threw open another door and motioned them inside while she watched down the hall. Once inside she closed the door and locked it, leaving them bathed in a soft green light of her staff. Her staff shifted to glow with a brighter white light, and Lebuin saw they were in an alcove with a flight of stone stairs leading down. The priestess hurried down the stairs, and with no other instructions, Lebuin and Ditani followed.

The stairs led to a large cellar filled with shelves; the priestess strode over to one of these. "Ditani, help me with this, please." She pointed at a shelf and then lifted one end; a soft click could be heard. Ditani moved where she indicated and helped lift and pull out the shelves. The shelves moved slowly to reveal a hidden door, and Lebuin heard the sound of water coming from beyond the door. They followed the priestess into the unknown.

In the soft light Lebuin was surprised to see that he was on a narrow ledge and there were boats attached to rusted rings sunk in the walls. Taking some sacks from a pile by the door, the priestess pulled a knife out of her robes and cut the sacks while talking. "Take one of the small boats. Go where the current will take you. You'll come out near the merchant docks. Do not wait. Leave the boat tied if there is time." She handed Lebuin and Ditani a pair of very rough shirts made from the old sacks. "Leave those robes here; they'll just mark you now. Take these, they will make you look more like poor workers—and put some dirt in your hair and get some grime on your hands and face."

Lebuin just looked at the sack in disbelief. *Poor-fitting robes, dirty sack shirts, grime! This is like the worst nightmare imaginable, hired assassins trying to kill me, people dying to protect me. There must be more than Magus Cune's revenge here. Lord, what is this all about?* Ditani had already tossed his robes aside and was pulling the shirt over his head. Lebuin slowly took the robes off, remembering to take his clasp.

The priestess saw the clasp and asked, "What is that?"

"Nothing, just an artifact I made. It keeps my clothes clean."

The priestess stared at it and then him in disbelief. "Keeps you clean? Why would you waste your time making something like that? Lady, forgive me, but that is completely useless!"

Lebuin puffed up. "It's my choice to make what I like."

"Lebuin, you cannot take that with you; it will ruin any chance you have of getting to safety."

Sighing, he nodded. "Yes, I know. It's just today was supposed to be very different."

The priestess nodded in sympathy. "Yes, yes it was at that. Give it to me, you can have it back if we make it through this alive."

Lebuin sighed again but handed over the clasp and then struggled into the rough shirt. The rough fabric scrapping his skin, Lebuin thought, *My Lord, this is harsh! I have seen workers dressed like this passing the Guildhouse. I never imagined I'd be dressed like one of them.* Lebuin looked at the priestess. "Holiness, how will Ticca find us?"

"Don't worry about her. If she lives, she'll find you."

Ditani had selected a boat and was waiting for him. "Where should we go?"

The priestess thought for a moment. "I am not sure, where was Ticca planning to take you?"

Ditani answered, as Lebuin cautiously climbed into the boat. "She was taking us to the Blue Dolphin, Holiness."

"Then I suggest you continue on that path. If she doesn't make it soon, you will need another Dagger."

Ditani found the oars and pushed off into the current. "Our eternal thanks, Holiness."

The priestess waved. "May Dalpha bless and watch over you both. Good luck." She turned and went back up the stairs with a purpose.

Lebuin rubbed an itch caused by the shirt. "Ditani, do you think we'll live?"

Ditani was concentrating on the currents and answered absentmindedly, "Time will tell."

Lebuin looked at his companion for a minute. *That was an odd inflection, it sounded like my dream. Was it Ditani I heard while I slept?*

Everyone keeps saying that today. Lord, can things get any worse?

Thankfully once they were in the broad current it was a leisurely trip. The waterway was lit by sunlight that came through a series of grates which were evenly spaced along the sides. Here and there were small ledges, unevenly spaced along the path. Most of the ledges had a stone staircase leading up and some had boats or barges tied to the same types of rusted metal rings. Above each stairway hung an engraved white stone, each carved in a language foreign to Lebuin. Some of the platforms had small wooden signs naming the establishment above. From time to time, workmen in boats would row past them, heading upstream, but most just used the currents to move their goods.

The canal soon joined with a larger channel, where traffic increased. Barges were poled and boats of various sizes maneuvered between them and the channel's banks; there was an intersection and more of those white stone plaques, laid into the walls, one on each side of the intersection. Floating in the water below them was a buoy with a sign showing street names he was familiar with.

As they traveled, more and more of the boats had lanterns out, shining bright in the gloom. Seeing that all the boats, including theirs, had lantern or torch holders, he looked at Ditani. "What is this place?"

"Have you never heard of the Delivery Channel?"

"Yes, but I thought it was a tributary to the river?"

"Yes, and the whole city is built over it; the water flows gently towards the ocean. The western docks have an entry system, so large craft don't have to fight the current. Most of the city's deliveries and goods are moved through the channel."

Lebuin looked at the construction and noticed that there were no seams except where the platforms were and where other tunnels intersected. "This looks carved from the rock itself."

"Llino is one of the oldest cities; all old cities have features like this, and no one today understands how they were made."

Lebuin looked from Ditani back to the odd seamless stone walls. "No one knows how to do this?" He asked, pointing at one of the white-inlaid stone signs. "So what language is that?"

"Again, Master, no one here knows."

Lebuin marveled at the engineering that this water channel under his very home represented. An itch reminded him of the sack he wore. *This is amazing. I haven't even left the city and I have already learned many things about this world. I can see the reason for Journeymen to journey. Only why do I have to have all of it coming so fast?*

Ditani maneuvered the boat near a wall where some sludge had built up. He purposefully let one of the oars pick some up and let it drop between them on the floor of the boat. He then cursed and started to throw it out by hand. A nearby group of workmen on a barge laughed at Ditani's seeming inattentiveness. Lebuin watched for a moment before Ditani looked at him meaningfully. Remembering the priestess' instructions, he bent down and helped, getting plenty of smudge on his hands and arms. He wiped his hands on his shirt and pants, following Ditani's lead. Finally Ditani pointed at his boots, and, grimacing, he proceeded to ruin those too. *And it does get worse. I have never been so dirty in my whole life. This stuff stinks, too. Stabbed, burned, chased, robbed of my powers, my clothes ruined, wearing an old oat sack for a shirt, and now river sludge on my whole body. This is worst day I have ever had, but also the most enlightening day too.*

The boat passed through an open gate made of steel that shone like a mirror. *Those don't look like they have aged, but they have to be as old as the city.* He tried to remember how old the city was. *The Duianna Empire was the first civilization in human history, and that was founded over fifteen thousand years ago if the reference books are to be believed. Then the accords were signed, breaking up the failing empire into roughly the current smaller countries of today, and that happened about nine thousand years ago. The Mages' Guild of Argos was founded just over four thousand years ago. This city is supposed to date from the time just before the Duianna Empire, which means that the city itself is maybe sixteen thousand years old, or possibly older. What civilization was here before we came? Why did they leave? And why do we know nothing of them and yet live in their cities which seem to have been built for us today?* Once past the gates they came out into the docks just as the priestess had said. Ditani found a place to tie up and they climbed on the docks just like the dozens of workmen milling around vessels of every size and shape.

Carefully, they made their way unnoticed through the docks until they came to Merchant's Road. Turning, they walked with the flow of foot traffic to the Blue Dolphin. Many workmen were heading there as well, it being the end of the day. Lebuin and Ditani joined the flow of workmen walking into the Blue Dolphin. *I think we overdid the grime; most of these men look cleaner.* Sniffing, he decided they were not really too far apart. Lebuin headed for the bar, but Ditani grabbed his shirt. "Aye, I see a clear spot, buddy," he said, indicating a place at a common table.

Lebuin rubbed the shirt and nodded agreement; they made their way over to the table and sat down. Ditani ordered dinner and took a couple of hyly mugs off of a passing tray. Putting one down in front of him he picked it up and sniffed. Taking a careful sip, he found it thick and lightly sweet. *Actually, this isn't as bad as I imagined.* He drank his fill, finding he was thirstier than he realized. Ditani watched and smiled at him, and feeling a bit better, Lebuin smiled back.

When the food arrived there was no napkin, nor water to wash with. Lebuin watched as Ditani produced a knife and cut a piece off a hunk of meat, using his hands. Ditani left the knife in front of him, and grabbing some bread, began to eat bare-handed with his dirty fingers. *Lord, I know I needed to learn... but really, this is almost too much.* Smelling the meat, his stomach made up his mind for him. He grabbed the knife, cut into the meat, grabbed some bread, and ate. As he ate he thought over everything, and realized Ditani had done more for him in one day than he had ever done in his life for anyone else. Smiling, Lebuin realized he really enjoyed Ditani's company, so he dug in and enjoyed dinner with his new friend.

Next to their table a bard stepped up to the small platform and struck up a jaunty tune. Lebuin grabbed a fresh mug of hyly and thought that things could get worse. But for now, this was a wonderful dinner after all. Ditani smiled at him and he smiled back. *Time will tell indeed. I just hope it is finished with today's tale!*

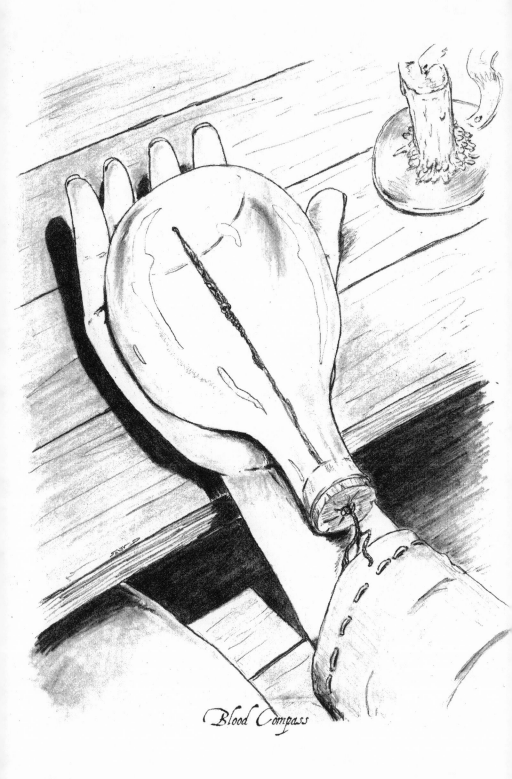

Blood Compass

CHAPTER 7

BLOOD TELLS TRUE

'*S*TEADY, CALM, WAIT FOR THE *right moment.' Her trainer had said that in every knife fight they had together.* Knives out, balanced foot, cautious on the approach, all key. The Knife apparently had similar training. They circled each other slowly, both measuring the other up.

"Who's paying you?"

He smirked. "Sorry missy, that is privileged information and where you're going it won't be of any use."

Confident bastard. Looking at his excellent disguise as a slightly wounded workman, she knew he was experienced. *He had to have been following us. Damn it! I shouldn't have let the priestess drape me in that hood.* She spotted the quick shift of his rear foot and was able to parry the first thrust. She sliced up with her dagger but he had already shifted and parried with his off hand. They exchanged a handful of feints, attacks, and parries, circling fast.

Lebuin and Ditani finally got through the door. She glanced over to make sure they were getting out, and smiled as she saw the door closing. Turning her attention fully on her opponent she saw he was circling towards the door. *I need to keep him occupied to give Lebuin time to get clear.* In spite of the danger, she launched a series of attacks to keep him from trying to run and pursue them. The Knife managed to hold her off. It meant he got into a better position; he seized the opportunity without hesitation. Feinting with his left hand, he changed direction at the last moment, and dropping low scooped up the loose end of her initiates' robe. Easily parrying her dagger, he yanked hard, pulling her off balance.

Damn it! These robes are going to get me killed! Gotta do something unexpected or I'm dead when his knife comes back around. Ticca was already off balance, so she let herself fall forward instead of fighting to stay standing as he expected. He had already reversed his knife and was trying for a neck strike, but without her counterweight he was also off balance. Ticca twisted and arched back, effectively dodging the strike. Unfortunately that exposed her mid-section and she was much too close. He delivered a vicious knee strike to her chest. The air was forced out of her in a loud yelp of pain and surprise. Releasing the robe, he sliced out, smiling wider as he managed to cut what felt like a bone-deep gash across her shoulder. Clenching her jaw on the pain, she managed to only squeak.

He smiled as she finally recovered from the maneuver by taking a couple of wild shots just to keep him occupied while she stepped past. *OK, bastard, you're not bad.* She backed up a little and he let her go. *Think you're winning, don't you... except I'm better than you.* She glanced at her shoulder; a bit relieved, she saw it wasn't as bad as it felt. It wasn't a deadly or impairing wound, unless that blade had been poisoned. *If his knives are poisoned I need to end this fast to get help in time.* Almost laughing, she thought, *Well, at least I'm already at the hospice.* She smiled back at him and saw his eyes light up with joy. *Yep, you think are winning. But you're not as fast or as well-trained.* "Not bad, but do try to keep up."

Ticca relaxed her stance, controlled her breathing, and moved with a fluidity and grace that would make any dancer jealous. Stepping forward, she delivered a series of thrusts and cuts, and he parried every one. She didn't give him time to riposte. She kept thrusting and cutting, faster and faster, as she warmed to the fight. He started backing away from the flurry of blows and she stepped forward with him, never stopping the attacks. He managed to get a riposte in about every third strike. She easily parried those and followed through with her own riposte. She smiled and looked him in the eye as the attacks continued. Finally his eyes showed real fear.

He had backed all the way to the wall. Sweat was pouring down his face. She paused. "Care to reconsider?"

"To hell with you, bitch!" He feinted left, but she saw his right moving to throw. She ducked under the thrown knife, thrusting up with her dagger and cutting the wrist of his extended hand. He was totally exposed; she simply reacted, knocking his knife wide and burying her blade to the hilt in his heart. Quickly stepping back, she pulled her knife out and let him fall face-first to the floor.

Backing up a few more steps she checked the room for more enemies. The only people in the room were a handful of patients, all stock still, mesmerized by the fight, and two acolytes. She let herself breathe a little before sitting down on an empty cot. She didn't put the knives away; she just rested her wrists on her knees dangling them in her hands. *Two days, two kills. This one was at least a reasonable fight.*

An acolyte approached cautiously. She brought her knife up quickly before dropping it again. "Lady, do you need me to look at your wound?" He looked like he would try to fly away if she moved.

Looking at her shoulder, she saw the blood was running well but slowing. Very gently and softly she replied, "Yes please, and do you have a rag I can clean my knives with?"

He moved to her side and handed her a square of cloth. She wiped and cleaned her blades while he inspected the wound. "I need to see it better; can you remove your shirt?"

She stood, shedding the initiate's robe onto the next cot. She then took her belt off and placed it on the robe. Finally Ticca turned her back and removed the shirt, and grabbing the towel he offered she wrapped it around her bare chest; then she sat back down, pulling the cot with her equipment close enough to grab it fast if needed.

Another acolyte started towards the body but she called him off. "No, don't touch him, I want to inspect him first." The acolyte obeyed and went to help the other patients.

Just as the first acolyte finished wrapping her shoulder with clean white cotton bandages the priestess came back through the door, her rod still glowing green.

"He's done, Holiness; unfortunately he didn't want to talk."

The priestess approached and inspected the bandaging. "Is it a major wound?"

"No, just sliced up the skin. I've had worse."

"Perhaps, but I think I can help." She lightly rested her hand on the shoulder and chanted a prayer. Soft warmth spread, and the pain eased considerably. "That will speed the process. In a day you can take the bandage off and it should be near fully healed."

"My thanks, Holiness." Ticca stood, dropping the towel and making the acolyte squeak a quick goodbye and rush off. She managed to not laugh, barely. Slipping her shirt on, she grabbed the belt. "I presume Lebuin is safe?"

The priestess nodded. "I set them on the Delivery Channel dressed as workers. They should have no problem making it to the Blue Dolphin via the docks. You can meet them there in about two marks."

Ticca thought about the situation for a moment and it felt good all around. "Thank you, I am worried, but I doubt they'll be watching the shipyards for workers." Settling her belt into place she stepped over to the dead Knife. She bent down and rolled him over.

He had four knives, a few coins in a cloth purse, and that was it. Searching him thoroughly yielded nothing more. The knives he had been using looked familiar. She tried to place them. Picking one up, she saw it was slightly longer than a dagger but still a bit shorter than the short sword she had fought with. It was single-edged and the hilts were a series of knotted black cotton bands over ivory or bone. *These look like those knives my Uncle and Trainer talked about. What were they called?* She thought for a moment and then it came back. *Odassi! The fighting knives of that group called Nhia-Samri who were pushing the pressure points to keep the anger high and the war going where my Uncle lost his arm.* She looked at them a bit closer and then put them down. *It might be, but this more likely one of the imitations Knives like to use to scare people; he didn't fight in the style my Trainer showed me they use.*

"He must have followed us from the Temple; I bet he was going to try to get into the hospice when we left."

"He might have done that after we left and then guessed at how you got out. He didn't get close until about a quarter-mark after we left the Temple."

Smart priestess; that is a pretty good observation. She thought it over. "True, that is also a likely scenario. Either way I still don't know who is backing this, nor do I have a place to start."

The priestess looked a little uncomfortable. "There is one thing I can do."

Ticca looked at her with interest. "What more is there?"

The priestess called for a bottle, a straight needle and surgical thread. "I can give you a blood compass."

I have heard of those, but no one ever said or even hinted that a servant of Dalpha would be able, much less willing, to make one. It would be very good to answer a few questions. "Holiness, that would aid me greatly."

The priestess received the items she called for. She quickly tied the fine thread to the needle and pushed that through the bottle stopper. Bending down to the dead man, she rolled the needle in his blood. She then carefully inserted the needle into the bottle. As she closed the stopper, she sang a mournful chant into the bottle, her lips practically touching the rim and her breath fogging the inside of the glass. The stopper jumped from her fingers, seating itself very deep into the bottle's neck with a slight hiss. The bottle glowed red for a moment, and when the light faded the fog on the glass had cleared completely. The needle hanging on the thread held firmly towards the door.

The priestess handed her the bottle. "This will last for three marks. After that the traces it follows will be too faint. It will lead you back on the path of his life."

Ticca took the bottle reverently. "Holiness, I know what it means to make this. I shall remember it. If you don't mind my asking, you're very competent in skills I wouldn't expect from a priestess. How did you learn these things?"

"I wasn't always a priestess." She pulled out of her robes a lovely old dagger with wings for a crossguard. The hilt was a carved piece of ivory with intertwining leaves and flowers, the pommel a nearly-closed oval of silver also engraved with the intertwining vines. "I am Boadua of Mostill Valley; Dagger, priestess, in service to the Great Lady Dalpha."

Ticca took in the dagger then looked into the older woman's eyes; there was life, cunning, and experiences untold in their brown depths. Ticca touched her dagger. "I am Ticca of Rhini Wood, Dagger in service to Journeyman Lebuin of House Caerni and the Guild of Lord Argos." After the moment passed Ticca grinned. "That's why the Great Lady called you for this task, why you brought us here and how you knew he was a threat."

The priestess smiled wider, nodded, and put the dagger back under her robes. "It was some time ago. I am pleased I still have some of the skills."

Ticca squared off to the experienced Dagger and put her arms out. "Sister, your service honors me and your name."

The priestess took Ticca's arms in hers. "And you have served well this day. Now continue with your charge, stay sharp, and may the Lady watch over you."

Releasing her arms, the priestess winked and turned to the task of cleaning up the scene. Watching Boadua efficiently taking command, she heard her Uncle's voice remind her, *'Some people spend an entire lifetime wondering if they made a difference in the world, but Daggers don't have that problem.'* Ticca set the bottle down and pulled her cloak out of her pouch. Shaking it out, she put it on and pulled it well over her shoulders so it could be pulled closed in front when she chose. Taking the bottle, she nodded farewell to the priestess. "Stay sharp." Being very cautious for more watchers, or archers in hidden places, she left the hospice. She was fairly certain there were no spies watching. *Stay sharp indeed. Just 'cause I don't see them doesn't mean they're not there. As my Uncle always reminded me, 'Daggers who are paranoid live to tell tales.'*

The path the bottle led was not unexpected at first. The Knife had indeed followed them from the Temple, moving back and forth from one hiding spot to another. It took longer than she liked to get back to the Temple due to the many zigzags. A full mark and a half had past. At the Temple she found he had not gone inside it but had been across the street, obviously observing both entrances. *Must have followed us on a hunch or got some warning we were no longer there.* From the Temple on it was a very simple path. He had come from a side street that paralleled the market. She followed his route to the merchant quarter. Ironically she found herself crossing Gold Street not more than three blocks from the hospice; he had come through an alley that led through a series of paths. The sun was already down and twilight was growing dim when she found what she hoped to find. Ticca wrapped herself in her cloak and moved through the dim shadows, when the blood compass indicated a nondescript door in the side of a house.

She circled the house and found that he had come from the opposite direction and stopped in the house. It was a nice rich merchant's house with two wings and two stories on a side street to Silver Road, with a large front yard and carriage round. What made it interesting was not the perfectly painted shutters, nor the very rich colored-glass double doors, but the fact that he had used the alley entrance, as had many others. The front of the house struck her as just that: *A front for something else.* She carefully left the area, making sure she hadn't been seen coming or going. *I need to think this through. This is where a Hand would live. I need to find out which Hand and who his clientele are likely to be.*

Once Ticca was clear of the area, she found a trash heap and broke the bottle there, leaving only scattered fragments. She took the needle and stopper with her. Breaking the string, she rubbed the needle in the dirt for a moment then threw it into another alley. Finally, the stopper went on a roof many blocks later. *May your afterlife give you all you earned, but I will not be one to keep you from it longer.*

Using the shadows, she remained vigilant for all observers and possible assailants the way back to the Blue Dolphin. She approached from the city path and spent extra time trying to find any hint of spying. She couldn't find a single lookout. *This is wrong. There has to be an observer. This is the one place I would go for sure. So it is the best point to get a lead on Lebuin's location.* Approaching by roof, she moved cautiously, keeping her cloak around her.

She had just about decided there really was no watcher when she realized that the roof next to her had a couple of tiles lifted slightly. *There you are. It isn't paranoia if they really are after you. Bet you have all sides covered too.* She moved back silently. She realized her boots were not making any sounds at all. *These keep getting more and more useful.* She moved smoothly away and then dropped into an alley.

Well, they know I am going to go in there. By now they might be worried that the Knife hasn't reported back. I hope Lebuin made it before they started watching, or even better that they didn't recognize him. Thinking it over, she couldn't think of a way into the building, other than flying, that could go unnoticed. Shrugging to herself, she pulled the cloak back, exposing the bloody bandage and affected a convincing limp as she stepped out to the street and simply walked in plain sight to the door. She imitated being wounded and trying to hide it. *Kind of silly pretending to pretend not to be wounded; but people see what they expect, and this will help make them feel a bit more confident in my lack of skills.*

Once inside, the smoke and sounds of the bar made her feel welcome and hungry. The smoke burned her nose, as it had for the last few weeks. *Whoever likes that odd herb is still here. I wonder what it is about it that they like so much, because it doesn't smell all that pleasant to me.* At the right-hand community table sat Lebuin and Ditani, talking and drinking. They were smiling and looked to be just fine, so she kept up the pretending to pretend and turned left, limping slightly to her own table. The table had changed; attached to the dagger holder was a metal coin. The coin was engraved with a few birch trees in the background and a pack of hunting hounds sitting looking straight out at her. She couldn't help it—some tears came to her eyes.

Sitting down, she unlatched the coin from the dagger holder and traced the etching with her fingers. The hounds were the same as the ones on her dagger; the coin was in the exact same style as her dagger. *This was my Uncle's when he was a Dagger here; Genne must have kept it all these years.* Holding back the tears, she put the coin back in the clasp, which was connected to the dagger holder by a pair of small screws. She pulled her dagger out and let it flip around her hand once as she laid it flat on the table.

Before she could signal she wanted something, a serving girl set a hot cup of arit in front of her from a tray of many drinks. "Care for dinner, Ticca?" The girl was eyeing her bandage with a concerned look.

"Yes please, thank you for the arit too. Would you let Genne know I'd like to see him when he has a moment?" The girl nodded and moved off, with a final glance at the bloody bandage, to deliver the other drinks on her platter.

Ticca watched the room for enemies. Some of the other Daggers, having already noticed her condition and weariness, had started to scan the room themselves. Seeing the already active scanning, her Uncle's voice echoed, *'Mess with one Dagger and you mess with them all.'* Time *to get a little help,* Ticca thought, and minutely nodded to the Daggers who caught her eye; in turn, they raised an eyebrow very slightly and she shifted her eyes sideways, idly running her hand over her dagger. When they signaled acknowledgment, she signaled that the inn was under observation; with a possible threat of Knife strike, and they grew even more alert. It didn't take long before all the experienced Daggers in the room had received and acknowledged the warning. There were three with daggers out that did not know the code; these were vouched for by one Dagger or another. *One of us will get to them and give them the code—good to know who is experienced.* Smiling, she thought of the more surprising Dagger history she had to memorize under her Uncle's guidance. *I would love to see their faces when they are told our traditions extend back beyond the known histories and into legends.* The Daggers slowed their drinking, and were inconspicuously sizing up the other patrons. Ticca joined in the exercise and by the time her dinner came out all the twenty-three non-regular customers had been identified and the Daggers were watching for any sign of trouble. *Now maybe I can relax a little. No Knife will ever attack in the Dolphin again, and any idiot trying to be a Knife will not like a room full of alert Daggers.*

As she ate, four of the non-regular customers left. Everyone else appeared to be enjoying the evening.

Genne came over, taking the other wall seat again. "Ya wann'd chat? Don' worry 'bout issues, ain't allowed."

"I know. I just I need a bath." Raising her hyly mug and blocking the view of her mouth from the room, she added softly, "And a room close to mine," before taking a swallow of the hyly.

Genne looked at her for a moment. "After yer bath, then." His eyes darted to Lebuin and Ditani then back to her. "We'll settle up inna yer room fer yer expenses."

He really doesn't miss much. Touching the metal coin on the dagger holder, she said, "I can't thank you enough for this."

"Dat, well..." He rubbed his neck. "Yer Uncle din't 'ave a chance ta collect it. I was a lad but I liked yer Uncle fine. Me pa said it migh' be needed again. So he stowed it. Took o'bit o'huntin' ta fine it. Glad I am ta have it out."

Ticca nodded, holding back more tears. Genne politely ignored the emotions, or maybe he was doing the same. He got up and went back to the bar without saying another word. Safe and comfortable, she took her time eating and drinking. It wasn't until she was just about to go up for her bath that Ditani and Lebuin spotted her table. She made as covert a "stay put" signal as she could, and thankfully they didn't move to follow. Getting up, she limped past them towards the stairs; when they looked she moved her eyes from them to Genne and back again as she went up the stairs to her room. *Lady, let one of them understand that. Course Genne probably has a means to that end too.*

In her room Ticca dropped everything but her knives and grabbed some clean, sturdy clothes; she closed the window shutters and then went out to the baths. One room was open with a hot, steaming tub waiting. She slipped inside, locking the door. Stripping, she put the boots on the rack, and her clean clothes over them. The knives she kept close at hand. Tossing the dirty clothes out the drop hole, she happily eased into the tub. It was wonderfully hot. She scrubbed everything, even dunking her head to rinse her hair. Then she soaked until the water grew tepid. Regretfully she stepped out, and, not feeling any pain from her shoulder, she peaked under the bandage; there was no sign that there had ever been a wound. She picked up her boots and kissed each one. "Thank you, Lady, for these little wonders, I cannot think of any tool besides my dagger that could be as useful." After dressing, she made her way back to her room.

Ticca was putting some things away when she heard a knock on her door. "Yes?"

"Ya asked for some hot arit." Genne's voice was a welcome sound. She opened the door and there stood Genne holding a large platter with an arit serving carafe, over a small candle to keep it hot, and some brown curly pastries. Behind him Lebuin and Ditani were just coming up the stairs. She held the door open as they all came into her room. Closing the door, she locked it behind them. Ditani took in the room with a nod of satisfaction.

Genne put the platter down on the table and poured a cup for everyone. Grabbing a pastry, he sat down and made himself comfortable. "Now dese are worth every pence." Closing his eyes, he drank a little arit and bit into the pastry. It almost looked like he had been transported to heaven. So everyone followed his example. The flavor was sweet, with a hint of chocolate, and something else that left a warm feeling that spread from the mouth out.

Lebuin looked shocked. "There is sharre in these."

Genne smiled. "Yep." Looking at Ticca, he asked, "What can I do fer ya?"

Ticca took another bite before answering. "We need to hole up for a little bit and plan our next move."

"So ya bring yer trouble ta my place?"

"Come on Genne, you know as well as I that no one would dare attack us here. Any Knife that tried would be cut down by his own kind at the mere mention of the idea."

Genne just nodded. "Who di' attack you?"

"A Knife, and he is dead, but we are being watched."

Sighing, Genne looked at the three of them. Then an almost happy smirk came to his lips. "Not like dis' is da furs' time. An' dis' place is always watched."

"Is there a room close by we can have for say, three weeks?"

"Yep, two doors down, same side. Fourteen crosses fer a cycle, wi' meals an' such."

"Done." Looking at Lebuin, she said, "M'lord, if you will, please pay him now."

Lebuin pulled his coin purse out and handed over the silver coins.

"Ya need'n more?"

She looked at Lebuin and Ditani and sniffed the air. "Yes, I am pretty sure they'd like to clean up." Looking at them, both men nodded thanks. "Please provide baths. Also," she looked Genne square in the eye, "for what you overcharged them this morning, how about finding them something a little more comfortable to wear?"

Genne actually looked embarrassed for a moment. "I dinna ask for dat. He put it out."

"True, but you didn't have to take it all." She winked at him. "This will make up for the misunderstanding."

Genne stood and motioned for Lebuin and Ditani to follow.

She leaned back with the sweet pastry and the arit. "M'lord, when you are done cleaning up, would you care to plan tonight or wait for tomorrow?"

Lebuin looked at Ditani, who nodded slightly. "I think we need to discuss some things tonight, if you agree?"

"That would be best. Please, when you're done come back here and we'll all share some stories."

The three men left her alone. With them gone, she closed her eyes and enjoyed the comfort of her own room. The pastries helped with that immeasurably.

It has surely been a busy few days. Remembering that she'd thought this morning she would take a few days to relax before putting her Dagger out, she laughed. Swallowing the last of the arit in her mug, she stood up and stretched. Grabbing her gear, she put away her belt and her pack in the armoire. Taking all of her knives, she pulled out a whetstone from her pack and went to the table.

She had just finished cleaning and sharpening the last knife when she heard a soft knock. Standing, she went to the door, knife still in hand. "Who's there?"

"Ticca it's us." It was Lebuin's muffled voice.

She opened the door and let them in and checking the hall was empty, she closed and locked it behind them. Genne had been pretty efficient and had provided simple loose pants and some clean-smelling brown cotton shirts. They both wore their original belts and gear over the long shirts. Looking at Lebuin's belt, it was obvious he had only worn it a few times before today. He had a silly cloth coin purse dangling from it, screaming to be stolen by the most trivial of cutpurses. *Of course he is a wizard, and if he was still dressed as I first saw him I think most cutpurses would think that was just bait.* The knife Lebuin sported opposite the "steal me" purse was a laughable, cheap steel knife obviously bought more for show than for any real purpose. Lebuin was easily every bit the pampered and pompous rich kid. His original clothes were very nice, but, like the simple fare he was wearing now, still hung loosely from his near-skeletal frame. Still, there was something about his face and eyes that gave her pause. *He would be amazingly handsome if he was a bit more filled out, with that brown hair and the piercing green eyes of his. I feel as if there is something potent hiding under that beard of his.*

Turning her attention to Ditani, she was surprised by the mixed feelings she had about him. *He looks like a typical Karkaian, but there is something more there.* The belt he wore was of excellent condition and well-cared for. It was by no means new, but still looked in top condition. The two knives he had were the longer variety favored in Karkai which were almost dagger-length. They were also double-edged but with a shallow grip and narrow hilts. In spite of being a servant, she was sure he was more used to giving orders than taking them, although he affected no outward sign of this. *He is much more than he lets on.*

The two men stood there for a moment; Lebuin was just a couple inches taller than she was, while Ditani stood another inch or two taller than Lebuin. As they both stood there with a blank look, wondering what to do, she was struck by how close they looked to another pair of men she knew, and an idea began to form in the back of her head. "There is more arit and pastries if you want." She pointed at the larger comfortable chairs. "Come, let's figure out where we are and what you'd like to do next."

Ditani stepped over to the table and with efficient servant-style action moved the whole platter to the smaller table between the comfortable chairs. She just slipped into a chair with her back to the window and waited.

Lebuin didn't move; instead, his brows moved up and down and his eyes looked up at the ceiling as he thought things through. Ditani refilled her mug as well as two others and handed her another pastry. She nodded thanks, looking Ditani directly eye-to-eye, and waited. Ditani met her look straight on and didn't glance down like a servant would. Ticca got a feeling that he was appraising her and found her admirably acceptable. *You are not what you pretend, old man, but I'll play along for now, until I know more.*

Finally Lebuin looked at her. "Ticca, shouldn't we be finding a less conspicuous place to plan? This has to be the most obvious place to find us. If there are more assassins they'll come straight here first."

He picks up fast. She nodded. "M'lord, you are right in the details and incorrect in your conclusion. You must be unaware of what the Blue Dolphin is."

"It's an inn where Daggers hire out of, merchants stay in, and workmen come for drink at night."

She nodded. "Yes, that is all true. It is also a Dagger Home."

Lebuin's blank look told her he had never heard of that. *Not really surprising, and, unless you work with Daggers, it won't really make sense.* Ditani didn't say anything but he didn't have the blank look that Lebuin sported. Her Uncle's voice reminded her, *'There are only two kinds of people that understand Daggers: Daggers, and the enemy; everyone else has a second-hand opinion.'* "M'lord, you may relax; a Dagger Home is guarded by all the Daggers who live and hire out of it. It will not be violated for fear of retribution. The last Knife who tried to kill in a Dagger Home was sent back in multiple small boxes and that launched an all-out attack by every Dagger in all the lands in every city against the Knives' Guild. Their entire Guild was nearly destroyed and most of the best Knives were dead before they apologized and swore to never again violate a Dagger Home. No soldier, Blade, Knife, guard, or spy will be anything but polite and respectful of privacy inside a Dagger Home."

"Are you saying Daggers are better than Blades, spies and Knives?"

"Most Daggers will tell you that Daggers are the best there are. It's true that Daggers are forged over years of training and experience; however, there are masters of other professions just as cunning, experienced and deadly. There are many more Daggers than there are of any other mercenary for hire. Also, Daggers have an ancient, traditional tie to each other. Our trainers instill a deep love of being a Dagger as well as a total commitment to the Dagger ideals of honor, courage and commitment. Daggers are more than friends or family, we are united by our commitment to each other and a history older than you would believe, going back into the time of legends. The soldiers, guards and Blades respect each other and talk about being a band of brothers. But Daggers mean it. We have a code, we have our secrets and we look out for each other. All others know this and tread lightly because of it."

Lebuin still looked unconvinced, but he walked over and sat down. As he took the mug of arit offered by Ditani, he stared at her. "You killed the mugger in the alley last night in mere seconds. You probably killed the Knife in the hospice too, didn't you?"

"How do you know about the alley?" She didn't bother to confirm the latter.

Looking a little embarrassed, he took a drink before answering. "I was watching from the Guild library. I was going to help, but you killed him before I could cast a single spell."

Ditani was looking back and forth between them. "You mean you knew her before today?"

Lebuin nodded. "I knew *of* her, that is why I chased her in the marketplace. I wanted to meet her, I thought ..." he trailed off and didn't continue.

Amused, Ticca prodded, "You thought what, M'lord?"

Lebuin leaned back. "Well, I thought maybe I could introduce myself, I really hadn't thought much past that. It's just you dress so amazingly, and the way you went from victim to assailant... I knew you had to be something special. I felt a strong need to meet you. I was more right than I knew."

Ticca's cheeks felt warm and she knew she was blushing. She noticed Ditani had an odd look on his face, and was covertly taking in the size of her room. *You know what this room and that table mean, don't you, old man? Why are you hiding it?* "Thank you." *Time for work, concentrate on the problem.* "We have a murky situation. Let me summarize it and if anything is missing we'll all add in the missing pieces we know, nothing held back, no secrets, your lives may depend on it, agreed?"

Both men looked down and thought about it. *They have almost the same habits, and given their features, they might even be family,* Ticca mused. Finally, they looked at each other and said, "Agreed," in turn, Lebuin first. *Agreed as far as you are willing to go, at least. Hopefully what you hold back won't be too critical.* Ticca thought about it for a moment then looked at Lebuin. Digging into what she knew about the Guild from her training, she filled in a few gaps in what Ditani had told her earlier.

"You just earned your badge of Journeyman, and have to go work in the field for some time looking for interesting ideas or uses for magic, you have some more important or powerful rival at the Guild who is hiring Knives to do what he cannot be caught doing himself. You never expected to be out in the world, and haven't prepared for it in any meaningful way."

Lebuin nodded. "Magus Cune isn't hiring Knives, he placed a sizable bet that I would survive with a 'lower class person of influence'."

"Which has the same results, just this would at least look like a friendly gesture. If you don't know the person is disrespectable or criminal, really a sinister move, cunning, too... and you," she continued, looking at Ditani, "just swept into town a couple of days ago with your master, and planned to have a pre-arranged meeting with a Duke about something, but he never told you what... Your master disappeared, without a trace, missed the meeting, and now has you, Lord Lebuin, and agents of this Duke out scouring the city looking for him."

Ditani nodded. "All of those things are true, and Master Lebuin offered to help, as he is in need of a path and hoped Magus Vestul might provide some guidance."

Interesting that you admit that you knew Lebuin's motives were not entirely altruistic. "Got it. Now as to myself, I have been working here at the Blue Dolphin for about six cycles for various merchants. I just finished a commission for my previous patron last night. Which, by the way, was why I was attacked and had to kill the Knife in the alley; he was involved with that affair and was going to try to capture and kill me. I was planning on taking some time to relax, when you were nearly taken out by that Knife in the market. From there I think we know the events pretty clearly."

"All except what you were doing today, and what happened to the Knife in the hospice."

"Yes, M'lord, true. Well we fought, he lost. I back-tracked the Knife to the location of his commission, and then I verified that this place was being watched by the elements who sent him. I pretended to be wounded so they would underestimate me."

Both Lebuin and Ditani leaned back in their chairs to consider that information. Ditani broke the silence first. "You haven't mentioned what you found out about Master Vestul."

"Ah, yes. Well I did track him. He did everything he told you he was going to do. Then on his way back here he was killed by a Knife, and his body was disposed of using Night's Fire."

Something passed over Ditani's face. *He doesn't look very surprised.* Ditani's features degraded as he took in the news, shifting to looking stricken. Covering his face, he sobbed quietly with tears spilling down his cheeks. Lebuin put his hand on the other man's shoulder and simply waited. *Lebuin suddenly looks very wise. These are a strange pair. The fresh recruit officer taken under the wing of the old sergeant friend, that's the basic relationship. But, there is more here. Ditani wept harder and fuller when he though Lebuin was dying, and this display for Magus Vestul is more like weeping for a friend who died after a prolonged illness. Not unexpected, but still hard to take.*

After some time, Ditani regained his composure and sat drinking his arit and eating a pastry while Lebuin and Ticca swapped details of their recent experiences.

"I understand why you took those boots off the man, but I can't figure out why you just left them at the hospice."

Pointing at her boots that she still wore, she asked, "What are you talking about? These are the boots here."

"No, they can't be. The boots you had on in the hospice were patterned shades of grey that would have matched that cloak the attacker was wearing perfectly. These boots are amazing too, but they are tan and brown fur, which is a good match for what you have on now."

Ticca looked at the boots. *Could they have yet another marvel? First they fit, then they climb, then they heal, then they move as silent as bare feet, and now he is saying they change to match what I am wearing? Lady, where did these come from?!* Taking them off, Ticca tossed them to Lebuin. "You're the wizard, can you tell me? I swear these are the boots I took off the man, the same boots I have been wearing since last night."

Lebuin caught the boots. "These feel unbelievable..." He looked them over closely. "They are amazingly clean considering you have been wearing them around town." He turned them over and examined the making. "I didn't realize we had the same-sized feet." He slipped them on and stood.

"You're right, they are amazing to wear."

Ticca was watching in shock as the now obviously larger boots shifted almost imperceptibly to a darker shade of brown, matching well with the pants Lebuin was wearing. *Oh my, they do change to match. I hope I can get them off him now.*

Lebuin sat back down and took them off easily, handing them over as if he handled such marvels every day of the week. *I guess he is used to these kinds of things.*

"Truly useful." He watched her closely as she put them back on. "Must be a simple spell based on coloration sampling. They also have the same cleaning incantations I use. The resizing to match the wearer is a really interesting trick. When I get my powers back I would love if you'd let me examine them a little more closely."

"Only if you promise to not harm them. They might be simple for you, but to me they are a Godsend and I thank the Lady for them."

"Oh of course, I just need to walk the enchantments for a few weeks to see if I can understand what they are doing, and possibly to learn a new pathway. That man who attacked you was certainly well-equipped. Do most Knives have cloaks that blend with shadows, boots like this, and burn to nothing when killed?"

Ticca snapped straight up, spilling some arit. "What do you mean burn to nothing when killed?"

"Well after you left, something in his pouch caught fire and it spread to consume his whole body. Leaving just the cloak, which being magical in nature might be a bit harder to damage than ordinary items."

"He had Night's Fire in his pouch? Is that what was smoking?"

"I'm sorry but I thought you said fire in the night earlier. What is Night's Fire?"

"It's a tool used by Knives that burns only the victim and any organic items, leaving almost nothing but some ash which is easily blown or washed away."

"Interesting, must be a rather unique set of chemicals. I'd love to get a sample. But, yes, I believe you describe exactly what happened."

Ditani had been staring silently past them both for some time. Standing up, he pointed and asked accusingly, "Where did you get that pouch?"

Looking back at her bed, she saw her pouch was sitting on the far side by the armoire. "I got that from the same Knife that attacked me last night. Same man who had these boots and the cloak Lord Lebuin has hidden in his room."

Ditani rushed past her and picked up the pouch, examining it carefully. "This is Master Vestul's pouch. I have put it away for him many times."

Standing up, Ticca stepped over and looked at the pouch in Ditani's hands as if new again. "Well it was on the Knife that I killed, he must have taken it from Magus Vestul when he killed him. I am very sorry, as he was a Knife, I figured there was zero chance of anything valuable being returned to a proper owner. So I took what I thought might be of use."

Ditani looked at the boots. "Those must be Magus Vestul's, too! They were a gift from an old friend of his. He treasured them and always put them up neatly."

Looking down, Ticca nodded. *Damn. Well they were nice while they lasted. I can't keep them, though.* "That explains why the Knife was so well-equipped; he had just taken all the best a powerful wizard had to offer. Ditani, I am truly sorry. These then belong to Vestul's kin, or to you as his servant." Taking the boots off, she held them out to Ditani.

Ditani looked at her for a moment and she could see in his eyes, he knew the code she had to adhere to. He shook his head and looked down to hide a smile of satisfaction. "Magus Vestul had no kin in the world and they would better serve you." He held out the pouch. "This pouch included. So by the right of blood revenge I give them to you freely. They are yours."

He is an odd fellow, for sure. Thank you, Lady, I really didn't want to lose these, and he has given me a clear conscience in keeping them. Ticca slipped the boots back on. "Thank you, truly. Yet I am still confused. I don't understand how a Knife could kill such a powerful wizard. Until today I thought, like everyone, that you were mostly invulnerable to weapons."

Lebuin was quiet for a few minutes and then he said quietly, "There are ways to penetrate a mage's defenses."

Ticca took the pouch back to the chair and cautiously opened it to the compartment with the papers. "If this is Magus Vestul's pouch then these are his notes, or letters, or something. They might give us a clue as to why he was targeted... for Ditani's sake." Handing them to Lebuin, Ticca sat down as he started to examine them.

Ditani sat back down too and looked over the papers with Lebuin. "These are the letters from the Duke. The others look like the master's quick notes, the ones he took before he would commit more careful notes to his research journal." As Lebuin moved through the papers, obviously able to read what they said, Ditani looked startled. "And those are the notes that Magus Gezu had me take to Master Vestul a few years back."

Lebuin looked up. "Well, these are intriguing hints at some significant discoveries. The letters from the Duke indicated Magus Vestul was coming here to share his latest research with the Duke for safety. Don't ask, I don't know what that means. It is just that the Duke in one letter agrees to ensure their safety. These papers were going to be handed over to the Duke."

"What about Master Vestul's key? He put it in the pouch when we left in the morning."

Ticca shook her head. "It isn't there now, most likely; it was left in the alley where the Knife burned up. It couldn't be destroyed by Night's Fire."

Lebuin shook his head. "No, it wasn't there. The rain washed the ash away almost instantly and I took the cloak. Are you sure it isn't stuck in a seam?"

Ticca shook her head, then stopped. *I didn't pull everything out of the vial compartment.* "No, not exactly, but I didn't search completely." She covertly shifted to the vial compartment while putting the pouch on the table between them. Opening it, she pulled the vial case out, as well as a few scraps of paper; and there under the paper was a Dolphin key similar to her own. Holding it up triumphantly, she exclaimed, "And here is his key then, as it isn't likely to belong to the Knife. Problem is we don't know the code to get in."

"I do," Ditani said.

Odassi

CHAPTER 8

KEYS OPEN PATHS

TICCA AND LEBUIN BOTH LOOKED at Ditani for a moment before asking simultaneously, "Should we go in?"
Lebuin asked, "Would Genne care if we looked in that room?"
"Genne has a hard policy about spying and thieving, M'lord."
Lebuin looked uncomfortably at Ditani. "Weren't you staying with Magus Vestul here?"
"Yes I was, in Magus Vestul's room."
"Ditani, that is perfect! It isn't stealing, or spying because it was a shared room, and Magus Vestul is dead. You said he didn't have any relations that would claim his legacy, right?"
Ditani looked pained. "Master, he was more to me than just an employer, I knew him well and we grew to be good friends... to speak so plainly of his murder." Ditani's eyes watered as he spoke.
Need to pull him along a little. Assuming a commander's mannerisms, but with a gentler voice, "Ditani, wouldn't your friend desire that we live to find the meaning to his death?" Waiting for him to mull it over, she kept her eyes firmly on him. Ditani nodded finally, looking her in the eye. For a moment she thought she caught a flash of light deep in his eyes, like a wolf's reflecting the light, and they were slightly larger than normal now that she was looking into them.
Ditani's voice trembled, but he answered, "Yes, Magus Vestul outlived all his relations and he had no children I am aware of."
Oh, this will kick him. Self-interest is usually a good motivator. "Well

then, it isn't thieving to enter your room and take your stuff. It also isn't thieving to claim any remaining personal belongings, as you were his servant and without an heir, a personal servant may claim everything. Congratulations, Ditani, you just inherited the entire legacy of a great wizard."

Instead of looking excited by the news, as she expected, Ditani looked scared. "Ticca, Master, no. I couldn't claim it all. I would be afraid to approach any of his research, and I wouldn't know what to do with his library. I do not want for much and have no need of his wealth."

What kind of servant would deny what is likely a small fortune? Looking at Lebuin to see if he was thinking the same, she saw he wasn't. Lebuin's eyes were lit like the noon-day sun.

Lebuin's eyes gave away that his mind was racing with possibilities. "Well then, Ditani, perhaps you would grant me what you don't desire. This could resolve many issues for me. I would be immeasurably helped by his library. I could even ensure his legacy of knowledge is not lost and complete what work he started but now will not be able to complete. I would of course give him full accolades with the Guild. His name would not be forgotten. Where is his research?"

If he follows through with the credit, it would be a good legacy. I hope we can trust this wizard.

"Master, everything save what was intended to give to the Duke is at his home in Algan. I know how to open it physically, and with his death, many of his magical protections should be gone as well. Perhaps with you to investigate it would work well. My wife will not believe our good fortune."

Lebuin truly smiled deeply for the first time. *Lady, he is a handsome man when he smiles.* "Ticca, Algan is leagues away up river, too far for Magus Cune's ally to continue attacking. If we can get there, all this mess could blow over, and I can find everything I need for years to come. There is even a Guildhouse there, so I have no need to return to Llino for some time."

Algan is a large enough city to have a Dagger Home. I could probably get some kind of guard or messenger commission back to Llino. Lebuin would be safe with his own base of operations. So all I need to do is get him there in one piece and, job done. Her heart agreed it was a good plan.

"True, it would solve that problem and some, if not all, of your questing requirements. What about who killed Magus Vestul? Do you want to investigate that?"

Lebuin's neck went a little red. "Well, yes, but I think that is beyond my ability. With your information I can write a letter to the Guild and let the council take care of it. I need cycles to recover, in which time they could have solved it and brought the guilty to punishment. Also, there is the matter of the price on my head."

He has coin, and it is a good point. "Very well M'lord. What would you have me do?"

Lebuin straightened, *He feels the power of leadership and likes it, I think.* "First help me collect what Magus Vestul had in his room, next I need some time to go over these notes before I write letters to the Guild. Can you get a note to my family's business and one to the Guild?"

"Of course."

"Then I'll write one tonight asking for a passage for all three of us and our cargo on the next merchant ship heading towards Algan. It will likely be a few days or perhaps a week before passage can be secured. Will we be safe here for that long?"

A week sitting in the Dolphin, that doesn't sound very entertaining. 'Course I cannot leave them totally unguarded, even here. "I can keep you safe here that long. The trick will be to get you and Ditani out of here and to that ship unseen."

"Well you'll have some time to come up with a plan. Now let's go see what Magus Vestul left behind."

"Ditani, where is Magus Vestul's room and did he leave the shutters open?"

Ditani looked at her. "It is the end room on this floor. Yes, I am pretty sure the shutters are open."

Lady, we are being observed, and open windows at night does not sound like a good idea. Genne said Magus Vestul was paid through the cycle, so we have three whole weeks before the room is reclaimed. She held up her hand. "M'lord, the room is secure and paid for three more weeks. The shutters are open, we know we are being watched. Let's wait until morning."

Lebuin sat back down, frowning. "You're right, and I'm tired. We can collect what we need in the morning without fear of observation. I think we all need to rest and consider the day."

Ditani nodded and the two men stood up together. Lebuin asked, "Can we safely go to the main room for our meals? I mean, how confined do you recommend we remain?"

Daggers will be there at all times, and they have been warned. Why would anyone risk the trouble when all they needed to do was wait for us to leave and deal with us only? "M'lord, I don't suggest you get too near the front door; beyond that I would say you can go where you will." She remembered the platform. "I would also not go out on the landing platform. Technically it is still the Dolphin, but you'd be exposed to a bow shot or another one of those lightning sticks."

"Wand."

"What?"

"Lightning wand. It was an artifact that contained the essence of an attack incantation that looked like lightning. Any such device is called a wand."

Laughing, Ticca stood up and escorted them to her door.

"Why are you laughing?"

"That explains why my Uncle called the switch he used to beat me with the 'Wand of Retribution'. I didn't get the reference until just now."

Ditani and Lebuin both laughed and were smiling as they left. Both grabbed two more pastries each and full cups of arit as they left, making her chuckle once the door was closed. *They might be more than they seem, but they are definitely men.*

Turning back to the room, she popped a pastry in her mouth. It didn't take long to dress and prepare her weapons. Placing her gear close at hand, she placed her dagger and one knife unsheathed where she could get them from the bed. Needlessly dusting off her boots, she pondered, *I wonder if these are the reason for the strange dreams I am having. Let's see if I have one without these on.* She placed the boots on the floor where she could put them on quickly if needed and stretched out on the comfortable bed. Checking the dagger and knife distances and location of her pack a second time, she laid back and stared at the ceiling a minute. *I have a commission, we have a plan, and there is a little travel included. All in all a good day.* Setting the lamp to burn low, she checked that the wick spring was wound tight and fell asleep, feeling warm and happy.

The Temple was lit by the many braziers around the large space. Acolytes and worshipers were kneeling or sitting in the pews. At the front, a choir of priests and priestesses sang hymns to Lady Dalpha. On the center dais the relics of the Lady were arranged around the golden lattice egg that contained the glowing sphere known as Dalpha's Light. The base of the dais was being cleaned by acolytes being overseen by a junior priestess.

Boadua paused in her progress, offering devotion to the Lady; she opened herself to the Dalpha's Light, and allowed her soul to share with the relic. Boadua felt her Lady's love and power and gave freely all that she could. Turning, she continued her measured gait to the door on the side of the dais. Opening it, she moved inside without hesitation. In the adjacent room was a large oval table surrounded by nearly two dozen comfortable, but business-like chairs. The chair at the head of the table had a much larger and ornate back and was occupied not by the High Priestess, known as The Great Lady, who normally sat there, but by Sula. Sula appeared to be a charming young woman, dressed in a simple cream-colored blouse, forest green skirts, with a wide belt and soft slippers. No matter where Sula chose to sit, to Boadua, that chair took on the aspect of a grand throne. Sitting next to Sula was the Great Lady Sayscia, who had removed her heavy robes of office and was dressed in a comfortable white and green frock with a soft leather belt. She still wore her tiara of office.

As Boadua entered the room, the two great ladies were bent over some papers on the table between them, debating some item that they were both pointing to on the pages. Sula's wide emerald eyes came up, looking at Boadua, and the conversation stopped. "Is he well?"

Boadua stepped around the table and sat opposite the Great Lady on the other side of Sula. "Yes, Holy One, Lebuin and Ditani have made it safely to the Blue Dolphin." Placing the sack she carried on the floor next to her she shifted to get comfortable in the chair.

Sula frowned slightly at Boadua. "I have told you to just call me Sula. It is my name after all."

"Your will, Holy One."

"Really, do we have to do this every time we start?"

"At least once or twice more."

Sula frowned, but her eyes betrayed the mirth she felt. "I hope so. You have confirmed they are safe at the Blue Dolphin?"

Boadua nodded, then, looking at the papers she realized there were more than at yesterday's meeting. "Have we really passed a new marker so soon?"

Sula nodded and pushed some of the papers closer to Boadua so she could read them. "My Mother indicated we have moved past many of the possibilities and allowed that we should know the contents of three markers. The attack on Lebuin was unprecedented even with the new packets. The last few days' events indicate we have avoided several possible failures. The key event remains unknown and impenetrable as far as these go. Magus Vestul died almost two years sooner than all previous attempts and nine years before the initial attempt. In the final packet we just opened, he surmised there was no way to succeed without that sorry event. The latest indicates we are taking a great risk in the hope the accelerated events will mean keys will have to wait a period before other events cause their need and continued motion. Thus giving us time to actually trace them to find the needed principal and figure out how to interrupt it. I pray his sacrifice is not in vain. Have you found who tried to kill Lebuin? Have we been discovered?"

Boadua leaned back in her chair, a little defeated. "I am as confused as anyone on this. I cannot find any news or hint that we have been discovered. Ticca's killing of the hired Knife before he reported back firmly and directly ended that possible diversion. I have consulted with numerous practitioners and none can fathom how he could have detected the hook, especially since he wasn't the actual target this time."

Sayscia leaned back in her chair, frowning at the news too. "Boadua, he appears to be a random element. We can find no indication he was key in any snap back, he just happened to be the Knife the Guild assigned. We therefore remain free of any closed loop. We are on a new path which is unique. All hints indicated the correct selections have been made. Actually we cannot agree if we are looping, which seems good to me."

Boadua skimmed over the new information. "Sula, how many packets remain?"

"Only one remains."

Sayscia and Boadua took a moment to take in the unexpected count. Sayscia spoke first. "Which means that the year or so we thought remaining is now gone?"

Sula shrugged. "Nothing indicates one way or the other. We must continue to act as we feel we should. We must also guard against directly acting or causing any specific action to occur based on this knowledge."

Sula looked over the papers in front of them again and sighed. "Lebuin is not only ill prepared, without any warning of what he must try to prevent, but now is totally stripped of his powers. We knew he should be ill prepared but there is no mention of being stripped of his powers. This is what we are worrying about. We have to remain external except where we specifically acted before to prevent becoming trapped. If we were to actively protect him, it would nearly guarantee becoming trapped forever ourselves."

Sayscia shook her head. "Sula, we don't need to act. I think we are well. Ticca is not involved due to any action on our part. So she would become involved regardless. Damega's progeny has much potential and is well-trained. If she remains under coin with Lebuin he will be safe."

Sula nearly bounced out of her chair as she sat up rigidly straight. "What do you mean by Damega's progeny?"

"Ticca is Damega's eighteenth generation granddaughter, and trained by the Traitor himself. You didn't know?"

Sula's hands cupped her cheeks in shock and she looked like she might be having a heart attack. "Oh Mother! How could I have done this?" She closed her eyes and sat rigid in that position for some minutes.

Both Sayscia and Boadua waited respectfully. While they waited, Boadua finished reviewing the new papers. Using Dagger signals, she silently asked Sayscia if she meant *the* Traitor. Sayscia signaled affirmative, and then it was Boadua's turn to lean back, thinking hard.

Opening her eyes Sula leaned back in the chair as if all the energy had been drained from her. "Sayscia, are you sure of this? How did you come to know this and I did not?"

"Sula, which part did you not know? That Ticca was Damega's progeny, or that she was trained by the Traitor?"

"Both; and just to be clear you mean Amia-Dharo the Nhia-Samri, who helped stop the war when you say the Traitor?"

Sayscia looked worried. "Holy One, I promised never to utter that name. He said it would cause a response, also the hundred crown reward for him by the Nhia-Samri is still posted annually."

"I am aware of the potential of the name. We are shielded here. However, I too will honor your promise. Now tell me how you know these things."

Sayscia considered for a moment. "In my youth, I fancied becoming a great and renowned hero-healer. I made sure to be near centers of conflict and Daggers. I never actually put out a dagger, but I associated with them enough that eventually I ended up an often added team member. This gave me much travel, excitement and some very trying times. Then the war started. I was quickly associated with a Dagger unit lead by Faltla of Rhini Wood. He was amazing, strong, smart, handsome, and everything a woman could desire. I could tell you many a tale of daring that Faltla and his men achieved in support of the southern alliance to help stop the war. I am not ashamed to say I was more than a little smitten with him."

Both Sula and Boadua leaned in closer with sparks in their eyes at the story.

"Faltla's unit was guarding a large command meeting at an encampment of southern alliance forces, when a surprise attack by a squad of Nhia-Samri came. We outnumbered them twelve to one, but they slaughtered all who didn't outright help with the evacuation. They cut through the ranks like a ship through water, and were heading directly for the general's pavilion, which was being hastily evacuated. Faltla and his squad attacked them. I watched as friend after friend fell. Every fall caused by wounds I could not hope to mend. But still they fought with knife and sword with such speed and skill that the Nhia-Samri experienced nearly equal losses. I shadowed the fighting in case I was needed.

"When the fight had reached the general's pavilion there remained only Daggers, Nhia-Samri, and myself alive on that bloody field. It was then that the Traitor was exposed. He had been meeting with the command staff and had made sure all the dignitaries were safely away. With the general who left last safely away, he came running back to the fight. He literally leapt over the general's pavilion, landing in the middle of the remaining Nhia-Samri squad.

"I am not ashamed to say I was horrified, terrified and struck dumb by the speed, ferocity and deadliness of the Traitor's blades. Faltla and the remaining Daggers rallied, seeing the Nhia-Samri beginning to fall faster than their own. It was a pitched battle. When the Nhia-Samri realized they were to lose, they turned as one on the Traitor. He could not withstand so many of his own kind; still, he was the second best Nhia-Samri in the world. He held most off, but one of the Nhia-Samri managed a blow with the side of his blade, cutting open the traitors head from the top of his skull and sliding down the bone and laying open the side of his neck, nearly cutting his shoulder in two. The cut only missed the main artery there by a hair, but still he was as good as dead.

"Faltla saw this and dove between the remaining Nhia-Samri to stand over the Traitor's body, calling for me to be ready. I have no idea how he knew I was near. The few remaining Nhia-Samri tried to take as many with them as possible. Faltla would not be moved, and so took grievous wounds that would cost him his arm at the shoulder; later he almost lost his legs to infection. In the end, only five remained alive in a field of thousands: Faltla and the Traitor, both badly wounded; Faltla's second, Sidur of Ashkash, Dagger in service to the general; myself; and a Nhia-Samri who lived to tell the tale.

"I ran from my hiding place to tend to Faltla, but he refused treatment until I had seen to the Traitor. I thought the Traitor was dead, but Faltla was right; I detected faint signs of life. So I managed, by the blessings of the Lady, to seal the Traitor's wounds, and after, Faltla's, which prevented them from bleeding to death. With Siddur's help we found a cart and got Faltla and the Traitor into it. We rode for several days before we were picked up by the remains of the general's forces. It was during that time that some of Faltla's wounds became infected. With the help of a surgeon we amputated Faltla's infected arm and saved his legs except for some toes. I refused to be relieved and tended personally to Faltla and the Traitor's wounds for over a cycle without rest, expending every bit of knowledge and power I had.

"During that time we came to know one another very well. We shared stories of our lives, families and dreams. We became as close as family. It was just before the Traitor left that Faltla revealed that his great-grandfather had summoned him just before the war started. Faltla's great-grandfather showed him proofs that they were of the Duianna line shared with Damega, and with a family history going long past something called 'the Migration' some fifteen thousand years ago. He charged Faltla to take up the care of these when he died. Faltla swore to do this, and I assume he has.

"The Traitor recovered completely in only six weeks and left to end the war. Faltla had to retire. I was assigned to the general's personal guard unit which had been placed under the command of Siddur, who had also been recruiting new Daggers. When the war ended I'd had my fill of adventure and came here, dedicating myself to our Lady.

"When I noticed Ticca carried Faltla's dagger I asked about it, and Ticca herself told me that she was the niece of Faltla, and said he had trained her in tracking since childhood; after Ticca's father died she told Faltla she desired to follow in his footsteps instead of in her father's. Faltla trained her as a Dagger from the age of ten, and when she surpassed his abilities, the traitor arrived and assisted in training her."

Sula, for the first time in either woman's experience, looked completely lost.

"I hired an unknown Hunter-Dagger who was blessed by my Mother, just to deal with placing the hooks. I had no intention of her getting involved any further. Now the progeny of Chaos itself, trained by Death Incarnate, is intimately involved. Oh Mother, can this be? How can this lead to deliverance?"

Boadua spoke up. "Well, that isn't all of it."

Sula and Sayscia looked at her in askance.

"I believe that Ticca is a Duianna, and trained by the Traitor. I recall hearing that the Duianna line breeds true. These things I now believe fully because I know this day she killed a Nhia-Samri one-on-one."

Sula leaned back. "Are you sure he wasn't just a very skilled Knife?"

"I cannot personally authenticate my proofs; however, I was required to use The Lady's Sight to keep track of the one who followed us from the Temple. I caught him as he was forced to move through a crowded section; but I lost him again a moment later. Being alerted, I forced him to expose himself momentarily and then I used the Sight to track him to the hospice. Further, the stories I have of the fight all describe intense nonstop blurring speed with ringing of steel on steel. I am sure the fight lasted at least a quarter of a mark as it took me just over twenty minutes to see Lebuin safely off and return. My own eyes as well as the acolytes' testimony proved I arrived only five minutes after the fight ended. Ticca managed to prevent Lebuin's would-be attacker from maneuvering in any direction but backwards until the wall stopped him, and she gave him a chance to surrender. He might have tried to use the feint death throw on her, but she was faster and killed him instead." Boadua slipped on her leather gloves and pulled two knives from the bag she'd brought. She carefully placed them on the table and pulled one out of its sheath, laying it on the table next to the first, with its maker's mark in full view.

The knives were well-made: straight, single-edged with a diamond-shaped blade with white bone and black cotton cross-wrapped hilts. Boadua indicated the knives with her gloved hands for emphasis. "These were his knives. While I know there are many imitations available, some remarkably good, these are far lighter than they look and there is power in the maker's mark."

Sayscia looked at them with horror. "Those are Nhia-Samri odassi blades."

Sula thought out loud, "Are they here to help or hinder?"

Sayscia looked at her in disbelief. "Help? Why would they help? What could possibly bring them here? Why are they trying to kill Lebuin? Could they know anything of these events?"

Sula's eyes burned with rage, staring at the odassi on the table. "We can answer none of these questions yet, but we will start to look for answers. I can't believe I am saying this, but hopefully Lebuin will keep Ticca's services. With his powers crippled for a time we cannot track him from a distance and I don't want to be close enough that Ticca will detect us. Given her nature, we cannot even trust an experienced Dagger to shadow her effectively. We must be extremely careful, especially with the Nhia-Samri involved."

Boadua smiled. "Sula, I can help with that, too." Producing a silver clasp tastefully decorated with blue and green gems, she placed it on the table. "This is an artifact made by Lebuin."

Sula looked from the clasp to Boadua's smiling face and back. Then she stood, offering her hands to Boadua. "Boadua, your service honors me, my Mother, and your name."

Blushing, she stood and took Sula's arms in hers. "Thank you, Holy One. It is my wish to serve."

Sula picked up the clasp. "Sayscia, please ask Magus Cune to come here as soon as possible. We need his aid again." Gesturing at the knives on the table, she added, "Boadua, please see that those are destroyed completely and as soon as possible. I am sure you know to not take them beyond the Temple walls again."

Sayscia stood, giving Boadua a meaningful glance, which she understood immediately, and they spoke together, "Your will, Holy One."

Sula sighed and rolled her eyes. She walked out of the inner door behind the head chair, mumbling just loud enough to be clearly heard, "I put up with much, Mother." The priestesses chuckled together as they separated for their tasks.

Urio-Larne read the report carefully for the second time. *This doesn't make any sense. What would pull him from his gaming houses to travel half-way across the world? He hates hot climates. What was so important? We must complete the assignment.* Shifting a little, he allowed himself to relax in the padded wing chair; there were perks to long service, after all. Looking up, he enjoyed the way the fire cast a glowing pattern on the richly-furnished library. Two large lamps on each corner provided ample light to see all the papers, charts, and tools spread in a neat pattern over the large oak desk. Putting the note down on a small stack of such papers, he considered the implications. Across from him his senior lieutenant sat straight-backed in the plain hardwood chair. "I don't think I have ever seen such a mess, Ossa-Ulla. Keelun killed Vestul before his meeting with Duke, which was reasonable, but only if information was obtained. However, we cannot locate Keelun and therefore we don't know if he learned what Vestul was going to meet with Duke about. Now Duke is alerted and stepping on our toes trying to locate Vestul. We had to eliminate three of his agents who discovered our involvement, three more than any such operation should require. Finally, you claim both Dalpha's and Argos's agents have become alerted to all this activity and in the same breath assert that they are totally inexperienced or inept to the point of being no real threat." Extracting a paper from the middle of a stack, he continued, "Yet this detailed report shows Argos's agent effectively stopping us, becoming angry at being attacked as though it were only an inconvenience, destroying a device I thought indestructible, and generally depicts a slaying of our agent with so much emphasis on destruction that it should be seen as nothing less than the warning and challenge it is."

Ossa-Ulla remained motionlessly rigid in the chair, his eyes burning with anger, but his voice was calm and respectful. "Sir, Palkni was indeed a good warrior, and he did manage to mortally wound Lebuin. I stand by all the profiles. Our information on Lebuin is extremely accurate. Lebuin is a tremendous dandy, more interested in his own comforts than anything external to the walls of the Guild. Lebuin was allowed to completely ignore all practical training. Ticca has no combat or intelligence experience in any military and comes from a fur-trapper background with dreams of glory. She is just a show-off out for personal glory, spinning her dagger as if it is impressive, when really it impresses no one but the other children."

Allowing a small frown of reproach to show, Urio-Larne responded, "Lebuin could not have been mortally wounded; he walked to the Blue Dolphin while avoiding your observers. If we were not already monitoring the Blue Dolphin internally we would never have known he arrived there."

Ossa-Ulla was showing some color at his neck. *Good, maybe you'll pay closer attention if you finally have a bad mark on your record. I cannot see how you managed a career of such perfection, but you have grown overconfident. At least this isn't a major operation; and little embarrassment will make you a better officer.* A soft knock came from the open door and both of them looked at the corporal standing at attention. He waved at the corporal to enter. "Report, Corporal."

The corporal stepped in and saluted crisply as he summed up his news. "Sirs, Dalpha's agent has retired for the evening. It has been confirmed she was wounded, with impaired movements." His voice took on a bitter and angry tone. "We have confirmed she killed Maru-Hue."

Ossa-Ulla snapped, "She caught him in a trap? That is not very likely, sir..."

He held up a hand to stop the lieutenant and nodded for the corporal to continue.

The corporal shook his head. "No sir, not a trap, she bested him one-to-one with odassi."

Ossa-Ulla stood up, shocked, his neck flushing a deep red. "She did *what*?!"

The commander picked two papers from one of the stacks. The tops read 'Ticca of Rhini Wood' and 'Lebuin of House Caerni.' Holding them out to Ossa-Ulla, he said, "I recommend you correct these profiles and put these fictions' authors on report."

Ossa-Ulla looked a little worried, taking the profiles. "Sir, I signed off on these, and I assure you she has only six cycles' Dagger experience on minor work. She is completely inexperienced. Lebuin is even more useless."

Looking calmly at his lieutenant, he pulled out another paper with a recent report. "She has taken a permanent table, she is under coin to Argos's agent, survived the confrontation, took out trained observers, and her sigil coin is not new. The Blue Dolphin in its five-hundred-year history as a Dagger Home has *never* let junior Daggers take a permanent table. Now we learn she has killed our third best warrior in a face-to-face fight. She is *not* what she appeared to be. Lebuin is the same; you have been fooled. I suspect Duke had a hand in this. I suggest you deal with this personally. We cannot be exposed. With Duke in town it becomes more than just a standing order. I believe you understand."

Ossa-Ulla snapped to attention and saluted. "Yes, sir! Personally, sir!"

"You are both dismissed." As the men did an about-face and marched out of the library, he wrote an order to recover Maru-Hue's odassi, placing it unsigned, like all his orders, in the tray for new orders; then he picked up his wine and drank. "What are you about, Duke?" he asked the empty room thoughtfully.

"Damn it, Ladro, find my friend!" He bit down hard on the leg of mutton in front of him, breaking the bone with an audible snap.

Having been Duke's long-time personal secretary meant he was entirely used to and unruffled by abusive language or violent displays of power. Having served Duke since a boy, Ladro was in tune with his master's moods, tactics, and most importantly, likely targets for his teeth. "M'Llord, we have been unable to locate Magus Vestul. By all accounts he simply disappeared between the tobacconist and the Blue Dolphin. What we need to discover is why so many competent agents have also disappeared."

Duke chewed the meat, letting the blood drip down his face for effect. He could eat as delicately as any courtier, but he was in a foul mood and it wasn't getting any better. At times like this Ladro had to admit it was motivating to Duke's staff if Duke let his baser instincts show a little. Swallowing, Duke said, "You have identified the various routes between the two, correct?" It wasn't a question.

"Yes, M'lord. There are only two possibilities: the longer but safer street path, or the shorter, being a cut-through alley that went almost directly to the Dolphin."

"Vestul was old, lazy, and probably as tired of this blasted heat as I am myself. He took the shorter route."

"The tobacconist's information agrees, and she was the last to see Magus Vestul that we know of."

Standing up Duke, nuzzled his bag over his shoulder from the hook it hung on. "Take me there now."

"M'lord, the Princes asked, most strongly, that you not involve yourself directly."

"The Princes can go to hell. This is my friend, and I roamed this little 'burg's streets thousands of years before those brats were born. God damn it, I helped *build* this fucking 'burg! If it hadn't been for the damned climate change, this would still be my primary residence! It's time those brat Princes learned they are not as all-fucking-powerful as they think they are! And full time this 'burg was reminded it's not as big as it thinks it is!" Turning, he kicked the door open so hard that it flew from its hinges and embedded itself in the far wall. "Now are you going to show me where your incompetent fools got lost, or do I have to roam the through the entire 'burg pulling these pitiful people from their beds to get my answers?"

Realizing there was no way to stop him, Ladro stepped out into the hall, grabbing his own cloak and shooing off the staff who had come to inspect the loud noises. Duke followed him out, snarling mad, with blood still running down his chin. A few of the newer staff actually took to heel at the sight. *Lords... this will take some smoothing over later.*

Together they headed towards the main doors. As they approached, the guards needed no warning to open the doors or the gate; both stood open, with eight guards at parade rest, four on each side. As Duke and Ladro exited the mansion, the guards snapped to attention. Ladro pointed at the four outside and indicated the direction they were going to take. The guards jumped into action, moving to warn off any carriages or pedestrians.

"Now see, that is damned good training, I like that." Then, looking at the guards remaining behind, Duke bellowed, "Are you waiting for an invitation from the Princes? Close the goddamned gates and GET BACK TO WORK!" The four remaining guards leapt to comply, especially motivated since it would cut them off from Duke and his foul mood.

At least the sun has set and it is cooling, hopefully that should ease some of Duke's mood. Looking at his master Ladro saw anger in his eyes, and worry. *Duke isn't used to worrying, especially about his oldest friends.* He quietly led his master through the city, with the four guards effectively getting carts and people out of their way; a few people screamed and ran, while others stood petrified at their passing. Many looked back and forth between him and Duke trying to ascertain exactly what was happening. *He's right, this city has forgotten him.*

They reached the arit and tobac shop in just over a mark. *Well, Duke at least makes the trip fast.* The blood on Duke's chin had either dried or he had licked some of it off. Either way he had shifted to quiet fuming instead of the loud, panic-inducing fuming, for which Ladro was very happy. He pointed at the shop as they approached. "That is where the tobacconist who last saw Vestul works."

Duke walked up to the little shop with its fenced-off patio and tables. Duke sniffed the air. "No, it can't be!" Duke jumped the little fence easily and yelled, "Dardalph! Get your lazy ass out here, and stop making me wait!"

A muffled cry came from inside the shop, followed by a crash like a stack of plates or mugs being dropped onto a hard stone floor. A short woman, who looked more like a barrel, came running out of the café. "Duke! Gadriel's teeth!" She ran faster than Ladro thought possible straight into Duke, slamming with an audible thud into his side. The woman immediately commenced laughing, patting his sides and hugging his front legs. Duke, in turn, lost his emotional control and was actually wagging his tail. The first two swings tossed a table into the street and some chairs towards the store.

Dodging back a little to stay out of the path of the tail, Ladro waited and watched. *Well, that is something I've never seen before. Wonder how long they have known each other.*

She started speaking a language Ladro had never heard before. Not unsurprisingly, given his thousands of years of roaming, Duke knew the language. The two of them had an excited conversation and all the while she alternated between patting Duke's sides and hugging his legs. All the patrons at the shop sat perfectly still, trying to not be noticed by the large intruder into their previously normal evening.

After the initial conversation started to slow, Duke's demeanor shifted back to the fuming mood he had arrived in. The lady became serious too and give him a lot of details as she pointed at various chairs and then across the street at an alley not far down; she also mimed some things and made signs with her hands which Ladro could not comprehend.

Duke actually licked her face once before jumping back out onto the street; then he looked at all the patrons, the guards, and Ladro. "If anyone here mentions my actions I'll use you for my next meal—especially you, Ladro." Looking at two of his guards, he said, "You two, put that table back in her yard."

Just ignore the threat. He really was surprised and the happiest I have ever seen him, including when I read him the letter from Vestul.

Duke moved with a purpose towards the alley and as he entered it he put his head close to the ground and sniffed back and forth. "There you are, you old bastard, now where did you go?" Duke continued to sniff as he moved down the alley, stopping from time to time to explore the wall or examine something. Raising his head, he looked at one of the rear guard. "Yilla, run back to Dardalph's shop and ask to barrow a pair of lanterns." The guard needed no further urging, and bolted to obey. "Good boy, that one." Putting his head down, Duke trotted along the alley, snuffing like a bloodhound.

They had just moved through an elbow section when Duke stood straight up and sneezed. Then he put his nose down again and moved very slowly. "No! Surely not, no. How could that be? I thought a ransom or draining. No! No! Nooo!" The guard was just coming back with the lanterns as Duke sat down and jerked his head to the sky, letting out an awful howl that shook dust from the walls and caused Ladro's ears intense pain. The guards and Ladro involuntarily pressed their hands over their ears, trying to block out some of the anguished howl.

At last, Duke looked down again at the spot he had been investigating and stood. He was angrier than Ladro had ever seen. He paced, and his mouth moved as if ranting with occasional obvious snaps of teeth like rending something apart. Ladro couldn't hear what his master said because of the ringing in his ears, and he felt relieved by this. This was not Duke of Greyrhan, the laughing story teller and gambler; this was something fearful, something that came out of a nightmare. Duke's teeth were bared while he paced. He snapped, he howled again, though not as loudly, and he raged. As the ringing in Ladro's ears abated, some of what Duke was saying started coming through. Ladro wished it hadn't, because Duke was talking in dozens of languages and Ladro was sure he was working through his complete vocabulary of profanity, curses and tortures.

By the time Ladro's hearing was good enough to clearly make out what Duke was saying he wasn't saying a word. Duke had sat down and was staring at Ladro and the guards with cold steel eyes. No one moved. After a while Duke snuffled the air and asked very softly, in a tone that sent shivers down Ladro's spine, "Can you hear me now?"

Ladro nodded. Duke motioned to the guard. "Yilla, bring those lanterns over here. Ladro, take one. You stand here, next to me, and you, over there." Yilla moved to comply, as did Ladro.

Duke then stood and went over every detail of the alley methodically. He found a grey clay pipe bowl and some brown paper, he found some violet cloth bits, he licked the wall and ground in places. He also found the scents of several people. He breathed especially deep of one scrap of violet cloth. After about a quarter-mark Duke turned and headed out of the alley, his head down, following some scent. He didn't speak a word, and his eyes remained wide with a burning anger.

The guards and Ladro followed silently as Duke traced the scent straight to the Blue Dolphin. Duke didn't pause, he simply walked through the doors, knocking one off its hinges and splintering the other. The sound naturally drew the attention of everyone present. No one moved. Duke stood in the doorway, smoke from the room pouring out around him to the heavens. Duke sniffed at the air, sneezed, and sniffed again.

A dozen warriors already had weapons out but held still. Duke stared at the occupants while they tensely awaited his next action. A number of Daggers who had weapons out put them away and waited for Duke. *Well at least the Daggers remember who he is.* It only took a moment before Genne reacted. Genne came out from behind the bar. "Here now, what do ya thin' yer about?"

Duke's eyes narrowed and he walked straight at Genne, who stood his ground. Genne was a large man, but Duke still towered over him easily by two hands. Ladro was amazed that Genne could so stoically stand, staring up into Duke's eyes full-on. He also noticed a number of Daggers tensed, with hands on weapons, at the scene. *Guess if you have your back covered by the very best it would be easier. Still it takes courage and self-confidence to stand against Duke. Of course the real questions are: do they prepare to back Duke or Genne; if Duke is still credited with creating the Daggers; and if they remember he can command the actions of the alliance?*

"Magus Vestul was my friend, and I am going to personally shred anyone I find out was involved with his murder."

"Duke please, we don' traffic in dat sorta work. Ya should know dat."

"A lot can change in a few hundred years."

Genne actually stood stiffer and taller. "Not da rules."

"Boy, don't talk to me about your rules! I was here when we laid them out. Someone here knows what happened and possibly why. I am going to find this person." Duke looked at the silent room. "Daggers out, you're hired, all of you. Find out who killed Magus Vestul in Drillian Alley. Find out why. Find out who paid for it. Twenty crowns for each answer, ten crosses a week each. Get moving!"

Ladro watched as six Dagger teams stood, pulling their daggers from the holders, each calling out their acceptance.

Duke looked at the ones who didn't accept coldly. "Very well, each of you are to report to me personally in the morning. Any other Dagger that wishes to accept has one more day to report in." Duke looked at Genne. "You can take damages from my counting. I'll be back, and I expect my table to be prepared." Turning, Duke walked out of the Dolphin. "It's time to remind this hellishly hot little 'burg who helped fucking build it."

Once they were a good distance from the Dolphin, Ladro sensed Duke was in a slightly better mood. Very quietly he asked, "Sir, why didn't you just identify the person you followed there?"

"Because someone there was smoking damned carmine-laced tobac. I won't be able to identify any odors for at least three days; it will be at least two weeks before I can track by scent again, three or four before I am back to my full tracking ability."

"Sir, shouldn't we have told the Daggers where to come to report in?"

Duke actually laughed at that. "Ladro, if they can't find me to report in, I don't want to hire them."

Daggers Up

CHAPTER 9

DAGGERS IN THE AIR

A WOEFUL HOWL RATTLED THE WINDOWS and shocked Lebuin wide awake. Sitting up, he saw in the thin light coming through the barely cracked shutters that Ditani was already peeking out the window as the howl continued.

"That sounds like it is just outside the window."

"No, M'lord, but the few on the street are covering their ears. It must be tremendously loud out there. These are thick windows and walls."

Getting out of bed, Lebuin stumbled to the window in the near darkness. Looking over Ditani's shoulder he saw a few people on the street begin to run away. The howling stopped, but it was followed by the occasional bark of a dog. A sense of dread came over Lebuin.

"Do you think that has something do with us? Could it be a demon hound summoned to track us?"

Ditani slipped around him. "I don't believe in demon hounds. Whatever it was it has stopped, and we are safer than most here. This has been a very trying day. With your leave, I'd like to get back to sleep."

Closing the shutter tight, Lebuin moved carefully in the dark back to his bed and lay down.

One day only since I was drinking hundred-year-old sharre with the head of the Guildhouse. All I wanted was to roam the library freely, to try to find new ways to improve the independence incantations. I was such a fool to not have seen all that was there. He traced the scar in the middle of his chest with his finger. *I almost died today. All that passed before was nothing; today I truly fought for my life. If I had given up I wouldn't be here. Who—or maybe better, what—was that entity that helped me? I am sure I was in the ethereal realm. Was that a God? I wonder if it was Argos Himself.*

Lebuin walked the day in his mind, unable to sleep. *The High Priestess used some kind of powerful artifact on me to help me live. I remember there were others there too. Powerful women. I am sure one was the High Priestess; the other that waited, perhaps that was Ticca; so who was the third powerful woman? There was a very powerful man too. This would be easier if I were still there, my mind was so clear. There were so many stories and books on metaphysical or spiritual travel and meditation in the library. I really wish I hadn't just shoved them aside as a waste of time. If I live I can examine them and maybe find a way to purposefully move between the realms.*

The bed moved slightly, and a muffled crashing sound woke him up. Lebuin sat up, realizing he had fallen asleep again. Ditani was sleeping and everything was quiet again. He listened and didn't hear anything more. *Someone must have dropped a tray in the hall.* Laying back down he was glad to find sleep came easily.

Someone was knocking on the door to his chamber, except this was an annoying person who didn't stop and in fact alternated the loudness of the knock. "I'm sleeping, go away."

Someone moved inside his room, alarming him. Lebuin rolled over and opened his eyes, trying to strengthen his shield, except there was no shield to strengthen. *What happened to my shield?* To answer that his mind groggily recalled the events of being stabbed, wearing an old sack shirt and purposefully rubbing river sludge on his fine boots. His hand came up and found the scar on his chest. Sitting up fully awake now, Lebuin saw he was in the room at the Blue Dolphin and not his chamber at the Guildhouse. He had on a loose pair of brown pants and a soft, carefully patched cotton shirt lay on the floor next to him. His boots were cleaned but would never again be the same. His emotions stirred inside and oddly he felt a deep sense of joy at the lessons in front of him. Smiling, he touched his ruined boots. *This is all I have to protect myself, simple cotton clothes and dirty leather boots, just like the majority of the rest of the world. Yet I feel a joy, like I am finally on the right path.*

Ditani had gotten out of his bed and walked to the door. "Who is it?" he asked softly to whoever was still knocking.

"Ditani, open up, this tray is heavy!" *That voice, it's the Dagger I thought I dreamed. Ticca, she said her name was Ticca.*

Ditani opened the door and Ticca strolled into the room wearing a light green, soft cotton tunic over a pair of black leggings. On her wide belt were more knives than he could count at first glance; somehow they were arranged so as to be complimentary to her look. Ticca's boots had changed into shiny black, very expensive-looking but functional riding boots. Her dagger was still set in the front of the belt at an angle, to allow motion while keeping it as straight as possible. *This lady has some very good taste; she manages to look dangerous and casually put together and yet still would fit in with any group of royals.* She was carrying a large tray of food which included a carafe being kept warm with a small candle and five mugs. Ticca put the tray down on the table, poured a mug of arit and grabbed a roll from the stack. She turned towards him and he smiled thanks, reaching out his hand. Instead of handing the roll and arit to him she sat down, picking up the mug and taking a drink of it herself.

"M'lord, I should warn you, I don't do domestic stuff. So don't expect it."

Ditani quickly made up for Ticca's lack of service by putting a mug on the night stand next to Lebuin and handing him a roll and some cut fruit. "Master, you should eat."

"Ditani, please just call me Lebuin, you too, Ticca." His voice matched his oddly joyful mood and he chuckled. Taking a bite of the roll he was surprised with its quality.

"Well you two, while you slept some rather odd things have been happening. None of it good, I think." Looking at Ditani, she added, "And you should have been a bit more precise in your details. Vestul didn't just come down here to meet *a* duke; he came down here to meet *the* Duke."

Ditani looked confused. "I'm sorry, I don't understand. I never meet the duke, and I think I told you everything."

Looking at Ditani like he was hiding something, she swallowed some more arit. Taking a bite of her roll, she stared waiting for something. Ditani ate some fruit and was avoiding looking directly at Ticca. A few minutes of increasingly uncomfortable silence passed as they all ate breakfast.

It was Ticca who relented first. She sighed and then continued, "Right, well, now we know Vestul came here to meet *the* Duke. So now we need to move out of here as fast as possible, before things get really ugly. We three will be leaving early this evening, so we have about three marks' travel time before dark."

Ditani was looking at her with a blank face and Lebuin decided to help out. "Ticca, I am sorry, you are moving a bit fast and I am not fully awake yet. Who is this duke and what is going to get ugly?"

Ticca looked at both of them for a moment before shrugging. "Short version for now, if we live another day we can talk more over the campfire. Did you two hear a strange noise last night and a crash sometime after?" Seeing that they both nodded, she continued, "Well, the howling was obviously Duke. I can say this because Genne is right this minute having two brand new doors put on the front of this inn to replace the two that Duke decided were in his way, and waiting to open them would take too much time. Word is he just walked through them as if they were not there, shattering one into small kindling and breaking the other in half, as well as ripping it and part of the door way clean off the building. Duke then had a fairly short argument with Genne, which technically he won, but Genne will debate that endlessly, so don't mention it in his presence. He then calmly announced he was pissed off, which was really no surprise, and that he wanted answers about who, why, and how Vestul was killed. He placed a bounty of twenty crowns for each answer and he hired every Dagger in the room at ten crosses a week."

The arit he just swallowed went down the wrong way at that last statement. Coughing, he put the mug down. "Wait, he offered a bounty of twenty crowns and hired every Dagger in the room? Who is this Duke, and what is he the Duke of to have so much coin? Is he a Magus? I mean, how did he destroy the doors?"

Ticca shook her head. "Lebuin, listen to me. This isn't a man. This is a creature that calls itself Duke. It is ancient in the extreme. It talks, it gambles, it drinks, it claims to be one of the oldest creatures in the world, second only to the Gods themselves, and it also claims it was human and a real duke a very long time ago. About five hundred years ago Duke left Llino for Greyrhan far to the north. But for thousands of years prior, Duke roamed these streets and also most of the kingdoms around here, conducting his business of smashing things he didn't like and acquiring things he did. As I recall, he had something to do with the Night Market too."

Lebuin remembered an old tale. "Wait, I recall a legend that Damega had a companion called Duke that was a wolf larger than any horse. Didn't they have a fight over something, and Damega killed it?"

"Not exactly. Damega and Duke did do a number of things together; in fact they worked together to build this very inn as the first Dagger Home. Duke taught Damega the Dagger code and morals and together they established the Daggers as we are today. But each had his own agenda and they finally had a pretty bad falling out. Duke left for the north and hasn't been seen since. There are some stories that Duke did show up for the war to help defend the kingdoms. This makes sense because he is part of the covenant that created these kingdoms. In fact Duke is the alliance's military commander as well as the most senior Dagger commander. But I haven't heard anything other than stories on that side."

Ditani leaned forward. "So this Duke was the wolf we heard howling last night?"

Ticca nodded. "I knew your Duke was looking for Vestul since he missed the meeting, as I ran into or passed some of his agents making the same inquiries I was. I guess he got tired of waiting in the back of the wagon and decided to get directly involved. I'd bet a cross that that howl was him finding Vestul's ashes in the alley. He then came straight here to hire a real army. I don't know how Genne could stand up to a horse-sized talking wolf that was looking to rend someone into small bits for a feast. I think whatever is going on here is going to turn into an open conflict with Daggers, Knives, and who knows what else, taking out whole buildings." Pointing at the door, she said, "Ditani, would you mind letting them in, please."

Ditani looked at her for a moment. "Let who in?"

A knock sounded on the door. "Why, our escape plan help of course. I took the liberty of hiring a couple of guard Daggers who like fights. They have been running some errands for us this morning."

Ditani got up and went to the door.

Before he got to the door Ticca warned, "Please don't let on we know anything about anything. They are trustworthy, but temporary help at best."

Ditani nodded, as did Lebuin. Then Ditani opened the door and two Daggers dressed passably well, if a bit rustic, wearing brown leggings wrapped with leather cross straps, knee high riding boots, light brown cloaks, and long cream-colored cotton shirts over mail coats with leather capitano hats. They both had knives and swords on wide belts. The taller was cleanly shaven while the shorter sported a neatly trimmed box beard. They both looked like they had recent haircuts. The larger one's clothes looked new, yet as if he slept in them and they had a ruffled, unkempt feel. They both wore a dagger on the front of their belts as Ticca did. Their daggers were a matched set with wide winged hand guards, hilts wrapped with blacked iron cord, and simple circular pommels. Overall the effect made Lebuin think of the warriors in sporting games or of hardnosed guardsmen who wouldn't take any backtalk. They smiled and put down their packs in the middle of the floor. The larger one spoke first. "Journeyman Lebuin, I am Risy, Dagger in your service. This is my partner."

The shorter Dagger did a half bow. "Journeyman Lebuin, I am Nigan, Dagger in your service."

Ticca smiled, pointing at the food and extra mugs. "Thanks boys, and help yourselves. Did you get everything done?"

They took seats at the table. Risy answered while pouring out two mugs of arit. "Indeed we did, everything you asked for is in our packs. We already dropped off our own sacks in our room upstairs. Your horses will be in the stables later today as per your instructions, and a bath is being drawn for me so I can apply the dye. Hope the herbalist got it right, I'd hate to end up looking like a ripe cherry." Both men chuckled at that.

Lebuin looked at them and then at Ticca. "Ticca, what exactly do you have in mind?"

She looked at him for a moment. "Isn't obvious? You four are going to switch places. We'll let the Knives attack Hair...uh...Nigan, and Risy here, while I escort you safely out of town on your mission."

"How exactly are we going to trade places? We don't look anything like them."

Ticca leaned over and opened one of the packs, then the other. Finding what she sought, she pulled out a wig that looked exactly the color of Risy's hair and tossed it to Ditani. "Try it on."

Ditani caught it, and after a moment of examining it pulled it on over his head. Except for the skintone he did look reasonably like Risy, and the wig had been cut to match Risy's hair, or perhaps the other way around.

"I get it; Risy is going to color his skin. But..."

Ticca held up her hand. "We have the whole day to go over the details while I get you two ready. In the meantime, I need you to write that letter you mentioned last night and a couple of others which we'll leave with them."

"Do we really need to get out so fast?"

"With Duke hiring an army to hunt down and kill some Knives, and with Knives trying to put a blade between your shoulders or poison in your drinks, yes, I would say we should get out of here as fast as possible without leaving a trail. If we go take care of your mission it will give things time to cool here." Looking at the other Daggers, she added, "Which reminds me, are you sure you don't want to take up Duke's coin?"

Nigan and Risy both shook their heads no. Risy answered, "No, thank you. I'll enjoy springing a trap on a Knife, or three, doing this; the all-out fight doesn't sound like a good idea to us. He is the Supreme Commander and all, but we aren't at war. Besides, I don't like dogs, and so working directly for a ten-foot-tall wolf just isn't a reasonable choice for me."

Nigan nodded. "That goes double for me."

Ticca stood up and went to the desk, pulling out paper, ink, and a pen. "Lebuin, if you please, I need you to write a few letters. One to your father as you planned, except the stated destination should be Breorchy, and you want to leave tomorrow afternoon, even if you need to divert a smaller merchant ship. Then you need to write a very short note to your father telling him to pretend Nigan is you and to see them off on the merchantman, and a third letter to the Guild. It should indicate that you are following a solid report on an odd type of magic by a shaman near Breorchy that comes from some papers you got from Magus Vestul's notes."

Lebuin looked at her for a moment. "Breorchy? I thought we…"

Ticca cut him off. "Yes, Breorchy, because that is exactly the opposite direction from where we are really going."

Looking at the two new Daggers, he thought, *I get it, she is planting false information everywhere. Breorchy is actually only slightly off-course from Algan, but should these two get caught and forced to talk the lead would still be wrong. She must have studied a lot of strategy to be able to come up with cunning stuff like this. I need to pay attention; this is a far better education than any day sitting in a classroom just reading about tactics.* He stood and went to the desk and began to write.

"I assume these are going to be delivered by Risy and Nigan, acting as Ditani and myself?"

"Nope, we will send the notes via two of the many urchins downstairs that hang out for just such messenger duties. The introduction note, that they'll carry themselves."

So she expects they'll get intercepted and read en route. "Maybe I should write two such notes to my father in case the one to him is held back when it is intercepted."

"You learn fast M'lord. And yes, that is a good idea, please do. If you two are done with eating, why don't you go to the baths and get ready? Don't forget to bring your clothes back here for Ditani and Lebuin."

"Ticca, do we have to give them everything?"

Lebuin looked over his shoulder to see what Risy was worried about. Then it became obvious, it was their dagger. Ticca thought about it a moment, then smiled. "Can you give them your older daggers? They were only slightly different and I doubt it will be all that obvious from a distance which is which."

Risy nodded at that. "That is much better; of course we'd like them back if at all possible. We did start with them, after all."

Ticca looked at them very seriously. "I swear to you, if we make it back, I'll do what I can to insure their safe return."

Turning back to the task of writing the notes, he finished the first and started the second as Risy and Nigan left to get ready. *I am not sure I like all this talk about possibly not returning. I would very much like to get back safely.*

Once the other Daggers were gone, Ticca moved the two packs to the beds and grabbed some fruit, which she munched while pulling everything out. There were some cosmetics, a straight razor, and other toilet items. She looked critically at Ditani. "Do you object to shaving your entire head to save your life?"

Ditani grabbed his shoulder length hair. "Um, well, I never fancied being bald. If you think it will help, I suppose it will grow back in time."

She nodded. "The wig can be glued in place if you do, which will help should things require prompt actions." Handing him some of the supplies, she told him, "Here, I'll take you to my room, where there is a private sink and toilet. I'll help you to apply this paste for a bit and then wash it off; we must be even and not miss anyplace visible. It should lighten your skin tone closer to Risy's. M'lord, when you have finished those letters you should eat more; once we leave it might be a long time before we get another good meal. We should check on what Magus Vestul brought and maybe take it with us."

"Ticca, Magus Vestul traveled very light, he only had his pack and that pouch you wear."

Ticca thought about it for a minute. "Really. Well then, once we are finished with the main work we'll get Magus Vestul's pack from his chamber and take it with us. I'll be back, and don't open this door for anyone but the four of us."

With that she left, towing Ditani along. Lebuin dutifully finished the notes, then pulled out some extra papers and for the first time in his life he voluntarily recorded a journal of everything that happened so far. Eating as much as he could while writing, he spent a considerable time trying to record all he had observed and felt when almost dead. When he was done he added some sketches of the daggers he had seen so far, then he added a drawing of his mother as he remembered her in the astral plain: pregnant, happy, and weaving her cloth.

Ladro sat patiently in the corner of the room. He had risen early, being unable to sleep well because of nightmares of Duke ripping people apart, and other thoughts brought on by what he had understood of Duke's litany of tortures. He sipped quietly from the now-cooling cup of arit as he watched his master sleep. Duke whimpered from time to time and a soft yowl came from him as he too obviously dreamed. His tail and paws twitched and his jaws ripped into another pillow. Duke had been chewing on a few pillows all night; there were feathers and lint all over his piled pillow bed. *I wonder if he is having nightmares too. Probably not, he has lived far too long to have those. Most likely he is dreaming of what he is going to do to the responsible people.* A shudder ran through his body at that. *I have never feared him before—sure, there were stories he told at his card house, and my parents, long in his service, had told some too. He is a good creature with his own sense of justice. Never have I heard of him harming innocent people. He lives by his military code of honor, courage, and commitment as if it were the only thing that can be counted on in the whole world. His code of conduct has always been to do right by everyone. Still, I never expected to be involved with one of his stories. I hope we get past this fast. I love him and he is good to me and my family, but he truly scared me last night.*

The sun had just dawned, with its first rays coming through the window, when Duke rolled off the pile of pillows that served as his bed. He laid there, his back to Ladro, on the floor chewing and licking the air. He tried to clean his eyes with his front paws and kept loudly chewing the air, spitting on the floor as best as he could. Looking at the mess around him he sat up. "Damn it. I hate it when I get so mad I chew in my sleep." He stood and shook violently, sending a shower of feathers and lint into the air.

His ears perked up and rotated to the window. "Excellent, glad to see they haven't gotten lazy down here since I left." Chewing the air some more, he added, "I need something wet, and bacon. I want bacon." Ladro smiled at that. Duke sounded more like himself. "Guards! I'm up—get my grooms, three bowls of water, breakfast with bacon, and Ladro. And tell the Daggers I'll see them one team at a time, in the order they arrived."

Heavy boots ran from the door as it was opened by the remaining guard. Duke smiled. "Good boys."

Ladro stood. "Yes, M'lord."

Duke growled and spun around, bringing his head low defensively, ears flat back and baring his teeth. His eyes widened, taking in Ladro. Shaking his head, he straightened up, sat down heavily, and huffed. His ears straightened up and swiveled to target Ladro. "How long have you been there?"

"I am not really sure, M'lord. At least a full mark."

Duke sniffed at the air and shook his head. *Probably upset because he didn't smell my presence.*

Duke looked at the floor, continuing to chewing the air for a bit. Then he looked at Ladro almost guiltily. "Ladro, about last night, you saw some things that only your ancestors have seen. Sorry I lost control for a bit."

"M'lord, it is OK. I have been thinking about it all morning."

Duke's ears perked up sharply and he cocked his head a little. *I hate when he does that look. It is so comical on him and he knows it.* "So what conclusions have you come to, Ladro?"

"M'lord, you did lose control and were madder than anyone I have ever witnessed. Yet where many I have heard of, or witnessed, would lash out and break something, or hurt a loved one, or rampage down the street, you planned what you would do to the responsible parties. I admit, your rant and the tortures you may have selected as appropriate terrify me to the core, and I beg you allow me to not be present should you act on those plans. Nonetheless, you did not touch any of your men or even damage something that was not within your own right to do so. I look forward to returning to your Tun Tavern, but now and forever, sir," Ladro stood straight-backed and squared his shoulders towards Duke, "*Semper Fi.*"

Duke straightened to his equivalent of attention, held it for a moment then nodded curtly at Ladro. "Well-reasoned and well said. *Semper Fi,* indeed. Vestul was one of us, and we will extract our justice for his murder. But right now I am more interested in the water I ordered. My mouth feels awful. Come on and let's get the day started, we have much to do."

Duke stepped out into the hall and indicated his bath to the guard, who moved fast enough to open it so Duke did not have to break stride. In a few moments a small group arrived with water bowls, and four women set to cleaning Duke's fur of the feathers with animal combs. Duke stuck his whole head into one bowl with his mouth open and just shook it back and forth, splashing water everywhere in the tiled room.

With the second bowl he did nearly the same. The third he stuck his snout in and chewed the water for a time. In the meantime, the grooms had efficiently cleaned his fur and were applying some special oils he enjoyed. It took only a quarter of a mark and Duke looked ready to greet the Princes.

"Ladro, I'll have breakfast in the formal dining room, and I seriously want bacon, so send someone out to get more—I think I'm going to empty the kitchens of it. I'll meet the Daggers as I eat. Have the staff offer them anything they please to drink. If any take up the offer for anything with alcohol in it have the staff give them a cross and dismiss them. Set yourself up in the study next to the dining room and see each team one at a time, with the outer door closed. Check their daggers carefully; I will want a full recording. Also, refresh your knowledge from my book of Nhia-Samri weapons, but do not let any Dagger see that book. Check all of their weapons, if you see anything listed in that book, bow to me when you present them. If a majority of their equipment looks new, motion them in with your right hand. Otherwise just open the adjoining door and announce them to me. Then I want you to leave the adjoining door open and as we talk, take notes. When done you will proceed as I say. Make sure the guards keep them in proper order. Clear?"

Ladro filed all the instructions instantly, as he had done his whole life. "Of course, M'lord." He opened the door and passed some instructions to one of the pages that stood there. Closing the door, he turned back to Duke. "Do you expect a Nhia-Samri to attempt to hire on with you?"

Standing and shaking, he ruffled some of his combed fur, which caused frowns on the grooms' faces. Duke smiled at them. "I have a reputation to maintain. Thank you, I truly love you all." Looking at Ladro, he replied, "Someone was smoking carmine-laced tobac in the Dolphin. There was no foreign merchant there that dealt with the Rhonian Empire, where that tasty herb comes from. Carmine is only used to flavor fish or poultry in cooking... There is no reason in the world to stuff it into a pipe except to burn out someone's ability to smell. Which by the way, I fucking discovered one night by getting so drunk we passed out, burning our dinners. I regret telling anyone about that, so unless someone was trying to slip some pungent-smelling poison into some else's food, in the main room of the Dolphin, filled with Daggers, I was expected. It was a deliberate trap designed to impede my tracking."

Ladro considered it, and, remembering the smell and smoke flavor of burned herbs, had to agree. No one would want to taste that herb smoke on purpose. Opening the door, two guards stepping smartly out of the way, two pages stayed against the far wall. *Everyone is on edge, no surprise, considering the tales of last night were probably already told to all the staff. Thank the Gods Duke long ago decided to only employ loyal families for life, or as long as they want. Otherwise this would have been a very bad day indeed, and we wouldn't be able to talk in our own home.* As they moved down the hall, a question occurred to him. "When did you realize you had been trapped, M'lord?"

"Right after I sneezed, trying to clear my nose after walking *into* the bloody trap."

Ladro looked at Duke, surprised. "You didn't even hesitate, you just walked in, and it seemed you did as you planned."

Duke smiled as he approached the dining room and the guard, anticipating his path, opened the door. "Never let the enemy know his plan is working."

"Because of this you believe Nhia-Samri might be here?"

Duke stopped, and gave him a look that said he should really keep up. "Ladro, you have lost three good agents completely. Vestul is dead and Night's Fire was used to hide this, and my tracking ability was taken away in a trap that could have only been for me specifically. Yes, the Nhia-Samri are here. Now the only questions are: What are they after? How can I kill more of them? And can I do anything at all to embarrass them in front of that little runt bastard, their Grand Lord Commander?"

With that he turned and entered the extravagantly decorated room with its massive oval table, large enough to seat forty guests. At the head of the table was a huge, eighteen-foot-tall throne that had no legs or arm rests; the beautiful gold and amber cushioned seat sat directly on the floor. The table was actually six hands higher than normal dining tables and all the elegant chairs arrayed around the table had longer legs, locking coaster wheels on each leg, adjustable height foot rests, and serving steps between each chair to compensate. The table held a huge serving platter on which were two dozen lightly roasted birds, arranged artfully around the edges of a pile of lightly crisped bacon that stood at least four feet high. The smell of it made Ladro's mouth water.

Duke looked at the pile and smiled. He breathed deeply and then growled. "Damn it, I want to smell it too. These three days are going to be painful." Duke arranged himself comfortably on the floor-throne. Looking at Ladro, he asked, "Would you care to join me?"

Ladro looked at the pile and his stomach was already begging for some. "M'lord, thank you, I'll have a bacon and egg sandwich in the study as I review the book you mentioned."

Duke smiled at his announcement of meal choice. "Very well. Give me a half mark to make a dent in this, then send in the first Dagger team as you complete your duty with them. There is no rush today. What is done is done, now it is time to find out what really is going on, and to insure real justice is served, with minimal losses. Our enemies here will be made to pay dearly, hiding in shadows or not."

Ladro closed the door, ordering the breakfast he was now ready for. He made a quick trip to the vault storage room to get the book on Nhia-Samri weapons. Taking the book, he went back to the study and slowly flipped through it, examining the engineering-quality diagrams and detailed technical description of each weapon, herb, and tool employed by the Nhia-Samri. After a half-mark, he locked the book into the desk drawer and motioned for the page to let in the first Dagger team.

A pair of Daggers came in, dressed and ready for work. They looked fresh and crisp, but according to their introduction, they had arrived here a full three marks before any other Daggers. One, called Elades of Stegea, had the silver hair and sun-darkened skin of a true veteran. The other, called Idanas of Stegea, had brown hair that was starting to go to grey, with a crisp tan that also spoke of years out in the sun. Both, however, had tight skin, strong muscles, and they walked with the fluid grace of highly trained warriors.

Ladro requested they place all their weapons and gear on the large desk for inspection. They didn't question the request, and promptly filled the desk with more weapons than Ladro thought possible, considering what little they were wearing. He inspected everything closely; their gear was heavily used but well-maintained. He drew quick sketches of their daggers, key weapons, and more unusual items. Ladro also took note of their names, homes, and Dagger training pedigree. These were long-experienced and highly capable Daggers with a prime table at the Dolphin, indicating that Genne, too, judged them very worthy of high ranking.

He then opened the door to the dining room and announced them to Duke. Duke was mid-bite and looked up, chewing a mouthful of bacon. Most of the birds had been eaten and the platter was down to about half of its original bacon load.

The Daggers walked into the dining room and stood just inside the doorway, waiting respectfully for orders. Duke finished chewing slowly. When he was done, he wiped his mouth on the mounted table napkin. Then he looked at the Daggers hard for a long moment. "I am impressed with your zeal. Arriving here a full three marks before the next team demonstrates commitment. What is the reason for the rush to wait?"

Both Daggers laughed politely at Duke's very old military joke. Elades took the lead and answered, "M'lord, the Dolphin is under observation by unknowns, Knives attacked another Dagger yesterday, and two seasoned Dagger teams have vanished over the last few cycles. We know enough of your true history to trust your goals and commands; we desire to serve with you."

Duke considered this answer. "You do me honor with your courage and commitment. You are Squad Alpha Team One. Which of you is lead?"

Without hesitation Elades stepped forward; Idanas simply remained in place.

"Elades, you are named Alpha Commander and need to select seven or more Daggers for team one, please do not break up a team. Of course you will also need to select two more fire teams for Alpha Squad and their leads."

The new officer nodded.

"Tell me, are you familiar with carmine?"

Idanas spoke up. "Sir, it is a spice out of Rhonia, which doesn't usually get this far south. I have some, if you need it."

Duke shook his head. "No, I don't need it, but you will. The initial objectives for your squad are: first, discretely find out if any shipment of carmine has come through here recently; second, familiarize yourself with its scent, look, taste and any indicators you can find from smoking it shredded mixed with tobac; third, discretely identify the Nhia-Samri agent, or agents, who are smoking it at the Blue Dolphin."

At the mention of Nhia-Samri, the Daggers' faces became as hardened steel.

Duke motioned to the far end of the room, where the two Daggers took up position. "While we wait for the next group I will tell you the command signals I prefer to use. It would be well if Alpha Squad consists of only seasoned Daggers. I will not allow the Nhia-Samri agents posing as Daggers to join Squads Alpha or Bravo." Turning to look at Ladro, Duke said, "Time to do this again with the next Daggers."

As Ladro closed the door he heard Duke say, "You may be free from restraint until Ladro brings in the next team. We'll have about fifteen minutes—tell me more about how you became Daggers."

Duke made the next lone Dagger Squad Bravo Commander, and the following team of three, Charlie Squad Team One, naming their Lead as Squad Commander. Ladro wondered where these odd names were coming from, but if the Daggers wondered the same they never showed it. Bravo Squad was ordered to find a way to locate and observe the observers of the Dolphin. Charlie Squad was ordered to begin investigations into the Night Market, Thieves Market, and any other illegal goods markets, to catalog everything that had been bought, sold or traded in the last five days. The next few teams ranged in experience, and the squad commanders debated which squad and team they would best serve. Every Dagger already knew that the squads were to be three teams of about nine Daggers, and each team had requirements of specialized skills based on the assigned objectives. Ladro found their total lack of egotism amazing, and even the new Daggers added into the conversation, not to promote themselves, but to clarify skill sets and experiences.

Then a team of two Daggers came in, calling themselves Apanal and Egal of Azaria. They had arrived about the middle of all the Daggers and teams of Daggers. They were dressed as expected; some of their equipment looked used, but most of it was new; then Ladro saw the small stack of chakram they each carried. These were weapons normal for the region they said they were from, but they were also a weapon favored by the Nhia-Samri. In no other way did they look out of order.

Opening the door, he bowed to Duke and introduced the Daggers. Oddly enough, no one in the room seemed to take notice or indicate anything was different.

Duke was working on his second platter of bacon and some of the other Daggers had food stuffs from the kitchens or fruits brought in for snacks. Duke smiled. "Azaria is a long way from here. I haven't been there in a very long time." Apanal and Egal just nodded politely and waited, and Duke continued, "How long have you been here in Llino working as a Dagger team?"

Egal answered for them. "Great Lord, we have only been here about three weeks. We hired on to a merchant vessel as sailors and guardsmen because we wanted to explore a bit beyond what we knew."

Duke nodded. "I understand the need to explore well. How long have you been working as Daggers?"

"Since we were children, five and ten years of age, Great Lord. We have been fortunate in our work and received good training. I am now nine and twenty years of age as is my life-friend."

"Interesting, Daggers tend to grow more roots as they age; you two did the opposite. So that means fourteen years of labor and experience?" Duke looked at Ladro, and Ladro, realizing it was a question for him, minutely shook his head. None of the equipment could possibly be old enough, and too much of it was too new.

As Ladro was standing directly behind Egal and Apanal he felt sure they didn't see him. Instead they both nodded and Egal said, "Very correct, Great Lord."

Duke looked at them and thought a moment. As he opened his mouth, Ladro prepared to run for cover, but Duke shocked him by saying, "Very good. It will take a clever eye and someone who is a little foreign to this city to lead Delta Squad. You shall be Delta Team One. Which of you is to be Lead?"

Egal stepped forward in a precise military step and stood tall. "I am Lead."

Duke nodded. "You will be assigned seven more Daggers or more, so as to not break up a team, for Delta one fire team, and you will assist in selecting the rest of Delta Squad." Duke then bluntly looked at Ladro. "And Ladro, I have told you before, stop with the infernal bowing. It is embarrassing; if you really must you can just wave them in."

By just after noon all of the remaining Daggers had been sorted into the five squads. Duke had reassigned one of the more veteran

Daggers to be Commander of the final Echo Squad when the numbers showed there would be the need if the team and squad numbers were to be kept to the stated sizes. Each of the squads was positioned at different locations around the room. The soft chatter of military people introducing themselves and establishing relationships made the room more alive than any feast of nobles could.

After the last Daggers had been assigned, Duke looked at the room and barked once. The room fell silent and everyone looked at Duke. "In a minute I'll dismiss you to the courtyard where some lunch is prepared for you to eat while I brief your commanders and team leads to provide orders and objectives. Commanders and leads are to remain close to the door and report in, one squad at a time. I will then meet privately with each team's lead for an initial one-on-one in designation order. Your leads will brief you as needed. Everything from this moment on is on a need-to-know basis only. Understood?"

The room resounded with a loud, "Yes, sir!" in unison.

This is amazing. Yesterday I would have sworn Daggers where more a rabble than a trained militia. I thought Daggers were just mercenaries and loners with slightly more skill. In one morning random Daggers have come together without a hitch or argument. I would swear these Daggers had fought whole wars together and were a standing army. They actually look happy to be assembled so. He couldn't help it; he glanced at Egal and Apanal. They were looking at Duke but also glancing around the room as well. Ladro quickly continued to scan the other Daggers as if he was taking notes, in case they spotted him looking.

Duke continued, "Each squad must report all findings back here daily. I expect each team to have positive confirmation of their squad's teams' locations and status every two marks. If any team misses a check-in it is to be considered an emergency 'man down' situation and reported back to me immediately, with appropriate actions taken per your squad's rules of engagement. You may communicate your reports with any member of my personal staff as if it were me, most especially Ladro here. Ladro is the only other besides myself that can give you new orders. Understood?"

The room resounded with another loud, "Yes, sir!" in unison. Egal momentarily frowned but quickly composed himself.

Duke stood up, putting his front paws on the table so he towered over the room like a giant and bellowed, "Where is the safest place to be?"

All the Daggers drew their daggers and held them high, yelling as one, "Behind the Daggers!" Ladro noted that Egal and Apanal were the last to draw, before his attention was drawn to Duke.

Duke yelled, "Do you want to live forever?"

"NO SIR!"

Duke yelled louder, "Semper Fidelis!"

The Daggers, almost in frenzy, yelled loudly, rattling the chandelier and glassware, "SEMPER FIDELIS!"

"Dismissed!"

My Lords and Ladies, what has he released here?

Unhorsing

CHAPTER 10

WALLS WORK BOTH WAYS

ORAHDA KNOCKED HIS BLADE SLIGHTLY to the side as he stepped inside Dohma's guard, landing a rib strike which was very painful even through the padded sparing armor. Orahda said, "Action is better than reaction," as he stepped lightly out of Dohma's striking range.

Wiping the sweat from his brow, Dohma signaled an end to the practice drill and rubbed his chest where it hurt. "Orahda, will you ever grow old?"

The weapons master nodded and lowered his weapon. "My captain, you wound me! I am nearly as tired as you, and you are getting on in in years."

Laughing, Dohma cleaned his sword and unbuckled the light leather armor, handing it to a page. "Don't bring my age into this or I'll go read your record."

Orahda had been weapons master for the Palace Guard since Dohma was a child. He was of average height, thin but with rolling muscles. He kept his wiry black hair tightly braided with beads tied to fall down the left side of his head and over his shoulder in the Karkaian style, although his skin was much lighter than any Karkaian, even with its deep tan. He was dressed in the same semi-loose leather pants and leather fighting vest with its high neck and no sleeves, which he always wore. Orahda thought armor was a waste of his time and energy and never bothered to wear it.

Orahda rarely taught any student directly unless they were exceptional in some way, but oversaw all the training through a small staff of trainers. Many nobles had their children join the Palace Guard instead of the Navy or Princes' Guard just for weapons training. This caused some problems from time to time as Orahda's training also instilled strong morals and honorable values, which some nobles thought were an impediment to political necessities. Of course many noble children grew to be fine guardsmen who Dohma trusted with his life, even when they left to inherit their parents' titles and responsibilities. Any who were found wanting were denied training by Orahda and eventually dismissed from the guard; this brought about many a heated political fight. Dohma had looked on Orahda like a loved uncle from early in his training and sometimes he fancied Orahda had similar feelings for him. Orahda oversaw Dohma's training personally. It was because of his attentions that Dohma was able to rise to the rank of Captain of the Guard.

Orahda grabbed a water pitcher and drank deeply of it. He looked as fresh as when they had started practicing nearly a full two marks before. Watching the weapons master drink, Dohma shook his head. *He should at least have the decency to sweat.* Orahda's hair was pitch-black, without a single strand of gray anywhere. *I wonder how old he really is. He hasn't aged my whole life and I would swear he looks only forty years. I am thirty-five and he was weapons master before I was born.* He watched Orahda's muscular arms flexing as the weapon's master moved, showing the banded steel of his muscles. His tanned arms were crisscrossed with scars. *His skin is probably tougher than the leather gear I wear.*

A messenger stepped up politely. "Captain, the Princes summon you to audience in the throne room."

"Better you than me, Captain. I'd tell them to get off their lazy butts and get in some practice. They are all starting to look pudgy."

Dohma laughed. "Only you can get away with remarks like that, which is probably why they don't summon you." *And I know they still resent that you never agreed to train any of them personally.* Grabbing his shirt and belt, he started walking to the throne room. On the way he got his shirt on over the light padded undercoat, slipped on his belt and ran his fingers through his hair. By the time he got to the throne room the sweat had dried and he was at least presentable.

He entered the throne room through the side door; guarded, as always, by the Princes' Personal Guard in their blue and silver livery. All three Princes sat their thrones on the shared semi-circle dais which took up a quarter of the circular room. Eight white marble pillars reached almost all the way to the domed ceiling, giving the room the look of a cathedral. Eight arched windows soaring two stories upward were placed between each pillar and completed the dramatic gallery. Between each of the arched windows were balconies with low banisters, used for musicians and by the ladies to observe the royal activities.

Dohma knew they saw him, and waited while they dealt with a Cabinet Lord's complaints of animal noises in the night near the docks. They told him it was being taken care of and waved him out. Once the lord had left, only the Princes, their personal guard, and Dohma remained in the room. Emman, the eldest prince, motioned for him to approach. He stepped to the front of the dais and knelt, bowing his head. "My Princes, how may I serve?"

"Duke has ignored our orders and went out on the streets last night. Further, we have had reports this morning that he has hired not less than thirty Daggers and caused considerable damage to the Blue Dolphin. You are to invite him here, immediately. You are authorized to take whatever measures you deem necessary to achieve this. We expect him here within two marks. You may go."

"My Princes, Duke is a Lord of Aelargo and entitled to the actions you speak of by the covenant of this land."

All three princes frowned at this and the marshal of their private guard placed his hand on the hilt of his sword.

"Captain Dohma, you are lucky we are alone. We shall overlook this comment. You have two marks to bring Duke before us."

Frowning, Dohma bowed and left by the main doors. *Oh this will not go well.* The royal foyer was filled with nobles, who flocked back into the throne room as he left. Dohma walked past the personal guards and sent one of his own guards, stationed outside the main palace doors, running ahead with orders to have a full detachment assemble at the palace. He ordered a second detachment to prepare for Duke's very-likely objection to whatever the Princes were about to tell him, to be stationed near the palace doors and ready for possible trouble. *With any luck this can be kept civil.*

Duke's own palatial home was only minutes from the Royal Palace. In only a half mark he was approaching the gates of Duke's residence with his detachment of fifty guards. Inside the gates he saw not less than a hundred warriors who were broken into groups and talking. Servants were just removing some tables that had been about the courtyard. *Damn, that is not thirty Daggers, that is a full platoon. It's too late to withdraw; I really hope he is in a talking mood. Something about him makes me trust him more than my own princes, even though I have only met him once.* Dohma stepped right up, stopping just in front of the eight guards at the main gate. "By order of the Princes, I must speak with His Excellency Duke at once."

The guards looked coolly at the fifty guardsmen he brought. One of them said in a most casual tone, "I'll ask if he is in." Dohma watched the guard walk slowly through the crowd of Daggers, taking his time. The Daggers all turned to examine his detachment. Sweat began to accumulate on his brow, and after a moment, the Daggers turned back to their conversations. Dohma lost track of the gate guard when a Dagger ran past him to a squad close to the gate.

Dohma concentrated to hear what was being said; something inside told him it was important. He had always had these little feelings, and long ago learned to trust them. The conversation was faint but not beyond his exceptional hearing, which he had trained himself to focus so he could follow conversations in a crowded hall at a distance.

"Commander, Ticca's patron has dispatched two communications, one to a merchant house requesting the diversion of any merchant ship to Breorchy to leave tomorrow; the other to the Guild, naming Breorchy as a likely source of information. She has also hired Nigan and Risy as guards. We spotted three horses being made ready for travel now. One is Ticca's, the others belong to Nigan and Risy. Bravo reports the watchers have also intercepted the communications."

"Damn it! That girl moves as fast as her uncle. I'd like to know what she has learned. This is all likely a diversion and she plans on intercepting the ship up river and taking her patron off the boat to proceed overland to their true objective." The commander looked directly at the Dagger who had reported in. "Three, move fast." At that the Dagger spun and ran out and down the street. The commander then gave an odd look at a Dagger wearing a turban standing with another group who had also been watching the exchange. The turbaned Dagger went back to talking with his own squad. The commander looked at the rest of his squad standing around him. "Two, pheasant shoot. One, ridge run with me." The Dagger squad ran out of the gate and also headed towards town, but down the street the commander and a strike team turned west while the rest of the team continued on the main road until out of sight.

A surprisingly short time later a page came running out. "Captain Dohma, *you* are invited in." The emphasis on 'you' made it obvious he was to leave his detachment outside. *Please Lord, let him be in a good mood today.*

He signaled his men to stay put and followed the page through the courtyard to an entry foyer as large as the throne room, with very expensive marbles and tasteful pictures on display. *Duke certainly has good taste. This is far superior to the over-the-top decorations of the royal palace.* Once through the foyer, a large, elegantly decorated connecting hall led into a formal dining room. As he stepped into the room he stopped, awestruck at the size of the table before him. It stood level with his neck. Looking down the table and feeling like a small child about to address his unhappy father, Captain Dohma saw the large wolf at the far end chewing on what looked (and smelled) like a man-sized pile of bacon. Duke sat in a throne that put every other throne he had seen to shame in its simple design, elegance and scale. *He really knows how to make an impression. And I have the feeling he is not happy today. This sure won't help his mood.*

Duke looked at him with steel in his eyes. "Captain Dohma, I was expecting you much earlier today. I am afraid you have missed lunch. As to the reminder you are here to deliver of the *little Princes'* request, you may tell the *little princes* to go suck on a hard candy. I will do as I please."

Dohma tried to speak, but his throat refused to allow air through. Coughing to clear it, he shook his head. "Excellency, I do apologize for interrupting your meal; however, the Princes request your immediate presence. I have been sent to escort you with all the honors due a lord of the realm."

Duke laughed and it sent chills down his now-sweaty back. "Oh, I bet they said that. You have a lot of nerve, Captain." Duke then stared at him for a moment, making him sweat a little more. Still, he stood his ground. "I like you, Dohma, so for your sake only I will accept this honor you bestow on me."

Thank the great Lord. "I thank you, Excellency. I assure you I am only here to escort you to the palace, with honors."

Duke wiped his mouth on a napkin the size of a small tablecloth which was being held in place on the table, near his seat, by a device of some sort. He then stood and walked calmly around the table and, glancing at his personal secretary he said, "Ladro, so that I may honor your earlier request, you may stay... just in case."

Ladro leaned backwards slightly as if he had lost his balance, his face going totally white. He swallowed a couple of times rapidly. *Duke just scared him deeply with that comment. What has Duke been up to this morning? Ladro is the last person I'd expect to be scared of Duke—he has been in Duke's personal service his whole life, from page to personal secretary.*

Duke walked past Dohma, heading for the exit. Dohma set aside his contemplation of Ladro's reaction and fell into step next to Duke out of his residence. In the courtyard, the Daggers stopped talking and looked at them as they came out. Duke walked casually straight to the gates, and looked back at the Daggers. "Time's a-wasting, folks. You have your orders. Echo, river walk."

Dohma's hand went to his sword hilt but the all the Daggers simply said, "Yes, sir," and went back to their conversations.

His guardsmen parted to let them walk through and formed up behind them as an honor guard. Duke walked with him back to the palace calmly, in total silence. *This is totally unexpected. I thought I'd have to beg him to come.*

When they reached the palace, Duke laughed, giving Dohma a knowing side glance when he saw the second detachment standing at honors just outside the palace entrance. Dohma signaled his men to stop at the palace entrance, with the other detachment, and followed Duke inside. He heard something from Duke that sounded suspiciously like a chuckle. Looking over at Duke, his large eyes sparkling with some private joke. Duke didn't break stride or say a word, forcing Dohma to race ahead a little just so he could be seen as the escort. Duke nodded politely to some of the staff and dignitaries as they moved through the entrance hall into the throne room's foyer.

Once at the entrance to the throne room, however, things changed. Duke didn't bother to wait; he sprang ahead of Dohma and simply walked past the princes' personal guards, shouldering the crossed halberds and men out of his way as if they were nothing more than reeds of grass. Not bothering to wait to be announced or addressed, he thundered out as he continued across the throne room, "What do you whelps want? I'm busy."

Looking at the nearly full room of nobles and dignitaries, Dohma realized it was much more full than normal. *The Princes must have summoned these nobles in order to make an example to them.* Everyone quickly got out of Duke's way; a few, upon looking him in the eye, bowed and then exited the room in haste. *Yes, that is a prudent thing to do. I wish I could do the same.*

Emman motioned the lord in front of them away. "Duke, we told you to stay in your residence and to not disturb our citizens. You went out last night and even damaged parts of our city. Now we have reports that you have hired many Daggers. We will not allow this to continue. You will pay the Daggers two weeks' service and tell them to disband immediately."

Duke stopped right where the marshal started to go for his weapon, and sat down, looking at the three princes with his ears laid back. "You are confused as to the order of things. I give the orders here, not you." Dohma detected an odd tone in Duke's voice and had the feeling that Duke was still laughing at something only he understood.

All three princes laughed at that, and so did many nobles still present, although the nobles' laughs sounded nervous. Elur, the youngest, shook his head. "You are wrong. This is our kingdom, and you have no authority here, except what we grant you."

Duke's voice deepened, and carried a slight growl to it. "Have you whelps even read the covenant?"

I have, and Duke's right. What is going on?

Elur laughed and his brothers chuckled too. Duke's ears came up in curiosity. Elur, through his laughter, asked, "What use do we have of a dusty old relic?"

Dohma felt a shudder of surprise and Duke was surprised too. "It is the cornerstone of your family's authority here. It is the charter that grants you the titles of the Princes' Regents, which you have dropped to stylize yourselves as 'the Princes'. Your family can't forget its duties; it is part of your very bloodline."

At this all three princes laughed. "Duke, oh Duke, you are the very best. Our family wrested this kingdom from the grasp of those fools long ago. I believe it was not long after you fled to the North. Our ancestors disposed of the last remnants of the ancient empire's ridiculous hold here. It was *our* fleet of ships that set sail from this port to create the true kingdom of the Sea Princes. *We* are the only authority in the kingdom now. This is no longer the *Kingdom of Aelargo*; it is now the *Kingdom of the Sea Princes*. You really should look at some modern maps."

Lord, they are traitors, from a family of usurpers. I know I have never liked them much; I swore to protect the kingdom from harm and to uphold the covenant.

Duke growled, which was enough of a warning. The marshal made a signal, and before Dohma could react, Duke moved. As Duke made to leap to the dais, however, heavy nets were thrown over him from the balconies. Twenty of the Princes' guards piled onto him, using their combined weight and the nets to pin him in place against the floor. More of the Princes' guards rushed into the room from the side doors, quickly grabbing and holding down the edges of the nets, effectively trapping the great wolf in front of the princes, who continued to laugh, joined by the remaining nobles.

Dohma's heart and soul screamed at the treachery he was witnessing. *What are they doing? He is a lord of the realm, how can I be party to this?* Looking at everyone in the room, he didn't see a single supporter. His hand moved and seized on the hilt of his sword, which the marshal took as preparing to aid them in subduing Duke, as he warned Dohma off with a smile of thanks. Dohma looked at the personal guards; they all had smirks or open smiles at this. He instinctively read them to the core and found them as traitorous as the usurpers. *The personal guard has known this all, and they are loyal to the usurpers.* Then his exceptional hearing picked up very soft chuckling coming from Duke. *What can possibly be funny about being trapped under twenty guards and a net?*

Emman shook his head and looked at Duke. "Poor Duke, to think you remain faithful to that dead line of lost kings. We long ago finished with that. Our ancestors uncovered Damega's true blood line and struck a deal; his body in exchange for the trinket that used to sit there." Prince Emman pointed at an alcove where an ornate gold book sat. "Of course the silly nobles at the time felt it best if we hid the fact that the kingdom's relics where being sold off, so they made that excellent facsimile."

Damega was heir to the throne? He has been styled a cut-throat thief and pirate. Could all I know of our history be wrong? This is too much—I must act. Looking around, he could see no way to help Duke or stop this. In his mind he heard Orahda's sound advice *'Steady, calm, wait for the right moment.'* He tightened his grip on the hilt of his sword, swearing he would kill the usurpers if he had the chance.

Duke's voice lost all humor and he growled, "You dared to remove the archive? It was for the royal and regent lines only."

"Exactly, you silly dog, and as we had all of the regent's line buried out back, combined with the last of the dead royal line, it was no longer of any use to anyone. So why not sell it?"

"Your ancestors betrayed Damega?"

"Of course. He was getting out of hand with all that silly talk of freedom, education, and comforts for peasants; not to mention trying to establish a hidden militia outside of our family's control. Of course I find it ironic that now, centuries later, we have built the schools and provided some of the securities for peasants that he sought to do. Aelargo was not nearly as rich, and those things do cost. Even more ironic that that militia has turned into a rabble of stupid mercenaries greedy for as much coin as they can steal from rich merchants and nobles."

Duke said something in a low growl. Dohma could only hear a little of it and it sounded familiar.

"Oh, you poor dog, are you having problems breathing under all that weight?"

Duke growled a little, and asked, "A last question: who traded your ancestors a body for a useless relic?"

Elur laughingly said, "Why, none other than High-Lord Shar-Lumen himself. Who else would be so stupid and powerful?"

The other two princes looked at Elur in surprise. "Brother," Emman warned, "You reveal too much."

Elur pointed at Duke. "And where will he take this knowledge?" Then, waving at everyone else, he added, "And these are our loyal subjects."

Just then a guard ran into the throne room. "The palace doors are being blocked!"

Emman stood and moved over to a window, asking in a very sarcastic tone, "Is it poor old Duke's little army of greedy mercenaries—oh, sorry, I mean 'Daggers'? I must see what this pitiful creature thinks will stop us." When he looked out, his mouth dropped open and he stared.

His two brothers stood and started toward him as the guard answered, "No Excellency, the palace wall is rising, and metal doors are rising out of the ground—right through the stonework sealing the surrounding walls!"

Several lords, and Dohma, rushed to the windows to confirm that the palace walls had indeed risen at least fifteen feet, and metal plates had broken through the paving stones, rising up out of the ground, fitting perfectly in the grooves into which the current gate doors had been mounted. As they watched, the current gate doors and stonework brackets were crushed, causing debris to fall around the now-sealed entrances. More metal plates, which had spikes topped with large balls of steel every fifteen or twenty feet, were sprouting from the top of the palace walls. As Dohma watched, lightning began to dance on the surface of the balls.

"What is that?!" someone asked.

"*That* is to make sure none of you get away," came an ominous, deep-throated growl from Duke. "You dare to brag about destroying the Duianna line and their loyal regents?"

The Princes turned, white-faced, and looked at Duke. "Guards, kill him!" they bellowed in unison.

A few nobles chose this moment to run out of the room. Duke pushed hard to one side, dragging the guards holding the opposite side of the nets towards him. Biting down on the net holding it and pushing hard with his legs, he used the slack he had made to create enough momentum to flip over onto the guards on the opposite side, crushing them with his weight. The guards who had been dragged with the net were catapulted, landing hard on the stone floor. Duke finished rolling, still holding the net with his teeth as he stood free; then Duke spun around, whipping the nets, sending the screaming guards who tried to hold on to it flying. Expertly, he spun around again, throwing the net over the guards who had been standing behind him.

The personal guards drew their weapons and jumped at him. He moved faster than Dohma thought possible for something his size. He attacked with teeth and paws, kicking two guards so hard they flew backwards a couple of feet, before landing on their backs with a sickening *crack* as their heads hit the floor. The princes bolted for a doorway, as did every other remaining lord and dignitary in the room. Duke grabbed another guard by the leg and used him as a club, beating away five other guards, and then threw the limp and broken body at some approaching guards, knocking them down as well.

Dohma smoothly drew his sword and ran it through the back of a personal guard. Pulling it, he spun, slashing the sword through the neck of another. The personal guards' attention was on Duke, letting Dohma kill five more before they noticed he wasn't on their side.

One guard managed to get in a good hit with his sword. Duke spun on him and took his sword arm at the elbow in his teeth. Dohma heard the crunch as Duke's teeth went through the steel armor and bone, neatly amputating the arm. Duke spit out the arm, still holding the sword, and turned to the doorway, where the detachment of palace guards where just starting to rush in, weapons at the ready.

Dohma cried, "Palace Guardsmen, the princes are usurpers and traitors! The Royal Personal Guard are all knowing accomplices." The remaining personal guard looked at Dohma in shock for a moment, just enough time for Duke to kill three more; knocking one down and standing on his throat while simultaneously picking another up, biting his midsection so the metal armor made a creaking sound and pinched off his screams; Duke used the body like a sledgehammer on the third. Dohma's guardsmen's shock wore off and they joined the fight. The few remaining personal guard were quickly dispatched.

Dohma walked around the room, killing any wounded, or pretending to be wounded, personal guards. He was pleased to see his own guards stab the dead bodies again just for good measure.

Duke watched him in surprise for a moment and then said something else which Dohma felt deep down he should understand but didn't.

When Dohma finished his work he stood in front of Duke and looked him in the eye. "Excellency, we," he indicated the guardsmen, "serve the Kingdom of Aelargo. We all swore an oath to uphold and protect this kingdom and its covenant. With the public confession of the usurpers, I name them, and all their family and followers, traitors. I, and all the royal guard, stand at your command as a true Lord of Aelargo."

Duke looked at him and then the guards. "Very good, Captain. You will detain every lord, lady and dignitary, informing them that I will be validating their status with the archives and all pretenders who confess before we discover them will be dealt with mercifully. As of this minute no one, save me, is to be obeyed until I order otherwise."

Duke looked around the room and smiled, although with the blood and gore splattered over his body the effect was not as pleasant as he likely intended. "Nice fight, boys. You aren't so bad. Now clean up this mess and start gathering everyone up." A thunder clap was heard in the distance, and Duke turned to look in that direction, his ears, eyes, and nose pointing like a hunting hound. It was almost as if Duke could see through the distance to the source of the sound. After a moment Duke looked back at Dohma. "I am sealing the city. Once the palace grounds have been searched and all supposed dignitaries are accounted for, I will open the palace gates and you can do the same for the entire city."

Sniffing the air, Duke shook his head. "Damn it, this is annoying. Echo Commander."

A Dagger casually stepped out from behind a pillar. "Sir."

Dohma and the other guardsmen stared at her like she was a ghost. *How did she get here?*

"Signal someone to find out what is going on at the west gate. Echo Squad, provide audible tracking queues, maintain noncombat distance, these bastards are mine. I want Emman first."

The Dagger said, "Yes, sir," and made a series of bird calls which were answered by another call outside the doorway.

Duke's ears swiveled towards the sound. "Stay out of my way I'll deal with those little bastards myself," he said, and then he leapt at the doorway, followed closely by the Dagger.

Everything was as tidy as she could make it, but Ticca went over the mental checklist a couple more times just to be sure. Lebuin and Ditani were fairly well disguised as Nigan and Risy, and both had allowed her to shave their heads to enable gluing the wigs in place with the gum. Lebuin didn't have the mass to properly replace Nigan, but with the padded armor under-layer he would pass very well from a distance. Of course, no one in the main room would be fooled for long.

Nigan and Risy had also transformed reasonably well and given that they were going to remain in the room and only go out to the dock very early in the morning. They should have no issue making a convincing Lebuin and Ditani.

It took a mark of practice before Ditani managed to imitate Risy's walk. Lebuin was a quick study and mastered the basic movements for Nigan in only a few minutes, surprising everyone, including himself. So the only issue was direct inspection at fewer than twenty feet. *I wish I could come up with a way out of here that didn't involve walking through the main room, but anything we do would raise suspicions and possibly an alarm. Well, 'preparation with boldness overcomes many obstacles' as my trainer used to say to me. This is going to really test that idiom. At least I got a solid night's rest without any dreams... I still feel marvelous with the dreams, but they are rather spooky in their detail and my ability to remember them so clearly.*

Footsteps in the hall, which sounded about right, and a knock at the door interrupted her thoughts. "Who is it?"

Ditani answered softly, doing a fair imitation of Risy's voice. "Ticca, it's me."

When she opened the door Ditani stepped in carrying two packs, then she closed the door and they all gathered around the table. "This pack is mine and still has just the clothes and other items I remembered. This one," he shoved the second leather pack towards her, "was Magus Vestul's, which I have never opened myself until just a few moments ago. You might want to look in."

She took the pack, noting that it was as well-made as the boots and pouch. The pack was closed with a metal clasp that had a nice black patina built up on it. It also had a geometric pattern engraved on it that looked a lot like the one on her pouch, but this clasp was not designed to rotate. Pulling it over, she noticed that although it puffed out like it was full, it was much lighter than an empty leather pack. Opening it, she looked inside and was taken aback by the view. The view was as if she was looking down and through an odd lens into a very large room stacked with boxes, trunks, shelves visible all at once. The sight made Ticca feel a little dizzy so she sat down. Lebuin, on the other hand, put his head down close so that his nose was almost inside of the pack.

His eyes darted around and around. "Now this is interesting." Before she could stop him he reached inside. She squeaked a warning, which he just ignored. As he reached inside, she saw the pack slightly deform, where his hand would be as if he was pulling something out of a normal pack. Lebuin pulled his hand out, holding a very large book that should have taken up the entire pack by itself. He grunted under the weight. "This is a little heavier than I thought." He put the book down on the table with a loud thud; next, he reached in and pulled out a fishing pole (it kept coming out of the pack, like a silly magic trick performed by entertainers in the market). He then put both items back into the pack. "I would say this would be most helpful for any traveling Magus. You could carry almost an entire small house of things in this." Looking in again, he frowned. "I don't see anything that looks like a magical artifact or incantation book; of course, I wouldn't have suspected the boots, or this pack, of being magical. Still, it might be a limitation we should observe until we are more familiar with how this works."

Lebuin blushed slightly and shook his head at himself then looked at Ditani. "I'm sorry, this is really yours now, I shouldn't have spoken as if was mine."

That is interesting; he is trying to follow the Dagger code as well as imitate a Dagger. He might not be as self-centered as I first thought.

Ditani shook his head. "Ma... Lebuin, that is an item for a Magus, I should not desire to carry it. It is yours, I am sure Magus Vestul would have desired it to be thus. He was a kind and good man. I know he always had wanted to have a family but, although he married a few times, he never had any children. Consider this a gift from a father to his son, to continue his work." Lebuin looked shocked and overwhelmed with emotion. He simply nodded and Ditani placed his hand on Lebuin's shoulder knowingly.

Ticca stood and forced herself to look into it again. As she moved her head closer, things she looked at directly came into focus. Putting her nose as close as Lebuin had, she could see every item in perfect detail. *Well that is how he was able to inspect the books so fast.*

"There is too much in here to inspect it all now. I believe we are all ready and it is a full mark past noon. We should get going so we can be beyond the farming communities by dark."

Lebuin was quickly putting some of his things into the new pack. "I have only ridden enough to be familiar with it. I really hope Risy's horse is as intelligent and cooperative as he said."

"Just try to look authoritative while you ride. Now remember, you two are following my command. That means you address me as 'sir', and you stay a step behind unless I direct otherwise by signal or orders. You pay attention to what is around; you nod to any Dagger who nods at you. We walk down, out and around, mount, and then ride for the western gate. Lebuin, you give two pence and Ditani you give a bell in tip to the stable lads. Any last questions?"

Ditani and Lebuin both shook their heads, slipping their packs over their shoulders as Risy and Nigan had demonstrated. "No, sir." Lebuin said.

Ticca smiled. "Not bad, I might make a Dagger out of you yet." Grabbing her pack, she gave them a final check and then opened the door. She stepped out and made sure they closed the door solidly. Taking a deep breath, she thought, *Lady, don't be offended but I desire very much to not meet you today.*

She assumed her command bearing, walking down the hall and straight down the stairs. Without looking behind she knew Lebuin and Ditani were following by the sounds of their footsteps.

In the main room she noticed the conspicuously empty Dagger tables. A few merchants looked at her and her escorts expectantly, but from her projected attitude of 'on a mission' they slouched in disappointment. *Wonder if they were looking for me specifically, or just any Dagger.*

As she passed the bar, Genne looked up at them and said, "Good luck, stay sharp."

Smiling back at him, she replied, "And you too. We'll be back, so don't rent my room out."

Smiling wide, he waved his hand in the air. "Nev'r crossed me mind."

The new doors looked a little out of place, and the repair work to the wall was bright white, compared with the yellowed wall it patched. *Duke sure leaves his mark.* The new doors looked a bit heavier, and when she pushed through she was sure of it. *Trying to prevent it from happening again, I bet.*

Outside, no one was near, and it was an easy thing to turn left and then to walk around the inn via the alleyway to the stables behind. Their horses were standing there, ready. Ticca went straight to hers, attached her pack to the saddle, and then checked the horse and tack over. Everything was in excellent condition. As she mounted her horse she checked to see that Lebuin and Ditani had managed to pick the right horses and were already mounted. *Good boys. We are almost clear. Now to get a few blocks from here and we will be clear of any prepared attacks.*

Riding out of the alley, she turned right, heading southeast. *Just have to make it past the market and then take the main trade road straight out of the gates.* She concentrated all her senses on looking for the attack. They passed by the Dolphin and she spotted movement at the roofline. Using her peripheral vision she saw it was a Dagger she knew. *What are you doing there? Must be working for Duke; but why watch the Dolphin unless Duke is somehow interested in whomever is after Lebuin? Let's see if he'll help.* She made a great show of exaggerated movements to adjust the reigns a little tighter, signaling with her hands as she moved them for assistance.

She didn't look up at the Dagger but he made a motion ahead of her and then vanished. *Oh, so you thought you were out of sight.* Paying attention to where he had indicated, she spotted a merchant who was adjusting his outer split shirt as if to correct its position; for just a moment there was a break in the shirt, revealing directly in her direction only the dagger under the outer robe. After fixing his shirt, the merchant started to signal something that started with the number four, but changed the message to a warning at her eight-thirty. *Damn it! Time to run.*

She glanced to her left rear to see a slim man in dark green tights, wearing a belt with at least three fighting-length knives and a sword on

200

LEELAND ARTRA

it, come running out of the house across the street from the Dolphin. He was looking directly at her. Behind him were two others dressed as valets, in blue button vests, two fighting-length knives and swords on their belts as well. The man in green said something and pointed right at where the western gate would be. He then pulled a knife from the back of his belt.

Damn it, they saw through the disguises! That looks like a throwing knife. Lebuin's too exposed! Her warhorse jumped instantly to her directions, spinning and lunging between Lebuin and the men. Ticca drew as she controlled the horse with her knees; she leaned out and slapped Lebuin's horse hard with her hand. "Ride!" Lebuin's mount jumped at the abuse and flew into a gallop. Lebuin, caught by surprise, was bounced around, his hands splaying as he grabbing desperately for the saddle horn, almost falling off. He managed to grab the saddle horn, hold onto the reins, and somehow managed to stay up for the moment. Using the momentum from slapping Lebuin's horse, Ticca ducked to the left as a knife passed over her, and would have hit Lebuin if not for his sudden motion.

She righted herself and held on with her legs, letting go of the reins to draw another blade. Guiding the horse with her legs they spun around again, and the horse leapt after Lebuin and Ditani as they raced away. A Dagger disguised as a workman on her left pulled a pair of daggers and ran to intercept the three attackers. Looking back, she saw that the three men were fighting with six Daggers dressed as workmen, sailors, beggars, and peasants. Before she lost sight of the fight two of the disguised Daggers had fallen, heavily wounded, and none of the three men who had come out to attack Lebuin were wounded. *What was a full fire team doing in disguise watching the Dolphin? And Lady, not that I am not thankful, but why the hell did they break cover to help me?* Her mind pulled her Uncle's favorite saying out to answer that: *'Mess with one Dagger, you mess with them all.'*

Unfortunately the roads in the city were not straight, nor were they empty. They rode as fast as they could while dodging carts and people. They had just made it to the gate when the Knife in green came running out of narrow alley just ahead of Ditani. *Damn it, who the hell is he and how did he get here so fast?* He was splattered with blood and had two fighting blades out.

"DITANI, LOOK OUT ON YOUR TWO!" Ditani's head thankfully snapped to the right location. *Thank you, Lady, he knew what that meant!*

The Knife sliced with his two blades at Ditani, who successfully dodged away only to lose his balance and fall half-off of his horse. The Knife turned toward Ticca as she turned her horse to ride him down. The war horse didn't hesitate and leapt at the Knife.

For a moment Ticca and the Knife's eyes connected and she read his immense anger towards her in that look. He wasn't afraid, and certainly didn't look at all like someone about to be trampled by a highly-trained war horse. He didn't try to dodge, but instead spun in place, sheathing his knives and twisting with a speed Ticca admired as she was carried directly over him. He managed to twist, step, and shift just enough that her horse made no contact with him as it passed over. Anyone else would have been crushed under the mighty weight and steel-shod hooves. *This guy is too much; he can't be a normal Knife. Why do I have to deal with three exceptional Knives in two days? If this keeps up I am going to demand more coin from Lebuin!*

Just as the horse passed over the Knife, he spun and jumped so that both his feet landed on her horse's rump. In one continuous motion he painfully grabbed Ticca's shoulders and pushed back off, pulling her right out of the saddle, and they both fell backwards off the horse. He let go of her just as soon as he had guaranteed she was going to be falling with him, which left him a small margin of additional flex in his legs to push off, adding more momentum to his own backward fall. Ticca's mind raced over the situation. *If I fall off this way I am going to break my neck, and if I don't this guy will finish me off.*

From the corner of her eye she saw him using his extra momentum to do a backflip, heading for the ground feet-first, legs bent to absorb the impact. *OK, that might work for me too.* Moving with her fall, Ticca bent backwards, putting her hands and back of her head on her horse's rump. She managed to kick the top of her saddle with one foot as she fell backwards, turning the fatal fall into a backwards summersault off the rump of her horse.

I do not like landing with my back to him. Have to fix that first. Landing, she immediately lunged forward in the same direction the horse was moving with the momentum she already had. The ring of a scissor cut of two knives behind her head told her if she had moved a fraction of second slower she'd be dead. Twisting in the air, she did a somersault half twist flip, landing in a much better position facing the Knife in green. She had her dagger and short sword out and ready.

The Knife didn't pause. Closing the distance instantly, his knives flew in vicious, deadly attacks. His face held a small smirk but his brows were tight with anger. His every move was deadly, and Ticca had little time to attack as she was forced to concentrate solely on parrying the flurry of blows. Over and over he attacked, and over and over she parried. Ticca was forced to walk backwards as he kept stepping closer, reducing her maneuvering room.

She had managed to get in the occasional riposte, but he slowly sped up. She tried to change the direction he was pushing her but he cut her off and forced her further back. Every three steps backward he sped up marginally. The Knife smiled evilly at her as she tried unsuccessfully to gain an advantage. Finally all she was seeking was escape. *Damn it, he keeps backing me up. This is revenge for killing the other Knife at the hospice. He is doing to me what I did to his friend. Except there is no wall to pin me against, just the open gateway; can I use that somehow?* Her mind raced, trying to find a way out of this situation alive.

Her arms ached with the strain of holding him off. She had never been pushed so hard, and yet somehow she matched his speed and strength. *I'm holding, but for how long?* She allowed herself to detach slightly to consider the situation. She was trapped in the fight. There was no way to disengage without giving him the chance he needed to kill her, which she was absolutely certain he was planning on doing. Ditani and Lebuin had made it out of the gate. She studied his technique, looking for a bad move. He made no mistakes; his knives flew in a nearly perfect pattern. He reminded her of her trainer. She saw the answer—her trainer had said that the reason he was the best was because he didn't always follow the pattern; there were moves within the moves. The patterns could be adjusted, but only by a true artist. Someone who knew the patterns, followed them, but didn't let them control.

They had backed up to the gateway and were in the shadow of the arch. The Knife hadn't increased speed in at least ten steps. *That's it, this is his best. Can I go faster?* She reached deep within and steeled herself. *Time to stop giving in to him.* She stopped taking defensive steps backwards, forcing herself to hold the line. His eyes widened when she held. *He is as surprised as I am. OK, now to be a great Dagger!* She held her ground, and letting herself relax into the flow of the fight, she found the calm of the patterns. Her blades sped up just enough that now he was forced to parry as often as she was. Now it was a parry, riposte, parry, and riposte. Then she pushed herself a little faster. He took his first defensive step backwards. She let her grimace turn into a smile and looked deep into his eyes. He wasn't afraid, but his anger had changed to something else. He stepped back again, but then he pushed back, making her step back. The fight went on back and forth. He was not an artist, but he was the second best she had ever faced. Ignoring the muscle complaints she let her hands flow in the patterns and new attacks emerged as she found different patterns within the patterns. "Who are you?" he asked. She didn't bother to answer, being busy with breathing.

A knife came from nowhere and nearly hit the man in green. He dodged it but that gave her a chance to slice his upper leg. Anger returned to his eyes. Another knife came at him and he dodged it but didn't give her another opportunity.

Something cracked loudly behind her but she couldn't look back. A donkey screamed in panic. Another knife, and this time he backed up enough to disengage for a moment and look around; Ticca allowed him to disengage so she could do the same. There were nine Daggers on the right side of the street, fighting with the two valets in blue, both wounded. Five more Daggers jumped out of another alleyway to her left and swarmed her and the man in green. As he fought them all, Ticca heard splintering wood behind her. Stepping further back, letting the other daggers occupy the Knife, she was able to look around.

A single solid slab of metal completely filled the gateway, rising slowly out of the ground, and as it slowly rose, the existing gates cracked and broke. It looked like there was a deep slot in the wall for this metal slab that had been filled in with stonework to mount the current gates. All of the stonework and other materials didn't stop the metal slab from rising. In fact, the metal slab was at least six feet thick and had already broken up through the huge paving stones which had been put over it. *That was the first cracking sound I heard, the stonework breaking away.* People had gotten out of the way as it was moving very slowly, having only risen about five feet so far. There was a farmer chasing his panicked donkey away from the gate.

Looking back at the fight she realized this had something to do with Duke. *Duke isn't paying me, and I have to get Lebuin his answers. This fight is theirs.* She spun and ran for the gateway, looking back in quick glances to follow events with the Knife, jumping up on the slab and sprinting across it. The Knife in green managed to break away from the other Daggers and ran after her. He was just about to the other side of the slab, which had only risen another inch. "Damn it! Close already!" she shouted in frustration, as she prepared to meet him again. He had just started to jump up on top. His foot hadn't yet left the ground behind when the gate snapped up so fast that the stonework in the slot was instantly turned into a cloud of dust and the remaining parts of the wooden door became flying tinder. The enormous slab of steel slammed into the top of the gateway arch with such force that large masonry stones on the top of the wall were thrown into the air like billiard balls. Ticca felt the shockwave hit her body, pushing her away from the gate slightly as the thunder clap left her ears ringing. She covered her head defensively and held her breath against the cloud of dust. She had to dodge several large falling stones as she backed away from the now-sealed city gateway.

Turning, she ran as fast as she could down the road. Her war horse had stopped only a few hundred yards away and another hundred yards beyond that sat Ditani and Lebuin on their horses, watching the events. She swung up in the saddle and rode over to Ditani and Lebuin, who were looking past her at the city with astonishment. Turning the horse, she looked back at the city wall. It was rising, and along the top more steel plates appeared, topped with spikes which held steel balls.

"Definitely need to give things time to settle down here." Ditani and Lebuin mumbled an agreement; the three of them turned the horses away from the scene and galloped down the road.

Sparing

CHAPTER 11

FRIENDS IN THE WOODS

THE FOREST WAS ANYTHING BUT quiet. There were noises and animal calls which sent chills down Lebuin's spine. They had ridden very hard and very fast for three days to get well away from Llino. Ticca had taken them off of the main roads a full day back, and now they were traveling over open country. Lebuin was sweaty and dirty, and muscles he never knew he had announced their presence with every move. *This has been a miserable three days. I wish my magic would come back so I could at least get some of this grime off of me. I cannot believe people live like this all the time. How can they ignore it?*

Looking across the campfire at Ticca, he noticed she didn't have the strained look she had worn for the last three days. Her brows were no longer drawn together in hard thought. In fact, she was looking at him as one might inspect a new farm animal, and it was obvious she was trying to decide something.

Looking left, he saw that Ditani was actually smiling as he busied himself cooking some hares Ticca had shot earlier with a sling. *How can he be happy? Today he was just riding along breathing deeply with a crooked smile. Now he looks like we are at the finest home enjoying a wonderful evening.*

The smells of the cooking meat wafted past him again. It was going to be a pleasant meal since there were herbs and spices in Vestul's pack, which Ditani had carefully selected. The roasting meat made his mouth water in anticipation. Looking up, he observed that it was a completely clear night and the stars were shining very brightly.

Ticca hadn't said anything yet and had leaned back against a tree, looking out across the clearing to the open sky. *She looks in a talking mood, and I really would like to start learning some things.* "Are we far enough that we can talk now?"

She looked at him and then back to the sky. "Perhaps. It has been three days since our escape from the city, and I haven't seen any sign of being pursued. The forest is alive, so nothing unusual is moving about. So yes, I'd say we can talk safely now."

Now I can ask the question that has been burning in my mind for days. "Why aren't all Daggers as skilled as you are?"

She laughed. "Heavens, that is an odd question to ask after everything we have done."

"I'm serious. I know I have little experience, but I am not stupid. You fought and killed a Knife at the hospice; you faced that demon in green and fought him to a standstill. He held off five other Daggers easily enough and broke away to chase you. In fact he looked like the Daggers were just insects that were annoying him slightly. If it hadn't been for whatever Duke did to close the city he would have attacked you again. So, why are you so good, or why are the other Daggers not as good as you?"

Ticca looked up at the stars and in a wistful voice answered, "I have had unique training."

"Obviously, but is it a secret? Can you share it?"

Ticca looked at him for a minute, her eyes going a little wide then slightly unfocused. "No one has asked me before." Ticca's gaze shifted to the fire. "I am only sworn to keep the source of my knowledge a secret. But no promise to keep the training a secret was demanded." She continued to look into the fire as if it were a window. "It isn't something he'd have missed, either."

Ditani took one of the rabbits and handed it to him, and handed another to Ticca. Taking a rabbit for himself, Ditani sat down and began to eat. Ticca sat up a little straighter and began to pick at the rabbit. They all sat and stared at the fire, quietly eating and thinking their own thoughts.

Ticca's voice caught both Ditani and Lebuin by surprise. "I see no reason I cannot pass on these skills. Of course, I am not really interested in being a trainer myself, at least not yet."

"Would you teach me?"

Ticca looked at him. "Lebuin, you're a mage—of what use is the sword and knife to you? You can shield yourself better than any fighter and kill with a look. Why learn the knife and the sword?"

"That is what I thought too. I think that is what Magus Cune was trying to teach me. I was just too naive to see it. Magus Cune nearly killed me with a sword in a magical fight. Magus Vestul was killed by a blade penetrating his defenses. I think mages might be, in general, too proud and overconfident. I recognize this in myself and I am disgusted by it. So I ask, would you teach me?"

"After five years training with my uncle, he had taught me everything he could and called on another trainer to complete my education. No offense, but I wasn't planning on spending that much time with you."

"I don't expect to learn all you know. It will be cycles before my magic returns. Should we start now, I might be of more use than just a target to protect." He looked directly into her eyes and gave her what he hoped she would see as a determined promise to study well. "I promise you, I am a fast study."

Ticca thought about this some more. "You make a good point, M'lord. It would be helpful for me to stay sharp and remind myself of the basics." Smiling, she looked at Ditani. "What about you, old man, will you join us in training? I know you can move fast enough, you dodged that Knife's sword well enough."

Ditani looked at them in surprise. "Me? I am an old servant who is looking forward to retiring. It was luck that let me survive. I almost fell off the horse doing it."

Ticca's eyes sparkled in the firelight. "Well, with some training maybe you won't need so much luck next time. My trainer always said, 'Be thankful when luck happens, but don't count on it.' Besides, I am told that the knife and sword drills keep men limber and active almost their whole life. Your wife might enjoy that." She stared at him, grinning wickedly, daring him to answer.

It was hard to tell but Ditani might have looked a shade darker in the dusky light. "Ticca, really, you go too far! But I agree, luck is a silly thing to count on. I do fancy keeping my joints limber, so I accept your invitation."

Ticca giggled like she had won a prize. "Algan is two or three weeks away by the trade road. It will take us at least a cycle to get there, traveling through the wilderness and avoiding contact. We can train for a mark every morning and evening. It won't slow us down too much. I think we should concentrate on the defensive skills." Tossing the remains of her rabbit into the fire, Ticca took off her boots and lay back on her bed roll. "Let me think this through and we'll start in the morning."

I can't wait! I don't know why but I have the oddest desire to master the knife now. Looking at Ticca, he admired her stamina, courage, and obvious intelligence. *This is a woman who will make a blazing trail wherever she chooses to go. I have been very foolish being more concerned with the outside of people than what was inside. With her help I may very well survive Cune's challenges. I intend to be a very different man when I next meet him.*

The evening was getting colder, and looking at Ticca, he saw she was still awake and looking up at the stars. "Aren't your feet going to get cold?"

"Better cold feet than odd dreams," she answered mysteriously.

"What do you mean by that?"

Ticca sat up and looked at him across the fire as if trying to decide something. He waited to see what she chose to do, and she looked at the boots and sighed. "I think they are causing me to see things when I sleep."

Lebuin looked at the boots too. "They are just an artifact, although one with a very useful mix of features. I don't see how including dreams would ever cross anyone's mind. Are you sure about this?"

Ticca shook her head. "No, but ever since I got them I have been having visions or dreams. They are as real as this is. I remember them clearly and in every detail. It is as if I am actually living the dreams, and when I wake up I am always confused about where and who I am."

"Do you want to tell us about them?"

Ticca frowned and thought about it. "Well, they are actually kind of girlish."

"Meaning that you are a girl in them?"

"Meaning I am another girl who is in love, and the dreams center around the romance. In the dreams I ...or she... or, well... in the dreams there are feelings and thoughts with immense love as I have only ever heard of. These dreams make me feel odd, and I am starting to believe such love may really exist."

"Are they the same dreams?"

"No, they are moving forward in time. Things evolve, as they do everywhere. I think the person I am reliving is the maker of the boots."

"Perhaps I can help you understand. Tell me from the beginning. You can of course leave out any, um... intimate details."

Ticca blushed. "Well there hasn't been any of that, at least none I was present for. I think the first dream might have been followed by a very excellent moment. At least, it was heading there when I woke up. This is about a woman who lives in a large forest city. Her name is Kliasa, and she trapped animals to make boots and travel journals."

Ditani sat up hastily. "Did you say Kliasa? Kliasa of Rea-Na-Rey?"

Surprised, he looked at Ditani. *Rea-Na-Rey, as in the Elven city of the forest? Why would you know someone from there?*

Ticca shrugged. "I haven't heard the name of the city said. I would remember if it was Rea-Na-Rey, still it might be the same."

"Ditani, do you know a Kliasa?"

Ditani looked at the ground for a moment and his shoulders sagged as if under a heavy weight. "Yes, she was a shining star like none before or after. We all loved her greatly. Magus Vestul loved her as a daughter; I loved her as a sister..." Ditani reached over and picked up the boots tenderly, as a man picks up his baby daughter. "She made these boots for Magus Vestul as a present. He mentioned how uncomfortable his boots were and she set about making him the finest boots ever, so that he would always be able to dance." Tears ran down Ditani's cheek as he softly caressed the boots. He then put them back by Ticca. "Believe me, you two have a lot in common, she would want you to have these. I don't understand the dreams; Magus Vestul never mentioned he shared her memories."

Everyone was silent for a while. Finally, Ticca looked at Ditani. "I'm sorry, I didn't know."

"How could you? You are young and the world hasn't been so unkind to you yet."

"I take it she is dead?"

"Yes, she died in an attack on her home. It was vicious, brutal, and long since avenged by even more brutal and horrible acts."

Ticca put her hand on Ditani's shoulder. "I am sorry. She was so happy and alive. Was it her lover who exacted revenge?"

Ditani nodded. "Oh yes, he did. He did things I shudder to consider. It is said he still bleeds from his heart because the wound never healed. This is why he shows no mercy, or regret, and is willing to do horrible things; things which anyone else with a dark heart would refuse as too dreadful." The fire seemed to dim and a cold wind blew over them as if nature itself stood in testimony to Ditani's words.

A shudder ran down his spine at that pronouncement, as if evil had touched their campsite. Lebuin thought about it. "Ticca, unless the artifact was specifically designed to share memories, I don't think the boots are the cause."

Ticca shrugged. "Well if I sleep with them on, I have dreams of her and things I have never experienced. I have spent days hunting in her forest and making a wonderful journal which was later given to Magus Vestul at a festival in his honor. It was Magus Vestul who finally called her by name, and I do recall him complaining about his boots. She resolved to make him boots; these boots. She is constantly worrying about this man she loves, trying to decide how to help him with his plans, which he hasn't yet shared."

Ticca retold the stories from her dreams. Lebuin paid especially close attention to the description of her feelings while making the journal. When she was done he asked her questions which she couldn't answer on the techniques used. "I'd love to experience that making myself. I might be able to learn those skills. This would be wonderful."

Ticca handed him the boots. "Give them a try, if you dare."

Taking the boots, Lebuin didn't really have to think about it much. He pulled off his own boots and slid into Ticca's. "You can wear my boots if you want. They are going to be too big, but they would keep your feet warmer."

Ticca looked a little put off, but took his offered boots and slipped them on. With that they all drifted off to sleep.

- - -

Sun was streaming in the window and he sat there enjoying the feeling on his face. Sitting up, he noticed something was different, something was not right. This was someplace he did not know. Looking around, he realized he was alone, but there was laughter, like dozens of perfect small silver bells, ringing outside. Standing, he moved to the window and looked out on an amazing scene. Dozens of children were running around, screaming and laughing. Some of the children were astride small deer; others were just running around. They all moved with a speed and agility he found hard to believe. What was even odder was that they were playing a game of chase and tag with a creature the size of a horse that looked like a wolf. The wolf laughed and yelled, jumping around with great agility, running and using trees to bounce off of, trying to avoid the children. The wolf was speaking the language of the children, and even though Lebuin didn't understand the exact words, it was obvious that the creature was playfully taunting them.

A presence was beside him; he looked and caught his breath. Next to him, smiling and looking out the window, was the most beautiful woman he had ever seen. She was dressed in a soft, fuzzy forest-green dress with long sleeves, which covered her from neck to toe. The dress hugged her form tightly from the neck to just below her hips, where it flared out into a wonderful skirt. The dress, while covering almost every inch of her body, still showed every curve of her perfect frame. It ended just above the ground, and peeking out were a pair of matching boots made of glossy leather, dyed a soft mossy green. Around her waist was a black leather belt, on which hung a small pouch and a much-used but well cared-for hunting knife.

"The children so love Duke, and he adores them."

Looking out the window again, he replied, "So that is Duke; I never would have guessed he played with children."

"Duke has many sides, as do we all, Lebuin."

"You know me? How? Who are you? Where am I?"

"You know the answers to all that already."

Nodding, he looked back at the woman. "You are Kliasa, this is a dream, and I suppose this is your home in Rea-Na-Rey?"

"Correct."

"I thought these dreams were supposed to be from your point of view."

"I will not let a man know my intimate thoughts. You come here out of curiosity, and a desire to know the making of my works. Ticca comes here for other reasons."

"So this isn't something you laid into the boots? Your mind is directing this? How can that be, you are dead."

"No, I am between."

Lebuin froze at that. "'Between'. Another entity told me I was 'between'."

"Correct."

"I sensed you there between; you were watching over us from the ethereal realm."

"That is a reasonable explanation. Yes, I was there. I lent what aid I could to help your survival."

"Why? What do you care?"

She looked at Lebuin with a mix of pain, longing, and secrecy. "I cannot answer that. There are limits to what I can tell you."

"How can this be?"

"You know the answer to that, too."

"The boots... you made them, they are connected to you, so you can use them as a conduit."

"Correct."

"So why haven't we heard from dead mages before through their artifacts?"

"They did not remain between."

"That isn't an answer. Surely some of them were not yet ready to move on."

"It is as much as I can say."

"So this is between two states of being?"

"You desire to know my secrets?"

"Don't avoid the question."

"I am not; I have answered as much as I can. Do you desire to know my secrets?"

This was unlike anything Ticca had said, but it was real. He could smell the flowers, he could feel the sun, and the wind tickled his skin. "I do."

"What price would you pay for them?"

"I can insure you shall be remembered."

"I do not need this. I am loved, and once I pass from here I will have no use for anything else."

Lebuin looked around. "We are between. Money has no meaning; you do not desire to be named. What can I offer?"

"I cannot affect things in your realm."

Lebuin understood then that she was holding herself here but unable to cause change, or manifest in the physical world. "What would you ask me to do?"

She smiled, and it was like lightning. "You see, good. Three things I will ask of you: Get Ticca to wear my boots, always, until this is done. Protect Ditani as much as he protects you. Finally, do not hesitate to risk all, for all is at risk."

Lebuin considered. "I can agree to the first two, but I do not understand your third request."

"You will, you have only to promise me these three things and I shall teach you all my secrets. We have passed the point of the necessity of your ignorance."

"What do you mean by that?"

"You will come to know that too, in time. I am aware of more than I should be, because of this place and of how I can interact through my creations. I cannot say more for fear of ruining hope."

"This is Rea-Na-Rey; you are a silver elf. Your secrets will be of little use to me."

Kliasa laughed, and it was as beautiful music with ringing tones, high and wonderful. "You know the name! Yes, this is Rea-Na-Rey, and I was what you humans call an 'elf lord'. I have hidden this from Ticca so she wouldn't be frightened." As Lebuin watched, Kliasa's form thinned slightly, becoming more elegant as her skin shifted to light silver. "I promise you will be able to learn and use the skills and secrets I share."

Looking out the window, he now saw the children were a mix of human and elf.

"Very well, I will do as you ask, provided what you say is true."

She smiled at him, and he was joyful. "Lebuin, we are between, it is impossible to lie here. Come, sit there, and we shall begin."

"How long will this take?"

"Time may pass differently here. I can give you as long as you need; I expect you will need at least a full year, perhaps more. Though it will seem like you have spent a year in study with me, only a single night will pass in your realm."

Lebuin thought about it and then smiled. "This will be the best dream I have ever had."

Kliasa motioned to him. "I picked this time because it was a wonderful one. We have three celebrations each year, and tonight's is the first. You will get to meet and know Duke and Magus Vestul as I know them. My love has already left, so there is no fear of any of my feelings for him intruding on this time. I have finished his boots and he took them with him, although he still doesn't wear them. There were a quiet few years after his departure that were full of happiness, which I can share with you."

Cycles passed and Kliasa was true to her word. Lebuin did meet the large wolf and laughed at the stories he told. Duke loved the children and was always playing with them or telling stories. Duke also had a deep love of Kliasa and came around often, just to chat with her; during these times Lebuin would sit and listen, or wander around the city as directed by Kliasa. Finally Duke left to build a better tavern, he said, and he had an emotional farewell with Kliasa. The summer festival had the honored guest of Magus Vestul; Kliasa introduced them and he found he liked him deeply. Lebuin learned that Magus Vestul had had many interactions with the elves, and they loved him completely for his sacrifices for them. All three festivals had ritual requirements on which Kliasa drilled him until he knew them perfectly.

They spent every day together; Kliasa taught him the art of making her boots and journals. She also taught him how to trap and prepare the animals. He roamed the vast forest with her. He learned her trap routes as well as she knew them herself. She taught him to use the sword, knife, bow, and sling as well as any elf. They spent marks every day sparring with weapons. She also taught him to read and write in the ancient language of the elves...

She truly passed on to him all her secrets. The training was much faster than he expected. Kliasa explained that this was because they were between and the connection of thoughts was superior, and so he understood what she was teaching better and faster than if they had done this in the physical realm. Kliasa also warned that although his mind knew all the skills, his body was without proper training, and he would injure himself should he push too far, too fast. She taught him the strengthening techniques used for recovery from injuries that caused long disuse and atrophy of the muscles.

A year passed and Lebuin knew the elven woods as well as he knew the library at the Guild. He understood the flows of energies that were part of the elves, and how they worked without the necessity of channeling because they were part magic themselves. He had mastered making boots that could change size, color, and texture to need. He knew how to make the journals' papers and inks that would create permanent records which would be nearly impossible to damage or alter. He knew how to fight and hunt as an elf. He knew all the elven traditions and rituals. And he loved Kliasa as deeply as Duke, Vestul, and apparently all who knew her.

He had almost forgotten about how it all started. One morning Kliasa came to him. "You have mastered all I have to teach you. It is time for you to fulfill your part of our bargain now."

"Kliasa, you are truly the marvel Ditani speaks of, I thank you for all your efforts. I will do all I can to fulfill my part."

She smiled. "Lebuin, know you are as much loved and cherished as I ever was. I am glad for this time we have had, I wish we could have more. You have things to attend to, however. I am better for having known you." She gave him a strong hug and then turned him around and pushed him gently out the door into the forest. "Be well Lebuin, and remember your promise."

- - -

Rolling over, the smell of hot arit came to his nose. He opened his eyes. *I am camped in the woods with Ticca and Ditani. Today we start weapons training with Ticca. This is going to be fun surprising her.* Smiling, he sat up, feeling immensely refreshed. None of his muscles complained and he felt strong and able. *Oh these really are marvelous boots, Kliasa. I think I will be making myself a pair as soon as I can... and I do remember my promise.*

Ditani was making some breakfast from the provisions and handed him a cup of arit. "Thanks, Ditani." He looked at the older man and felt a warm friendship for him. "Ditani, I ... I mean ... Well I'm glad to have you with me." Ditani looked him in the eye and nodded in response as a wide smile grew on his face.

Ticca was already up and doing her morning stretches barefoot. Lebuin swallowed some arit and joined her, also taking the boots off and doing them barefoot. Ditani set aside the breakfast to stay warm and joined them too.

Lebuin followed along as she did each motion slowly, as she had done in the days before. He found that some were already familiar from what he had studied with Kliasa. In fact, most of the warm-up was exactly as he had learned. The only problem was that his physical body hadn't had the benefit of the year of training his mind had. It wasn't long before he was sweating and his muscles were fatigued. Ditani had also followed and had the same difficulties in the same areas he did; however, Ditani was obviously in better shape, so when they sat to breakfast, Lebuin was the only one sweating profusely.

Ticca smiled, putting her boots back on. Looking at him as she ate, she commented, "You both did pretty good."

"Yes, well, there is a reason for it."

She raised her eyebrows. "Oh? And what would that be?"

"I have studied these moves, I just haven't done them. You are doing some differently than I remember, though. There are also a few moves I didn't know before."

"Nose stuck in books too much. Well, we'll get you over that. What about you, Ditani, how do you know the same patterns as Lebuin here? You both stumbled in the same places, so I assume you both have studied the same patterns."

Ditani laughed. "My people are taught this from youth, we call it 'the Path'. Many of my people do it every day together in open fields or parks. I haven't done it myself in a few years, but I remember many of the concepts it contains. Only warriors are taught the full martial aspects of it. Most only do it for the exercise and stretching."

"Well then, you two are going to be at least proficient by the time we get to Algan. If you both already know this, it is only a matter of removing the imperfections and adding the missing components. I still need to get you both to stop being so dramatic."

"What do you mean? I thought we needed to learn the moves?"

"That is what many think, but really it is about eliminating wasted motion; for example, in a fight, most people swing widely and block with more motion than needed. Really a very little diversion is needed to cause someone to miss. The less energy you need to redirect an attack, the more energy you have to sustain yourself. Most people who do these patterns tend to add drama to it, exaggerating some of the moves. You both were doing that. What is needed is the absolute minimum."

Lebuin nodded. "Ah, I see, conserve strength and let the opponent waste their own, thus tiring faster."

Ticca nodded. "Right. Now, if we are finished with breakfast, grab your knives and we will do some practice drills based on the patterns. These will likely be some of those martial aspects you spoke of, Ditani. So, congratulations, you are both entering the warrior caste."

"Shouldn't we use wooden sticks or something?"

Ticca smiled an evil little smile. "No, this will encourage you to concentrate on getting it right."

Lebuin swallowed hard. *No kidding.* Once she started the training he almost laughed. She had them standing facing each other, doing something like the Path, but also very slowly. It was like a dance, where he did one side and Ditani did the opposite.

"You will learn all twelve patterns from both sides by the time we are done. Since you know the patterns already these will come very fast. However, you must both concentrate on always, and I mean *always*, doing them exactly correctly. If you make a mistake, recognize it, stop, and do it correctly."

After Ticca was satisfied they had learned the first pattern, she made them switch sides and practice, paying close attention and correcting any mistakes through example. After he and Ditani had learned the first pattern dance from one side she traded places with him against Ditani and did the drill again and again, each time moving slightly faster. When Ditani made a mistake, she stopped as if frozen until he fixed it, and then they continued. Watching Ticca and Ditani, Lebuin was struck by how much it looked like the fight she had with the man in green, only much slower. Once she had set a certain pace that still couldn't be called fast, she stopped.

"This is the speed you will use to practice all the patterns. You will see that they can be strung together in a loop where you do one side, then the other, and then the next. A complete workout would thus be doing the Path once correctly, at a speed that would complete it start to finish, in half of a mark; followed by the patterns for a complete loop in another half mark or perhaps a full mark. Meaning you can do the entire practice by yourself in one mark. If you do both the weapon and the barehanded patterns you will need one and a half marks to complete the entire set. You do not need a partner for the pattern dances, but it is best if you can have one. Once you have learned these you should do them every day for the rest of your life. So from now on I expect you to do this in the morning every day as we travel, and I will teach you more each evening."

Lebuin repeated some of the pattern dance then looked at Ticca. "This is the fight you had with the man at the gate."

"You have an excellent memory, M'lord. This is one of the twelve practice patterns based on the Path that use weapons. There are also twelve hand-to-hand practice patterns that are also based on the Path. The fight we had used components of all of them as the situation permitted."

"So the Path is a foundation of fighting techniques, with and without weapons?"

"Correct. The Path is a fighting technique and a mental training exercise. If done correctly, it calms the mind, and eventually, your body will respond within the Path."

"What do you mean?"

She pointed to a spot in front of her. "Stand there." He did. "Now, try to attack me." He just looked at her stupidly. She smiled that evil smile. "Don't worry, I won't hurt you."

"I'm more afraid of hurting you."

"Yes, I know, I need to beat that out of you. When you are fighting it will usually be for your life. Therefore, you cannot hesitate as you did when thinking of trying to help me from the safety of your high window. Come, try to shove me, push me, kick me, or come at me with a knife, Lebuin."

The jab was dead-on and she knew it, too. He felt embarrassed at being reminded of his inactions. So he thrust his knife at her midsection, but not so hard that he couldn't stop it, and then she wasn't there. Her midsection had turned and shifted slightly out of the way, so his knife was passing a hair's breadth from her shirt. Her arm came up just as in a move from the Path, and he saw it was binding his own arm so that as her other hand came around, it would have broken his arm backwards at the elbow... except his knees had lowered, and he was moving his arm to turn it into an elbow jab to her belly, being supported by his other hand. Ticca twisted away from that using a different move from the Path, pushed his jab down and pulled him forward and off balance while bringing her knee dangerously up towards his groin, his own knife pointing at his chest while still in his hand. She stopped, but not before Lebuin had already shifted a little, so her knee would have hit his inner thigh instead. She held him there, slightly off-balance, his knife pointing at his chest, and because of her hold, his arm and the knife were entirely under her control.

"Do you see now?"

Shocked, he looked at the result of the maneuvers he had been learning but had not understood. "Yes, I clearly see the result. Are all of the patterns as dangerous as this?"

Ticca nodded. "The Path was long ago perfected, and there are variations but the core, which I am teaching you, is the same in every one. Every move is a dodge, a strike or a parry. The Path is the essence of all fighting styles, distilled to its purest form. It is also a form of meditation. I'd bet you will replace any meditation you do as a wizard with a much slower version of the Path. You might try doing it very slowly. I have been told many wizards that learn the Path do this."

"Are there no other patterns?"

"Of course, but this is the base, all others have extra moves which are wasteful or for show."

"So learn this, learn them all?"

"Pretty much. If you master this one, the others are but extensions, in slightly different order using different names for the moves. That is enough for now; we have ground to cover."

"Before we go, Ticca, I have an obligation to settle."

She looked at him oddly. "What can you do out here?"

"It isn't so much what I can do, as what I need you to do."

She waited, looking oddly at him.

"Ticca," he swallowed. "The boots are not the source of your odd dreams, but they are the conduit."

"This sounds interesting, let's get some arit and talk."

They walked back to the camp and Ditani made fresh arit. Lebuin swallowed and started, "I didn't learn the Path from a book. Kliasa taught it to me, along with many other things, in exchange for some promised favors."

Ticca sat perfectly still, listening.

"You see, last night I spent over a year in the great forest learning everything Kliasa knew, learning the ways of the elves, learning their city and people. I met Duke and Vestul on their visits to the elven city. I know how to make boots such as you are wearing now. I know how to make that journal you spoke of. It is all true. Everything you witnessed is truth."

Ditani made a sound, causing both of them to look at him. His head was down and he was staring at the ground. There were tears on his cheek. They both looked away, giving him his privacy for his grief. *He knew and loved her, and to hear I spent a year with her must be a real blow.*

Ticca looked back at him. "How can this be?"

"Ticca, there is a place where we all go after dying; between this realm and that is another one. I think it is the ethereal realm; Kliasa called it 'between'. She is purposefully holding herself there with all her power. She can connect with people through her artifacts. Ticca, she wouldn't tell me why, or what she wants to teach you; but she did say she has much to share with you only. She begged of me to convince you to put her boots on and to never take them off till the conclusion. It wasn't until we were finished with training today that I was able to see all I learned in the last year, overnight, was accurate."

Ticca shook her head, stood up and started pacing back and forth. "That is the second time a powerful entity has told me to do something while referencing an 'end'."

Confused, Lebuin looked at her. "What do you mean?"

"The High Priestess of Dalpha told me, in the Temple, to come back and tell her how this ends, if I can."

Lebuin frowned and stood, starting to pace himself. "You know, when I was dead I had a strange experience that I wasn't sure was real… but, now I am sure of it. There are powerful beings who are working towards an end. They all fear some major catastrophe and there is something about it that keeps them from getting involved directly. They are being forced, either on purpose or by circumstances, to stand back."

Ticca nodded as they paced together while Ditani sat and watched. "Lebuin, I think we are on the verge of something very important. I just don't know why. We are blind, but many people are trying to give us hints… Why us?"

Lebuin shrugged. "I don't know, but I trust Kliasa totally. It is impossible to lie in the ethereal realm. She wants to share something with you. She wants you to have the boots, and all she asks is that you never take them off until after the end."

Ticca stopped and looked at him. "Well, as odd as this sounds; I think I will agree. My trainer always said, 'Knowledge is the most powerful weapon you can hold.' If Kliasa really is holding on, just to tell me critical things, it would be silly to ignore her. Besides, I like how I feel in the morning after sleeping with these things on."

- - -

After that the days fell into a pattern: martial practices in the morning and evenings, with long days of riding in between. As they rode, Ticca would teach them of Dagger tactics, signs, and the Dagger code. She also recited many of the Dagger histories, which she demanded they recite back to her repeatedly until they had them word-perfect. Lebuin was surprised to learn that Duke had started the Daggers and based them on an organization of military specialists. They were respected throughout the world before they had been forgotten during the Imperial times. There was a lot of emphasis on not losing sight of any one of the three guiding aspects of honor, courage, and commitment. Oddly, the commitment wasn't to the Daggers but to doing the right thing, having the courage to stand up for the right, regardless of the consequences, and the honor to always step up. There were a considerable amount of signs, tactics, and other skills that could only come over years of dedicated training. With every word, Lebuin felt as if he was growing and becoming what he should have been from the start.

Lebuin only required some simple practice to teach his physical body the skills his mind already knew, and sling, bow, sword, and knife came fast. Ditani mastered the sling and already knew knife and bow. They hunted as they rode so that they always had excellent meat to eat in the evening. He also found he liked the Dagger code of honor, courage, and commitment. The whole idea of upholding a high moral code resonated with his soul. He would recite the things Ticca told him over and over again in his head, making sure he would never forget.

After they had learned the Dagger skills, Ticca added survival techniques. When they came across wild vegetables Ticca would point them out and they would collect some for the next few days. It was discovered that food put in the pack did not spoil, at which point Ticca and Ditani taught Lebuin how to hunt deer and they spent some time preparing smoked jerky from the venison. Apparently there were deep family secrets to the jerky preparation methods; Ticca and Ditani spent a lot of time arguing over which was better. Ditani was willing to share his with Lebuin, but Ticca kept hers a secret. In the end they grudgingly admitted that each was an 'adequate' preparation. Lebuin laughed at them, as both tasted delicious.

Some mornings Ticca would be a little confused on first rising, but they all knew the cause. Ticca said nothing more about what Kliasa shared with her; during the second week, though, Ticca said something to Lebuin in the Elven language and Lebuin responded immediately. They were both surprised that Ditani also spoke the language, although he had to concentrate. For the remaining time they spoke nothing but Elvish. Ditani quickly remembered the language and was soon speaking as fluently as Ticca and Lebuin.

After a few weeks Ticca declared them ready for more advanced training and started teaching them how to fight together against a single opponent or how to fight against multiple opponents. So their morning sparring was spent fighting in pairs against each other, rotating until they had all had a turn fighting two-on-one or one-on-two.

During the second week Lebuin's powers started to return. He slowly and carefully exercised them while they rode and each day they grew stronger. With the physical, magical, and mental exercises, he felt better and more alive than ever before. Lebuin found himself dreading having to return to the city life. Of course he did miss baths and clean clothes, but not as much as he'd thought he would. He also found he enjoyed the diet they ate; simple roasted vegetables with seasoned fresh meats from their hunting. They ate better than any noble every day as far as he was concerned. Also Vestul had obviously been collecting herbs his whole life, there was a huge collection. Ditani knew most of them, and experimented with others.

- - -

They were on the road almost six weeks before they came to the first outer farmsteads of Algan, and Lebuin had bulked out considerably. Lebuin had decided to shave his beard so he and Ditani looked a pair, both with similar dress, clean shaven, and with similar haircuts. Lebuin had also gained a dark tan that was not too far from Ditani's natural look.

Looking down the hill, they could see the main road was a short way off. Out of habit, he asked in Elvish, "Should we take the road? I doubt anyone here is expecting us." Looking at Ticca and Ditani, he added, "Or would recognize us, for that matter. I would swear Ditani is years younger and I know I have put on weight I never thought I'd gain."

Ticca looked them over, answering in Elvish as well. "You certainly have changed a lot. I would say that what you were was merely a shadow of what you have become, Lebuin."

He smiled back at her, in the easy way they had come to know each other. "Thanks. And you certainly look better for those city pounds you have lost, too."

"If you two children are finished complimenting each other, what say we get on with what we came here to do."

"Yes, father," they said together and then laughed. Ditani looked at them and laughed too.

Ticca looked on the farmland and the road. "Ditani, you said Magus Vestul's house was in the city. We might as well just ride down there and take the road in."

Lebuin thought about it and frowned slightly; Ticca noticed and asked him with a look what he was worried about. "Well, you certainly know more about tactics than I ever will, but that would be an obvious approach. So wouldn't it be less conspicuous to ride in from, say, the opposite side?"

Ditani nodded in agreement and Ticca smiled. "You are doing well, except for one problem; three Daggers or a Dagger and two disguised patrons, fled Llino. It might be reasonable to assume we three came from someplace else, and by coming in from the opposite side and we'd give that impression even more. However, we are going to go straight to Magus Vestul's house to essentially claim it. There won't be much hiding once we have done that. So why hide now? If they are here, they'll know we are here, regardless of which way we come in."

"You have a point. If we are to settle Ditani's claim we'll have to identify him and ourselves as proper witnesses."

Ditani thought about it. "We don't necessarily have to announce our presence. Vestul was often gone for cycles or years at a time."

Ticca thought about it. "Well, how long do we need to stay in the house? I thought our basic plan was to spend some time here cataloging and getting things in order. After all, they were only hunting Lebuin in Llino, and aside from you, there is no real indication he was coming here."

"Yes, except we have since learned that something larger than just Lebuin's quest for knowledge is going on. We haven't really talked about it much, but those were not ordinary Knives that attacked as we left."

"Ticca, Ditani has a point. We haven't explored those Knives that took all your exceptional skill to hold off. Is that ordinary for Knives?"

Ticca shook her head. "No, I don't think so. I really don't know who they were, but if I had to guess I would say they were Nhia-Samri. I haven't said that because it makes no sense at all. How could Magus Cune hire the Nhia-Samri to hunt you? Also, if they were Nhia-Samri, why haven't they been on our tail the whole way? They are skilled and would have had no trouble picking up our trail."

"I suggest we move back a bit and talk this over. There are some questions we need to work our way through."

They moved back into the woods and found a good camping location. After camp had been set up they sat down around the fire.

Ticca started. "This all started with Magus Cune placing a bet in your favor with a villain. That villain then sent a Knife to kill you to win his bet. We saved your life; I am involved by mere chance. But the resources employed are excessive for any bet, no matter how large. Seriously, hiring Nhia-Samri to observe the Dolphin to track and kill you? That would be a king's ransom in gold."

He and Ditani thought that over. Ticca continued, "Ditani is involved because he came with Magus Vestul to meet with Duke. Now, those two are serious power players and whatever game they are involved in could explain the Nhia-Samri. So what if the first attack was the bet, but the second and third attacks were directed at Ditani, because of his involvement with Magus Vestul and Duke?"

"But why not track us down these past few weeks?"

"That is odd; unless in pulling the disguise they mistook us for Daggers being sent by Ditani out of town. Later they may have discovered that it was Ditani fleeing, but then they got into it with Duke, which delayed them long enough that they actually lost our trail."

"If that is the case, they would be waiting here for us to get whatever they think I have."

"Ditani, you have everything Magus Vestul had, I have his pouch and boots, and Lebuin is carrying his pack. Nothing was left. So if they are after what Vestul was taking to Duke, it must be those papers, which we cannot figure out without consulting Vestul's library."

Ditani nodded. They all thought about it for a bit. "Honestly, Ticca, this is just a random game. Either they are at war with Duke and not here, or they are waiting for us. If they are here it will be to capture us, and something they believe we carry, regardless of if we have it."

"We need to find a way to determine if they are here, without getting caught. I doubt we'll get so lucky as having an ancient gate seal them off from us again."

"Lebuin, I have an idea. If they are here they will want to capture all three of us. They'll be covert. I know I can spot them. What if I ride into town by myself? I will speak to the mayor as a representative of Ditani and gain access to the house. I can then go there, get something silly and ride back out of town. We'll meet deep in the forest. If they are there they'll have to assume I got what we needed and so follow me. I'll make myself damned hard to follow, giving me time to spot them. If I do see them, I'll take them someplace and lose them before finding you two."

Ditani nodded. "So long as you don't try to get into the tower it will be perfectly safe. There is an office off the main entry that has a safe. I can give you the keys as proof and instructions for specific papers there. It is my safe and office, so I know what is there. To the mayor it will be proof as much as to anyone else."

Nodding, Lebuin said, "I can connect us by an incantation so I can see what is going on around you, know which direction you are in relation to me, and also give you a pull to guide you to us. We only need work out some signals so that I know when to give you a slight nudge. This way you don't have to know where we will be at all, and we can come to your aid if needed regardless of where you are."

Ticca looked at him. "Have your powers returned at that level?"

He nodded. "Yes, this would be no problem for me. I still have a number of weeks before I dare touch water, but I have enough control of air for something like this."

Ticca smiled that evil grin of hers. "I like this plan. Let's do it. We'll need a couple of letters from you, Ditani."

Lebuin pulled out his pack and retrieved the travel writing desk with its papers and ink. Handing the portable desk to Ditani, he started to concentrate on the necessary incantations he would need to connect and watch Ticca.

A few marks later, Ticca was riding off towards the road as he and Ditani packed up camp and set out deeper into the forest. Lebuin double-checked to make sure he could see Ticca and everything around her. She stopped at the edge of the road and made the hand signal; he gave her a gentle tug back towards them. She smiled and kicked her horse onto the road heading for town.

The Royal Vault

CHAPTER 12

FATE IS CIRCULAR

DOHMA SMILED AS HE ENTERED the palace foyer. He had been feeling better and better about the events of the previous days. *Sure, the city is sealed tight as a drum, and an ancient terror or hero has seized control of the city. Daggers are now considered officers of the throne, all eighty personal guards that survived the first day by hiding are being tried as traitors. The pretenders' families are all accounted for, and in the royal prisons, the three pretenders were simultaneously and gruesomely executed in public, witnessing each other's deaths over a full day. And every noble in the city is under house arrest or in the prison because of attempts at bribery or escape. For some reason the townspeople were enjoying all these events. They have been extremely cooperative and even giddy at the changes and orders. I feel better about serving here than I have ever felt. I am proud to be an instrument of true justice.*

He stopped for a moment to watch fifty workmen removing the paneling that had been put up in front of the actual palace foyer walls. Behind the ornate plaster with its overly-gaudy embossed golden inlay were walls of towering marble, with an intricate pattern that looked familiar. Once a larger section fell, it became clear that the pattern was an old seal like the one on the covenant. *They spent hundreds of years slowly hiding our history and past. How could so many generations remain so corrupt? It's hard to believe, but the evidence is mounting that each generation of usurpers was actually more ruthless and more corrupt than the previous one. Pirates; this was a nation run by pirates. They robbed on the seas, calling it 'patrol tariffs', but really, the navy was manned with mostly cutthroat pirates. It is no wonder, then, that so many nations tried at times to break our hold on the merchant lanes. According to the records, the responses were far more brutal than anyone here knew. I hope we can establish a more peaceful relationship with our neighbors. I suppose the excessively gruesome and lengthy executions will provide some good faith in that direction.*

Duke had ordered every wall of the palace to be hammered on, and if any wall cracked it was to be broken down, to reveal the true palace that was hidden underneath. It was a strange order at first so Dohma followed the workmen around as they pounded on the walls. The majority of the palace had been plastered or tiled over, which explained why it was all brash. Behind the façades were wondrous friezes showing the history of the ancient city. There were some interesting pictures, to be sure. The building of the city was depicted, with representations of the Gods watching over the construction. What was amazing was that there were representations of buildings which floated over the sections of the city walls; which were hanging down from these buildings, being moved into place as complete sections, instead of being built up one stone at a time, as buildings were built now. Also, there was one mural that looked down on the finished city from a great height, showing multitudes of people moving about the city. Where the central market was now was a field, with smooth rounded buildings which stood off the ground on legs that ended in immense wheels, as if they were meant to move, except there was nowhere for them to go. In almost every picture of the city could be found the representation of a large wolf, which had to be Duke. Even more interesting was that in a number of pictures the landscapes were covered with snow. *No one has ever mentioned that it used to snow here. I wonder what happened that could cause it to become so much hotter that it never snows, and when it happened.*

Whole generations of princes of the Empire where represented in detail. The faithful regents' line was also represented in one grand hall. It was obvious from examining the art that the princes he had known were not of either line, which is why they tried to hide it.

Dohma continued into the throne room, which now held no thrones but a large bench-table on the floor in front of the dais. Duke's massive chair sat behind and at the center of the table. There were three seats to his left and two to the right, for the yet-to-be-named new regents. In the center of the room, a circular table had been brought in and on it were books and maps of the city. Twenty highly educated and respected merchant scribes and sixteen clerks were meticulously tracing the city records and carefully cross-checking each item. Seven royal scribes who had been promoted from Duke's staff sat at a second table, which was filled with the notes and records being created by the research at the center table. The royal scribes were also consulting the ancient records and carefully preparing to write an accurate history from whatever point was determined to be the beginning of the false histories. All of the noble lines were being cross-checked, and family trees were being rebuilt, refuted, or confirmed.

Duke was looking over some books at the center table and spotted him coming in. He walked over to Dohma. "Captain, I must say your family is amazing! Your sister is a most able accountant; I am surprised she was only a junior assistant in the financial offices. How she can keep years of accounting records in her head at once is a mystery I care not to learn for fear it would make me boring at the tavern."

Dohma laughed, and his sister, who was currently only partially visible over a pile of books, looked up, recognizing the laugh. She too smiled and ran over to give him a hug, and then returned to her work. Duke had found her during the bureaucratic purge. After working with her for only half a day he had appointed her in charge of the treasury and financial records and then simply walked out of the room. Dohma wasn't surprised to hear that she stepped up and took charge without a single protest, as he knew from the guard reports how efficient and respected she was.

Duke smiled. "Ah, the joys of the bean counters! The Lords and Ladies be blessed that we have them so I don't have to do it myself. Do you realize that those penny-pinching little cockroaches kept a complete set of records of every bribe, graft, and embezzlement, going back generations? For the descendants of people smart enough to usurp power without suspicion they were oddly stupid."

Dohma looked at Duke, confused. "Excellency, I don't understand half of what you say. Was there something you needed of me?"

Duke laughed. "Sorry Captain, short version: we have accurate records where truly smart thieves would have left none. They thought they had outsmarted the world, and so became stupid bureaucrats. We will likely be able to sort everything out in time. Your sister is a great help; thank you for recommending her as someone in the financial office I could trust." Duke motioned to the other side of the table where Dohma's brother was busy with the scribes and clerks resolving noble lines, coordinating communications with the officers on the docks, and keeping the merchants informed with estimates for when their goods could move again. "Also your brother, who was the head steward, is doing well coordinating all the extra activities. I am deeply grateful to you and your family. Your family is making this whole job a lot easier."

Dohma bowed. "The honor is to serve your Excellency."

When he looked back up Duke was giving him a peculiar look. A crashing sound of masonry falling drew his attention. Both Duke and Dohma looked to where a pillar that connected the dais to the wall was giving way under the workmen's hammers. "Ah, at last! Come, Captain, this is what I called you for." Duke stood and walked to the back side of the dais, where the wall section, which had been hidden behind the pillar, was now revealed. There was a recessed, high-arched doorway with a large steel door which had a bolting mechanism with a wheel and two grips so it could be turned easily with two hands. The workmen cleared the doorway itself quickly and Duke made a motion at it. "Captain, if you would please."

Dohma stepped up to the hidden door and grabbed the handles to open it; however, a very strange tingling feeling in his hands caused him to let go and jump back, looking at his palms. He bounced off of Duke, who had moved up very close behind him. His hands looked fine. He looked at Duke, who encouragingly said, "Just some built up static, Captain, nothing to worry about. Please open it up." Stepping back up to the door, he took a breath and grabbed the handles again, ignoring the odd tingle. He expected the mechanism to be frozen with age but it turned easily. There was a sound of many bolts being pulled back as he twisted the wheel by the handles. He pulled, and the door swung open silently.

Looking back at Duke, he saw that the wolf was still standing close and had been crouched slightly, as if getting ready to spring into action against some foe. Duke relaxed, sat down and just stared at him, thinking. Dohma stood there waiting. After a time Duke looked at the door. "Well, that cinches it."

Confused, Dohma looked at Duke questioningly. "What, your Excellency?"

Duke motioned to the darkened room beyond. "Captain, lead on please."

"Should I get a lantern?"

"Not necessary, just step in; we need to talk in private."

Dohma took a step into the dark room. He could make out a fine, polished stone floor and the beginning of a case by the light pouring in from the throne room. As he stepped inside, the room brightened as a series of panels along the top of the walls lining the entire space slowly lit up, like the sun rising. The box panels looked like they were shallow wood planter boxes which obviously contained something that poured out a bright white light up onto the white ceiling, providing excellent lighting without shadows. The room was larger than he had guessed, being a long rectangle that went away from the throne room. The room was forty feet by nearly a hundred-and-a-half in length. The door was in the center of the shorter wall. The walls were lined with shelves of books and artifacts, and down the center of the room were more shelves, as in a library. At the far end Dohma fancied he saw huge chests.

Duke stepped into the room, which was more than spacious enough for him, and the door closed behind him on its own. Off to the right was what could only be described as a lounge area. There were a dozen comfortable chairs, low tables, and foot stools, arranged as in a smoking room. There was also a wine cabinet, a tobac humidor with a glass front, and a small bar with dozens of bottles of varying shapes and sizes, all containing liquids. There was even a small sink with a faucet sat next to that with racks of drinking glasses.

"Dohma, it is time you were truthful with me."

Dohma spun and stared at Duke. "Your Excellency, I have never told you a lie! I am your servant and would never conceal anything important to the state from you."

Duke looked at him. "Well, that is about the answer I would expect from a Prince's Regent."

Dohma felt the blood rush from his head and he was dizzy for a moment. Duke just sat and watched him. Upon regaining his composure Dohma said, "Excellency, I am just a guardsman, nothing more. I was not part of the usurpers' family. I am from a humble family of servants."

Duke shook his head. "Only a regent, an heir to the throne, or I could open this room. That is why they sealed it up from view. They probably tried to break in through the walls and ground, but discovered that this palace is not made of stone but something they had no chance of breaking. The door was always kept behind a tapestry, so most didn't even know this archive was here. I suspected something like this, but without the true archive, or other artifacts that have been stolen or sold off, I couldn't confirm my suspicions until this door was exposed. By opening it you have proven your bloodline. I know you are not me, so are you a regent or an heir?"

Dohma pointed at the closest chair. "Your Excellency, I need to sit."

"By all means, relax. I see an excellent spirit there in that first rack—in the blackish bottle with the wines. Pour yourself a small glass and sit down."

Dohma was too confused to think. He took the smallest glass he saw and poured himself an ounce of the fine-smelling liquor. *I definitely need a drink.* Holding the drink, Dohma practically collapsed into a chair. Looking around, he absently took a drink of the amber liquor. Fire blazed in his mouth; it moved with speed out through all his limbs and into his head. He felt power such as he had never thought possible. He felt as if he could fight a hundred men and not be tired. He felt his muscles relax and their energy suddenly restored.

His thoughts became crystal clear. He had been drawn to join the guard because his brother had joined the staff and his sister had taken up with the scribes. He had known his place from an early age, and had gravitated to the covenant and studied it deeply. He had been drawn to learn the laws of the land—some he hated instinctively, but others he knew to be right and just. His other guardsmen had followed him readily enough. He saw he was a natural leader and tactician. He could easily be a regent. He knew for certain he was not an heir, as that ancient line would be bolder and stronger than he. He wasn't sure how he knew this.

He looked at the empty glass and then at Duke, who had been watching him closely. "What was that?"

"That was a several hundred year-old sharre."

Dohma looked at his hand as if it was a traitor. "Excellency, that was a priceless treasure I just squandered."

Duke shook his head. "No, that was a needed medicinal hit to the head of the Prince's Regent to put him in working order. Just one of the many perks of your new position."

"How can this be? My family are just simple servants!"

Duke tilted his head slightly. "Well, I didn't expect to have to explain this... But, you see, a boy and a girl, when they are between about thirteen and sixteen, meet someplace private and they..."

"Excellency please, that is not what I meant!"

Duke laughed. "But that is what happened. Obviously some young scamp of the regents' line had a tumble or three with a servant girl, at just the right time to save the line. If it had been the other way; a servant boy having a tumble with an already recognized regent's daughter, the result of that tumble would have been welcomed into the family immediately, of course, and then promptly killed off with the rest. Since then your family has served the kingdom as best as it could. Your family probably remained close and did much to help keep all those fine records we are finding out there. Although your ancestors didn't know it, the behaviors, loyalty, skills, and talents are kind of built-in. You are almost everything you were born to be. Only now you will complete yourself, as will your brother and sister. I have found the missing regents, and glad I am that your bloodline is not lost. I suspected you because of your actions before and during the transition of power, and also I liked you, which usually takes a few years and a couple of fights."

Dohma shook his head. "I don't want to rule."

"That is good, because you will find you don't *rule* so much as guide. Kingdoms have a life, and they need to be guided, but really they tend to work just fine without much interference. Lord Dohma, how old were you?"

"I'm thirty-five, why? Wait, why did you say 'were'?"

Duke looked worried. "Do you have children?"

"No, I am not yet married. I have dedicated my life to the guard." Then Dohma realized what Duke was worried about. "Excellency, my brother married young and has a wonderful son. My sister is twenty-six, with two children, a son and a daughter of her own born before she turned twenty. We are, however, all that remains of our family line, as many uncles and aunts were killed young, in the war."

Duke shook his head. "Well at least there is something to work with here. No one can breed many kids anymore. Your sister is lucky to have had two children. You must make sure the little lads spread some wild seeds as soon as they hit puberty. Permit the girls to marry at sixteen to their heartthrob; trust their instincts for a husband. Remember the law that your line produces no bastards. Marry them to the ones they get pregnant if you must for propriety, but adopt and embrace all bastard relations. With careful work we can insure the safe continuation of the line."

Dohma felt an old feeling of excitement and energy, like the days when he first joined the guard. Except this energy was still growing in him; somehow he felt younger. He stood and looked at himself. He felt different. "What has happened?"

Duke smiled. "The truth, a little mental adjustment, realization of an internal need; oh, and by the way you're now about twenty-three. But don't tell anyone, you can easily hide the backshift once at this age range. So you have about seven years to woo some damsel into your bed and make some brats of your own."

"Twenty-three! Why does that only give me seven years, what happens when I turn thirty?"

"It is too long of a story for now. It isn't by design or malicious intent, and the Gods try to compensate. I know you noticed older people never have children. The truth is men over thirty and women over twenty-five are sterile. The doctors will tell you it is just how nature works, and they are right, but for the wrong reasons. The Gods have purposefully and truthfully—as far as they tell it—directed possible blame at themselves with some of their teachings. The reality is that magic is dangerous for all creatures from our original lands, but is life-giving to the elves, dwarves, Gods, and creatures of magic. The ambient levels had to be balanced very carefully: just high enough to allow the creatures and peoples of magic to live, and just low enough to allow the creatures and peoples of our lands to live. But even at the safer lower levels magic still has some side effects; one specifically is that it sterilizes humans.

We really didn't have much of a choice, and the Gods try to make sure people live without much of the diseases of old age, giving everyone a good chance to at least know their great-grandchildren.

The end result is that from puberty men have about fifteen years of fertility; women only have about ten because they generate all their eggs up front. Kind of poetic justice for being too prudent, I think. So you must marry a woman who is as young as possible—eighteen or so would be great. It won't be difficult once you are formally announced and installed as a Prince's Regent. Every remaining noble will be tossing their daughters at you like candy. Trust your instincts there, too. When you meet the right one you will know."

I can't believe I am having this conversation. If magic is detrimental to humans and others need it to live I can see why this is kept quiet. "How did you restore my youth?"

"Me? Oh no, it wasn't me, it was the sharre; that bottle was old when they bought it, so add on the five hundred years it was locked in here, combined with this room's design to preserve everything and *voilà*—roughly six or seven hundred year-old sharre at least. I wouldn't suggest squandering it to a drinking binge; the results might not be as good as you think. I suggest keeping it a family secret, and then one glass only in the direst of situations. I would guess each swig of that is worth at least twenty thousand crowns."

Dohma felt a little dizzy realizing he had just consumed something so valuable. Then he looked at Duke, who wore a real smirk. "Seriously, getting too old without making the proper number of kids is a dire situation?"

"Hey, I am improvising here. We are just damned lucky you are who you are—and yes, I still think this was an appropriate use. Are you going to start questioning the word of a lord of the realm?"

Captain Dohma stood up in front of Duke. "If I feel I must."

"Good answer. Now that we have confirmed that sharre is as old as I suspected please pour another glass of it and pour it down my throat."

"Excellency, is that wise?"

"You've stepped up to the new role pretty fast, *Lord* Dohma."

Am I questioning Duke? Looking within, he knew he was right. Those feelings he had always had, which helped him make the right decisions, were now even stronger. *I am a Regent and I have responsibilities. I will not allow timidity to prevent me from protecting the realm.* He looked squarely at Duke. "You showed me who I am. I serve willingly and gladly. You didn't answer my question."

Duke smiled. "Very good. I must admit that the whole bloodline thing is a bit stronger than I suspected. But this is good for everyone. As to my request, and it is a request now, for a shot of that treasure. There are Nhia-Samri agents in the city; they laid a trap for me, robbing me of one of my greatest senses, that of smell. We have garments from one of their officers and I need to track him down. They know all of this and are probably taking actions to cover their tracks. That sharre will give me back my full sense of smell in moments instead of the few days more I would have to wait otherwise. Which means..."

"That we might be able to ferret them out of their hole," he said, finishing Duke's sentence while pouring another glass. "The Nhia-Samri are accomplices in the usurpers' actions and have committed an act of war with the kingdom by killing the last heir." Walking to Duke carrying the small glass he held it up to Duke's open mouth. "Excellency, may you make them pay double for their crimes." Dohma poured the amber liquid into Duke's mouth and stood back.

Duke swallowed and stood up, shivering. Duke's whole body started to glimmer and he shook his head and sneezed. When Duke looked at him, his eyes were glowing like twin lanterns; then the light faded and the glimmering stopped. Duke sniffed the air and smiled. "It has been a very long time since I had sharre that old. Boy does it carry a hit."

"Did I glow like that?"

"Of course, but not as much. My physiology causes it to be a bit more dramatic for me. However, yes, you did, and that is when I realized how old it really was. Originally I only expected it to be a few hundred years old, and let me tell you, even at that age it packs a punch. Now, would you mind letting me out of here? You really don't want to see how I have to open this door."

Unsure if Duke was joking, he decided it was indeed time to leave. He needed to talk to his family, find a new Captain for the guard, and start thinking bigger. Looking at the books as he moved to the door, he knew it was time to learn. "What are all these books?"

Duke looked at them. "Records, histories, secrets. You will find them all very interesting reading. First, however, you need to concentrate on that section over there, and this section here," he said, pointing at two different areas.

Opening the door, Dohma asked, "Why, what are those two sections?"

"The first section contains the instructions for controlling the city. Congratulations! You get to read the owner's manual. It is really boring stuff, mostly about required maintenance. You will find a few interesting things there though, please pay attention to it all. That second section is untouched noble family trees that were kept accurate, at least until the regents were killed off. We will be able to determine the precise timeline by comparing those to the other records we already have. I bet your sister will be more interested in that than you. You must learn who your nobles are and establish a functional and trustworthy bureaucracy. Nobles with much honor to lose and enough money to be immune from bribery make great heads of offices."

With the door open, Duke walked out and stopped, and lifting his head high he breathed in deeply. "No, that can't be!" he said, then he barked and ran. *Can the Nhia-Samri already be here?* Dohma ran after him, calling for more guards. Duke cut through the room, jumping over a couple of surprised clerks and through some doors that lead to the servants' hall. He slid on the smooth floor and bounced off the far wall, using it to change his direction so he could turn down the hall. Dohma somehow managed to stay not far behind the giant wolf. At the end of the hall were a pair of doors that led to the kitchen. Duke stopped short of them, sitting down and sliding on his haunches through the doors and into the kitchen. Thankfully, they were not locked. Dohma, breathing hard, came up behind.

Duke was sitting there, on the floor, looking at the surprised kitchen staff, a team of Daggers with wide smiles, Duke's secretary, Ladro, and a beaming head chef. The head chef crossed his arms and tried to look annoyed. "Excellency! I was going to surprise you with this!"

One of the Daggers said, "Well the hound is back, time for that hunt we had planned." Dohma smiled at that. *Yes, and I suspect they will not be ready for you.*

Duke gave a look of retribution to the unrepentant Dagger and then looked at the head chef. "I am surprised! The heavens know, I am surprised! To have my sense of smell return to that odor was like the Gods themselves, descending to reward me for this day's work."

Five guardsmen rushed in, weapons ready, as the chef placed before Duke a platter of some kind of pastries which were tall brown spiraled rolls topped with a thick white icing. There were five other trays of these rolls that had just been pulled out of the oven. The Dagger lead waved his hand at the guards. "Put the weapons away boys, this was only a culinary emergency."

Breathing deeply, Dohma took in the odor of these odd rolls. They smelled like nothing he had known before, yet his mouth watered at the unusual scent. "What are those?"

Duke bent down and shoved the tray over his way with his nose. "These, Lord Dohma, are *cinnamon rolls*." He said it in such a way as to make the mere name a word of worship. "They are to be treasured by not letting them get cold before being eaten completely. This will be another perk of your new position." Looking at Ladro, the Daggers and the kitchen staff, he added, "I don't care how you did this, but thank you. Now, hurry up and give some to everyone and make sure to put some on a plate for me!"

The cooks did as instructed and everyone, including the guards, watched respectfully as Duke bit into one, closing his eyes with delight as he chewed loudly. Breathing heavily to cool the roll, he mumbled around the food, "Ah, they are still very hot! Oh wonderful, wonderful, it has been too long."

Once Duke had finished the first cinnamon roll everyone took a careful bite of one. Dohma had to admit, they were better than anything he had ever had before, except for the sharre. Truly enjoying the flavors, he watched Duke slowly savor two more; *he sure is an odd creature.*

When they had finished, Duke licked his lips for some time. "Can't think of a better way to start a hunt. Commander Alpha and Echo, river walk." The Daggers, busy licking their fingers, as one looked at Duke, smiled and ran out of the room without a word. Duke stood and nodded to Ladro and the cooks. "Thank you again. I will find some way to properly thank you for this. Now, if you will excuse me, Lord Dohma, you need to go read a couple of books and take care of other business as you best can decide. I'll be back to confirm your position in a more public ceremony later." Duke looked at the guardsmen. "I name your Captain, and his sister and brother, Regents of the Realm. Their children are named Regent heirs by direct bloodline only. Witness this to all staff immediately; and now I will see about those pests we discussed, Lord Dohma." Smiling, he turned and trotted out of the room and down the hall towards the front entrance, letting out a chilling howl, announcing a hunt had begun.

"Good hunting my friend." He said to the empty space where Duke had just been.

He was surprised when Duke's retreating voice called out, "Thanks... Now get busy!"

Turning, he saw Ladro was trying to stifle a laugh. *Busy doesn't begin to describe it.* Looking at the guardsmen he saw they all were suppressing deep emotions as they looked on him, some with watering eyes. *I wonder if they are just proud that one of their own has been given so much or if something inside of them knew who I was all along and is now joyous at the confirmation. This whole bloodline thing Duke talks about is a little strange.* Walking out of the kitchens, he headed back to the throne room. *I think I might look at some of those books, after I talk with my sister and brother.*

Behind him the guards had formed into a personal escort.

* * *

"Two days. We have been cut off from almost every outpost, lookout, and direct operative. We are almost blind and stuck here hiding now for two days! Duke has Daggers out everywhere! The Daggers are watching for us and the guards are answering to the Daggers! This is totally unacceptable! When I told you to see to this personally, I didn't mean 'expose the whole operation and get us locked into this backward little city'! One thing! We only needed to get one thing and you missed it! Then you expose us, to kill off a possible witness, who wasn't even a primary target. Now we are stuck, out of communication, and have no way to continue operations." Urio-Larne paced back and forth in his library as he continued to rant.

Ossa-Ulla knelt with his head down and back straight. In supplication to his master's rage, his knives were laid bare on the floor in front of him as the tradition demanded. He was naked from the waste up. *Years of perfection ruined by a deceiving charlatan of a woman who hides behind her appearance of youth to trap men. If I am allowed to continue I will rend her in the old style. She will see her own entrails pulled out slowly over days and used to feed animals while she still lives.* He looked at the knives. *If I get the chance, that is. Urio-Larne is within his rights to demand complete repentance of me.*

"The Daggers killed two of our very best, you only just managed to escape, and that was in rags." Urio-Larne stopped in front of him. There was the sound of snapping fingers over his head, followed by something being handed to Urio-Larne by one of the two men standing at attention behind Ossa-Ulla. Urio-Larne shook the ripped green vest and shirt wadded together within his field of vision. The cloth was stained with blood—some of it his own—and had cuts from the Daggers' knives. "Rags! Rags! There are whole sections missing from these! This isn't some stupid hound! This is Duke! Duke, and you left him rags to scent you by! You came here! Rags! This was the worst and most thoughtless action of a cadet. It is impossible to think of anything you could possibly have done worse!" Throwing the clothes on the floor in front of him, Urio-Larne started pacing again.

Two days of this and each day it gets worse. More news or events come because of the start. Yet he does not decide my fate—it is as if he is waiting for something. He hasn't made up his mind yet. He is trapped and embarrassed. How could I have known she was so good? We didn't even know we were surrounded by Daggers! I should have guessed that, or at the very least considered it. The first group fell so easily. Ticca, that devil woman, who is she really? That was a trap at the gate and we walked right into it. I am shocked that the Daggers would sacrifice their own to bait a trap. It was very well played. I will never underestimate them again. The group that pinned us against the gate was well prepared. She was the commander though, I am sure of it. She played her part perfectly. She led me to the gate, causing my men to follow, and then as soon as everyone was exactly where she had planned she had Duke close the trap. Very well played. I bet she is in the palace right now helping to determine how to best to hunt us down. Ticca, I swear I will rend you in the old style.

Someone stepped to the threshold of the library and waited respectfully. Urio-Larne paced back and forth several more times. "What is it?"

"Sir, we have managed to spray every part of the neighborhood and the path Ossa-Ulla took returning here three times now. We shall not be able to do a forth."

"Why not?"

"Sir, Duke hunts."

"Not possible! He took a full dose of burned carmine. He won't be able to track effectively for at least another three or four days."

"Sir, signal relay reports Duke has begun untangling the scents at the west gate."

"We must prepare for discovery. I am not sure if three treatments are enough to stop him; two have proven ineffective before, we only know positively that six with time to dry are enough. If he comes on the area before the chemicals finish working he'll know it has been cleaned, which will give away the general area. After that, this whole area of town will be torn apart looking for us. Damn it! We must execute a complete shutdown." He spun and walked over to Ossa-Ulla. "This is worse and worse. Do you realize that having such a public fight in an open space which Duke could and did have placed off-limits means he will gain all three scents? Further, you exposed our observation post for the Dolphin. Duke has claimed and sealed that too! There was no chance to clean that! Many of our warriors will be cataloged by him and there will be absolutely no hiding them!"

Urio-Larne stepped to his desk and back. He heard papers being shaken over his head. "Ossa-Ulla, you are given a reprieve."

Surprised, Ossa-Ulla looked up but remained kneeling.

Urio-Larne shook some papers at him. "Warlord Maru-Ashua commands me to reinstate you as Nhia-Samri. He allows me the privilege of naming your rank. He also suggests that I send you out of the city, to a less conspicuous location." Urio-Larne paced again and then smiled. "We will evacuate you to outpost Llino Twelve. From there you can take an assistant and proceed to Algan. I want every part of Magus Vestul's house in ashes before anyone gets the idea to search it. Do you think you can handle lighting a fire in a small city filled with old people and children, Second Lieutenant Ossa-Ulla?"

Two ranks? You strip me of two ranks?! I am barely more than a cadet. Looking firmly at his Colonel, he answered, "I will serve well. And after?"

"Return to Llino Twelve via Rhini Wood. Find out more about this Ticca. You are in no way to make contact with Ticca's family in Rhini Wood, nor are you to do anything more than intelligence gathering. I expect a complete report in four weeks."

Picking up his swords, he sheathed them respectfully. Bowing once all the way to floor he stood and walked out of the room to prepare for the journey. Bitterly, he thought, *I shouldn't need a second chance. But I will take it.*

Preparations didn't take long. Within a mark he was fitted with a breathing system. The underwater breather was a set of tubes that attached to a float which could be changed to look like a small piece of wood or floating garbage or reeds or whatever was appropriate for the water it was to be used in. The breather would allow fresh air down one tube only and the second tube exhausted his breath by small holes under the water, making bubbles which were too small to be spotted except up close, and then they would look like they came from a water animal. A simple valve switched back and forth based on his breathing allowed him to breathe in good air and vent the bad. It also had a helmet made from glass and wire which allowed him to see very clearly. He knew if he went too deep the glass would shatter and likely kill him.

He was also handed the weights needed to stay submerged. The water was extremely cold, especially near the bottom, but his constitution could deal with the shock. Once in the water, he walked calmly down the bottom of the Delivery Channel, careful of the traffic and his breathing system. His papers, some clothes, and supplies were sealed in a water-tight harness that was strapped to his back. Once in the harbor, he carefully dropped some of the weights until he was able to easily maintain a good depth at just under the fifty-foot reach of the breathing system. Swimming slowly, he found the harbor was blocked by gates made of steel bars which were impossible to squeeze through.

He searched the docks for a way out, and finding none, he sat by a gate underwater, breathing slowly. *Sooner or later they have to open the gate for a merchant; that will be my time.* The day wore on and he grew very tired. The sun passed out of sight and he felt the tides pulling him into the gate. He let the water pressure hold him there and rested. Sometime later a ship was approaching—he could hear its movement in the water and behind him; he felt the gate swing silently open. After a day of struggle, escape was as simple as relaxing and letting the tide sweep him out of the city. *Duke, I have escaped you. But, the Lords permit, I will be back.*

He stayed underwater until he was sure the ship was out of sight and he was far from the city. Slowly, in the dark, he surfaced in timed stages as he had been instructed. Surfacing to the starry night sky, he paused to enjoy the sight and then struck out for shore, which he could hear in the distance. He was east of the city where the marshes merged with the river and sea, creating the great swamp lands. When his foot hit the muddy swamp floor he knew he was close enough to shore to stand, but there was no dry land in sight. Taking off the heavy gear and the water pack he rearranged everything so it could be easily carried.

Looking up at the stars, he found the ones he needed. A little observation and he knew which way to head. He had studied the detailed maps of the marshes and was able to guess where he was. He also paid close attention to any sign of predators, as the marsh contained hunters that could kill a man before he could cry out.

I need to avoid contact, so I will have to skip the trader routes. He concentrated on remembering the maps. Then it came to him. *There is an abandoned fishing home not far off. I might be able to rest there.* Turning, he confirmed the landmarks and then began carefully navigating through the swamp beds. He stayed vigilant for any of the numerous predators. After just over a mark, he spotted the leaning house in the darkness. The house was little more than a dark outline against the greens of the swamp trees and shrubs. He approached cautiously, looking for signs of other people or predators.

The house was empty. A small thrill of success went through him and he gratefully climbed onto the solid grass-mound. Finally being able to stand on dry land, he found some old fishing net, made a hammock, and strung it as high as he could between two strong palm trees. He then hung his stuff high in the tree and climbed into the hammock, falling asleep almost instantly.

The morning sun woke him up. Looking down he saw that a couple of predators had come through to investigate his scent. *I must have been exhausted to not have woken up when they came looking for me.* Looking up at the tree where he had left his pack he saw it was still safely in the tree. Getting up, he took the hammock down and put the netting back where he had found it. Grabbing his pack, he put on the simple traveling clothes with his knives hidden under the shirt. It was four days to the outpost if he walked. *I don't want to spend another night in this swamp. It doesn't matter how tired I am, I need to move fast right now.* He started the walk ten, jog ten travel pattern that he had been taught. *I should get out of the swamp by sunset and then another half-day will see me at the outpost.*

The day moved on about as fast as he did. The running and walking became like a meditation. He carefully reviewed every decision he had made and action he had taken since being informed that Magus Vestul was to be intercepted before he met with Duke, the information he carried in his pouch at all times to be sent to Hisuru Amajoo unread, in no way was a Nhia-Samri to come into direct contact with Magus Vestul, and anyone not Nhia-Samri involved was to be eliminated without a trace. That assignment had fallen to him. He had found a Knife capable of killing Vestul and stealing his pouch, which would hold what Hisuru Amajoo desired. The Knife killed Vestul but did not make it to the meeting, having vanished himself. Which meant the Knife was still to be found and eliminated without a trace. Ticca had appeared by surprise. Ticca had been seen in a number of key locations over the past cycle— too many locations to be a coincidence. When it was discovered she was acting for Dalpha's Temple he had decided she might be involved, which would mean the original orders applied to her. *A real puzzle was how was Dalpha's Temple involved?*

Ticca had left the Dolphin boldly wearing Magus Vestul's pouch. *I should have seen that as a warning. In hindsight she was clearly baiting a trap. She wanted to pull us out and expose our involvement. Her trap worked perfectly; I was a fool and fell into it. I ordered her to be removed and the pouch recovered immediately by one of our own. I cannot see how she managed to hire or involve that mage. That he is a special operative is clear. How did they communicate? Unless Dalpha's Temple was communicating with the Guild... I had not ordered the Temple to be monitored. It must have been coordinated through the Temple. The foolish-seeming mage stepped in just perfectly and laid our involvement open to the world. She played me for a fool. She pretended ignorance and efficiently ran down exactly what had happened to Vestul. Her speed at recreating Vestul's movements was another clue that she knew more than we thought. She was just going through the motions, and again I fell for it. She had his pouch, which meant the Knife either sold us out or more likely she caught him and extracted all he knew then killed him. I am still missing something, I am sure of this; she didn't need to spend the day tracing Vestul, unless that was just a ruse to throw us off. That must be it—she was blinding us. Interesting techniques, by publicly hunting what she already knew she confused me, which led me straight into the gate trap. I need to learn from her brilliant tactics. What is her next move? If I can get ahead of her I can turn her own trap on her.*

By the time he reached the outpost he had managed to puzzle out every aspect of Ticca's traps. *She will work with Duke to destroy all of our operations in Llino. Then, knowing little or no warning was, or could, be sent to our command, she will turn to Magus Vestul's home. Urio-Larne will be forced to destroy the command post and all but the most critical records. He'll get as many as possible out, probably by facing Duke and Ticca directly. If I hurry I can beat her to Vestul's Algan home.* Smiling, he realized he had the chance to get ahead of Ticca and Duke. He was free of the city before they expected, through the impenetrable defenses. *I will destroy it and then wait; they will not expect a burnt shell. She'll come in by herself to keep suspicions down; but seeing the burnt-out house she'll realize she has been expected and will have to move fast to recover. She'll be concerned that we recovered from the house what she tried to stop us from gaining in Llino. She'll race back to get support; they'll have a secret camp set up beforehand. If I capture them I can gain the information we need and present that to Warlord Maru-Ashua.*

I need someone who can play the part with me. The perfect operative will be a top-rank fighter with speed, mage-neutralization training, and who can sing and play an instrument well so we can pose as bards. I'll need to make sure to burn the house a day or two before we get to town, so as not to arouse suspicion. Small villagers are narrow-minded and superstitious to a fault, if there is a fire and there are new people in town it will be blamed on them. Smiling, he laughed. *Of course in this case they'd be right.*

The outpost had no new communications from Llino. The

commander of the outpost read Urio-Larne's orders carefully before allowing Ossa-Ulla his pick of the outpost's gear, horses and personnel. It took a day of careful interviewing before he hit on someone that would work. Fate was friendly and he found a gifted fighter, mage, and musician in the form of a beautiful woman named Runa-Illa. She was perfect for his plan. He gave her a short brief of the guise they would need and special equipment needed, along with the gist of his plan without precise details. She accepted the secrecy without comment and prepared their equipment admirably. All the equipment, new or old, had been distressed to look well-used and reasonably maintained. She chose to take a hammer dulcimer to complement the only instrument he could play better than most traveling musicians, the twelve-string guitar. It took two days to assemble everything, and he pressed her hard in fighting practice to help prepare her for Ticca.

Pre-dawn on the third day after leaving Llino, he and Runa-Illa mounted the light but fast horses loaded with all the right clothes, gear, and instruments of a pair of traveling bards. As they left the outpost, Ossa-Ulla took the lead, riding at a fast canter south until out of sight of the outpost and far enough to let them cut past the southern farms of Llino. Then they turned west and kept the horses moving at a steady trot. As they passed Llino the sun had just started to rise. The early morning light showed a series of smoke columns that could only be from a section of the city burning. Stopping to roughly triangulate the sources he knew that the command post was burning. *Ticca, I will rend you in the old style.*

Runa-Illa was also studying the smoke columns with a questioning look, yet she respectfully remained silent as good subordinate should. He broke the silence. "Llino command is destroyed. We are going to complete their last order to prevent the Dagger responsible from gaining any critical information. Then we are going to capture, interrogate, and kill her."

Runa-Illa looked at him with cold green eyes which burned bright with her soul. She slipped off her horse while drawing her odassi. Kneeling, she held them out in front of her, blades crossed near the base just above the copper bands. Putting her head down, she said softly, "I serve, command me."

He slipped off his horse and drew his right odassi. "Your service is honorable." He touched his odassi blade at the point where her blades crossed the stamped mark on all three odassi glowed red. Sheathing his odassi, he mounted. "We must make best speed for Algan. We have to beat them there."

She stood, sheathing her odassi, and mounted as well. Turning their horses, they spurred them back to a trot. Using the trot-walk travel pattern they would be able to get to Algan in perhaps a week and a half. Ossa-Ulla knew he had to get there in less than thirteen days so he could burn the house then wait a few days before the "traveling bards" got there. *Ticca will be leaving Llino in two or three more days and will hurry, but not as fast as we move.*

The Hunt Begins

CHAPTER 13

HUNTERS HUNT

"**N**O, I SWEAR THAT PRIESTS and priestesses just appeared from the alleys the moment the three men ran that way." He pointed west to indicate the direction. "It was like magic. I didn't see them before or during the fight, but then I was busy watching the fight more than looking at the other spectators. The high priestess herself came out of Drillian's Alley last and had that golden artifact from the Temple. She ran when called by a healer and touched it to the wounded person the healer indicated. Some acolytes came with stretchers and started taking the wounded away. The high priestess walked between two of the stretchers, concentrating, with a frown on her face and that thing glowing like the sun. That's it—except for the blood on the street I might not have believed I saw it at all."

Elades considered the baker's statements as compared to the story he had already assembled in his notes. The baker was only one of a dozen near or direct eyewitnesses to the fight in front of the Dolphin. In fact he was the most factual direct eyewitness of them all. If it hadn't been for the immediate arrival of the healers most of Echo Squad would be dead. Instead only two had suffered wounds too serious for direct healing, and they were still alive at the Temple. One of those was expected to make a full recovery. *How in the Lord's name did they know to be here? I have been refused admission to the high priestess three times now, and the healers just say they go where needed. Forgive me, Lord, but sometimes holy types can be really annoying.*

Allua, one of his squad's Daggers, ran in and leaned over to whisper in his ear, "Sir, the hound is ready. Alpha and Echo are ordered to river walk for him."

Shocked at the news, Elades stood. "Thank you very much, Nualli Baker, I appreciate your help with this. Do you desire compensation for lost work?"

The baker stood. "Thank you, but my assistants are likely doing OK in my absence. I am glad things are finally getting cleaned up here. I live for the true Princes and their Regents."

Elades smiled and waved him out. Turning, he saw more of his men had already stepped into the room as the order was being rapidly passed. Looking at Allua, he asked, "Where?"

"West Gate."

"Of course; and Echo?"

"Already informed, sir."

"Ridge run to within four blocks, then river walk on Duke's lead." No one waited a breath longer and they all bolted, most grinning with excitement. Elades couldn't keep from smiling himself. *I don't know how he did it, but if he can truly hunt now we might finally have the advantage. Playing catch-up is even more annoying than dealing with holy types. Sorry, Lord, but you know it's true.*

They poured out of the building, using every alley, door, and window, heading in many different directions. Of course, once out of sight, they each took a separate path, turning toward the western gate at their best speed.

Elades approached the west gate from along the wall. He was stepping over another dead bird, cooked by the lightning-balls on top of the walls, when he noticed that it had something on its foot. Stopping, he picked it up. The bird was charred, like it had been in a very hot fire, especially its wings. The legs, however, were relatively untouched. On one leg was a small canister containing a sliver of paper; he took it off of the bird and pulled the sliver of paper out of the canister. It was in some kind of code. *I need to show this to Duke.* Looking up, he saw the silver balls at the tops of the long spikes that topped the wall sparking with lightning occasionally. *Well that explains those things. Interesting counter-intelligence device, for sure.* For the dozenth time, he wondered what the effect would be on a person trying to climb over the wall. *We'll have to scout the outside of the wall carefully for bodies when Duke opens the gates. This might be very interesting. I should also have our patrols look for more carrier birds.*

He continued to the gate and arrived within minutes of Duke, who was sitting next to the gate, looking at the area quietly. Duke turned and walked to the gate and then sat down. He looked at it curiously, then said something, and the six-foot-thick, fifty-foot-wide metal slab slid down rapidly, with a slight grating sound like a knife being dragged over rock. It sank until it was a few inches below the street level, making a slotted line in the road across the gateway. The slotted line was where it had been paved over, hiding it from view. *Must have been done when the pretenders figured out they couldn't control it and put in the more normal gate system.* Duke said something else and it slid up just as fast, closing without much more than a soft *thunk. That thing has to weigh as much as a large house; what kind of machinery could lift such a weight so efficiently and evenly?* Duke then opened it and closed it a few more times, and each time it moved at a different speed. Not once, however, did it close with the speed and power it had when it had cut Ticca off from the Nhia-Samri, who had then managed to fight clear and escape.

After experimenting with the gate, Duke moved around the periphery of the fight area, which was still being guarded by a dozen city guardsmen. Duke stopped at each guard and Dagger asking them to hold their hand out to be sniffed. After getting each person's scent he continued his circuit, snuffling the ground. There were key points where he stopped and snuffled around dramatically before continuing around the scene. One spot near the gate Duke spent more than a minute following the scents. Finally he followed the fight path to and from the gate a few times before also examining the steel gate where the Nhia-Samri had pounded on it in frustration.

Duke looked around. There were a number of people watching the event with interest. Duke called out, "Alpha and Echo Commanders, front and center!"

Elades jumped down into the alley, past another of his men, who was concealed in the shadows watching the alleyway diligently. Once down, he walked out to Duke, around the fight area, which everyone was under orders to not cross for any reason. Echo's commander, Sonnua, was coming up the street.

As they came to Duke, Elades took command as was appropriate, answering for both squads. "Sir."

Duke glanced curiously at the bird in Elades's hand for a moment. "Commander, evacuate the vicinity for a space of three blocks in all directions. Pay what is needed to compensate business owners. I want three detachments of guards made ready. Place one of those detachments on the perimeter here. They are under orders to not allow anyone to re-enter, but not to raise arms to anyone who refuses or who exits after the evacuation. They are to take careful note and request firmly a piece of clothing, hat, or coat to be returned later of anyone exiting late or re-entering. Again, they are not to raise arms if refused, just take careful note. Bravo Squad to assemble at the center square with the other two detachments. Elades, remain here; and Sonnua, please attend to this."

Elades turned and signaled for Alpha to remain on guard while Sonnua started giving orders to the guards present.

Elades turned back to Duke, holding out the bird. "Sir, I found this in route." Holding out the small paper and canister in his other hand, he added, "It had this."

"Feed me the bird."

Elades tossed the bird in the air and Duke snapped it like a dog catching a tasty morsel from the table. Duke chewed it whole for a few moments, then swallowed. "Not bad. Mash and corn fed, definitely a prized bird. Give that message to Ladro, with orders to make a copy for the royal scribes and for Delta's commander to decipher."

Elades smiled. *Yes, let's see if the Nhia-Samri agents will feed us good or bad intelligence. I wondered when we were going to deal with them. But they have done a good job so far, nothing even out of order, other than paying a little too much attention to other units' orders.*

Duke looked around as the guards were escorting everyone from the various buildings, making sure they walked down the side of the main roads and out of the area. "Elades, give me your hand."

Elades held out his hand and Duke sniffed it carefully. "Good. Also, have anyone else involved with that fight come here immediately."

He signaled for Alpha to report in individually. Over the next twenty minutes Duke took a good smell of every single member of Alpha Squad. By the time he was done the streets were completely silent. Duke motioned for Elades to remain still and sat in the middle of the empty street with his head held high. Although Duke's eyes were closed his ears rotated back and forth rapidly. Once or twice his head would snap around in a direction with his ears perked in the same direction like a pointer dog. *He's waiting for something or someone. But, what? The area is evacuated.*

Duke stood with his head pointing up at one of the buildings down the street, which looked like a rich merchant's home. "Alpha, deer hunt!"

Duke burst forward like a released arrow, straight at the building, while a dozen Daggers came out of the alleys all around and ran at top speed in the direction Duke was heading. Elades felt his heart rate jump and he followed Duke as fast as he could. Duke didn't bother heading for the main door; he ran right at the building. When he was ten feet away, he leaped high into the air, bursting through a lower window. Three other Daggers, with Elades, ran right up under the window and then partially up the wall, managing to grab the window ledge. From there they pulled themselves up and followed Duke inside.

Elades swung himself into the library with a kick. Landing, he rolled, coming up to a fighting stance and drawing his daggers. Duke had barreled through the library, knocking a table and some large chairs out of his way and crashing through the closed double doors. Elades checked that the three others were up and ready. He smiled when he recognized his second, Idanas, as well as Nullo Sidurson and his brother Essen—his best knife fighters—were the three with him. Together, the four of them followed Duke at a cautious run.

Through the doors was a large, round, two-story room with stairs going up both sides. Duke ran through the middle and jumped up, just clearing the banister to land half-way up the stairs. Elades signaled for two to follow Duke and Nullo to stay with him. Together they ran left and then up the nearer stairs. Idanas and Essen ran across the room to follow Duke up the far stairs. All four of them reached the top together. From the first floor the front and back doors crashed loudly as they were kicked in by the rest of the squad.

Duke turned right, towards the street, barking loudly, "First floor alley-side, second floor street-side," at the top of the stairs, then barreled through a set of large white double doors. Duke's growls sounded like a whole wolf pack. Below the sounds of more fighting could be heard. Elades waved Idanas and Essen off to a pair of doors to the left of the ones Duke had forced; then he and Nullo dove into the room where Duke was already fighting.

There were three Nhia-Samri in what looked like a spacious sun room, with large windows overlooking the gate and street. All three were dressed simply, but had odassi blades out and were circling Duke cautiously. Duke dove at one, who dodged out of the way, while the other two tried to spear him. One of them managed to stab Duke. Duke grunted with pain and twisted around, pulling the attacker off-balance as his blade was stuck in Duke's side. Duke's teeth succeeded in grabbing the end of his attacker's leg, which was all Duke needed to yanked the warrior around; Elades had to admire the guy's tenacity as he didn't yell out or panic instead he tried to stick his other knife into Duke's head.

Duke saw the coming attack and yanked his head around hanging on to the guy's leg. The Nhia-Samri was whipped around violently, like a doll. The Nhia-Samri must have had a death grip on his blades; the one stuck in Duke's side was ripped out, causing a spray of blood that arced around Duke, following the sword.

Elades stepped up to Duke's wounded side and blocked a second attack by the remaining Nhia-Samri on that side. They exchanged a rapid series of knife thrusts and parries. On the other side of Duke the sound of another knife fight told Elades that Nullo had engaged the third Nhia-Samri. Exchanging knife strike after knife strike, he fought his opponent. They circled each other and Elades saw that Duke was slamming the one he had up and down on the floor, turning him into nothing more than a bloody pulp of a man. Duke flung the pulped man out of the window into the street and turned to Elades's opponent.

Duke made a snap for Elades's opponent, which forced the Nhia-Samri to dodge. That gave the opening Elades had been waiting for. Elades swiped his dagger at the Nhia-Samri's neck with all his entire strength behind it, half decapitating the man. Blood sprayed out and over Elades and Duke as the Nhia-Samri fell.

Not pausing, Elades turned and jumped over Duke's tail to the other side of the room where Nullo had been cut on his arm and leg but was still fighting the Nhia-Samri there. Duke's ears twisted toward the hall, he barked and launched out of the room, giving them more space to fight. Elades stepped in and attempted a double-cut strike at the Nhia-Samri's head, which he blocked, leaving his lower belly open. Nullo didn't hesitate, plunging both of his knives into the Nhia-Samri's gut. The Nhia-Samri tried to cut down on his killer, but Elades quickly parried the attack and kicked him backwards off of Nullo's blades to fall by the window.

Grinning, they turned and followed the sound of fighting to another room where Duke was standing on one Nhia-Samri's arms, pinning him down, while snapping at another who was trying to get Duke off. The Nhia-Samri who was pinned was ineffectively kicking Duke as hard as he could from below. But Duke ignored it. Two other Nhia-Samri were fighting Essen and Idanas individually. Nullo jumped into the fight to aid his brother. Elades whipped his dagger at the Nhia-Samri who was attacking Duke. His dagger imbedded into the Nhia-Samri's throat, making him fall backwards into a chair, landing in such a way as to look asleep except for the dagger sticking out of his throat and the blood running down his front.

The distraction gone, Duke growled. Looking down, he turned his head sideways to take the whole pinned Nhia-Samri's head into his mouth. The Nhia-Samri screamed as he saw the wolf's teeth coming down. Duke bit down hard, crushing the skull and cutting off the man's scream. Duke, still holding the head, pulled upwards with a twisting motion, ripping the man's head right off his body. Duke spun, slinging the head out the window into the street.

Nullo and Essen had finished off the Nhia-Samri they were dealing with and were turning to help Idanas. Except that Idanas performed a masterful triple-cut maneuver, ending in a down strike that cut the Nhia-Samri open from neck to waist. The Nhia-Samri fell back, screaming, as his blood and guts burst from his opened front. Essen ended the Nhia-Samri's suffering with a rapid cut to the neck, which partially decapitated him.

Duke looked them over and smiled, "you can't control who comes into your life, but you can pick the window you through them out of."

Idanas nodded and grinned madly at Duke then turned and jogged out of the room with Essen following and went down the stairs. Duke turned and listened intently for a moment. Then he sat down; licking his lips clean he turned to licking his wounds. "Good way to start. I think they got a signal off, warning the others."

Nullo, who had been examining his wounds, looked at Duke, surprised. "Did you expect to have the element of surprise?"

Duke looked at him and then laughed. "Well, now that you mention it I had hoped for it. But you're right, not likely to happen anyways."

Elades looked at the wound on Duke's side. It wasn't very long and it had stopped bleeding. But he knew it had been deep stab. "Will you need medical attention?"

Duke stood up and shook like a wet dog, sending blood droplets everywhere. "No, it is already healing. Let's get back to the gate and continue this hunt. I want to kill more Nhia-Samri today if possible."

As they exited, Idanas came and reported four other Nhia-Samri had been killed on the first floor and the house was clear. They left Idanas with one team to search the house for intelligence, not expecting to get any, and then walked back to the gate.

Duke stepped up to the edge of the scene and sat down, looking at the street as if reading a book. "Run me through the events as you have assembled them again."

Elades provided a narrative of the complete fight, pointing at various locations as he went through the events. Duke didn't interrupt but looked hard at each place Elades pointed to. After he was finished Duke thought for a bit. "Elades, did you see Ticca ride over this Nhia-Samri?"

"No, sir, but I have the description from nine separate witnesses to the event."

"Damn! That had to have been a hell of a maneuver to pull off. You came to the fight after they had already been fighting for at least three minutes?"

"More like five, sir. I cannot be sure, but that is what I feel is about right from the descriptions."

"Ticca fought this guy head-to-head for five minutes before your squad got here. Then four of your squad tried to hit him with thrown knives, which he avoided, while still trying to kill Ticca. By your reports she only started Daggering six cycles ago. That is a pretty damned good performance for one so young and inexperienced. Any chance he was letting her go, just making it feel hard for her?"

"I don't think so, sir, unless he was an unbelievably good actor; he desperately wanted to kill her. Five of us engaged him long enough to let Ticca break away, but he walked over us and gave chase. I tell you there was rage and hate in his eyes. I truly believe he wanted to kill her and he went practically berserk when the gate cut him off from her. He shouted some pretty intense oaths while he pounded on the closed gate with his knives. If he was acting for her benefit, that wouldn't have been needed. By that time all of Alpha Squad was present and we still couldn't stop him, sir. He fought as fast and hard with all of us as he did with Ticca; if he was any better he'd have had an easier time getting away from us. I am seriously impressed with her speed and knife skills. She is better than any of us."

Duke was staring at the gate as they spoke. "Did they say anything? Especially Ticca?"

"The Nhia-Samri asked her who she was. She didn't answer him." Thinking back, Elades concentrated. "You know, I think she did say something."

Duke looked at him. "What did she say exactly, Elades?"

Elades thought about it, making the moment clear in his head. Ticca had run and jumped up the five feet to the top of the closing gate. The Nhia-Samri lightly wounded him and a couple of his squad. He had knocked them aside and started to run for the gate. Ticca had reached the far side and did a jumping half twist flip, landing ready to fight. She didn't look happy that the Nhia-Samri was already giving chase. She then exasperatedly called out for the gate to hurry up and close.

"Sir, she said, 'Damn it, close already!' from the far side of the gate."

Duke looked at him. "Are you sure?"

Elades nodded and Duke turned back to the gate. He said something and the gate smoothly slid open. Then he said something else and the gate began slowly closing. When it had reached about five feet high Duke looked at Elades. "Commander, please say it the way Ticca did."

"Damn it, close already!"

The gate continued its slow, steady rise.

After a few moments Duke said, "Damn it, close already!"

The gate snapped shut in the blink of an eye, slamming so hard that more of the loosened masonry was launched into the air to fall down at random. Duke yelped in surprise, jumping backwards at the sudden motion and the immense thunderclap it caused. Elades, having witnessed this before, still jumped at the sound as well. They both looked up and saw the incoming masonry and dodged the falling rocks. When the rain of rock had ended, Duke sat down and looked at the gate in genuine surprise, his mouth open. "Well that is a new one. Hell, that isn't in any of the texts. I wonder which fucking idiot added that ability. Now I have to test every damned city. I wonder what other inspirational commands that idiot allowed for."

Elades was a bit confused, but he knew that wasn't unusual for working with Duke.

Duke looked down. "We have a serious problem. New standing orders: if Ticca comes back, do not oppose her in anything, and I need to know every move she makes."

"Yes sir. Who is she?"

"That is a good question, and we are not the only ones asking it. There are several possibilities, and some of them worry me greatly. Especially since it was either her scent, or our man in green, that I followed from Vestul's death-site to the Dolphin. There were only two key scents where Vestul died, besides that of Vestul himself." Duke turned around, putting his back to the gate. "Now back to our business. Whatever she is up to she'll deal with it. I have some Nhia-Samri to deal with presently. Let me see that cloth you have stored."

Elades went over to a doorway belonging to an empty house, where they had locked up the ripped clothing from the Nhia-Samri while trying to grab him. Elades was glad senior Daggers had been here with him as they knew enough to not touch the cloth too much and to keep it sealed. Just inside the doorway were three large steel bowls from a nearby bakery with inverted bowls on top as covers. He carefully picked up the first set of bowls so as to not disturb the cover, and placed them on the ground in front of Duke. Duke exhaled deeply bent down and pushing the top bowl off breathed in deeply through his nose. He then stuck his nose right into the cloth and whiffled through his nose as he moved the rags around with his snout.

"Damn it! It was Ticca I followed from Vestul's body to the Dolphin. This guy was nowhere near there. That is NOT what I expected. What the hell is going on here? This guy attacked Ticca at the Dolphin, was ridden over by a horse, jumped up on that horse, pulled Ticca off of it, and they both landed like a circus act and fought like devils for over five minutes. But for what and why?" Duke put his nose down and walked back and forth around the area, snuffling like a bloodhound. He stopped where the two Nhia-Samri, along with the one in green, had fallen. "Uh huh, well now, that means that these two are his accomplices."

"We have their clothing as well, sir."

Duke looked up. "I was going to ask for those next, but first I want to make sure I am in top shape for this. I don't think we'll get a second chance here. I believe I have them pretty clearly. Bring out their clothing so I can confirm this."

Elades went back to the same house and brought back two other sets of bowls. Duke scented from them. "Yep, that is exactly what I predicted from the scene. I'll call him target B. This one is what I expected too, he'll be target C. Of course our man in green, who is definitely a senior officer, will be target A. OK, that confirms everything is working as good as ever and I know everyone involved. But, none of these Nhia-Samri were the other scent I got at Vestul's assassination location. We are still missing one player here. I need answers. So time for a good old-fashioned hunt."

With that Duke began moving back and forth, up and down roads and alleys. He didn't leave immediately, but went to the roofs by jumping on smaller buildings and then up on larger ones. After carefully examining their structures, he finally jumped down.

"We have been observed; I have a couple of other scents to key on. Which means they'll be ready. Once we have left the area you can let people back in. Have the guards keep things peaceful. Send word to Bravo that once I engage they are to fish hunt as fast as possible. I would prefer if it was within five minutes."

"Shouldn't we just have everyone with us, sir?"

"No—there is an entry point at the city center that I have briefed them on." With that, Duke stuck his nose down and started down the alleyway the Nhia-Samri had fled though after breaking away. Duke ran with speed, only stopping occasionally to spend some time moving back and forth on major streets. The Nhia-Samri was not stupid. He spent a great deal of time crossing back and forth on busy streets. He had to have picked up a cloak someplace to hide his bloody and ripped clothing.

Duke moved with confidence down streets and alleys; however, eventually he stopped. He then moved back and forth many times at an alley entrance. "This has been cleaned. There is a chemical agent I don't know here, I can still smell it. It isn't dry yet. Two guards here, no one is allowed out. Anyone may come in. I want guards below in the Delivery Channel at this point too, with the same orders." Duke howled like a hound on the track and then ran with speed up and down streets and alleyways, making it difficult for the Daggers to keep up. He would stop and call out, "Pair of guards here and below! No one is allowed out!" He would then run back. Eventually there was a six-block square, around which a new perimeter had been established. The sun was setting but Duke didn't stop, and he kept howling from time to time. He began carefully moving up and down through the area. Occasionally he would stop and spend a lot of time snuffling a section of the streets. He never varied from his pattern. He also howled seemingly at random.

A number of people became very upset when they were not allowed out. However, a Dagger quickly showed up and explained by whose order they were being detained, which generally made everyone decide to patiently wait.

Finally Duke had finished with every street and alley in the six-block area. The sun was fully gone from the sky and twilight was just ending. Duke sat down near one of the main entry points through the area. "Commander, more guards—I want this entire area sealed. Anyone can leave, if they strip down to nothing. Nothing, and I mean nothing, is allowed out of this area. Order some basic clothing for anyone leaving. They are only allowed to wear a shirt and pants we provide out. If they don't like that there are a number of empty houses where they can sleep. Bring food and drink for everyone."

Duke walked away from the perimeter guards and directly across the park square. He knocked loudly on the door of a medium-sized house which commanded a view of the blockade. The house had a small yard and a full carriage circle in front. When a butler opened the door, Duke just pushed past him, yelling, "Everyone out, go find an Inn, I am using this place tonight!"

A rich merchant stepped out of the library with a book in one hand a glass of amber liquid in the other, and an annoyed look on his face. He took one look at Duke, however, and made no argument. He ran, calling to his wife to bring the children as they were going out immediately. His wife came down the stairs, yelling at him, asking if he had lost his mind. When she saw Duke sitting in the main entry, she screamed and ran back up the stairs. After that it only took a few minutes before the entire house was completely abandoned. As the merchant left, he bowed deeply to Duke. "Excellency, please help yourself—there is wine and excellent meat in the larder. We shall find lodging until you are satisfied."

Duke smiled, "You are generous and I will; however, do not hesitate to send a bill to my home for any damages or replacement foods. I need a command post near the fight." Duke then turned and used his tail to sweep everything in the room to a corner, breaking a number of statues. "Commander, get his dining table and bring it here, empty. Send a message to Ladro saying that I am hungry and tired and need my maps of Llino here as soon as possible. I want all team leads for Alpha, Bravo, and Echo here in one mark. Also, double the guards on the upper and lower perimeter; call in Charlie and Delta if needed to provide some relief. I want rotating Daggers checking every point of entry at least every twenty minutes."

With that he lay down on the side of the room and put his paws in the air, closing his eyes. Within a few minutes Duke was snoring while men rushed around to fulfill his commands. In one mark everything had been accomplished. The team leads all stood around the main room while Duke continued to snore. Ladro had brought some of Duke's staff and the maps had been placed on the table. There was also a long stick like a fishing rod with two belted leather hoops attached near one end.

Elades was considering if he should wake Duke when like a clock striking the mark Duke made a snuffling sneeze, rolled over, sat up and started looked at the maps as if he had been doing it for some time. "Listen up. The area has been heavily cleaned of all scents. Although very effective, I could still make out a point or two, but nothing definitive. Either this is new, or perhaps this is the first time I got to them before that agent fully dissipated, which is more likely."

Echo lead asked, "Do we go door-to-door then and raise the whole area?"

"No, there is a bit of a surprise here. Ticca was through here too. In fact she spent a lot of time wall-hugging." Slipping his paw into the two hoops on the rod Duke bit the leather tips and pulled them tight. He then used the stick like any military commander used a pointing stick. Slapping the map at a precise location with the tip of the stick, he said, "Ticca came into the area here." He then moved the point along a route straight to a point near the middle of the area. "She went up to here and spent a great deal of time circling this house." He pointed at a large house that fronted one of the many park squares in the city. "She then exited by the same route she came in. She did not approach the house."

The commanders looked at the map with interest. Elades pointed at an alley near the house where a doorway into the house was indicated. "You howled three times here. Why?"

"Nice catch. Every time I howled I had target A's scent. He has been all over this area, especially on the path towards the Dolphin. I was howling to scare the crap out of any damned Nhia-Samri who were watching. I wanted them to know I had a hit. I suspect they know where they have been and so were able to understand my warning taunts."

Echo lead asked, "Won't that eliminate our element of surprise?"

Duke looked at the men. "Commanders, do you really think we are going to surprise them?" Elades chuckled and Duke gave him a 'stop it' look.

Everyone looked serious at that. Many shook their heads 'no.'

"So this is going to be a direct attack?"

Duke smiled. "Oh yes, yes indeed. I want to kill every single one of them. No one gets away this time." He pointed at places around the house. "They will be sneaking people out to attack us from behind. All units will hold at the edges of the perimeter except for two teams, which will be split in these locations. I will attack first. When I call for aid, one squad at a time will enter. This will flush them all out except for those who have been ordered to hide. Once we are finished, we will burn everything for two blocks around that house. That will flush out any hidden Nhia-Samri. Bravo, you will stop anyone trying to escape using the Delivery Channel. When we are finished you are going to send two teams to do a fish hunt under that house. There will be a sealed trunk someplace on the bottom within this perimeter. I want the contents of that chest captured. It will be booby-trapped, so be careful. Once opened you will take everything out, being careful to not touch it with bare hands; use cloth gloves only, which are to be thrown into the water when done. You will secure some lead weights so they won't jiggle and place a single sheet of paper with a dictation I will give you later into the trunk and then put it back where you found it. We attack at dawn."

Duke looked around while everyone pondered the plan and orders. When no one had any questions Duke said, "Excellent. Now, get to work. Tell everyone to be well-rested and to eat lightly tonight. Dismissed. Ladro, dinner please."

Elades coordinated much of the logistics. Once everything was lined up he found a quiet corner and got a few marks' sleep. Ladro woke him. "Duke is up." Rising, he did some quick stretches and joined the growing number of people in the entry-hall-turned-command-room. Duke was reviewing last minute details with the Bravo Squad Commander as Elades walked up.

Duke didn't even look around to see who it was. "Elades, Charlie Squad is going to back up Echo and maintain the perimeter. Grab some food from the next room and some arit if you want. We'll have final briefing in fifteen."

Turning into the dining room, he saw some other tables had been brought in and the staff was making breakfast sandwiches along with a selection of fruits and drinks. Grabbing an egg sandwich from the platter, he poured a cup of arit and ate quickly. Stepping back out, he saw that all the leads were present.

Duke looked at him and nodded. "Dawn is in two marks. Twilight needs to have zero movement. Even though they know we are coming, there is no need to advertise where everything will be. I have moved some people around based on injuries and manpower needs. The plan is still the same. Any questions?"

Everyone shook their heads no. Duke nodded. "Come." Duke stepped outside and in the street all the Dagger squads were assembled, except for a few who were on patrol. Elades looked at them proudly. Duke stood, looking at them all in the eyes. On both sides of the street beyond the Daggers were two full detachments of city guards. The night was made as bright as day on the street and courtyard by dozens of lamps.

Duke yelled, "Daggers! Now it is time to demonstrate once again what we are. These Nhia-Samri have betrayed the kingdoms time and time again. They are bloody mercenaries who work for the nefarious cause of that little bastard, their Grand Commander. We have proved to them once before that they are our inferiors. They have not forgotten that, for now they hide in shadows, afraid to show us they are here."

Duke paused as the Daggers and guards yelled support to his last statement. Looking over the crowd he continued, "They took coin to assassinate the last true heirs to the thrones." The Daggers and guards yelled out at that. Many drew their weapons and held them at the ready. Duke grinned wolfishly. "This is war! Remember, the object of war is not to die for your cause but to make the other bastards die for theirs! *Semper Fidelis!*"

The Daggers, as one, held their daggers high and yelled: "SEMPER FIDELIS!"

Duke nodded, then yelled, smiling, "What the hell are you doing still standing there? Get back to work!" The Daggers broke and moved in many directions at once, as the leads launched from the small guest platform to coordinate. Elades had taken advantage of command to be in one of the teams that would directly cover Duke; from the beginning he stood his place. Duke watched as some Daggers had to stop moving to order the guards to their stations. Duke shook his head. "Commander, if I had two full divisions like these Dagger squads I could take this war straight to Hisuru Amajoo now and win. Go get your two teams in place."

"Yes sir. We'll be there."

"I know you will."

Elades jogged over to where his two fire teams were waiting. "Time to earn our coin." They nodded and moved silently into the blockaded area. It took almost a half mark to get into positions. Elades looked over the quiet street and the simple house. It was large two-story house with its main entrance on Silver Street. There as a perfect front yard and nice patio with a covered carriage platform in the front. It only had a small, three-foot-tall white fence. The front doors were very large stained-glass doors which Duke could easily walk through. The windows all had whitewashed shutters; the whole house looked like some picturesque, perfect example of what a rich merchant would own.

The pre-dawn twilight came and the front doors opened. One man dressed in the loose garb and armor of a Nhia-Samri officer with his knives in the cloth belt stepped out. He wore red-painted armor plates with a black helmet which rose to a point. His feet were bare and behind him stood row after row of Nhia-Samri, also wearing their traditional armor.

The officer walked out boldly to the middle of the front yard where he was completely exposed. He held his hand up and the waiting Nhia-Samri marched out of the house, forming five ranks, four wide by four deep, directly behind the red-painted officer. One Nhia-Samri in the front right corner of each rank held a square banner with some symbol on it. On the front left corner of each rank stood a Nhia-Samri officer with a distinctive armor pattern and coloring.

The Nhia-Samri commander yelled, "Duke, I know you are out there. Come forth!"

Duke's voice came out of the distance, "OK, we'll do it that way. Hang on a second; I am not getting younger, you know." After a few minutes Duke appeared, slowly sauntering down Silver Street. Behind him were the four squads of Daggers in a loose formation. The Nhia-Samri waited, but Elades could see that the officer frowned at the obvious insult of having to wait. Duke eventually got to the middle of the square, where he looked behind him. "Wait here boys, I have to deal with this upstart." The Daggers filed out into general ranks as Duke walked up to the house and pushed open the gate—which was not locked or barred—and walked up, sitting down in front of the officer. Duke was wearing a mantle of office in the form of a golden collar of linked plates which joined in a V over his chest, where the collar connected to an emblem made of a single large emerald. He also had a pouch over one shoulder and what looked like a silver sack tied to it. Looking over the assembled Nhia-Samri, he said, "Ah yes, I see you are ready to surrender. You don't have anyone shivering hidden in a dark hole someplace?"

The officer frowned deeper. "No, Duke, do not insult us. You know we do not surrender; however, we have not yet begun hostilities.

Therefore there remains the possibility of peaceful settlement."

Duke licked his chops. "Actually I think we started hostilities pretty formally when your man attacked our citizens." Duke twisted his neck to pull the silver sack from his pouch and tossed it at the feet of the Nhia-Samri officer. The officer bent down and opened the sack, looking into it with an expression of anger and horror. Duke casually added, "Plus yesterday I chewed the head off your gate-watching outpost commander. Doesn't that count?"

The officer straightened and looked at Duke with outrage and a mix of something else Elades couldn't identify. "What is the meaning of this, Duke? Why do you insult us so boldly and force the conflict?"

Duke looked at him squarely. "You killed one of mine. One whom you knew was off-limits. Your own petty bastard Grand Warlord killed another one of mine, and the last heir to the realms, in exchange for a trinket that would no longer work. You are up to something, and I am going to find out what it is. Your choice is surrender all you know and I will let you walk out of here alive with your armor, weapons, and provisions to get you back to Hisuru Amajoo. You can carry a message from me that the Nhia-Samri have exactly four cycles to abandon every outpost, every station, every tie to the realms because after that time I will hunt them just as you hunted the orcs to extinction. If you do not accept my offer I will begin my hunt with you and yours; and your heads with my message stuffed in every mouth, and every odassi, broken, will be sent to Hisuru Amajoo. Either way you will carry my message to the bastard Shar-Lumen."

The Nhia-Samri officer actually staggered backward a little at Duke's declaration. He never once took his eyes from Duke's. After a moment Duke asked, "What is your decision?"

The officer straightened standing taller. "Either way we are likely dead. There is no surrender, no compromise. One path holds honor, the other disgrace. You leave me no choice. The Nhia-Samri are absolute. Do you desire time to prepare?"

Duke used his front paw to tap the emerald. The mantle dropped off, and as he bowed his head allowing the pouch to fall beside it. He then stood and did what could only be a described as a bow to the officer. "So be it. No, I do not."

The officer returned the bow and drew his odassi. Duke launched at him, but he dove under and rolled back to his feet while striking at Duke's underside with one of the blades. The blade slide through Duke's fur but had no effect. Duke landed and spun, diving low, trying to get the officer's legs. The officer danced out of the way, stabbing out. Duke twisted, preventing the stabs from making contact. The officer leapt at Duke before the wolf could come fully around. This time a blade managed to strike into Duke's back shanks.

Duke growled. "First blood is yours. Last blood will be mine!" He spun and nipped at the officer, who was forced to dodge; Duke predicted the dodge and adjusted for it. His teeth managed to grab part of the officer's armor. Duke flipped his head and the officer was thrown five feet to land in a pile. Duke spun and lunged at the pile. The officer tried to roll out of the way, but Duke was too fast and trapped the officer's arms under his front paws, just as he had done the day prior at the gate.

Duke yelled, "For Vestul and the Realms!" Biting down, he ripped the officer's head off by the exposed neck.

With the death of their officer the Nhia-Samri screamed as one, drawing their odassi and rushing Duke. Duke leapt high and over one whole rank, yelling, "Daggers! Do you want to live forever? Get to work!" *Not exactly the codes we agreed on, but what plan ever survives the first engagement?* "All Daggers attack!"

Four squads of Daggers rolled forward, screaming and drawing weapons. The two waves met loosely on the street and park directly in front of the house. Knives sang everywhere; Daggers and Nhia-Samri fought viciously. Duke spun, grabbing a Nhia-Samri by the arm and throwing him into a group of others. Duke didn't waste any time, he dove right after him, yelling, "Hey, I'm not done with you yet!" Duke bowled over ten Nhia-Samri who tried to cut and stab him, but he danced around them, stepping on chests and heads like a prancing war horse. Ten more Nhia-Samri lunged as one against Duke before any other Daggers could get there. The wolf howled with pain and instinctively bit at what had hurt him. A Nhia-Samri lost his arm to that bite, but he stabbed again with the other. Duke jumped aside; picking up one of the ones from the ground and using him like a club, he smashed the one-armed Nhia-Samri away.

All of the Daggers attacked in groups of three to each one Nhia-Samri, as ordered. The technique worked very well. Nhia-Samri were falling at a tremendous rate, but so were the Daggers. In the distance Elades saw some people leaving the house rapidly, carrying boxes. "Echo! Get the escapers! Don't lose what they are carrying!"

Twelve Daggers jumped out of combat and gave chase. Elades fought with Nulla and Essen; they killed Nhia-Samri after Nhia-Samri. Still the fight went on. Looking around, he saw that at least two dozen Daggers were down. Duke was dealing with six Nhia-Samri by himself; it looked like there were six Daggers downed there too. "Duke's lost his support, move it!" They tried to force their way to Duke, but the numbers were just too much. It took too long. Duke had dozens of wounds and was bleeding profusely by the time they got to him, but still he fought on.

The Daggers rallied around Duke. The Nhia-Samri on Duke were obviously the better fighters, it was hard to get past their guard. Duke yelled in frustration, "You don't hurt 'em if you don't hit 'em. Merge six-to-one! Don't worry about me!"

With that he rolled over a pair but they stabbed him deeply and he fell. Another Nhia-Samri sliced Duke's side open as he fell. The Daggers all screamed. Teams began fighting harder and harder. The Nhia-Samri were down to about a quarter of their original number, but the last ones where tough and half of the Daggers had fallen as well. Elades cut across one, who managed to parry as Nulla stabbed him. Turning, they tried to attack the back of a group of three Nhia-Samri who were covering each other. "Two more sets here, now!" Some other Daggers joined the fight, but they couldn't get in. Daggers were beginning to fall faster than Nhia-Samri.

Elades tried to coordinate some of the chaos, but it was looking like it might be a toss which side would win. A loud outcry was heard. Elades looked over and it looked like every street and alley was disgorging guards, and at their lead was Lord Dohma. The guards screamed and dove into the fight. Dohma and three other guards joined Elades' group. "Lord Dohma, you need to not be here."

"I outrank you, Commander. I serve the realm. Now kill these bastards, damn it!" With that his blades fairly flew, as well as Nulla's, and the Nhia-Samri were finally losing the fight. One of the three guards with Lord Dohma fell. The other two guards, grinning madly and fighting expertly, were both killing Nhia-Samri warriors and protecting Lord Dohma. *Those are some well-trained guards. I didn't realize the weapons training they got included that kind of hand-to-hand fighting.* Blood flowed freely, making the ground slippery, and the gutters were filled with the red liquid of life. The last of Nhia-Samri fell, with ten guardsmen on him, including the two that had been with Lord Dohma.

Before the last Nhia-Samri hit the ground, dozens of green-robed healers and even more white-robed acolytes from the Temple of Dalpha had appeared; they began treating the wounded guards and Daggers. Elades saw the High Priestess come down the street carrying the Light of Dalpha, which glowed like the sun. Next to her was a beautiful woman in a green dress and cream blouse who looked more a princess than a healer. The High Priestess started responding to cries from her healers and moved with great speed, carrying the Light of Dalpha where needed, bathing the wounded in a bright glow of energies. The princess like woman was also a magical healer; she moved as fast as the High Priestess, bending and touching the indicated fallen Dagger or guard with her bare hand which glowed for a moment before running to the next in need.

Lord Dohma was lending a hand to the healers and was being guarded by a Dagger and three guards. Elades looked for Lord Dohma's two personal guards from earlier, as he wanted to congratulate them, but he couldn't see them. Looking over the field of bodies, Elades saw that Duke was not moving and ran over to his fallen body. Feeling the wolf's bloody side, he found a faint pulse, but Duke was bleeding from dozens of wounds and a two foot long open cut on his side was peeled back revealing bones and muscles while blood poured out like a river to the ground. "Duke needs help!"

The strange woman in the simple green dress rushed over. She ran her hands over Duke's bloody sides and even stuck her hand into the deep cut which went down his side. She looked worried and then glanced at Elades for a moment. Her large eyes took on a determined look and she turned back to Duke speaking very softly into the wolf's ears. "Oh Duke, beloved of Argos. There is need too soon to wait." She knelt and embraced the great wolf's bloody neck in a hug. Her hands and arms glowed with a soft green light which spread over the whole of Duke's body. Duke's larger open wounds closed before his eyes. *Lord she is the most powerful healer I have ever heard of!*

Duke's head lifted slightly and he groaned. "Did I drink too much again? I have an awful headache." His eyes were glazed slightly, and as he looked at the girl his eyebrows furrowed together. "Dalpha, where's the aspirin? And why'd you change your hair?" Then Duke's eyes closed and his head slumped to the ground but the wolf was breathing deeply as if sleeping.

The woman smiled at Duke and then shakily stood looking at Elades with her deep emerald eyes. She looked very pale and her legs seemed unsteady. "Worry not, he'll be a little mobile in a few days and normal within two or three weeks." She turned and started to walk away, her legs wobbled unsteadily as she moved off.

Elades noticed that her clothes, arms, and hands were still perfectly clean. "Who are you?"

"A healer, of course," she answered over her shoulder.

Elades looked at Duke and then back, but she was gone. *Damn! People are vanishing a lot today.* He looked around and couldn't see her anywhere. *Who in the Lord's name was that? Damn it! I hate dealing with holy types! Sorry, Lord.*

Duke's nose started twitching like it itched. Duke mumbled "Blood?" His head rolled slightly upright and he opened his eyes. His eyes were clearer and he looked around not moving his head but sniffing deeply. Duke's eyes slowly cleared and he raised his head to get a better view. "Oh ya, the fight. Commander, report."

Elades couldn't help it, he felt relieved to see Duke was going to be OK. He stepped up to his commander and placed his hand reassuringly on Duke's shoulder. Elades looked around before answering. "Casualties— many; number of dead—not known; combat efficiency—we won."

"Good boys. Now burn it all down. There will be nothing but traps there. Collect all the heads and odassi. Don't handle the odassi with anything other than thick-gloved hands. Make sure to keep the commander's head and odassi separate. I'm going to take a little nap now." With that Duke put his head down on the bloody ground and closed his eyes once more. Elades heard Duke softly chuckle and say "yep, that should about do it. Bet they remember me now."

Delivering The Message

CHAPTER 14

JOURNEYS BEGIN WITH A STEP

"**M**ILORD, HIS EXCELLENCY REQUESTS YOUR presence."

Dohma looked up from the papers his sister had been showing him. The valet before him wore Duke's livery but was very young. He was short, with a perfectly soft, smooth face with the friendly happy smile of a child raised in a good home. The boy's name popped into his head on cue. "Of course, Brolle, I'll attend at once." Dohma handed the papers back to his sister, grinning. "Duty calls, Sis." She frowned at him as he stood, stretching. *Any excuse for getting away from paperwork. I can't see how my brother and sister can spend all day looking at papers.* Moving to follow the boy he asked, "Is he up yet?"

"No, milord. His appetite returns but he still has pains when he moves."

Brolle lead him out of the palace and down the main road to Duke's residence. *Hard to believe it has only been three weeks since I walked this very path with guards at my back to order Duke to the palace. Now I give the orders and Duke is a trusted friend.* Duke's guards opened the residence's gate on cue so that he didn't have to break stride.

The courtyard was a very busy place. Two new hay carts had been shined and polished, their sides replaced with a fine-grained wood, oiled and rubbed to a beautiful rich look. The wheels had been painted a glossy black with red trim. If it weren't for the gruesome materials being carefully arranged on the first cart he might have taken it for a party cart for an extravagant celebration. Instead, one cart was being loaded with the severed heads of the Nhia-Samri after a slip of paper had been rolled and inserted into each of their mouths.

The second cart held just as strange a sight. Four blacksmiths had been called in and instructed to use their thickest gloves in handling the odassi blades. They worked in pairs. Each blade was carefully lifted by one blacksmith and held in an exact position on an anvil. The second blacksmith would then position one of the commander's odassi at a specific angle so the angled straight-edge at the tip was squarely across a symbol on a copper band that was at the base of the odassi blade. Then the two blacksmiths would look at each other to be sure each was ready. Finally the one holding the commander's odassi would strike the back of the blade with a hammer, driving the commander's blade through the copper band. The effects of this were dramatic to say the least. The commander's blade would spark and glow red; the second blade would make a sound not unlike a cry of pain. Fire would explode from the symbol and the copper band would snap open; the blade fractured in a perfect line down the middle. When complete, the commander's blade looked as if nothing happened. The other blade was split, and the copper band remained attached but with its edges curled outward. The broken blade would be placed in the cart reverently and then the process repeated. On the side of the yard were some other tools Duke had special-ordered, which would be used to break the band of the commander's last blade when the last odassi band had been split.

Not really sure what it is about those blades, but seeing this I am not sure if I should be more afraid of them or that Duke knew how to do this. The boy ran ahead a little to open the door for him. Once again he walked through the beautiful foyer, which was a complete contrast to the scene in the yard. Following where the page pointed, he walked to another set of doors, which the page jumped ahead and opened for him. Stepping through the doors, he was in a grand hallway that lead to Duke's private rooms. He marveled again at the size of the doors and the unique large handles that would allow Duke to open and close them himself if he wanted to. *Everything in this place is scaled to Duke, which makes it just grand by design.* Two guards were stationed at both ends of the hall as well as a pair flanking the large double doors to Duke's sitting room. A guard quickly opened the door for him, letting him walk in unimpeded. *The level of service Duke commands is amazing. These people serve him with a speed and rapidity I didn't think possible, and they all love him, which tells much about that old wolf.*

Ladro was sitting at a secretarial desk with two stacks of papers, one on each side, with a single sheet of paper before him, all destined for the mouths of those heads. Ladro put Duke's seal on the one in front of him, placing it on the left stack and taking an identical paper from the right stack and carefully reviewing it. *You really have a flair for dramatic overkill. I can imagine the effect of receiving a message stuffed in every mouth of the severed heads of their own men. Thank the Lord and Lady you are a friend and not an enemy.*

Duke was lying propped up on his side on a pile of pillows in a large mound against one wall. The wolf's head came up as he walked in. "Ah Lord Dohma, thank you for coming directly."

"Excellency, I live to serve. What do you require?"

"I thought you should like to take a light snack with me and listen to a report I am about to get."

Dohma noticed that a table had been placed near Duke's head with a comfortable chair. The chair sat on the wall side of the table, angled to be able to observe the room as well as comfortably speak with Duke. "Both sound far more entertaining that what I was doing."

Duke chuckled then winced. "Oh don't make me laugh, my innards are still re-aligning and it hurts. I take it you were doing your administrative duty."

Dohma took the initiative and sat down. "If that is a polite way of phrasing 'boring paperwork', you are most correct. I cannot imagine why any pirate would desire to take over a country. It is far too much work."

Duke put his head down on a pillow that kept his head significantly raised. "And that is why Damega and possibly most of his ancestors ran away at every mention of resuming the throne. He felt he could serve people better by being with them, and he got to have an adventure or five." Duke pinned him with a serious stare. "You, sir, need to learn to delegate."

It was Dohma's turn to laugh. "I know how to do this. I was Captain of the Guard after all. I know well the usefulness of empowered people.

The problem is we still haven't sorted out who we can trust. My family will not allow corruption to reign in our government again."

Duke looked at him quietly for few moments. "Dohma, close your eyes." It was a sign of how much he trusted Duke that he complied instantly without even thinking about it. "Now listen carefully, do not analyze anything. I want you to answer my questions with the first thing that comes to your head. Do not talk except to answer my questions."

"Do you understand?"

"Yes."

"Good. Now, what is your name?"

"Dohma Gerani."

"How old are you?"

"Thirty-five."

"What is your sister's name?"

"Ellua Garana."

"How old is your sister?" Duke went on, asking simple question after question. Every time he answered, Duke asked the next. There was no pause. Finally Duke asked. "Who should be Dockmaster?" Dohma answered instantly, "Baroness Morthan." His eyes snapped open, looking at Duke, who was smiling.

"There you go—name Baroness Morthan Dockmaster. That is one job you can forget about."

Dohma shook his head. "But we have not yet validated her family is not a pretender line."

"You will find that Baroness Morthan herself comes from a true line. That she might have married a pretender line is not important. I believe her husband is dead, so her title remains from her marriage. She is likely a countess in her own right. Nonetheless you can trust her and her progeny with responsibilities. Does she have any adult children?"

Why did I name her? I don't even know her. I think I met her once, maybe twice, for only a few moments. I did like her though. Thinking for a moment he recalled, "She has two sons, both serving as officers in the guard. They have both been favored by the weapons master with personal tutoring." *Which is why I made sure to meet the Baroness at a celebration party for the guards.*

"So what should her sons do?"

"Well, Eorji would do well to oversee the tax enforcement office, and his brother Illiam really should remain in the guard. He will be an excellent career officer." *Wait, why did I say that?* He looked at Duke, confused.

"I told you trust your instincts; they'll be right. All you have to do is listen to yourself. Feel free to accelerate your research into these people to confirm your hunches, as it will make you more and more confident in your hunches in these matters. Now you have a Dockmaster and a head of tax collections. That should reduce the paperwork considerably." Duke smirked at him.

"Sorry Excellency, this really is going to take some getting used to."

"Oh of course it is. Now eat."

Dohma looked down and the once-empty table was loaded with food and a selection of drinks. *When did this get here? Duke's staff is efficient... and too quiet sometimes; I guess when you have to keep from waking a wolf while working it's only natural you'd get good at moving quietly and efficiently.* He helped himself, as he really was hungry. While he was eating he looked around. Aside from Ladro continuing to check every page before affixing Duke's seal, the room was empty. Duke was resting with his eyes closed, breathing softly and evenly. "Didn't you say something about a report?"

"I did, but you came faster than I expected. It will still be another half-mark at least before Elades gets here with the report. So relax and enjoy a little rest, you've earned it. By the way, I have wanted to say you did a very stupid, commendable, brash and courageous thing leading your guards into the fight. It saved the day and many of our people. Thank you, but please don't do it again till you have some rugrats."

Dohma choked on his bite. *Oh ya, I need to ensure the line. That will take some getting used to, too.* "I had a hunch."

Duke chuckled and grimaced again. "Ouch. More like you didn't like being left out of the fight. You were in the right place at the right time, and willing to do what was needed. You'd have made a good Dagger."

He enjoyed the swell of pride that came with that. *High praise from Duke. He really takes Daggers very seriously.* Dohma chewed on his food for a while, thinking about the Daggers and guards. "Excellency, I have been meaning to ask you. Did you really start the Daggers with Damega, like the pretenders said?"

Duke smiled. "I didn't start them, I just continued them."

"You can't just drop that, it demands an explanation."

Duke looked at him with a serious look in his eyes. "The Daggers are continuing an honorable and proud tradition of military service that goes back further than you would believe."

"My ability to believe has had a lot of exercise recently. Try me."

Duke moved to get more comfortable. "We have time, so alright, you get your wish. Just the short version though. Daggers, like the knives they are named after, are not just born—they are forged by masters over time with great care. If anything goes wrong they don't become Daggers. All Daggers start learning a profession as they grow. All are very knowledgeable, and some are even learned scholars. Because they are the people they are, they see to the physical as well as the mental, and tend to end up getting some military experience in a guard or army somewhere. Then, if they want to be Daggers badly enough, are right in the head, and haven't been perverted by their associations, they get picked up for more training by an experienced Dagger."

Duke was looking at the ceiling and he lost himself in his explanation. His voice changed slightly, getting softer and somehow more dramatic. It seemed as if Duke were actually travelling further and further away and leaving only his voice behind to tell what had become of him. Dohma noticed that Ladro had not changed papers yet and was holding very still, with his head shifted to hear every word of the coming tale.

"Long ago I was just such a man. I was born to a family that had an honorable tradition of being Daggers so far back it was already lost in time and legend. Hell, one of my ancestors earned a Dukedom for his service. But although this made our family rich, he made sure his children grew up with the right values of honor, courage, and commitment; his children did the same. So it was that in my family we all served when our time came—woman or man, we served. I enjoyed the work, and though not necessary made a full career of it, rising to a very high rank before I became as you see me now." Duke chuckled ironically. "In fact it was because of my commitment to the Dagger ideals that I stuck my nose in where I wasn't supposed to and ended up as you see me now.

"You see, a disaster of a magnitude you would find hard to imagine was in progress. All our lands and those of the peoples of magic, including those of the Gods, were threatened with total destruction. The Gods, with the secret aid of our government, were trying desperately to find a way to save everyone or at least some. The result was that our people, along with many of our creatures, were migrated to many new lands with the help of the Gods and the peoples of magic. This was no small task, and it cost all dearly in lives as well as cultures and resources.

At first our original government and civilization held together and we worked with the Gods, elves, and dwarves to build cities and establish ourselves in this new land. It was then we discovered the unexpected results of living with magic we spoke of earlier. Our populations began to shrink and the resources needed to sustain our old ways were simply not feasible, given what was left in knowledge, power, and people to do the work. The old government and militaries started to break down. We did all we could to create a sustainable, safe society, and thus a new empire was born."

Duke's eyes glossed over as he went back in his mind. Dohma had one of those feelings. *He is going to reveal something important. I must concentrate, this is a key.*

"Eventually even that empire was too large to sustain itself and it began to fall. As a final effort to prevent total chaos, the Emperor created the concords which established the smaller kingdoms you now know. Damega learned all this and much more. It was he who showed me what I didn't understand before. Damega was the one to finally break through my optimism for humanity and proved to me the true state of things. People are people, and a few thousand years wasn't going to change that. It was humanity's struggle against its greed and thirst for power which caused empires to fall and change. People are born with certain behaviors and attitudes built-in, which are filtered by their experiences through childhood events, resulting in adults of all types. Most are good, yet some are bad, and enough are really evil. Without a proper balance the majority of good people suffered at the hands of the truly evil controlling the bad. From time to time a hero emerged. But one person was not enough to balance the world. We were missing an organization of men and women with the abilities, training, and commitment to do whatever it took to do what was right. People committed to a higher standard, who could be looked up to and trusted by the majority of good people and feared by the bad and evil, keeping them from making bold sweeping moves. An organization that had to reach out across kingdom borders to touch all realms. That is when I realized every world needs Marines. You see, the three tenants of a Dagger are honor, courage, and commitment.

"Daggers are required to live and exemplify an ultimate standard in honorable ethical and moral conduct. Honor encompasses and requires many traits and behaviors. A Dagger must never cheat, steal, or lie, but that is not enough. Each Dagger must cling to an uncompromising code of personal integrity, accountable for their actions and holding others accountable for theirs; and above all, honor mandates that a Dagger never sully the reputation of being a Dagger.

"Then there is courage. Courage isn't just blindly doing idiotic things for glory. For a Dagger courage is honor in action, a moral strength, willing to do what is right, regardless of the conduct of others. Courage means willingness to take a stand for what is right in spite of adverse consequences. Every day a Dagger can wake up and smile, knowing they did right and will do it again.

"Finally, Daggers have commitment, which is a total dedication to the Dagger ideals and to the world as a whole. Some call it 'all for one and one for all'. But that is too simple an explanation, because commitment includes the ideal that if you want a job done right you give it to a Dagger. To a Dagger, commitment is a combination of a relentless dedication to excellence and selfless determination. Daggers never give up, never give in, never willingly accept second best. Excellence is always the unachievable goal that must never be forgotten or abandoned. There is no such thing as an ex-Dagger—once a Dagger, always a Dagger, because commitment never dies.

"I was a career Dagger officer and I tried to live by that standard always. But after coming here I had become the hero, just one soul, who could only be one place at a time. Damega showed me we needed Daggers everywhere.

"I taught him all I was, all I knew, and he embraced it like none I have ever seen before or after. He was an unbelievably good template for others to work towards. I was only the trainer; Damega was this world's first true Dagger, son."

Duke sat silently and Dohma noticed tears beading off of Duke's eyes. *He misses Damega. If Damega was the first Dagger then Duke probably thinks of him as a son; which means he had an argument with his son and went away, only to...* Dohma sat up as the realization hit him. *The pretenders said Shar-Lumen delivered Damega's dead body. Oh Lord—in Duke's eyes Shar-Lumen killed his son! Worse, he killed him before they made up.* Dohma sat respectfully quiet, watching Duke in his silent remembrances of things long past.

Duke pretended to adjust the pillow, but Dohma knew he was cleaning his eyes. Duke's ear twitched. "Ladro."

"Yes, sir?"

"Get back to work."

"Yes sir." Ladro smiled and put Duke's seal on the document in front of him, grabbing the next.

I wonder if Ladro knew this all before. Still there is something I wonder, which will distract him from his mourning of Damega. "Why did you call them Daggers instead of Marines?"

Duke's eyes snapped open and he looked at Dohma for a minute. "How do you know that name?"

"You said, 'That is when I realized every world needs Marines.'"

Duke chuckled and grimaced again. "I need to watch it around you. After nearly fifteen thousand years this place had forgotten that name and many others. There was a pattern here of calling mercenaries Blades, brokers Hands, and so on. So using a name like Green Berets, Seals, Star Legion or Marines would not have invoked any special feeling, and hell, I haven't seen a beret since just after the migration, why the hell would I want to introduce that silly headwear again? Damega came up with the idea of sticking his dagger in the table to call attention to himself over other mercenaries. Those we started training did the same, so calling them 'Daggers' just made sense."

Thankfully, before Duke could go back to remembering, Elades stepped into the room. Duke looked at him and nodded.

"Excellency and Lord Dohma, we have broken the code used by the Nhia-Samri. We have deciphered most of the materials captured when we took the Llino Outpost."

Duke smiled. "First, what was that bird carrying?"

"Sir, the bird's message was 'abort and track.'"

"So the whole mess with Ticca at the gate would not have happened; which means we wouldn't have been able to track them down so efficiently. Excellent, this will make sending the commander's odassi home so much funnier as they won't know he didn't get the order. Continue."

"The majority of the materials are expected logistics. We now are aware of two other outposts nearby. One is situated to record all merchant traffic."

Duke nodded. "That is not surprising. Monitoring the merchant traffic will reveal much about who is in favor and not. Anything else?"

"Two items of extreme importance, sir. The first is that we have answered two of your primary objectives. Specifically, who killed Magus Vestul and why." Elades pulled out a paper and held it to read it directly. "'Llino Outpost, you are instructed to intercept Magus Vestul before he meets with Duke. He is carrying vital information on his person in his pouch at all times. The pouch is to be seized and sent to Hisuru Amajoo unopened. In no way is a Nhia-Samri to come into direct contact with Magus Vestul, and anyone not Nhia-Samri involved is to be eliminated without a trace.'"

Duke started a low rumbling growl. "That answers why but not who."

"Sir, according to the reports, the second-in-command, by the name of Ossa-Ulla, hired a Knife named Keelun who vanished at the same time Magus Vestul did. They suspected Ticca intercepted him since she publicly wore Magus Vestul's pouch the next day. She trapped them by hiring a mage named Lebuin who blocked their assassination attempt on her to recover the pouch. They were not sure if Magus Vestul was dead or alive. The final report, addressed to a Warlord Maru-Ashua, written for delivery when the documents were recovered, suggests the theory that Magus Vestul hired Ticca prior to coming to Llino. Ticca arrived early and pretended to be inexperienced while making similar arrangements with Magus Lebuin, who they also suggest is a Guild special operative, perhaps even a Dagger himself. Ossa-Ulla is blamed with falling for the entire trap and exposing their presence; the commander also accepts blame for not more directly overseeing Ossa-Ulla and allowing this to happen."

Duke's tail wagged in spite of the growling. "This is very good news—one of ours completely foiled them. But if correct, she failed to protect Magus Vestul. She could not know of the Nhia-Samri element until too late and that would throw any Dagger for a loop if unexpected. Hell, I didn't know they were here. This has been a very surprising trip. But why didn't she just report to me if she was working with Vestul? We have confirmed she is carrying his pouch, so she must still be operating under some instructions we are unaware of. He was coming to give me something important. Now we know it is some kind of data, most likely that damned research project he has been so secretive about for the last few decades. But how did Shar-Lumen learn about it when even I didn't know?"

Elades looked slightly worried. Duke picked up on it. "There is more, what is it?"

"Sir I don't think we killed Ossa-Ulla. The local commander wanted to kill him for his mistakes but Warlord Maru-Ashua wouldn't condone the request. Instead he was demoted and the commander sent him out on a mission outside Llino the day before you started the hunt."

Duke did not look happy. "Details, please."

"Sir, Ossa-Ulla was ordered to take an additional agent and proceed to Algan to burn Magus Vestul's home to insure any possible copies of the information sought would not fall into your possession. He was to then proceed to Rhini Wood and gather intelligence on just who Ticca is, before reporting back to the outpost just east of Llino. He left via the Delivery Channel using something they call a breather."

"God damn it! When the hell did they get scuba gear? We have been letting ships out since before the hunt after careful inspection. If they have scuba gear there is no need to be on or near the ship he could just wait at the gate."

"Sir?"

Duke looked at Elades. "Sorry. Scuba gear allows one to carry a supply of air underwater. There is no need to surface and one can stay underwater a very long time undetected. It is pretty complicated and I thought forgotten."

Elades frowned "Sir, Ticca was supposedly heading to Breorchy and that is in the general direction of Algan."

Duke's eyes went wide. "She is going to Algan to recover everything!

Ossa-Ulla and another Nhia-Samri are also going there. I bet he is pissed off enough to try to trap her. How good are Nigan and Risy? And didn't you say Lebuin was still in town?"

Elades nodded. "Lebuin is at his father's merchant house with his servant. They haven't been able to arrange a ship due to the blockade and such. As to Nigan and Risy, they are good but probably not good enough yet."

"Fetch Lebuin now." As Elades darted out of the room Duke looked at Ladro. "Ladro, arrange a covered wagon with four post horses and fill it with pillows. I am going to go to Algan as fast as possible."

Ladro looked up. "Sir, you need to heal."

"Damn it! I'll heal en route. In fact, I'll likely be able to move faster than the wagon on my own in another week. Time is wasting, go now." Ladro grabbed the stack of sealed papers and exited quickly.

Dohma was thinking when Duke interrupted his thoughts. "Have you finished reading the city instructions?"

"I ran through them quickly, but I couldn't quote you any of it."

"You need to be able to open and close the gates and turn off the defenses when you are ready; any issues with the commands?"

"No, I know where to look and the pronunciation guide is straightforward enough."

"I would like for you to see me off to the gate. I want to make sure you can open and close it. I'll be taking this Lebuin with me. He is central to this somehow. Oh, and for all the Gods' sake, do not ever cuss and request something of the city. In fact tell your whole family that cussing is not allowed ever again for them. I cannot be sure what the city will do if you get spitting mad and start yelling out commands in any language."

He looked at Duke, confused.

Just then the guard opened the door and all four blacksmiths were there.

Duke looked at him. "It would take too long to explain. I'll explain it later, if not to you, to your great-grandchildren." He then looked at the blacksmiths. "Tell me you cut the correct one last?"

"Yes Excellency. We took special care before doing it."

One of the smiths produced another split odassi. "We brought both for your inspection." They brought the two swords close to Duke so he could inspect them.

"Very good. All the others are done and counted?" The smiths all nodded. "Good, any final questions on the last process?"

They all looked worried but answered. "No, we understand."

"Very good, everything else is proceeding well. Go ahead, there will be no further need of that."

The smiths nodded and left, leaving only Duke and Dohma in the room. Duke looked over at him. "Any more questions?"

Dohma leaned back with a glass of wine. "Thousands, but for now I think you need the rest and I need to think. Should I stay longer?" he asked hopefully.

Duke nodded and smiled. "If it won't be too much of a bother. I'd like you to be here for the interview with Lebuin." With that he put his head down and closed his eyes.

Ladro came back in quietly and sat down at the desk, continuing to process the papers. It was less than a mark before Elades came back with a very odd look. Dohma looked closely at the man. *He's embarrassed about something. I wonder if Lebuin already got out of the city.*

"Sir."

Duke lay there, waiting. "Yes, Commander? You look like you got caught sneaking off with the cookies. What is it?"

"Sir, Lebuin wasn't there. Ticca really pulled an excellent switch." He waved his hand to the guard at the door and two men walked in. The tall one was dressed in simple clothing bearing the Mage's Guild sigil. The other wore an excellent double-breasted blue vest over a light blue silk shirt with large pleated sleeves, loose gray leggings tucked neatly into shiny light brown riding boots with silver buckles. However, both had wide belts with swords, fighting knives and a dagger prominently displayed. "Sir, these are Nigan and Risy."

The taller one stepped up. "Excellency, I am Risy, Dagger in service to Journeyman Lebuin. This is my partner."

The shorter, well-dressed dagger did a half-bow. "I am Nigan, Dagger in service to Journeyman Lebuin."

Duke just stared at them for a minute and everyone started looking a little uncomfortable. Finally he sat up slightly. "Risy, you are not in service to Ticca or Magus Vestul?"

"No Sir, Ticca is our commander and we are all in service to Journeyman Lebuin, although technically our service is up. Still, we felt we should try to complete the original objective, just in case."

"Can you tell me your mission, please?"

"I don't see why not. Journeyman Lebuin just earned his badge, sir. He has some rival in the Guild who has caused some Knives to be on his tail to trip him up. He hired Ticca to help him with the Knives and to see him safely through some quest for a new type of magic for the Guild. Ticca hired us to impersonate Lebuin and Ditani, laying a false trail while she snuck them out for the primary objective. We were only to be a target and to get a chance to have at some Knives. After that our coin is done, and I think with where everything is we did a good job, sir."

Duke was looking at the floor, mumbling, "Ditani, Ditani...could it be?" He looked up at Risy. "You do look like him. Boys, you did a very good job. In fact too good. With this information you must forgive earlier comments I may have made about you abandoning Ticca to fight alone at the gate. I now see that it was Lebuin and Ditani whom she was buying time for. Elades, go get that cart ready; we must leave as soon as possible. Tell Bravo they are to assume primary role here, Alpha is going with me. Alpha, prepare and report in at the west gate in one mark. The remaining Daggers will take orders from Lord Dohma until my return." Elades left at a sprint. Looking back at Nigan and Risy, he added, "You boys missed a good fight."

Nigan smiled wickedly. "No chance of that, sir. We wouldn't miss the preliminary skirmish for nothing. We slipped in with the guards and helped protect Lord Dohma here. And as you are heading after Ticca, if it is all the same to you sir we'd like to join up—might be more fighting."

"Your service honors me. No time to go back to the Dolphin, and I assume you gave Lebuin and Ditani all your gear. You'll find all the gear you might need and some horses in my stables. Pack for maneuvers and report to the west gate in one mark."

Dohma just stared at the two Daggers in shock. *They were in my guards just for a fight and protected me? Now they want to follow Duke to help Ticca. My Lord, Daggers really are living up to what Duke described.* Then the first part hit. "Preliminary skirmish?"

Duke saw the look on Dohma's face and started laughing hard. "Oh ouch! Don't make me laugh, damn it!"

Sayscia wrote a few instructions for the healers on the supply report. Setting her quill down she carefully set the report in the stack of similar papers for her secretary. Looking at the desk she sighed. *So many wounded beyond our abilities, I can't believe another war is starting.* She was reaching for another report when she heard the familiar tread approaching in the hall. Smiling she leaned back and waited.

After placing a pack just outside the door Boadua came into her office dressed in sturdy brown leather riding pants. She had a cream-colored cotton shirt on under hard-formed leather armor which protected her chest and back, with a leather skirt to protect her thighs. Over this she wore a wide belt with a short sword and belt pouch. On the front of her belt she had a dagger with a lovely silver pommel; its ivory hilt engraved with intertwining vines and winged cross-guard sheathed in another carved piece of ivory with intertwining leaves and flowers.

Sayscia looked at the travel pack resting on the floor behind Boadua in the hall just outside the door. *Lady she means to leave.* Sayscia stood and looked at Boadua seriously. Boadua looked fit and ready in her old costume; yet she stood uneasily looking at Sayscia holding a neatly folded green cloth over her right arm.

Boadua stood straight, looking Sayscia in the eye. Sayscia knew what it all meant and that there was no chance of changing Boadua's mind. Boadua carefully placed a golden-chained amulet on the desk and held out the green cloth. Sayscia's eyes watered, her heart felt heavy and her spirit sank taking in the stance of her friend and trusted second.

"Duke is leaving, and Alpha Squad needs a senior medic."

Sayscia stepped around her desk and gently took the green priestess's mantle from Boadua. "You are still a priestess of Dalpha."

"I am a Dagger first, Sayscia. You, more than most, know what that means."

Sayscia sighed. "Yes, Boadua, I do. Commitment never dies."

Boadua shook her head. "No, it doesn't."

Sayscia didn't bother with the traditional parting. She grabbed Boadua in both arms and squeezed her hard through the leather armor. Boadua returned the hug generously. "You stay out of the fighting. You're the medic, so you have to be there to put them back together. If you get yourself killed you can't do that."

Boadua sniffled and then held Sayscia at arm's length, by the shoulders, looking at her eye-to-eye. "You aren't my commander now. But, I promise you I'll do everything possible to bring them, and myself, back."

"You can take all you need from the temple supplies."

Boadua smiled. "Thank you, I have."

They both laughed and wiped tears from their eyes.

"Very well, but I also want you to take this." Sayscia moved quickly to the storage locker on the side wall. Opening it she took out a leather pouch and filled it with a number of small individual vial boxes, each one containing a precious vial of Dalpha's Draught, sealed and packed in the box with cotton felt. This store was part of the war preparations Sula had ordered on her arrival. Turning, Sayscia held out the pouch.

Boadua looked at her for a moment, then took the pouch and slung it over one shoulder carefully. "I'll try to not need to use these."

"I know. But better to be prepared, right? Plan for the worst, expect the best?"

Boadua nodded. "Thank you for not making this difficult."

Sayscia waved her out. "Just make sure you come back. If you get yourself killed I'll be seriously mad at you when we next meet. This isn't 'goodbye', just 'until we next meet'."

Boadua nodded, smiling. "Until we next meet." She turned and stepped out, grabbing her pack, and walked off rapidly towards the front of the Temple, wiping her eyes with the back of her hands.

Sayscia rolled the green mantle into a tight roll and hugged it for a time. Her work forgotten, she stepped out into the hall and started walking. In her mind she reviewed all that had passed in the last few cycles. Sula, Dalpha's own daughter, arriving without warning—at first she'd felt it was a blessing for the Temple. But, Sula had immediately ordered preparations which could only be for a war or worse. They labored to find and train new acolytes, and to prepare large quantities of medical supplies. Then Sula had started going out on mysterious business. After one of those outings Sula had returned with Magus Cune and introduced him as her direct agent saying the Temple was to send notice to all of Dalpha's hospices to give Magus Cune anything he asked for without question.

Then a box was delivered that contained sealed messages. The first message scared her to the core, as it accurately described events that happened the next day, warning that every care was to be taken to not take actions without Sula's or Dalpha's approval, as the consequences could lead to the destruction of everything she knew. Sula then had shared that she had hired a new, inconsequential hunter-Dagger to identify specific people and place a tracking hook keyed to Sula and Cune.

Cycles of careful preparations followed, and then came the whole emergency rush to heal a new Journeyman. That servant called Ditani had just ran into the Temple, unceremoniously grabbing Dalpha's Light, handing it to her, and pushing her physically out while screaming she had to move faster to heal Lebuin. Sula, who had walked out into this and with only a single look had taken up the servant's side, had provided the last physical push through the doorway to the hospice and then dodged back into the Temple as if she needed to hide.

Then the revelation that the great Magus Vestul had died, knowing he was to die, and was also the source of the mysterious packets of information. She'd discovered Sula crying publicly in the Temple the next morning and had consoled her as she cried for a full day after that, occasionally calling out Vestul's name and asking her mother what could possibly be so important to require such a sacrifice. How Dalpha herself had come into the Temple and asked to be left alone with her daughter. After that interview Sula had radiated rage and determination. Sula's rage had cooled, but the new determination in her eyes never wavered.

Sayscia didn't pay attention to where she was going. She realized she had climbed the entire stair to the tall tower without noticing the journey. From the high tower over the Temple Sayscia saw that the dock gates were open once again. She watched dozens of ships preparing to or already setting sail. Looking at the docks, she smiled, seeing them once again busy with commerce. Squeezing the green fabric in her hand, more tears came to her eyes. She stepped to the western side of the tower and looked out into the distance. She saw, just over the western wall, what could only be Duke's carriage heading west, escorted by a thirty warriors on horse. The western and southern gates were open and farmers were bringing in much-needed food for the city. Her eyes tried to find one particular Dagger with Duke; she found her by the color of her snowcap blanket, appaloosa horse, and the green cloak she wore, which was the same color as the mantle Sayscia held. *Lady, watch over her and let her come home.*

"She'll be back."

"You don't know that, Holy One."

Sula stepped up to the bannister with her. "She rides as if born to it."

Sayscia laughed. "She was, and she had much practice over the years."

"Duke has cleaned the city of Nhia-Samri, and now goes to help Ticca and then kill more."

Sayscia nodded. "Yes, Holy One. Please watch over her."

Sula put her hand on Sayscia's shoulder. "I have Magus Cune's help. I will do what I can."

Sayscia nodded and softly said, "Once a Dagger, always a Dagger."

Sula was gone and the platform was empty; alone, she watched as Magus Cune rode up to the Temple on a huge black warhorse with white socks, leading another stallion, which was a beautiful cream color. Both horses had travel packs and gear. Magus Cune also had a backpack that looked a little heavy, a large black sword swung at his side and a black-hilted dagger with a pentagon pommel on the front of his belt. Sula came out of the Temple and walked gracefully down the stairs, taking the reins of her horse from Magus Cune and mounting smoothly. The two of them rode down the street towards the west gate.

Just at the corner Sula stopped and looked back up at Sayscia. Sayscia felt her heart warm with hope as Sula smiled and held her hand high. Sayscia held hers up in return.

She stayed there on the tower, watching the western road until long after even the dust trails of Sula and Magus Cune had vanished. She realized a warm presence had been with her as she watched. She turned around, and behind her stood a tall woman who looked much like Sula except she had blazing red hair that fell in curls past her shoulders; she was wearing a simple green dress of woven wool that covered her from her neck to the floor. On her wrist was a beautiful shining bracelet of woven gold and silver over black leather gloves that went almost to her elbow over the dress's long sleeves. A golden chain belt wrapped her waist, with a sapphire buckle that allowed the ends of the belt to hang down to her knees in front. Around her neck, over the dress, was a simple golden chain with a medallion made of a large sapphire with the same symbol as that was etched over every door and altar in the Temple. She wore a simple, soft, loving smile that extended to her brilliant emerald green eyes, which were slightly larger than normal.

"It is not over Sayscia, it is only begun. You have done well and we have hope. The first step has been made and the ground is solid."

Sayscia knelt, holding out Boadua's mantle. "Lady Dalpha, Boadua has left to go with the Daggers, as their medics were killed. Though she has resigned, please do not forsake her."

"Sayscia, be at peace in your heart. All the Gods are watching with great concern and care. Boadua remains my servant as much as my Lord's servant. She burns with commitment, honor, and courage. She is doing as her soul tells her and is deeply respected for this. All must do this now if we are to have hope. Rise, you of all my faithful need not bend knee to me."

Sayscia stood and looked into the eyes of her Goddess, Dalpha, seeing and understanding that all the Gods would help if needed and possible. Her heavy heart lifted with hope.

"Good, you understand. You must now burn all the packages left to you by Magus Vestul. There is danger in their continued existence with my daughter gone."

"What of the unopened one?"

"There is the one you know of and three more in the vault that were hidden from all. They must be destroyed as well. Fear not, our Lord knows their contents if needed. Burn them in the great fire, collect the ashes and mix them, then sprinkle them into the river below."

"Yes My Lady, your will." Sayscia moved to the stairs and just before she started to go down she saw that Dalpha had moved to the same spot where she had been standing and was looking westerly. *Even the Gods are worried.* With that, she hurried down to the Temple to destroy all the precious knowledge which they had been given, and which had saved so many lives already.

Memories of the Last

CHAPTER 15

LESSONS COME WITH A PRICE

THE TRADE ROAD WAS NOT too busy. Carts of hay, fruits, vegetables, and other products were flowing towards Algan, while still other carts filled with iron works, tools, and wooden crates flowed away. She pushed her horse to move around the various carts, keeping a careful eye out for anything unusual. The farmland slowly turned into vineyards, which in turn, slowly became more industrial enterprises, such as large barns for animal traders and wood shops.

The sun was close to setting as the city came into view. The road was bracketed by inns and cottages, mixed with the large country estates of the wealthier citizens. The road widened and was very busy with people moving about on their various errands.

Ticca slowed the horse down to a comfortable walk. As she passed through the city gates, she looked at the masonry around the gatehouse and the walls. She could see that the gatehouse was not the same as the walls themselves. She also noted that the heavy, iron-banded, wood gates were held in place with hinges set into masonry, which was inside of similar slots to Llino's, though thinner. *So Algan has gates like Llino, but they don't use them, or probably even know about them.*

The sun was setting, so she started looking for an inn. She turned into the courtyard of a large one with a sign showing three green doves flying in a circle around a mug, with the name 'Three Green Doves Inn' underneath. It was a short distance inside from the large city gates. A small boy ran up to hold the reins of her horse.

Ticca pulled a copper pence from her belt pouch and handed it to him. "Give him a full wash and brush-down. He needs his shoes cleaned, and I want good hay or oats only. Understand?"

The boy pocketed the pence and stared at her dagger for a moment. Then he looked her in the eye and smiled. "You a real Dagger?"

Grabbing her saddle pack, she nodded. "Yes, I am."

"I'm going to be a Dagger someday too. Don't worry, I'll take real good care of... uh, what's his name?"

Ticca smiled. *Bright boy, and a good one too. He might just do it, if things work out right.* "His name is Rild. Don't give up on that dream; it takes a lot of work."

"I know. My da' is in the guard and says I can join in a few more years. In the meantime, I am studying smithing and horse husbandry. I promise to take good care of Rild for you, ma'am. I can also clean your leathers, too, if you want." She nodded. He saluted her and turned, walking the horse off to the stables around back.

Slinging the saddle pack over her shoulder, she stepped into the inn. She was reminded of the Dolphin. There was a large room with a single hearth that boasted a large fire. The room was filled with the smoke from dozens of sources, and people of all classes were talking or playing games. Next to the fire, in a corner, was a rather beautiful lady, expertly playing a dulcimer as she sang an old ballad. Many of the patrons had stopped talking and were entranced by her performance. There were two servers, so Ticca took a small, empty table, putting her pack and saddle pack under the table where she could keep her leg against both. Two people took note of her entry; a rather handsome man at the end of the bar, and the bard in the corner.

A server noticed her relatively quickly and came over with a platter of hyly. "You're new. Are you hungry? We have some of the best stew in town."

"That sounds perfect. I'll take one of those mugs, too. Do you have any rooms still open?"

Putting one of the mugs of hyly down in front of Ticca, the girl shrugged. "Don't know about the rooms." Indicating a man at the end of the bar, she added, "I'll let Illari know you want one." She moved off to serve others.

Ticca relaxed, drinking the hyly and taking an inventory of the patrons. She noticed that the bard would sweep the room with her eyes from time to time. *Smart bard, keeping track of the drunks and other possible problems... Especially when you consider how good she looks. I bet she has issues almost everywhere she goes.*

A male server brought her a large, wooden bowl of wonderful-smelling stew, placing a wooden spoon down on the table with it. While she ate, the dulcimer played on through a series of old songs. *She is really very good. These are hard tunes, and she hasn't missed a note.* Tapping her toe to the beat, she finished her dinner.

Something was wrong, and Ticca couldn't figure it out. Taking a quick glance around, everything was as expected. The bard had shifted slightly, and was actually facing more generally in her direction. The same male server came to take away the bowl and spoon. As he left, the handsome man from the end of the bar approached and pointed at the chair opposite her. She nodded, and he sat.

She tried to stifle a smirk at his over-the-top Gracian machismo. He had strong, brown eyes, the expected ever-present dark, stubbly beard, and a handsome, slim face. He sported a white, billowing-sleeved, open-neck shirt, showing off six gold necklaces over his black, wiry, chest hair, and wore several gold rings on both hands. His hair was well cared for and greased back. He smelled of pine soap with a mix of some top-quality cigars. He had the Gracian look that a lot of ladies, for ages, had thought to be the perfect look for romance.

"Hullo, my name is Illari. I own this place." He had an accent that emphasized his vowels and elongated the 's' sound. In fact, he sounded exactly right for his look.

"Ticca. Do you have a private room?"

He gave her an obvious look from head to toe, and might have even judged her worth correctly. "We do, Lady Ticca. How long would you need one for?"

"Just the night. I want a good room."

"Of course, Lady Ticca. I have an excellent room that I am sure you will enjoy. For you, ten bells, including your dinner and breakfast."

Wow, this place is expensive. Judging from the rest of the room, it didn't seem the patronage was all that high scale. *Trying to fleece the one-nighter, are you?* "Three bells."

Illari smiled widely. "Ah, you are not a silly traveler then, are you? Four bells, one pence. It really is a good room."

Reaching down, she grabbed her packs. "Show me, and if so, I agree." As they left the room, she noticed the bard in the corner glancing at her. Everyone else was either paying attention to their meal, their companions, or the beautiful bard.

Illari showed her through the bar and up the stairs. The second floor was composed of two long hallways, and he walked down the left to the very end. There was a wide door with a slightly better lock on it than the others. He produced the key and opened it, stepping back to let her enter.

As she stepped inside, she was impressed. It was a spacious room with windows on three walls, to the front, back, and side of the inn. She tossed her packs on the bed and stepped over to look out the windows, at the bustling street. The bard was leaving the inn, heading deeper into the town, her dulcimer slung over her back. She glanced back, and Ticca quickly dodged to keep from being spotted. Ticca was sure the bard hadn't seen her in the window, and watched through the sheer curtains as she turned right, a couple of blocks down. "Your bard has left early."

"Ah, she is often requested by wealthy people for dinners and such. She keeps a small room downstairs. She'll likely be back later tonight, if you liked her."

Ticca shook her head, as her instincts were telling her something was wrong. "No issue. How long has she been here?"

Illari moved to a door. He thought about it. "She has been in town for about four days now. Yes, that is about right, because she came three days after the big fire. You have a private bath and toilet here." He opened the door, and Ticca looked in.

Surprised by the toilet and bath, she re-valued the room. *OK, so this is a really nice room.* "Big fire? Was the city burned then?"

Illari carefully moved her pack to the floor, grabbed the bed covers, held up his hand for attention and then rapidly whipped the covers off, revealing the cotton sheets. "See, no bugs. I pay good money to mages to keep this entire inn free of little biting things. I really do not like getting bit in the night." Looking at her with an intensity only a true Gracian could get away with, he added, "Unless, of course, it was a beautiful lady such as yourself, doing the nibbling, aye?"

Ticca smiled and blushed, in spite of herself. She nodded and pulled out five bells. Handing them to the innkeeper, she said, "You won't have that worry with me tonight. You said there was a fire?"

Illari's smile never faded, but he shrugged with some disappointment and looked at the money. "I'll give you your two rings' change in the morning, Lady Ticca." He flipped the covers back onto the bed. "Oh yes, we had a very big fire. It burned down six lovely homes before the guards and citizens got it out."

"That sounds bad. Does it happen often here?"

Illari headed for the door. "Oh no, Lady Ticca, this is a nice, clean city. Sure, we have a fire from time to time, like everyone else, but this happened on a very windy night, which caused the fire to jump. If Magus Vestul had only been here, it probably wouldn't have happened at all. But alas, he is traveling someplace romantic, I am sure, and he will be sad on his return." He opened the door, handing her the key.

Alarm bells started ringing in her head. Keeping a casual tone, she asked, guessing at the coming answer, "Does Magus Vestul protect the city from fires?"

"No, Lady Ticca. You see, the fire started at his house, so if he had been here, he would have stopped it quickly, yes? Ring if you desire hot water or something from the kitchens... And of course, if you need me," he said, giving her an obvious, intense look, "I'll be downstairs."

Ticca was too surprised to respond, which he must have taken for a gentle 'no,' because he gave her a friendly, crooked smile, shrugged again, and closed the door. She heard him humming the jaunty song the bard had been playing earlier, as he walked back down the hall.

Magus Vestul's house burned down a week ago? That cannot be a coincidence. She carefully closed and locked all the windows. Next, she closed all the shutters, but left just enough space to look out onto the street. She noticed a bell-pull by the door. She pulled it, and started taking some of her stuff out of the packs. A few minutes later, a soft knock came at the door. She opened it, and there was a kitchen girl there. *Well that tells me who the bell summons. I was worried it might be Illari.*

The girl looked at her expectantly. "Yes lady, you need something?"

Ticca nodded. "May I have some hot water for a bath, and do you do laundry here?"

The girl nodded. "I'll fire up your hot water, milady. It will take about twenty minutes to warm. I can do your laundry tonight, if you wish."

Pulling out another bell, she handed it to the girl. "Yes to all of that, thank you. Is this enough?"

"Yes, lady, it is more than enough."

"Ah, good. You may keep the rest."

The girl did a little curtsy and smiled, running off down the hall. In thirty minutes, she came back with some towels, and showed Ticca how to open the hot water sluice from the boiler mounted on the roof. "I put a bucket of coal out for your boiler, lady, so it will stay warm all night. A boy keeps all the boilers full and stoked until late, and then checks early in the morning, so you'll have really hot water in the morning. This here," she pointed at another valve at the bottom of the tub, "will send the water into the sewer when you're done."

With that, Ticca stripped down, wrapped herself in one of the towels, and gave her clothes to the girl, who promised to have them clean in the morning. Once the girl was gone, Ticca locked the door and took her knives into the bathroom, putting them on the cabinet, close at hand. She then grabbed one of the Llino tobac shop cigars, putting it on the bath table, too. Testing the water, she found it was surprisingly hot, and she added a little cold water to make it just right. Letting the towel drop to the floor, she climbed slowly into the hot tub, and let herself enjoy it for a few minutes.

She scrubbed herself down, drained the dirty water, and then opened the hot water again and filled the tub a second time. Taking the cigar, she bit the end off and lit it from the table lamp, and again, climbed into the hot tub. Leaning back, she relaxed, enjoying the cigar and the bath's heat soaking in. When the cigar was long finished and the water started getting cool, she got out and drained the tub. She dried herself with the other towel and took her knives out to the main room.

She dressed in her only clean clothes and slipped the boots back on. Taking all her gear, she arranged it around the room, with her knives out and ready. She climbed into the comfortable bed and fell asleep, feeling very relaxed and comfortable.

- - -

She was sitting by the silver lake at the edge of Rea-Na-Rey. The sky was clear, and the moons were reflected in the calm waters. Next to her, sat Kliasa, who was staring out over the waters.

"Hello Kliasa."

"Ticca, I am worried for you."

"Yes, I know. I have walked into a trap, and only appear free at the moment; it can close at any time."

Kliasa nodded, turning to her. "I saw through you, the bard. She is Nhia-Samri, as you guess. You are in extreme danger. They have been waiting for you, and have already destroyed Magus Vestul's home."

Ticca sighed. "Yes, I expected this, which is why I asked Lebuin and Ditani to stay in the forest. We need to know what is happening." Turning to sit facing Kliasa, she continued, "I have lived most of your life with you, but you have withheld some things. Your love is Shar-Lumen, the Grand Warlord of the Nhia-Samri, isn't he?"

Kliasa nodded. "You figured it out, but you have shared a large part of my life, and you know me better than anyone except the Gods, themselves. You have seen Shar-Lumen before he became evil. You have seen the wonders he has done and the good man that he was."

Ticca didn't answer; she waited. Kliasa looked up at the stars. "This is painful to share."

"They are going to try to kill us. Why?"

"It was only after your fight at the gate that I knew the Nhia-Samri were involved. I cannot answer your question, because I do not know. In fact, no one knew until your actions exposed them. Before you go further, you need to see three things. Then I shall hide nothing more of my past from you. You may then ask, knowing I will answer, if I can. This will be painful to you, too. Once you see, you cannot forget it. You must be strong."

Ticca thought about it, deciding that, painful or not, it was necessary. "Kliasa, I love you as a sister. I am sorry, but I must know."

Kliasa nodded, and her face grew tense as she steeled herself. *Lady, what have I asked, that she is so afraid of, even now that she is beyond?* Ticca felt her own palms sweating as her heart raced in anticipation. The world shifted.

They were sitting at the high table in the middle of a solstice feast. Elves brought dishes of fine foods, and dancers were entertaining the crowd. Kliasa was next to her.

"This is the beginning of the Nhia-Samri." Kliasa pointed at a group of men. The men had shaved heads and wore white, loose clothing and saffron sashes over one shoulder. They sat, enjoying the dancers, and were eating very little of the fare. What they did eat were only vegetables and fruits. Shar-Lumen was speaking with the leader. Shar-Lumen stood as the dancers stopped, and stripped to his waist, pulling two knives. The men did the same. They stepped to the center of the circle of tables and began a knife fight demonstration.

Kliasa sighed happily as Shar-Lumen held off two, then three, then four of the men. Then the fighting stopped, and the master of the men stepped up, bowed to Shar-Lumen, and produced two knives. They fought to the cheers of the crowd, except that Shar-Lumen was forced to back up a step. The elves gasped, and then the man started fighting differently, and Shar-Lumen was put on the defensive until finally, he was disarmed. The elves applauded, and Shar-Lumen bowed to the master, smiling and laughing. He joined them as they sat and began eating fruits again. Shar-Lumen was talking intensely with the master of the group, who considered what was said.

Kliasa explained, "They call themselves monks. They value life and honor above all else. They know many fighting forms, and that was a demonstration of a very old style that was thought lost from this world. They are peaceful, loving people whom the elves respect. Shar-Lumen left with them to learn their ways. He wasn't exactly pleased at being beat this night. He is a very proud man, but at this time, he was also willing to admit when he was wrong, and to learn from it. It was in their home, he found the old tombs that spoke of men called Samri that held honor above all else. These men ruled for millennia, calling themselves Warlords. Shar-Lumen decided he liked it so much, he adopted all of it and began building a vast empire of Samri. Nhia is an ancient name of this world, so he called them Nhia-Samri or Samri of Nhia."

"Yes, but that doesn't explain the evil. Losing at a fight, and getting taught the new techniques, does not make someone evil."

Kliasa sighed. "No, but you need to know that the Nhia-Samri hold honor above all else. They are still trained and conditioned to follow the original pattern of the old Samri. It is the Grand Warlord who sets the tone for all. So long as he acts honorably within their code, they will follow him to their deaths."

Kliasa looked down, her lips going white, and her face tense. "Now, I will show you the seed of evil and the evil itself. Are you sure?"

Do I really need to see this? She is very worried it will ruin me. 'Knowledge is your greatest weapon,' said her trainer's voice. Looking at Kliasa, she nodded yes. Kliasa closed her eyes, and tears appeared. Before the tears slid down her cheeks, the scene had changed.

It was the winter solstice celebration, with all the elves laughing and drinking sharre. Kliasa was again seated at the high table. Ticca, however, was off to the side on a small hill, overlooking the scene. She was a little confused, and then she saw it:

Silently, a guard was knifed from behind. Ticca looked around, and the entire area was surrounded by ugly brutish warriors. They were slightly shorter than the elves with misshapen mouths, twisted yellowish teeth, and flattened foreheads; they all had irregular fangs and were heavily muscled beast like men covered with lumpy boils and scares. The brutes were running into the crowd, stabbing everyone in range. A whole group of them swept the high table, grabbing everyone there and dragging them off, screaming. The elves regrouped and retaliated quickly. All had blades out, and the sound of intense fighting replaced the happy music of the celebration. The elves and brutish warriors fought hard, and apparently, evenly. The elves fought with grace and skill. The brutish warriors fought with force and superior speed.

Kliasa was being dragged off, along with the elven lords and ladies. A detachment of elven warriors intercepted them as Ticca ran to see what was happening. The fighting was horribly bloody, and all but three of the high table occupants were freed. Kliasa was not one of them. She had been carried off by a small group, in a different direction; Ticca followed them, her heart racing.

They carried Kliasa into the forest, kicking and screaming, as she tried to use her magic. Finally, when they were a long way from the city, one of them laughed and pointed at Kliasa. Ticca didn't understand what he said, but she screamed when the brutes began to beat and play with Kliasa, like a toy. Ticca tried to attack them, but her attacks simply passed through the warriors; she was only an observer.

Waves of horror tore through Ticca's wretched heart. Sweat oozed from every pore in her body as the adrenaline poured into her bloodstream. She sobbed as she watched Kliasa brutally raped and tortured. Her heart felt such agony, she wasn't sure she could survive the stress.

The more Kliasa fought, the happier the brutish warriors became. It didn't stop with that first attack. When they stopped to rest, as they traveled, over and over again, the brutes played with her. Ticca followed them for three days, suffering Kliasa's pain with every breath she took. Eventually, they came to a mountain village filled with ugly creatures like the brutish warriors. They carried Kliasa, beaten, bleeding, and broken-spirited, to a large, central building with a cavernous entrance and a bonfire burning in the center. Kliasa was tossed to the ground in front of the leader.

The leader laughed and grabbed her by the hair. Kliasa made a gesture, and a magical blast burned the front of the leader's body. He laughed and began his own torture, raping her again on the spot, to the cheers of all the creatures present. It was then that a cry came from outside, and fighting was heard.

The leader grabbed a sword and stabbed Kliasa through the stomach. He threw her, screaming, into the fire. Ticca fell to her knees, her soul screaming out for mercy. She heaved, but her empty stomach had nothing to send forth. The pounding of her heart was only intensified by the crushing sensation in her chest. The sound of her heartbeat was deafening in her ears. Ticca's body convulsed with sobs, as she watched what her mind didn't want to comprehend.

Elven warriors, in their shining silver armor, burst into the room and began killing everyone present, but the brutes soon pushed them back out. Kliasa, still clinging to life, managed to roll out of the fire, burnt almost beyond recognition. She lay on the ground, trying to gather some magic to heal, but was too tired and damaged to succeed. The fight continued while Kliasa's breathing slowly became shallower as she died. Ticca watched helplessly, her head pounding. Ticca wrapped her arms around her chest and shoulders, in a futile attempt to comfort herself.

The elves fought hard, but the creatures were too many. Then Shar-

Lumen came running into the room, his clothes caked in snow, as if he had somehow come from the top of a mountain, to this hot forest. He slew every creature in his path, running straight to Kliasa. He screamed, and pulling an emerald out of his pouch, bent close to Kliasa, as the emerald began to glow. Kliasa opened her one good eye and smiled at him, cracking her burnt lips. Pain was evident in her contorted face. Through mangled lips, she managed to cough out, "You are too late. I will await you, my love. Don't forget to wear my boots." The emerald in Shar-Lumen's hand blazed white, and then broke into pieces. Shar-Lumen screamed his anguish at the Gods as Kliasa sighed deeply, and then breathed no more.

Shar-Lumen went berserk. He killed every creature in the village, even the women and children, constantly screaming his heart out. The elven rescue party stood back, in shock and horror.

Orcs, these are orcs. I heard they were ugly and the Nhia-Samri hunted them to extinction. She shuddered at the implication. *Shar-Lumen took out his revenge on the entire race. My uncle told me there was a standing bounty of one cross for every pair of orc ears and scalp delivered to the Nhia-Samri. Every bad-mouthed mercenary in the world tried to cash in on that bounty. The entire world hunted orcs for years. The entire race was made to pay for the death of one.*

With tears still flowing from Ticca's aching eyes, she fell to the ground. *This is too horrible. How could this have happened? Why did they take Kliasa, only to kill her? An entire race, good and bad, paid a terrible price. It is too much.*

"They were brutal, wounded beings. The council had blocked them from moving into our forest. There had been a meeting that had not ended well. The orcs swore to teach the council a lesson. As I was sitting at the high table, they thought I must be one of the council. If it hadn't been me, it would have been another." Ticca looked up, and Kliasa was standing there crying, even though her burnt body was also on the ground in front of her. "Millions have died because of where I sat."

"Kliasa, I am so sorry. This was far more than I ever imagined!"

"I tried to warn you. But now that you have seen this, you need to see one thing more."

"There is more? I know what happened; I know why Shar-Lumen

hunted orcs. It was blood revenge, an honorable cause, but the scale…"
She shook her head, unable to find more words.

"Yes, the scale. You need to understand the scale."

Ticca stood on a hill. The burnt body of Kliasa was gone. Kliasa
stood whole and safe next to her. "Where are we?" Kliasa only pointed to
a small village on the edge of a lake or sea. There were human peasants
farming, children running in fields, laughing. By the water, old men
were busy repairing fishing poles and making new line. A number of
fishing boats were just pushing out for the morning. It was absolutely
beautiful, peaceful, and almost perfect.

A movement caught her eye. She saw warriors moving out of the
forest. Behind her, a man stepped out, and on his belt, were two odassi
blades. Another ran up to him. "Sir, scouts have located the hunting
party. They report that the objective is in the second house. The hunting
party did not survive the interrogation."

"Well done. Signal the attack ships to take out the fishing boats, once
we have secured the objective. We do this by the numbers. Precision,
lieutenant, precision."

"Yes sir." The lieutenant ran off as more warriors appeared out of the
woods, on the far side of the village.

This vision did not have the same quality as every other thing she
had experienced. It was clear, but it became blurred at the edges of the
village. Only the area to the surrounding forest around the village, and
the village itself, was clear and sharp. Ticca looked at Kliasa. "What are
they going to do?"

Tears still flowed freely from Kliasa's sad eyes. "You must see."

Shivers running through her body, Ticca reluctantly turned back. It
didn't take long. At a signal from the commander, men marched down on
the village from all sides. As they approached, the kids stopped playing
and ran for their parents. When the warriors reached the villagers, they
pulled their odassi and slaughtered everyone. Women screamed and ran,
carrying babies or children, but warriors ran them down and slew all of
them without pause. Men tried to fight back with gardening equipment,
and were simply cut down. There was no one capable of standing against
one, let alone dozens, of these highly-trained warriors. Bile rose in Ticca's
throat, and her stomach cramped, as she choked out cries of anguish at

the scene.

An officer ran up to the commander. "Sir, the enemy is resisting, but we are winning the objective. So far, no casualties."

Resisted? Enemy? These farmers are being spoken of like a veteran army! How could anyone accept these kinds of orders?

The commander pointed at the fishing boats. "Make sure those enemies do not get away."

The other bowed and ran off, shouting more orders.

It took only minutes, and everyone visible in the village was dead. The warriors then broke into the houses, where more screams could be heard, but suddenly ended. Finally, a group of warriors dragged a fishing net filled with orc children up the hill, to the commander. "Sir, objective confirmed. All targets have been dealt with."

The commander looked at the frightened orc children. He pulled out a golden sphere with a crystal mounted on it. It glowed, and Shar-Lumen was standing there. The commander bowed. "Lord, objective achieved, these are the last."

Shar-Lumen walked around the children, his eyes cold and merciless. "Burn them." Looking at the village, he continued, "Burn it all. To think these animals managed to infect others to try to help them. Yes, we'll have to burn it all, Commander. Burn it to ashes. Burn as my love burned to death after being brutally raped and stabbed. Raped, stabbed and burned to ashes. That will be a complete blood revenge, Commander."

The commander motioned, and oil was dumped on the screaming orc children, followed by a spark. Ticca, gasping and sobbing, watched the children writhe in the fire. When she could take no more, she spun around, turning her back and covering her ears, trying to block out the torturous cries of the children, as tears continued to flow across her face. Still, she heard Shar-Lumen, "Once it is all burned, return to Outpost Thirty-five. You and your men are to be commended for your excellent performance and commitment."

Ticca was back by the silver lake. Kliasa was holding her gently, and they both cried for a long time.

Kliasa kept her in Rea-Na-Rey for almost a year. They practiced knives and walked the forest paths. They talked little, and slowly, Ticca managed to regain herself. The knowledge was almost too much for her to bear. But she knew. She knew why Kliasa was holding herself here. Originally, it was just to wait. Then, it was in the hope of healing her love back to the good man he had been. She also knew that the origins of the Nhia-Samri were rooted deep in the past, with skills and knowledge thought forgotten or lost.

Finally, Ticca was sitting by the silver lake enjoying the sun, when Kliasa walked up. "You have healed. Your spirit is bright, and though not as cheerful as it once was, I don't see any darkness."

"Must be handy, being able to read people like that."

Kliasa laughed. "You might be able to do the same one day. But it will take many years to develop."

"Well, you are right. Thank you for keeping me here 'til I dealt with what you showed me."

"Time is something I can give you here. The elves have always been good at healing wounds; even those of the spirit. It took me longer than you might think to recover myself, even in this place. But I am well again, and I have forgiven."

"If that is so, why is Shar-Lumen still bleeding from the heart? Why doesn't he heal?"

"Because he is stubborn and refuses to be consoled. He took my boots off the day I died. By the time I had healed myself, and learned how to communicate through my creations, he had removed everything I ever made for him, from his body. He has never put anything I made for him on since then. I think he has them in his chambers, where he can cry over them every night. If only he had put them on, or held them and slept, I could have tried to mend his soul. Now, I think it is too late. The evil has destroyed all the good in him."

"So whatever is going on, he is at the center, and I need to find a way to stop him."

Kliasa nodded.

"What is this thing Vestul was working on? Why does Shar-Lumen want it? If we destroy it, will that stop Shar-Lumen?"

"I don't know. No one knew Shar-Lumen was involved until you exposed the Nhia-Samri. I only know some of the details, because Vestul wore my boots or wrote in my journal often. He never slept with them, and his mind was too shielded for me to penetrate when awake. So he never knew I was still here and watching. In fact, it wasn't until you came along that I even knew I could communicate with someone in the physical realm. Your first night was simply me wishing I could talk with you, because I saw in you a kindred spirit, and it has been a long time since I talked or shared with another lady."

"But you now believe the Nhia-Samri to be central in whatever is going on?"

"It is very possible. There are still a few things I know I cannot say; the Gods themselves warned Vestul, and thus me, as well."

"Well, I doubt we can kill him, which would be a quick end, unless he has embedded his orders into the Nhia-Samri. There is no way I could beat him in a fight, fair or not."

Kliasa shook her head. "No, do not try to best him or kill him from surprise. He cannot be surprised, and he is the best there is. Not even the Gods could beat him in a fight now. He has almost become a God himself. His powers have expanded, and he has gathered knowledge and applied it in scary and ingenious ways for over a thousand years. He may even be immortal, like Duke. None can say."

"The key is the Nhia-Samri. If I can convince them he is no longer honorable, they will not follow him."

Kliasa shrugged. "It might be the answer. But again, we do not know. I love you, Ticca, and I trust you more than you will know for a very long time. I hope you and Lebuin are the keys to salvation. I don't know how. But I have done all I can to help you two grow, and to have the ability, knowledge, commitment, and courage to do what is needed. Like the Gods, I am launching you like arrows at the heart of a catastrophe which I cannot see clearly. It might mean I am sending you to kill the love of my soul, because we must stop what is happening. If that means sending him to meet me here, then my long wait will be over. You have my blessings and my prayers to do what you feel to be right. If you need me, I'll be here for you, at least, 'til the end, and perhaps longer."

Ticca nodded and hugged Kliasa. "Thank you, sister, for everything." She lay down on the soft grass and closed her eyes.

- - -

When Ticca opened her eyes, the sun was streaming through the cracks in the window shutters. It was early morning, and she was in a Nhia-Samri trap. She stood up feeling marvelously rested. She did her morning stretches and a short version of the Patterns that could be done in the smaller space of the room. Grabbing her gear, she packed quickly and made sure all her knives were in the right place.

Unlocking the door, she headed to the main room of the inn. *Time to see what they have planned.*

In the main room, a few patrons were quietly eating breakfast. She took a table and was brought a platter containing fruit and porridge. The girl from the kitchen came out and handed her clean clothes, and started to count out three rings' change. "No, you keep that." The girl smiled, curtsied, and went back to the kitchens.

After she ate, Ticca put the clean clothes in her pack and walked out to the front. Her horse was already there and ready. *This is a good inn. I'll have to stay here again if I come this way.* She tied her saddle pack to the horse and climbed up, taking the reins from the lad. "Which way to the mayor's residence?"

"You can't miss it, lady. Just follow the road to the center of town, and on the right of the central square will be his residence."

"Thanks, and don't give up on that dream. If you come to Llino and I am still there, you'll find me at the Blue Dolphin."

The boy's eyes widened in surprise. "You're a Dolphin Dagger?! Lady Ticca, I shall find you, I promise!"

"Careful with your promises. Daggers take them very seriously."

"Yes, milady, I know."

"Good. Then I expect to see you there in about five years. Make sure you learn well, what the guard has to teach first."

Turning, she rode out of the courtyard and headed for the center of the city. It was still early, and there was almost no traffic, except the early deliveries from the mills and bakers. As she rode, she felt as if she were being followed, but she made no indication of her suspicion. Pretending to be doing a little sightseeing, she tried to spot her follower.

At the center of the city, was a large park square with a wide road around it. The entrance to the mayor's residence was very conspicuous. Its lovely white walls were of the same material as the wall of the city, and it had an ornate gateway.

Riding into the mayor's courtyard, she was met by servants who took her horse off to the side, and then took her name and business need. She was asked to wait in a comfortable room with large windows that overlooked the courtyard. The mayor, himself, came in promptly. He was much older than Ticca imagined, but he walked straight and tall. He wore an excellent, double-breasted jacket over an older-style shirt of cotton, with a stiff collar and thin, black, silk tie. He approached her, holding his hand out.

"Lady Ticca, I am Rualli of Algan, the Mayor of Algan."

Ticca stood and took the offered hand. "I am Ticca of Rhini Wood, Dagger in service to Ditani of Karkaia."

"Please, come this way. My office is just across the hall. May I offer you some arit or tea?"

Ticca smiled. "Arit, please."

The Mayor smiled widely at that, and showed her to a large office lined with bookshelves, which were white, like the walls of his home. On one shelf at shoulder height, she noted there was a gold-bound book in a recess all to itself. It rested on a holder that kept it elevated at a good angle for display, as well as reading. The book looked almost identical to a book her uncle had. The mayor stepped around his desk, indicating a chair for her to take. Once they were seated, a tall, balding servant in well-worn, well-maintained clothes brought in a large platter with some cheese and a pot of steaming arit, with two cups. He placed the platter on a sideboard and poured two drinks, offering one to Ticca, and the other to the mayor, who took his, and sipped a little right away.

Ticca took a whiff of the unique and wonderful smell. "I haven't had this before."

The Mayor smiled. "It is a special blend we manufacture here. I own an arit-bean farm and arit factory here."

Ticca took a sip, and it really was very good arit, smooth, with a hint of spices. She set it aside and pulled out the papers Ditani had written. "Your Honor, thank you for the wonderful arit. I wish I was here with better news."

The mayor looked concerned as he took the papers and read, while drinking the rest of his arit. He put the cup down and covertly wiped his eyes as he finished reading. "Oh, Lady Ticca, this is sorry news for many reasons. Magus Vestul was not only an excellent friend for my entire life, but more, I loved him like an uncle."

Ticca nodded. "He was such to many people."

The mayor nodded. "It is even worse that only a week ago, his house was burned almost to the ground. There is little there for Ditani to inherit, unless he can get into the tower, which is only charred on the outside, but we couldn't force the door. Thankfully, it did not continue to burn or explode, as many here worried."

Drinking the rest of the wonderful arit, she looked at the mayor. "May I inspect the property, so I might give Ditani a full report?"

The Mayor stood. "Of course, what is left is still of value. It is an excellent location, and Ditani might yet build a new home there or sell it to a merchant. Please allow me to take you in my carriage." He rang a bell, and a servant stepped into the room. "Ollai, please have my carriage readied immediately. I will be taking Lady Ticca to Magus Vestul's property."

Ticca stood. "I have a horse, Your Honor."

He waved his hand. "We'll have a groom bring it for you. I insist such a lovely lady travel with me, so I can show you the marvels of our city personally."

Ticca blushed. "If you insist."

They left shortly in an open, two-horse carriage, with the mayor sitting facing forward. Ticca had maneuvered to sit facing backwards. As they went through the city, the mayor proudly pointed out many interesting features and spoke of the city's long history. Ticca made polite conversation while memorizing everything he said. She also tried in vain to find whoever was following her. She still had that feeling. They arrived at a gated home with a very large yard. *Wow! This is a lot larger than I expected. Something about this is familiar.*

As they stepped down from the carriage, the familiarity became even more intense. Ticca looked at the wide street that led up to the small avenue, which ended at the arched gateway to Magus Vestul's residence. As they walked past the gate onto the property, a large fountain sat in the middle of the drive, just inside the gate, past which was a large, square area with a little lawn and some trees with a bench. Back behind the burnt husk of the house, there were some glades of trees, so she couldn't even see how far back the property walls went. Looking around, she realized she was standing in the exact place where the Night Market was in Llino. The fountain was exactly where the statue of that girl was. *If you pave over the lawn and build residences where the walls are around this, it would be the Night Market. I wonder if the city has the same general plan as Llino. If so, the Night Market could have been a rich residence at one time.*

They walked up to the burnt remains of the once large, two-story house. A stone tower stood at the rear left, back of the house. The exterior was burnt, with smoke stains all the way to the top, which would have been a full story above the main house. The right side of the house was close to the outside wall. Ticca could see that the next house over the ten foot wall was also burned badly; however, there were dozens of workmen there cleaning and repairing it. At the base of the tower, was a blackened door.

Ticca tried to follow Ditiani's directions, and found the safe laying on the ground amidst dozens of burned books. She rolled the safe over and used the key to open it. Inside, was nothing but charred papers and melted silver and gold. The fire had gotten very hot.

Walking over to the door of the tower, she noticed it looked somehow familiar. Getting closer, she saw that it had six sliders at eye level, like a Dolphin Dagger-room door. *Now that is interesting.* Rubbing the door to remove some soot, she found the outline of a key hole. *This is the same kind of door used at the Dolphin. We would need to know the pattern and have the key to open it.* Stepping back, she looked up at the tower. There were windows, but they all appeared shuttered. *Well, it is buttoned up tight. We'll need to get Lebuin here to see if we can open it.*

Feeling eyes upon her, Ticca turned, and only the mayor was there, toying with a burnt beam of wood. She looked around with her eyes only, keeping her face directed at the mayor. On a rooftop, exactly where she had sat those nights observing the Night Market's activity, there was an abnormal bump to the roof line. *There you are. We think alike.* Walking back to the mayor, she shrugged. "Well, Your Honor, I am sorry to leave your company, as I would surely like more of that fine arit; however, I must go and report this to Ditani at once. I suspect he will want to clean it up and sell it. But I cannot be sure."

The mayor nodded and led her back to the carriage, where a groom brought her horse over. The mayor took her hand and held it for a moment, and he bowed to her. Turning, she mounted up and rode out onto the street at a walk. But once out of sight of the Mayor, she kicked the horse to a fast canter, and kept it going as fast as possible out of the city. Once on the open road, she kicked it to a full gallop, and raced for the farmland. *They'll follow. I need to be ready.*

The horse was in great condition, but she allowed it to walk for a while, then urged it to a fast canter again. Reaching the point where she originally came onto the road, she kept going for another mark, before turning to go overland. Although she saw no one, she couldn't shake the feeling of being watched.

Reaching the forest, she maneuvered the horse, keeping it moving. After nearly a mark, she felt the gentle tug that told her which direction Lebuin was in. She signaled for him to run. The tug came again, but she signaled only for him to run. He gave her two tugs to answer yes.

Ticca's expression brightened as she began looking for the right spot. It took almost half the day before she finally found what she was looking for. There was a great clearing with a large rock outcropping on the far side, which could be used to surprise someone who passed too close to it. The outcropping was part of a small hill. She angled the horse for the hill, passing close to the rock outcropping, and then turned up the hill. Once there, she rode up the hill, and then found a place to tether the horse, where it had some grass to eat and a small stream nearby.

Dismounting, Ticca slipped the small bundle out of her shoulder pouch and shook out the cloak. Putting it on, she made sure the hood was fully over her head, and then she made the loop back to that rock outcropping, hiding her tracks as she moved. She moved rapidly, but with precision, her hunter instincts and training taking all of her concentration. The hunter knew she was both the bait and the hunter. Her prey was smart, so she had to be smarter. It took only a half mark to get back to the rock point.

She cautiously edged her way up to look into the clearing. Once in position, she settled in to wait. They were tracking her. She could feel it. They were only a mark behind, at most. In fact, the pursuit came sooner than she expected. A lone rider came out of the edge of the forest, into the clearing, cautiously. He looked around at the clearing and up at where she sat, hidden, and a frown crossed his face.

I know him, that is the Nhia-Samri I fought at the Llino gate! Well, at least, I know I can match him, but this is going to be harder than I thought.

He dismounted smoothly and examined her tracks, and then got back up on his horse. He sat for a short time thinking, and all this time, he stared directly at the outcropping where she was hiding. She held perfectly still, breathing very slowly.

At last, he looked down at her tracks and slowly started across the clearing, following them. As he approached, her muscles tightened, ready to surprise him. Something kicked her hard from behind. She yelped in surprise, and she tumbled off the outcropping, to the ground, a few feet in front of the Nhia-Samri from Llino.

As she tumbled, she drew her dagger and short sword. Throwing the cloak back over her shoulders, she rolled into a ready stance.

He smiled down at her from the horse, and on the outcropping, stood the beautiful bard with her odassi out. "Ah, Ticca, forgive me. I haven't properly introduced you. Ticca of Rhini Wood, this is Second Lieutenant Runa-Illa, my second. I am Second Lieutenant Ossa-Ulla." He casually slipped off his horse. "You don't really have a chance. I wish I could offer you reasonable terms. However, we both know you wouldn't take them, regardless. After all, a Dagger never willingly accepts defeat, right?"

He drew his odassi slowly. Ticca waited. Very calmly, he stepped forward, and in an even tone, said, "Now to see how good you really are, before I rend you in the old style." He bowed and waited.

Why not, he will want all of us, so he'll just be trying to capture me to use as bait... Might be able to take advantage of this. She undid her cloak, letting it drop to the ground behind her, and returned his bow. He smiled and attacked. She parried his blows and kept an eye on Runa-Illa, who stood on the outcropping like a judge. They fought as she looked for his weaknesses, and he looked for hers. Blow after blow were exchanged, and thrust after thrust. Finally, she found a hole and exploited it, to deliver a cut to his side.

Without pausing, he increased the speed of his attacks. The patterns flowed, and she found new and unique ways, and stepped beyond them, but he adapted and was able to counter her. He, too, began to adapt new approaches.

He is learning from me. Damn it! I am teaching him to fight better. Her trainer's voice came to her: *'Don't waste time in a fight. End it as fast as possible, or else, you might lose by example.'* That had never really made sense, until now. She realized that in not trying to kill directly, she was in essence, training him. She needed to be a killer first and foremost, when fighting.

Damn it, I shouldn't have wasted time thinking he'd want to capture me. Too late, she realized that he was much better than she thought. *I can find out what we need someplace else. The easy way is going to get me killed. If I can't best him now, we are all in trouble. Never mind getting information from him. If I lose, then Lebuin and Ditani will be lost, too.* She didn't bother thinking about it anymore; she pushed and began delivering heavy, killing blows.

Ossa-Ulla smiled and parried them, while returning the same. "Now you are fighting like a Nhia-Samri. Who trained you?"

Ticca didn't answer. She pushed and pushed, but he had already learned too much from her, and she couldn't break through. He had learned her moves, her style, and was able to adapt to match. Still, he couldn't get through to her, either, as she also learned his. They fought and fought. They both were sweating and moving around, when he finally caught her off guard, and his blade sank into her hip. The pain flared, but she ignored it and used the moment to slice his overextended arm. The battle was ending. They were chest-to-chest, and he let go of the blade imbedded in her hip, and grabbed her wrist with his free hand.

Instantly, Ticca knew she had made a fatal mistake. *Oh crap! I let myself get into a strength-versus-strength position, and he has the upper body strength and speed to use it.* Pushing her back hard with his knee into her crotch and with his hand holding her wrist, he lifted her off the ground and then slammed her down on her back, landing on top of her. She gasped, trying to regain her breath. His body was on hers, his nose touching the tip of her nose, and his cold, blue eyes were looking directly into hers. She could feel his breath on her lips. She couldn't defend, as his other blade knocked her dagger aside and pierced her shoulder. She screamed just before passing out.

Aelargo Outpost

CHAPTER 16

BEGINNING IS A SINGLE STEP

DITANI WAS COOKING SOME RABBITS they had bagged earlier. Lebuin decided to take advantage of the lull in conversation to check on Ticca, as he had roughly once a mark since they had parted company. She had gone to town, had dinner, and now had a room for the night. This time when he checked, Ticca was just climbing into a bath, and after a moment of marveling at how beautiful she was he rather guiltily stopped looking. He shifted, looking at Ditani to see if somehow Ditani could see what he had witnessed or done, only to notice his pants were far too tight. *Oh my Lord, I am fully aroused. I never really considered Ticca that way. Lord, don't let Ditani see this.*

He turned around as he stood, so that his back would be to Ditani. "I am going to... ah... practice a little while you cook."

"Milord, we just finished practice."

He moved off slightly, coughing. "I... ah... want to test something with magic."

Ditani called after him, "OK, don't go far. I'll call when the rabbits are done." He wasn't sure but he thought he heard Ditani chuckle. *Oh Lord, he noticed.*

Walking a short distance, he played with some light telekinetic tricks. His air powers were really back to nearly full strength. He had even momentarily cast the cleaning incantation he used and was enjoying not feeling as grimy. *Now if I can get water involved I can even heat up some river water or a pool to take a comfortable bath out here. I wish we had all gone to town; I could use a nice bath too.*

Pulling his knife out, he toyed with hitting stick targets that he floated around. Watching the knife fly he had an idea. "Ditani, can you put those rabbits aside for a moment? I need someone to help test something."

Ditani came walking over. "So you really are testing something?"

Lebuin laughed. "OK, Dad, really I didn't mean."

Ditani waved his hand. "It was only natural. She is taking a bath?"

Lebuin laughed, nodding. "OK, so you wanted to test something."

"Yes please, grab these sticks and throw them in any direction you want, but wait for a moment or three so I don't know when you are going to do it."

Ditani shrugged, taking the sticks he made like he was going to throw one but didn't. Instead he tossed the one in his off hand, using an underhanded toss. Lebuin threw his knife fairly accurately but still it was slightly off. He gave it a telekinetic kick to both adjust its course and to accelerate it. The knife pierced the stick efficiently and they fell together to the ground. Ditani whistled. "Did that knife just change course?"

Lebuin nodded. "Yes, I just thought of this. I have been using telekinetic magic since I was about eight for all kinds of things. I just realized that I can do it almost instinctively so I thought it might improve my combat skills if I used it like a third hand or to improve accuracy on moving targets."

Ditani walked over and picked up the knife stuck through the stick, pulling it out. He tossed the knife back to Lebuin. As Lebuin caught it Ditani drew his knives. "Let's see if you can really use it as a third hand. If so it would be a real advantage because it couldn't be seen."

They sparred for another mark, until it got too dark. Lebuin slowly figured out how to use his magic while knife fighting. It was most effective against Ditani. He wasn't so sure how it would be against Ticca, but he smiled to think of the next time they sparred and he could try it. "If you don't mind a little extra practice I'd like to do a half-mark more in the morning like this."

Ditani nodded as they walked back to the camp fire. "It really is a bit shocking at first. I couldn't find a way to defend against it. I think you have found a real advantage should we have to fight for real."

The night passed peacefully enough. When they got up he checked on Ticca again. She was eating breakfast. So they did the Path and various dances. When they were finished he checked on Ticca again and she was standing in a burned-out ruin of a house talking to a well-dressed man. "Uh-oh."

Ditani looked at him. "What is it?"

"It looks like Ticca is inspecting a burned-down home. Yes—she is opening a safe with the key you gave her. Magus Vestul's house is burned to the ground."

"What about the tower? That is where his library is."

Lebuin concentrated. Thankfully Ticca moved to a metal door and rubbed on it, exposing a key hole. "It looks like a Dolphin door."

"Yes, that is the door to the tower."

"Well then the tower is still there, and is untouched except for smoke stains."

"Well then, we might yet discover what we need."

Lebuin broke contact. "Well, I'll check again in a bit." They checked their traps and found they had bagged some more rabbits. Carrying these back to camp, they sat down to relax. Lebuin checked on Ticca again. She was riding in the forest, fast. He gave her a small tug, to which she gave the emergency 'run' signal. He stood and gave her another tug. She repeated the signal. "Ditani, pack, we have to move." He gave her the two-tug 'yes' signal.

Ditani sprang up and began packing their gear. Lebuin kept his Sight on her as he helped clean the camp. They did everything to erase their presence as Ticca had taught them. They then led their horses on foot through the forest.

"What is going on?"

"I don't know, but she is riding fast through the forest and she is some distance east of us."

"East, that is back towards Llino. She isn't coming here?"

Lebuin concentrated; Ticca had actually changed her direction after his first directional tug to angle away from them. "No. In fact, she is moving away from us."

"Are we going to help, against her instructions?"

"Of course. I hired her, not the other way around."

"Good! Which way?"

Lebuin pointed and they carefully followed Ticca, making sure to leave no trail.

Ticca stopped and Lebuin did too. "Wait, something is happening, I need to concentrate."

Ditani started watching for trouble.

"She has taken a position on a rocky overhang. She has some kind of cloak on that is blurring my vision of her slightly... someone is coming. It looks like she is going to ambush them. Wait! She just jumped off of the ledge in front of him, instead of jumping him from behind? Why would she do that?"

Ditani stepped closer. "Was she pushed? What is happening?"

"I didn't see anyone near her but I couldn't see clearly through that cloak of hers. They are talking. I think it is the Nhia-Samri assassin she fought at the Llino gate and it looks like they are going to duel... yes, now they're fighting." He watched the fight, giving Ditani a running commentary, when Ticca's face told him something was wrong. "Something is changing. They are changing their fighting styles slightly. She beat him before, but this time I think Ticca is in trouble." He watched as the man stabbed her in the hip. She cut at his arm, but he grabbed her and then lifted her to throw her on her back as he landed on top. Then he stabbed her through the shoulder and she went pale, closing her eyes. "No!"

Ditani grabbed him. "Is she dead?"

"No, they were not mortal wounds, but she is unconscious. Wait, he is talking. He's binding her wounds. Now he lifting her and is tying her to a large tree. He is using very strong knots and strong ropes pulled very tight. He is cutting open her leggings and is treating her stab wound with a salve."

He started moving again. "We need to get there, and she is at least a day away at this speed. There might be more of them, we will need to be extra careful."

They moved stealthily and steadily toward Ticca's location. Lebuin kept his mind partially open to her the entire time. At first it was difficult to maneuver and watch Ticca. But eventually he got used to it and they made better time. "She is waking up. They are talking again. My Lord, he has a whip and is using it on her! He must want to know where we are. Faster!"

They continued easterly as fast as they dared. When they got close, Lebuin used his precise knowledge of where Ticca was to allow them to circle widely around. They found a safe location to leave their mounts and slowly crept up, using every skill Ticca had taught them, until they were within hearing range of the clearing. They could hear the assassin talking to Ticca in a cold voice that sent chills down Lebuin's back. "Stay awake please, this really isn't fun unless you are awake to feel it all. Would you care for more healing? Let's close up this wound here, huh. I think I should maybe give you a little energy boost. Here is a little more stimulant—that'll keep you going a bit longer, aye?"

Lebuin's blood boiled as they separated to come from two sides. Moving silently, he timed it so that he and Ditani would emerge at the same time. His steeled himself, blades out to free Ticca. Hopefully she was in good enough condition to move.

Stepping out, he saw that Ticca was trying to spit something out and her clothing was in ruin from all the shallow knife cuts and whip strikes. He grabbed the assassin with his telekinetic incantation and lifted him off the ground so he couldn't move and rushed to Ticca's side to cut her ropes.

"Lebuin, run. It's a trap. RUN!"

Lebuin looked up at the man he was holding five feet off the ground. "He can't do anything up there."

"Not him, behind you!"

His heart skipped a beat as the hairs on the back of his neck suddenly stood on end at the warning. Fear-fueled adrenaline surged through him, letting him start to duck and spin around as a knife cut deeply across his shoulder. He screamed in pain as he lost control of his powers momentarily. The Knife he had been holding in the air dropped and landed well, as if expecting the fall. Lebuin's training paid off as his feet found footing and his knees bent without real thought, lowering him below the worst of the strike. *Damn it. If I hadn't moved that would have really been bad.*

He now was crouched facing a beautiful woman who, like him, had two blades out ready for a fight. For the forest, the woman was amazingly well-dressed. She had a forest-patterned silk shirt over formed padded armor. Her light green leggings were the color of the grasses. She had well-worn but excellently cared for calf-high boots with dull brass buckles. She was wearing a cloak that blended perfectly with the forest. She shifted, bringing her other blade around. He was in the totally wrong position, so he reflexively used his magic as he had practiced with Ditani and it worked, deflecting her blade. He riposted rapidly and she actually had to dodge backwards to avoid the strike.

Ticca's voice, dripping with anger came unexpectedly from his left rear. "Damn it! When I say 'run' I mean 'run'! You two are going to get us all killed."

He glanced over and Ticca was no longer tied to the tree behind him. In fact she was diving for her knives by the fire. Her hands and feet were still tied but since the rope had been stretched around a tree it wasn't exactly a hindrance to her movements without the tree there. *How did she get off the tree?*

The lady assassin in front of him didn't give him any more time to think. She stepped in and started attacking him furiously. It was all he could do to block her attacks. Lebuin stepped back, trying to get more space, and she stepped in, keeping the fight close enough he could smell her perfume. She was fast and as they fought she smiled wickedly. He used every trick he had learned using his telekinetics and variations of the patterns that Ticca had shown him. They caught her off-guard and she spun away. *I actually am doing this! Lord, I never would have believed I could fight like this!* Glancing at Ditani and Ticca he could see that they were doubling up on the first assassin. Ditani had a couple of cuts on his arms and his side. But they didn't slow him down.

I need to stop this so I can help them, that guy might be too much. The girl sheathed one of her knives and parried his attacks one-handed. She was concentrating very hard, trying to open her belt pouch. *Whatever is there is not going to be good for me.* He pushed himself to go faster. She tried to step backwards to gain space. He knew if he let her get to the pouch it might be over for all of them. So he stepped in close to her. She was forced to block some of his attacks with her open hand by hitting his wrist. *That is a neat trick. I should have Ticca teach me that.* While he was admiring her bare-handed technique he missed what the other hand was doing. Her blade hit his so hard his hand stung and one of his knives went flying away.

She smiled at this change. *Can't give her a moment. I need another knife.* Which is when he spotted that her blade was sheathed with the hilt right in front of him, so he grabbed it.

Ticca dodged as Ossa-Ulla tried to slide his knife across her chest. She stepped back in, trying to get inside his attacks and grapple with him. Keeping it body-to-body was giving her an advantage. He was as fast as she was, but he didn't have enough training in extreme close combat. Ditani was doing a good job of not becoming a pin cushion and was helping to keep him busy. Still, the two of them were having a problem ending it. He kept slipping between the attacks and counter-attacking.

Finally, the break she was looking for came. He stepped into a depression that he wasn't expecting. This caused him to have to shift his weight back to the other foot momentarily, leaving him stuck with both legs grounded. If she hadn't been up close she would have missed the chance. She took it, viciously bringing her knee up dead center into his groin. He flinched in pain and jumped backwards. This gave Ditani an opening to cut downward, planting the point of his knife into Ossa-Ulla's shoulder. Ossa-Ulla was seriously hurt, but not out of the fight. He dropped to the ground, doing a reverse roll, and coming back up as fast as she could step forward to continue the attack.

He must have been in an insane amount of pain but still he did a lunge back towards her and Ditani, stabbing at them both. To keep from bouncing off of Ditani, Ticca was forced to dodge against her stance. Ditani, thankfully, dodged the opposite direction while parrying his knife. Although desperate, the maneuver gave Ossa-Ulla exactly what he needed; a moment to regain his stance.

Ossa-Ulla jumped back again, landing hard enough to probably jar his genitals back into place. Ticca moved fast, taking three steps up to him, not giving him any time to recover. On his odassi blades were narrow half-inch copper bands at the base, stamped with some kind of symbol. As she brought her dagger up, these symbols exploded with a shining golden light, which surprised Ossa-Ulla more than any of them. It was too late to stop her attack. Ticca's dagger drove past Ossa-Ulla's stunned defenses, and directly into his heart. She pulled her dagger out, preparing for another strike, but he was frozen, looking at the glowing symbols on his odassi.

He looked back up at her and smiled. "That explains it. You're Gods. I have fought Gods and almost won. There can be no higher honor." Then he fell to the ground dead, smiling as if he had been given the most precious gift of his life.

Ticca spun around and saw that Ditani was staring at Lebuin, who was holding an odassi blade with its symbol glowing brightly. In front of him Runa-Illa was standing, her other odassi in hand, its symbol glowing brightly as she stared at Lebuin slack-jawed and wide-eyed. Her face went suddenly white and her eyes became even wider; she sucked in her breath, dropping to her knees before Lebuin, holding her arm out perfectly straight, her remaining odassi flat between them with the tip raised at a forty-five degree angle. Her head was held down respectfully.

"Forgive me, Lord. I am yours to command."

- - -

The Warlord was sitting in his throne talking with his tactical advisors when his odassi began to vibrate in their sheaths. Standing, he drew the blades and the maker's marks were glowing, a bright golden hue that made the whole room as bright as midday. None of the other odassi present reacted and the advisors looked on the Warlord questioningly.

"The Gods have taken Ossa-Ulla and Runa-Illa. Summon my officers; we must determine the meaning of this."

The mayor of Algan was sitting in his office enjoying another cup of arit as he heard a large carriage draw up. He smiled when his attendant came in. "Ah, is Othulm here already?"

His attendant looked a little white. "No sir." He opened the double doors wide as a large wolf wearing a golden chain mantle of office, with a large sapphire sigil and a red sash of lordship, limped into the room. "I am ordered to announce His Excellency Duke, Lord of Aelargo."

The mayor dropped his cup in shock and stood slowly. The wolf stood taller than any horse, and stepping up to the other side of the desk, shoved a chair out of its way, sitting down slowly.

"Your Honor, has a Ticca of Rhini Wood been here yet?"

Behind the wolf in the foyer he saw five Daggers. One was extremely well-dressed, like a lord himself. They all stood silently watching the proceedings.

He felt himself going a little light-headed and tried to sit back into the chair.

- - -

Someone was waving ammonia salts under his nose. He waved his hand to knock the offensive bottle away. Opening his eyes he saw his valet. "Ah, Palthum, I had the strangest dream. I thought a talking wolf came into my office."

The valet held him firmly and lifted him into his chair. After that he moved aside and the wolf was still there.

"You Honor, I must apologize for causing such a reaction. However, I am in a bit of a hurry. Are you well now?"

The mayor looked at his valet and his attendant, then back to the wolf. He sat up straighter and tried to find something to snap him back to reality. "I need a drink please."

The wolf looked at a Dagger. "Nigan, get the mayor a brandy shot, please."

The well-dressed Dagger stepped quickly over to the small bar and sniffed at a couple of the bottles there before pouring one into a small glass and bringing it over. He handed it to the valet. "Here, this will help." The Dagger then looked back at the wolf. "Sir, we could have just come in ourselves."

The wolf shook its head. "No, then you would have brought him out and this would have happened in the yard instead of someplace with a soft carpet and brandy nearby."

The mayor took the drink and then sat up a little straighter. "You are Duke, as in *the* Duke from long ago. It was said you were immortal but I didn't really believe most of what I read or heard."

"Ah smart fellow, that is good, as most of it was highly understated anyway. Now Your Honor, if you are feeling better I only need to know if a Ticca of Rhini Wood has been here, and if so, what happened."

The mayor looked at his valet and waved him off. "Excellency, yes she was here early yesterday morning. She had papers showing that a Ditani had inherited Magus Vestul's property due to the untimely death of Magus Vestul. Unfortunately-"

Duke cut him off. "The house had already burned down. So she left town rapidly. Which way did she go?"

The mayor nodded. "I believe she left heading east. The guards reported she was moving fast."

Another Dagger stepped up. "So she knew it was a trap. How did we miss her?"

Duke thought for a moment. "She cut off the road for the forest. She must have been trying to get them to reveal their presence. She could then lay a trap or lose them. We are one day behind her and her pursuers." Duke looked back at another Dagger. "Alpha Two and Three, rabbit hunt east." Two Daggers bolted towards the front courtyard. Moments later several horses galloped out of the courtyard.

Duke looked back at the mayor. "Did she take anything from Magus Vestul's house?"

The mayor couldn't get more surprised. "No Excellency, she inspected it only briefly. She opened a safe but the contents were totally destroyed. She didn't open the tower door, which is still sealed."

Duke thought about this. Then he looked at the town's relic. "Did Ticca come into this office?"

He nodded yes.

"Mayor, please put that on the desk in front of me."

Not understanding the request, but understanding that saying 'no' wasn't an option, he stood and carefully lifted the sealed gold-bound book and gently placed it on the desk before Duke. "This is the ancient relic of Algan. It has sat in this house since the beginning of the city. However, it opens for no one."

Duke looked at it carefully. He raised his front paw and placed it gently on the top of the book and said "Aperi." The seal on the book's center lock turned a quarter turn and all the locks fell open.

The mayor looked at the book and then at Duke, who put his paw back down. "The stories are true. You were here at the beginning."

Duke smiled but didn't answer. "Nigan, open it to the last page please."

Nigan stepped forward and carefully opened the book, then flipped through the pages. The pages were heavy rich paper but Nigan turned through an impossible number of them to find the last page. He laid the book open on a half-empty page. There were neat lines of print in a foreign language half-filling the page. Duke looked down and read it. "*Oh Damn It!*" He looked up—there was shock and surprise in his eyes.

After recovering from the shock Duke howled once like a hunting dog. "Nigan, close that book and put it back where it came from!"

Duke touched the sapphire on his mantle, which opened a release, letting it drop to the ground. He stood. Ducking, he shrugged out of the sash. The Daggers had already moved to make a hole for him the moment he howled. "*Not again!* Alpha, follow if you can, this might be a deer hunt." With that he spun and sprang out through the foyer.

Turning around the mayor saw the wolf had exited the house and was already on the other side of the courtyard heading out the gate turning east.

Nigan quickly closed the book and the latches sprang up by themselves, relocking. He ran with the book to put it in place. Turning, he touched the brim of his hat. "Thank you, Your Honor, please excuse us. Urgent business." He bolted to catch up with the other Daggers, who had already left. There was the sound of many warriors whooping as the rest of the horses galloped out to the street, also turning east.

He sat down and his valet stepped over and picked up the mantle and sash. "Your Honor, what should we do with these?"

"Keep them very safe. I have no doubt someone will be by to collect them. We haven't seen the last of any of them."

Two officers carried the trunk between them as they walked respectfully behind Eshra-Zunia. They marched together down the hallway lined with the swords and armor of hundreds of defeated enemies. At the end of the hall, before the two tall iron doors with their broken shield handles, stood eight honor guards, four on each side. They did not move, and Eshra-Zunia stepped between them, pushing the doors open before her, hard and loudly. She stood there, feet wide, hands on her hips, frowning into the room. Twelve officers were in conference with the Warlord, but their conversation stopped suddenly as she opened the doors.

The Warlord stood, placing his hands on the hilts of his odassi. "What is the meaning of this?"

Eshra-Zunia paused a moment to emphasize her authority over the others, except for the Warlord himself. They quickly realized their oversight and stepped back from the table, bowing. The corner of her mouth turned up ever so slightly. The corner of the Warlord's lips raised marginally in a quick smile as he almost imperceptibly nodded to her, commending her for reminding the officers of their places. She lowered her eyes respectfully for a moment, thanking him for the high praise.

"Lord, Llino has opened its gates and traffic is flowing normally. We have retrieved the document cache. None remain of the outpost."

The Warlord thought on this for a moment. "What of Duke?"

"Lord, he has abandoned the city with a squad of Daggers. He is heavily wounded and rides in a pillowed carriage pulled by four quarter horses. He pushes for speed westerly."

"Are you sure none survived?"

"I am sure. My Lord, just after Duke left a pair of ornate open carriages drawn by white mares also left, bearing west. Each driven by a small boy wearing white, emblazoned with Duke's sigil. We intercepted them, as they were clearly for us. On our approach the boys stopped the carriages, descended and bowed respectfully, then began walking back to Llino." Her face hardened. "The first carried only the heads of our warriors stacked high and visibly surmounted by the head of the Llino station commander. His head was pinned in place with his own odassi with broken bands for all to see. In each mouth was a paper; I checked only two."

The Warlord's face flushed red with anger. "Broken bands!" The Warlord paced furiously. Then he stopped and looked at her with anger burning in his eyes. "Why only two?"

"Lord, they were identical. I needed look no further at the atrocity to know every mouth carried the same message." She held out a bloody paper.

The Warlord motioned and a servant came from the side, taking the paper and running to bow before the Warlord, holding it out. The

Warlord took it and read. He sat down on his throne heavily as he finished it. "We must warn Hisuru Amajoo."

"Lord, I have already sent our fastest courier with the second copy, a description of the two carts and the commander's broken odassi. Hisuru Amajoo will know these details in not more than ten days."

The Warlord looked up at her and nodded. "Very good. You only mentioned the contents of the first, dare I ask the contents of the second carriage?"

Eshra-Zunia, feeling light-headed, took a moment to gain the strength to answer. Softly she said, "Lord, the second contained every odassi—we counted and checked the records—every single one, with its band broken by the commander's odassi." The Warlord stood, enraged, the veins on the side of his neck pulsing with anger as he grimaced, his face turning dark red, his eyes narrowed with intensity. At this the twelve officers cried out, falling to the floor, prostrating themselves before the Warlord, as did the honor guards, the men with Eshra-Zunia, and Eshra-Zunia herself.

The Warlord screamed, drawing his blades. He held them high and bellowed, "DUKE! YOU HAVE GONE TOO FAR!" The room was filled with a bright yellow-orange light from the Warlords' blades and he brought them down on the large stone table before him. There was a tremendous explosion of light and sound.

After several minutes of silence the Warlord said, "Bring me the document cache."

Everyone remained prostrate, as the two warriors who had carried the trunk quickly stood, taking the trunk and placing it before the Warlord, backing away rapidly to prostrate themselves once again behind Eshra-Zunia. The Warlord didn't even bother trying to unlock it; he sliced the lock off with his still-drawn odassi. Sheathing the swords, he lifted the top. After a moment Eshra-Zunia heard the sound of a paper crumpling and the Warlord yelled in frustration, kicking the trunk away. In a voice so calm she felt cold to her very core the Warlord addressed her. "Eshra-Zunia, assemble all my generals here in two days. I will present you as the new Warlord. After that I must go to Hisuru Amajoo and offer myself to Grand Warlord Shar-Lumen. We are at war." The Warlord walked out of the room.

Once he was gone Eshra-Zunia stood and looked. The table was cut completely in two and the trunk lay off to the side of the doorway on its side, empty except for three ingots that had spilled out, which appeared to be made of lead. One of the ingots had landed standing on its side showing perfectly Duke's sigil stamped on its top. In front of the throne was a crumpled sheet of paper next to the bloody message. She stepped around the broken table and picked up the paper, curiously smoothing it out. The other officers slowly stood looking at her.

The paper read:

'Warlord, I owe you nothing. You owe me everything. Give my most personal regards to the Grand Warlord when you see him next.—Duke.'

She stood, stunned at the implications. *Duke must know he stripped the Warlord of every possible honor with these actions.* For the first time in many years she felt fear. *I will be Warlord in two days and then I must battle Duke.* The image of the cart of severed heads leading the cart of broken swords sent shivers down her spine.

She picked up the bloody paper and looked at the assembled officers. *They deserve to know.* She barked "Attention!" The officers and her escorts' heels clicked together as one as they stood at attention. She stood tall and straight, reading the message delivered by their dead brothers' mouths in a clear voice.

'There is no honor left to the once-great Nhia-Samri. The Nhia-Samri have committed an act of war on all the realms in the direct assassination of the last heir to the throne and are now our enemies. I am with honor and will not offer silver for two ears and a scalp. Any that renounces their odassi before me, my representative or Dagger officer shall be pardoned. You have four cycles to abandon every outpost and hidden observatory in all the realms safely. After that I will hunt any that remain without mercy. When the realms are purged I will come and level Hisuru Amajoo. Grand Warlord Shar-Lumen will be made to pay for his treachery. The Nhia-Samri sun is setting forever.

Field Marshal Rolly Duke Bensure, Admiral of the Star Legion, Duke of Wellingshire, Imperial Lord of Aelargo, Supreme Commander of the Imperial Armies of Duianna'

CLIFFHANGERS

LIKE A KNIFE TO THE HEART!

I have a love-hate relationship with cliffhangers. I love and appreciate well-executed cliffhangers. I hate when I suddenly run out of words and have to wait for the next book to get published. I also hate when I finish a book with a cliffhanger and I haven't written the next book, because I too want to see the rest! I admit I have prodded my favorite authors to hurry up from time to time. If the next book isn't available yet, trust me I am slaving over the keyboard to get it neatly wrapped up for you. Feel free to prod me to move faster! If the next book is just about ready for publication you can find the first chapter or two on my web site (www.LArtra.com). If the next book is already out you can use my website or go to most ebook sales sites and use their "Look Inside" or "Preview" feature to get at the first chapter or two. You can also find more information about this series at the official Facebook Golden Threads page: www.Facebook.com/GoldenThreadsTrilogy.

ABOUT THE AUTHOR

Leeland Artra lives in the Emerald City (Seattle, Washington) with his wonderful wife and idea-inspiring kids. He spent the first half of his life as an avid science-fiction/fantasy reader while becoming a US Navy-trained computer scientist and self-taught table-top gamer. After twenty years of thinking he should publish he finally got serious, pulling out all the notes and ideas he had stored, and set down to learn how to be a professional writer. He soon discovered he got as much joy from writing fiction as he did from reading it. His goal is to transition to full-time writing someday. In the meantime he works as a software engineer and architect at Expedia. In short, by day he helps people take fabulous vacations, and at night he helps people take even more fantastic trips of the imagination, which he finds to be very symmetric.

A PERSONAL NOTE
FROM LEELAND

I hope you enjoyed reading this book and found the deeper, more complex world history hinted at fun to try to unravel. I spend a lot of time engineering the history and mechanics of my stories. If you enjoyed this book please consider leaving positive feedback at the eBook retailer you purchased it at or Goodreads.com (or both). If you blog about it please send me a link. The more positive feedback I get the more time I can spend writing the next story! I love interacting with my readers, so if you feel like chatting with me about this story or others please visit me. You can find me at:

www.LArtra.com
www.Facebook.com/Leeland.Artra
www.Twitter.com/LArtra
www.Goodreads.com/LArtra
www.Smashwords.com/profile/view/lartra

LEBUIN'S LEXICON

LANDS/PEOPLES

Curcumveni Desert: A vast wasteland of unforgiving desert which spans the entire Duianna continent from east to west along the southern edge of the Halias-Ne Mountains. No known safe path exists across this desert and it is plagued with strange deadly creatures.

Dulgruim: A dwarven kingdom on the southern tip of the Duianna continent, bordered on the north by Karakia. Capital: Or-Anithi-Umta. Abbreviation: DU.

Karakia: A mixed nation of tribes spanning the central part of the South Duianna continent from the Darain Ocean on the east to the Occiduis Ocean on the west. The northern border is the Curcumveni Desert and on the south the Dulgruim Nation. Capital: None. Abbreviation: KA.

Laeusia: A human kingdom which lies between the Duianna Empire and the Kingdom of Yalthum.

Nae-Rae: An elven kingdom spanning the eastern third of the North Duianna continent, bordered on the north by the White Ocean, the south by the Burga Mountains, the east by the Darain Ocean, and the west by the Duianna Empire. Capital Rea-Na-Rey. Abbreviation: NR.

Nasur: A human kingdom on the southeastern edge of the North Duianna continent, bordered on the north by the Onasa Channel, the south by the Halias-Ne Mountains, the east by the Sea Princes' Kingdom of Aelargo, and the west by the Western Burga Spine Mountains. Capital: Thilis. Abbreviation: NA. Known to be friendly with the Nhia-Samri.

Niya-Yur: The world. The elves called the world Nhia in ancient times. The dwarves called the world Garduan-ka-Gadriel (loosely translated means Gadriel's Flesh).

Oslald: A human kingdom on the southeastern edge of the North Duianna continent, bordered on the north by the Burga Mountains, the south by the Sea Princes' Kingdom of Aelargo, the east by the Onasa Channel, and the west by the Darain Ocean. Capital: Stegen. Abbreviation: OS. Strong supporter of the Duianna Covenant.

Rhonia: An island kingdom in the northern Darian Ocean, famous for rare and pungent spices and unique animals.

Sea Princes' Kingdom of Aelargo: A human kingdom on the southeastern edge of the North Duianna continent, bordering on the northern edge of the Halias-Ne Mountains between the Darain Ocean and the Kingdom of Nasur. Capital: Llino. Abbreviation: AE. Commands the largest known navy and tightly controls all sea trade.

Yalthum: A human kingdom spanning the entire west coast of the North Duianna continent from the Halias-Ne Mountains on the south to the northern ice fields. Yalthum is as old as the Duianna Empire, has never attempted to expand its borders, but has bitterly defended its borders and western sea lanes.

GODS

Argos: The All-Father God of the Universe, who oversees the magicians in all lands; is considered the chief deity.

Dalpha: Goddess of healing, woods, and the elves, represented by large temples in almost every major city in the realms.

Gadriel: God of the dwarves.

Lothia: Primary Goddess of Karakia, and wife of Argos, she often takes the form of a large raven.

PLACES

Algan: Inland farming city on the western border of the Kingdom of Aelargo.

Alorn Mountain: An ancient volcano now dormant on the north western point of the Kingdom ofAelargo.

Blue Dolphin Inn: Dagger Home and merchant's inn that has a huge stainless steel hoop mounted on the roof with a platform which the owners and legends claim was the main port of call for the Emerald Heart.

Breorchy: Onasa Channel port city on the northwestern border of the Kingdom of Aelargo.

Burga Mountains: A blue mountain range which cuts east-west across the southern part of the North Duianna Continent from the Darain Ocean to the Onasa Channel.

Burga Spine Mountains: A blue mountain range which cuts north-south from the Onasa Channel to the Windy Pass.

Delivery Channel: A waterway system of all ancient port cities which connects one or more rivers together to flow under the city, creating a simple, smooth-flowing, barge-friendly means of transporting large loads.

Dorn Hills: A large range of hills on the north edge of the border between the kingdoms of Aelargo and Nasur.

Eralci: An unknown kingdom or city in ancient times now lost.

Greyrhan: A province of the Duianna Empire in the far north just south of the great ice fields.

Halias-Ne Mountains: A thick rocky mountain and volcano

range which cuts the entire Duianna continent in half, spanning from the Darain Ocean on the east to the Occiduis Ocean on the west.

Llino: The Sea Prince's stronghold and capital. Notable places: Blue Dophin Inn, the Night Market.

Loren Sound: An inlet of the Darian Ocean bordering the southeastern part of the north Duianna Continent.

Miumi: Port trade city on the Loren Sound on the eastern border of Oslald.

Night Market: A unique black market in Llino in which any service or goods may be purchased through brokers known as Hands. The market opens every day at sunset and closes at sunrise.

Onasa Channel: Inlet of the Loren sound which traverses through hundreds of miles of canyons northerly to the great Empire Lakes, generally salt water transitioning to fresh water near the Empire Lake outlets. Also known as the Onasa River.

Rhini Wood: The old-growth forest along the northwestern edge of Bear Foot Sea in the Kingdom of Aelargo. Also the name of the village and farming lands in the same location.

Windy Pass: A series of hills and valleys which separate the Burga Spine Mountains from the Halias-Ne Mountain Range, bordering Nasur on the east and Laeusia on the west.

TITLES/POSITIONS

Apprentice: Any tradesman under training for a guild (Mages' Guild included).

Blade: A professional soldier, mercenary fighter, sword master.

Councilor: A member of Leading Council of the Argos Guild of Mages.

Dagger: Professional warrior specialists for hire that hold to a strong set of ideals based on commitment, courage, and honor.

Guard: City soldiers, general police force.

Hand: Broker or facilitator for trade in various goods or services, usually illegal.

High Councilor: Chairman of the Leading Council of the Argos Guild of Mages.

Journeyman Mage: Title of a mid-level magician for the Argos Guild of Mages; carries a unique badge of office and is seen as a direct representative of Argos.

Knife: An assassin or hired killer, strongly controlled by a secretive guild

Magus (pl. Magi): A higher magician who has achieved the rank of master in the guild

PEOPLE AND THINGS

arit: A strong, bitter drink made from roasted beans of the aritia tree which only grows in tropical climates.

blood compass: A magical artifact made with blood which is capable of retracing a person's life. Its construction is taboo in many lands and illegal in a few. It is effective for as long as the subject lives and for many hours after death.

Boadua of Mostill Valley: A senior priestess of Dalpha in Llino.

cycle: One complete cycle of the moon Tempa. Each year has twelve lunar cycles divided into the four seasons winter (Samag, Noelag, Foilleg), spring (Gearra, Marta, Abra), summer (Sealen, Ogmen, Luchen), and autumn (Lunas, Sultas, Fomas).

dagger table: Various inns and taverns allow mercenaries to hire out from them. A Dagger table is reserved for only Daggers. Daggers signal they are open for hire by placing their dagger into the table standing up. Senior

Dagger tables have a Dagger holder mounted on the table and, in Dagger Homes, can be owned exclusively.

Damega Drakeruin: Legendary warrior who started many of the Dagger traditions. Although very mercenary he is always portrayed in a 'Robin Hood' fashion. A good-hearted rogue, who refused any offer to settle down. Supposedly found or was gifted the Emerald Heart, a flying ship.

Ditani: A Karakian servant to Magus Vestul.

Dohma Gerani: Captain of the City and Palace Guards in Llino.

Dolphin dagger doors: Unique doors use only at the Blue Dolphin Inn in Llino for Dagger and special guest rooms which are considered unbreakable and thief proof that require a combination and a special key to open.

Emerald Heart: Legendary flying ship of Damega Drakeruin. Legend has it that it flies faster than any creature and is home-ported in a secret place far in the north.

Faltla of Rhini Wood: Ticca's Uncle a retired tactics Dagger that served in the Realms' War and trained Ticca from birth.

Genne: The current owner of the Blue Dolphin Inn the original Dagger House in Llino.

Hisuru Amajoo: The city fortress home of the Nhia-Samri.

hyly: A semi-sweet liquor made from honey.

Kliasa: The daughter of House Elaeus of Rea-Na-Rey

Magus Andros: A fifty year master mage of the Argos Guild of Mages and Lebuin's mentor at the Llino Guildhouse.

Magus Cune: A twenty five year master mage of the Argos Guild of Mages and Lebuin's nemesis for all of Lebuin's twenty years at the Llino Guildhouse.

Magus Gezu: A seventy year master of the Argos Guild of Mages that died in the summer of 15348.

Magus Nillo: High Councilor and a sixty year master mage of the Argos Guild of Mages and Lebuin's mentor at the Llino Guildhouse.

Magus Seriel of Eralci: An ancient mage who wrote the secret tombs of magic Lebuin acquired and studied.

Magus Vestul: An immortal master mage who predates the Argos Guild of Mages. Close friend of Duke. Lives in Algan.

mark: A period of time equal to a twenty-fourth part of a day and night and divided into 60 minutes.

Nhia-Samri: A shadowy, ruthless mercenary group of warriors of unknown size which fight with inhuman speed and agility.

Nigan: A combat specialist Dagger that works out of the Blue Dolphin Inn in Llino. Partners with Rissy and is called "Hairy" by Ticca.

odassi: Single edged magical weapons of the shadowy faction of warrior mercenaries called the Nhia-Samri.

Risy: A combat specialist Dagger that works out of the Blue Dolphin Inn in Llino. Partners with Nigan and is called "Frumpy" by Ticca.

Sayscia: The High Priestess or The Great Lady of Dalpha in Llino.

Shar-Lumen: The shadowy Grand Warlord of the Nhia-Samri.

sharre: A sweet wine made by the elves from unknown ingredients. If kept properly it grows more potent over time. Five to fifty-year-old sharre is very robust and gives a little energy, as well as making people drunk extremely fast. Sharre over one hundred years old can heal wounds, revive tiredness, and sharpen the mind dramatically. Sharre over five hundred years old is thought to restore youth.

Sula: A priestess healer of the Temple of Dalpha.

The Traitor (Amia-Dharo): The second-in-command Nhia-Samri who betrayed the Nhai-Samri in a great war and helped the Alliance Nations end hostilities. Second most deadly warrior in the world.

Ticca of Rhini Wood: A hunter Dagger that works out of the Blue Dolphin Inn in Llino.

vanedicha: A poison which induces a trance if a small amount is inhaled and kills in less than a minute in larger doses. Victims are unusually truthful when revived from a vanedicha-induced trance.

OTHER ITEMS OF NOTE

Argos Guild of Mages Sigil: A stylized gold dragon with the five silver waves behind it.

MONEY

For over 10,000 years all of the nations of the Duianna continent as well as many trade nations on other continents have done trade based off of the Duianna Imperial Money System. The money system was further cemented by the Covenant of Duianna. Although prices may shift slightly and the value of various precious metals will fluctuate the currency has remained stable. Any attempt to undermine the currency is seen as a capital offence in every nation known.

Copper Ring (r)
Ring: 1
Pence: 4
Bell: 6
Tyme: 12
Chera: 24
Cross: 48
Crown: 960
1 lb 99% base: 360
Coin (oz): .044
Approx Size: 1/2 Penny

Copper Pence (p)
Ring: 1/4

Pence: 1
Bell: 1-1/2
Tyme: 3
Chera: 6
Cross: 12
Crown: 240
1 lb 99% base: 90
Coin (oz): .178
Approx Size: ~ nickel

Palladium Bell (b)
Ring: 1/6
Pence: 2/3
Bell: 1
Tyme: 2
Chera: 4
Cross: 8
Crown: 160
1 lb 99% base: 220
Coin (oz): .073
Approx Size: ~ dime

Palladium Tyme (t)
Ring: 1/12
Pence: 1/3
Bell: 1/2
Tyme: 1
Chera: 2
Cross: 4
Crown: 80
1 lb 99% base: 110
Coin (oz): ..145
Approx Size: < nickel

Silver Chera (c)
Ring: 1/24

Pence: 1/6
Bell: 1/4
Tyme: 1/2
Chera: 1
Cross: 2
Crown: 40
1 lb 99% base: 140
Coin (oz): .114
Approx Size: > dime

Silver Cross (s)
Ring: 1/48
Pence: 1/12
Bell: 1/8
Tyme: 1/4
Chera: 1/2
Cross: 1
Crown: 20
1 lb 99% base: 70
Coin (oz): .229
Approx Size: ~ quarter

Gold Crown (g)
Ring: 1/960
Pence: 1/240
Bell: 1/160
Tyme: 1/80
Chera: 1/40
Cross: 1/20
Crown: 1
1 lb 99% base: 180
Coin (oz): .089
Approx Size: ~ dime

ACKNOWLEDGMENTS

First and foremost thank you to my readers. Without you I cannot continue to write and every day I enjoy chatting with you online. My readers' comments and reviews inspire me to work ever harder to produce good stories and fantastic characters.

Next I must send a huge thank you to my great friend Charles Berry who started as my very first beta reader and continues to inspire me with new ideas. Thanks for the long chats on character development and possibilities. Also, a huge thank you for donating the audio trademark and music for the promotional videos!

I have not the words to thank Elle Casey and Lindsay Buroker for taking an interest in an unknown new writer and answering my questions, no matter how trivial. Very early in my learning to be a professional writer I read everything I could from other successful writers on how to do this job. That you two took an interest in me and mentored me with suggestions and great references for professional services really propped me up at times!

To one of the greatest editors of all time, Alexis Arendt (Wordvagabond. com) a tremendous thank you. Your hours of toil, words of support and editorial comments made this book a reality. Looking down I humbly apologize for the number of reflexive sentences. You are the best!

To Kitten Jackson (kittenkjackson.com) an amazing editor with a unique view on my work. I really appreciate you stepping out of your comfort zone into the weird genre of fantasy. However, now that you are properly addicted to the genre the world is a better place. Thank you for sneaking my book into your tight schedule.

The unbelievably great art work, formatting, and cover work for this book was done by Glendon Haddix, Tabatha Haddix, and Steven Doty of Streetlight Graphics (www.StreetlightGraphics.com). Steve Doty is the principle sketch artist, and in spite of my promise to keep revisions to a minimum he still redid a number of sketches until I was simply awestruck at seeing an image of something I had only imagined. I am really sorry I caused so many eraser holes because every piece you made was amazing from the beginning!

To my loving wife who at first wasn't sure about what would happen but supported me anyway- I love you. You took care of so many things and let me spin my threads on the keyboard. Also to my son who kept me off the keyboard often enough that I didn't miss out entirely on your fifth and sixth years of life! Talking to you and playing games gave me a lot of interesting ideas that I hope you remember as you read these stories.

Finally to everyone else I cannot possibly list from my life, who are my friends and family. You all inspire me, make me laugh, and support me when I'm down. I love you all! Stay Sharp and don't forget to call from time to time.

OTHER WORKS BY LEELAND ARTRA

GOLDEN THREADS TRILOGY

Book One: *Thread Slivers*
Book Two: *Thread Strands* (available August 2013)
Book Three: *Thread Skein* (available March 2014)